The Woods of Arcady

The Woods of Arcady

Book Two of The Sanctuary of the White Friars

MICHAEL MOORCOCK

TOR PUBLISHING GROUP

NEW YORK

THE WOODS OF ARCADY

Copyright © 2023 by Michael Moorcock

A Tor Book
Published by Tom Doherty Associates / Tor Publishing Group
120 Broadway
New York, NY 10271

www.tor-forge.com

Tor® is a registered trademark of Macmillan Publishing Group, LLC.

Library of Congress Cataloging-in-Publication Data

Names: Moorcock, Michael, 1939– author.
Title: The woods of Arcady / Michael Moorcock.
Description: First U.S. edition. | New York : Tor, Tor Publishing Group,
    2023. | Series: The Sanctuary of the White Friars ; book 2
Identifiers: LCCN 2023007699 (print) | LCCN 2023007700 (ebook) |
    ISBN 9780765324788 (hardcover) | ISBN 9781429944854 (ebook)
Subjects: LCGFT: Fantasy fiction. | Novels.
Classification: LCC PR6063.O59 W66 2023 (print) | LCC PR6063.O59 (ebook) |
    DDC 823/.914—dc23/eng/20230301
LC record available at https://lccn.loc.gov/2023007699
LC ebook record available at https://lccn.loc.gov/2023007700

Our books may be purchased in bulk for promotional, educational, or business use. Please contact your local bookseller or the Macmillan Corporate and Premium Sales Department at 1-800-221-7945, extension 5442, or by email at MacmillanSpecialMarkets@macmillan.com.

First published in Great Britain by Gollancz, an imprint of
The Orion Publishing Group Ltd, Hachette UK

First U.S. Edition: 2023

Printed in the United States of America

0   9   8   7   6   5   4   3   2   1

For Peake and Tolkien, respected predecessors

The woods of Arcady are dead,
And over is their antique joy;
Of old the world on dreaming fed;
Grey Truth is now her painted toy.

—*W. B. Yeats*

Part One

Emergence

In this world, a species can only thrive when everything around it thrives too.

– David Attenborough

1

The Smell of Roses and of the Sea

THE DREAM, THOUGHT Harold Blackstone, staring through the grimed glass of his Smoking compartment, has to exist first; only then might one create the actuality. Which, like America, could become quite different in time. How did desire, imagination and memory work? The train had made one of those mysterious brief halts, as if to catch its steam before starting off again. It shuddered, hissed, and waited. He lowered the window to look out. A signal. What did it mean? Here, surely, one reality had already inspired the creation of another.

The train lurched and restarted its journey. He was intoxicated by the proliferation and powerful scent of the wild roses, the hedge lilies and herb robert in the thickly wooded embankments of the single track as the train rattled and squealed and sent smoke through the lush Sussex countryside. Sometimes the insects were so thick in the air he could hardly see past them. The train could be travelling through mythical England. He enjoyed the idea of the red, blue and brass smoke-spouting engine appearing from a grassy tunnel to be greeted by astonished fifth-century Celtic knights. Wasn't there a scene like it in *A Connecticut Yankee*? They believed a roaring dragon emerged from its lair. Would they have attempted to tackle it or would they have galloped off in panic? Blackstone had a pretty good idea what he would have done.

Perhaps what we called ghosts were glimpses of the future or past. He had once been impressed by Frazer's – or were they Wells's? – fashionable notions about the idea of a fourth dimension, another Universe! Or did we all, as James suggested, each live in a universe of our own, a kind of 'multiverse'?

The lazy little country train snaked up out of the valley and for a short while ran along a crest of the downs. He saw the sharp blue of the sea beneath the paler sky, a cool horizon with one misty pleasure boat shimmering as if airborne. They were frequent in the summer, often carrying an entire minstrel show for the evening run. He was no snob. The thing was probably quite jolly in the sunset. Now, he thought comfortably, reaching for his newspaper, he could relax and stop thinking about Oxford, Mrs Heaney and all the rest of them. He could forget that wretched paper arguing for MacDonald's destructive influence on adult fiction. He could get back to his novel or go over a Balzac translation the publisher was shouting for. He hoped he wasn't turning into a dabbler like his father.

Suddenly the train squealed, shuddered and came to another mysterious stop. Like most of his fellow passengers, Blackstone felt grit, smelled steam and stuck his head out of the compartment window. An expanse of hedges lay ahead. A row of inquisitive heads popped from windows up and down the train. Either they avoided eye-contact or exchanged comradely complaints against the railway company. Somewhere on the horizon the sea joined the sky. The scene froze for a second. The train made an encouraging murmur and shook itself. He sat back in his seat, abandoned his book and checked his watch. A brake from the house would meet him. They appeared to be on time. This was the 3.18 local from Brighton, which hugged the coast until Worthing and now turned inland. To be sure, he took another look at his timetable. He picked up his pocket guide. Lower Wortham was the nearest station to Moat Hinton, all that remained of a walled Anglo-Saxon settlement and its ancient church. Blackstone was looking forward to the excavations.

He had been surprised to receive his cousin Constance's letter asking him to what she called a 'family symposium' at her big house near Lower Wortham, which she had renamed The Follies after inheriting it. Connie was the only one of their branch of the family rich enough to keep it up. Old Sir John showed little interest in his British property. Her one insistent point was that Blackstone should not tell his father about the symposium. Old Doctor Blackstone's actions and statements had been self-contradictory since the BEF left for France.

"This is about little Nell," she had said when he telephoned. Little Nell was the last to youngest of Doctor Blackstone's large English family. Blackstone was Nell's eldest brother's son, closer to her age than his father's brothers. She had always seen him as an ally within the family. He could, as Constance had it, 'talk' to Nell. She could be a bit highly strung but so imaginative! Of course they all loved her, though Ethel disapproved of her wildness. Nell had married a rather nice engineer with an old-fashioned Yorkshire name, who drove a sporty two-seater Blackstone rather envied. And now, he gathered, she was with child. That should settle them down. Presumably this event had something to do with Constance's letter. He fell back in his seat, lit a pipe and wondered if the child would make a good character. An innocent eye on the adults, perhaps? Like James and Maisie. A fresh vision of the world. What might the child be like? Blackstone could only speculate. The second boy, his young cousin, would further complicate his large and rather well-known family. What on earth could this 'symposium' be about? Something to do with the War?

With a sigh, the brave Merchant Ventura Pearl Peru straps herself back into her gene-harness and, flipping toggles, swings the omniphone to her gorgeous lips. Screens are coming up jazzed or blank and her ship has suddenly developed an itch. "Calling in and calling out. Peru, Peru. Multiverse, are you hearing me? We have time and gravitational upheavals not 18-bars from Ketchup Cove. No sight of our *Spammer*. I don't think public readings of *The Stranger* are going to do it for this one, mes pards. I'm coming in! Fix me a bit of that Moroccan fudge. Oh, you'd better hope you have some of that *White Album* left. We need a conjunction."

ACHTUNG, DAHLIA GARDENS!!!

AND HERE I am, trying to tell the truth, really. I was born at 18 Dahlia Gardens, Mitcham, South-west London, on 18 December, 1939, delivered by Dr Dylan. You couldn't have been born into a more suburban suburb. We were twenty minutes from Trafalgar Square. Detective stories abounded with frustrated, mild-mannered, usually homicidal, clerks who lived where I was born. P.G. Wodehouse had respectable romantic novelists and pretty actresses lodging in 'Dahlia Gardens'. The name was synonymous with bourgeois and petit bourgeois. By the end of the war the Germans had sent more rockets our way than anywhere else. We thought they understood where the realm's power was but actually they were rerouted by MI5. I slept securely in a Morrison shelter. My mother held me up to the window. Chuckling, I watched the dogfights. Ruins everywhere. My mum laughed and joked so I smiled, too. Thanks, MI5.

With all my imagination, all the resources Nature gave me: sturdy peasant genes, a taste for travel and reading, a certain

London intelligence, a good visual imagination, a talent to entertain, not because I was needy but because I probably wasn't. I suspect it does have infantile roots. I enjoyed the mutual fun of it. *All together now!* No tragic mask hidden here. My reading tastes were already broad. Unfortunately George MacDonald, and most of those 'child-speakers' who were directly influenced by him, left me feeling irritable and condescended to. My working life would be more successful than I had ever expected. My only disappointment is that I never made it into the Country Music Hall of Fame.

At school I loved to make people laugh by hamming up a bit of Shakespeare. Everyone enjoyed it. Belmont, my tiny nearby prep school, was run by a pair of terrifying dykes in tweeds and pudding-bowl haircuts. At least they weren't cruel. And they weren't into B&D or I would know it now by the very bad knots they tied when in exasperation they secured me to the bannisters. Belmont was a day school, exactly a mile from home. I got thrown out of one boarding school for keeping kids awake with my stories but at Belmont I just encouraged the other kids to bunk off, having discovered that the first class was the only one which took roll-call. After lunch, the world was your oyster! We were eventually exposed by a toady we'd let in on our truancy scheme.

At eleven, having failed my 11+, I was sent to Pitman's College to learn how to become a journalist. I had known that I wanted to write since I was eight or nine and I worked to that specific end through the last four years of my schooling until I only specialised in typing English and a little French. At fifteen, having said I would work evening classes to get to university, I went to work for Messrs Balliere, Tindall and Cox, publishers of medical books, in Henrietta Street, Covent Garden, next door to Victor Gollancz Ltd, publisher of angry lefties and myself from the '80s until now.

I lasted a day. I wasn't used to the foul language and badinage of the post room. By the following week I had abandoned publishing to the sink of depravity and got a job in the City. I went to work as a messenger for Flexhill Shipping Company. Every morning I took a train or a bus to grey London Bridge, about thirty-five minutes door to door from our somewhat posh leafy suburb of Norbury, where Kingsley Amis and Martin Stone grew up, where my mother and I lived for the rest of my childhood and where I formed a lasting friendship with Brian Alford, who became a brother. In 1961 they discovered the London to Brighton Roman Road. Legions had marched past the wondering yokels of Croydon town's north borough. We had known relatively undramatic security, progress and civilisation for at least fifteen hundred years.

Brian could make anything but wasn't much of a reader. He, too, fell in love with Crompton's 'Just William' books. Previously, when the subject of reading came up, he would mention *Treasure Island*. Until we started working we were inseparable. Building elaborate old Guys to display for our fireworks money and then burning them at the stake on November 5th, carolling at Christmas, odd-jobbing in Spring, full of sweet blossoms and promise, and Summer, endless warmth and the smell of tarmac, building tree-houses in the long days of July and August, almost overwhelmed by the smell of grasses, leaves, flowers and the trails of tiny animals. We pretty much made extinct one large black-and-orange newt resembling a tiny dinosaur. We went scrumping on allotments and orchards, trespassed in the grounds of posh schools and monasteries and played in the two nearby woods.

My tolerant, sensible mother loved Brian, cared about him and disapproved of his own mother who seemed perfectly happy with our informal adoption of her son. It saved Mrs A. money, after all, when my mother fed and clothed him and took him on holiday. He only lived a street away in the houses once designed to accommodate the workers who built the suburb and intended for eventual use of the poor who served the bourgeoisie who bought the mock Tudor residences. These nostalgic miniatures were grouped around a small 'village green' dominated by a red-brick mock Norman Baptist Church whose stained glass and lead meant money to kids who grew up scavenging ruins, although the place was never actually ruined. We had preyed on their Boys' Brigade, whose band marched with their noisy instruments around the neighbourhood every Sunday. By the end of one year they were marching hatless and we had a respectable collection of their pillbox headgear. Almost everyone felt a sort of friendly contempt for churchgoers. But now at fifteen I had no time for adventure. I was a working lad.

Again luck and circumstance came together. The job had been advertised for an office junior but really I was working as a messenger. This job gave me time to read and to dream and explore. Ships stretched for miles in the Pool of London and beyond. Every vessel had a creaking cargo crane or two working for that last gasp of imperial glory. Goods for and from an Empire. Ghosts of the future. Stevedores yelling, docks managers squawling and seabirds shrieking everywhere. There was a well-known picture of the Pool and a big cargo steamer being brought in by her famous tugs. One of which was *The Moorcock*.

Flexhill's office was above a tea and coffee warehouse of creaking staircases and a view over the ruins near Billingsgate. The wonderful smell of coffee countered the smell of fresh fish. Men and women still wore hats to work. Bowlers for men with rolled umbrella, briefcase, newspaper. Hairdos replaced pillboxes but handbags and heels were still *de rigeur* for women. The security of the uniform. As a junior I wore blazer, white

9

shirt, tie and flannels. Pretty much the same as my school's without the badge and cap. A raincoat in winter, like everyone else. Only Saturday afternoon and Sunday off. It was not hard work. It gave me a lot of time alone. Much of it was spent reading. Sometimes I would walk to explore the city around me.

Lost in thought about my fanzines, *Burroughsania*, *Jazz Fan*, *Albion* and *Book Collectors News*, I could always escape the job's longeurs. I kept a book handy because much of my job was sitting on buses or trains, in shipping offices or consulates from the East End to the West End. If I finished one book, I simply bought another. Walking or waiting. From booming ships, raucous stinking pubs of the City to the hush of Kensington's tree-lined Embassy Row, the undemonstrative authority of nation states. Then, armed with bills of lading, I returned to a City which actively disliked colour.

Every morning except Sunday, I descended from the bus or railway carriage at London Bridge. I would walk past the Monument, pass through the busy fish market whose white-coated porters carried piled boxes of cod on bobbin hats, their special headgear of tarred leather. Then I used the dirt paths through cleared bomb-sites, piles of stale-smelling rubble filled with pink and purple fireweed, trails blazed through broken concrete, the steel reinforcements resembling defiant fingers reaching skyward, and past the Customs House where I imagined Tom Paine working.

The nineteenth century might have been bombed to the ground, save for some battered Victorian Gothic, but the Palladian eighteenth century was still alive! St Paul's, too, and the Old Bailey, the Monument, the Tower of London. Tower Bridge was the only landmark less than a century old. I found it easy to understand the old city. It was so small! No wonder everyone knew Defoe or Johnson! Busy times in Coffee Houses and Pudding Clubs. I could hear their voices sometimes, their English oddly accented as they exchanged friendly ribaldries and filthy anecdotes. If I got the chance when the tide was out, I explored the Thames shore like a mudlark. I loved the river's generally friendly stink, still carrying the spiced scents of India, China and Africa with the briny smells of fresh fish just as I'd enjoyed the wealth of blooms and vegetables from Covent Garden. The scent of flowers and the sea. London smelled of Empire, then, still. The might of the salty ocean, the subtle overpowering smell of old roses.

A few islands of Portland stone in the City had survived unsullied since the eighteenth and nineteenth centuries. One moment you would be in the bright light of the bombed sites and the next you would be in the dark canyons of the surviving offices. There were still rows of buildings standing around Leadenhall Street and the lettering on dark doors and windows continued to be black and gold Victorian in stony narrow streets barely touched by the sun. Boot shops and book shops, sandwich shops and newsagents, travel agents and shipping agents, import and export firms, tobacconists and teashops, men's conservative tailoring, as if their little unbombed islands were the whole city, never touched. And here were the offices of all the famous shipping companies. Cunard, with its Piccadilly showrooms near the Ritz, had a more serious and sober office in the City. Blue Star Line, Union Castle, German-American, French Lines, Italian-American, Fred Olsen Lines, Norwegian Atlantic, Turko-Black Sea Lines, usually with a beautiful English oak scale model of their flagship in a brass-framed window. Laymen judged the ships by their number of funnels. Years later I'd see the models for sale in Portobello Road and feel sadness for their passing. The originals could sometimes be seen at the docks, but increasingly I visited ships which had known their glory days before the war. They had names redolent of greater decades, before America took over so many of their routes – the All-Red, Imperial Route, the Empire Lines. Old and even a little embarrassing. I heard the big Cunard passenger liners, which we never saw in London, were getting a bit shabby. The ferries, stinking of beer and vomit, that limped to Ireland and the Continent, were no longer what they were. Like the ferry that took me to Paris with my girlfriend, Maria, in the Autumn of '55, our first trip abroad. We were both fifteen and I was supposedly her girl-friend and would be until her dad learned the truth when she got back to London.

Under the Seine's quays and outside Le Mistral Bookshop before it became Shakespeare & Co., I played my guitar and, whenever I collected enough francs, bought another book from the cheap shelves. George Whitman, the grumpy American proprietor, didn't mind. I brought trade in and *was* trade at the same time. Maria was just happy to be there, enjoying the ambience. We came home after three weeks and split up. That was also traditional. But I would remain loyal to Paris as the other city of my heart.

In those days cities were more distinctive. Paris smelled of coffee and Turkish tobacco. London tasted of vinegar and sour tea and Glasgow of strong beer and Birmingham faintly of curry. Today they all have McDonald's. Glen Coe's Revenge on the world for the Highland Betrayal. They all smell the same. Makes you want to move to another planet.

In the horrible heat of August I resigned my shipping job. As the company prospered so staff had been added until the single big room, with only three windows on one side facing what was becoming a building site, had over twenty people in it and we were beginning to behave like crazed rats. I became employed by a firm that was to have a serious effect on my life. I joined Harold Whitehead's, Management Consultants, as office junior, promoted to junior consultant. Round the corner from St James's Park, Buckingham Palace, a short walk from Victoria Station, in Princess Street, Whitehall, and across from a functioning brewery whose big dray horses still came and went, delivering Whitbread's to the world. For a while it was so peaceful, so easy on the eye, that I felt I was in heaven.

My immediate boss was Major Fry, ex-Indian Army adjutant, now the firm's accountant. After my mentor, Mr Jelinek, he was the most even-tempered, sweet-natured, most principled man I knew. Everyone at Whitehead's loved me and had plans for my education and promotion. ("Don't join the army, old boy! Whatever you do!") Meanwhile, I had limitless use of the office electric Roneo duplicator. It's what we used before photocopiers. They even gave me stencils and paper. My production of fanzines of every sort, but chiefly about books and music, soared. The quality improved. I came in contact with science fiction fandom and broadened my talent pool. I met fellow spirits, like Pete Taylor, Barry Bayley, George Locke, Vince Clarke, John Wyndham, Brian Aldiss, Arthur Clarke and Sam Youd ('John Christopher'), John Brunner, Bill Temple and even C.S. Lewis at the Globe, Hatton Garden, every month, when fans and writers mingled. And I devoted more time to our skiffle group rehearsals and a couple of gigs. We'd formed the group before I joined Whitehead's but now we got a few appearances as The Greenhorns. My main memory of that period was trying to wrestle a tea-chest bass onto a double-decker bus, because none of us had access to a car. I had a tendency to sing long Woody Guthrie songs which didn't go down well at church dances and social-club events. But I wrote to Woody and Pete Seeger and got replies!

Thanks to my Edgar Rice Burroughs fanzine, I would soon join *Tarzan Adventures* as assistant editor, in Brooke Street, Holborn, alongside the red-brick Gothic Prudential building and across from one of the last sixteenth-century blocks of half-timbered shops in London, forming the frontage of Staple Inn. I bought my Sobranie cigarettes there. *The Old Curiosity Shop* was just down the alley behind it. Actually it wasn't the original but it pretended to be. It looked right.

You can read a lot of my life story in collections like *London Peculiar, London Bone* or *Letters from Hollywood*. They're close memoirs of different times in my life. They're easy enough to find. I've written slightly fictionalised accounts of the London district I called Brookgate, a general area bordered by Leather Lane, High Holborn, Grays Inn Road, St Paul's and down to Fleet Street and the River. Until Soho, that was my territory: Blackfriars Bridge to Southwark and the surviving riverside warehouses of the Pool, the settings for so many British noir films. After work I began meeting my friends in Soho. Pete Taylor, Barry Bayley and I became pretty inseparable. We never had much money for anything but books, cigarettes and beer, so we played a lot of chess. For 3*d* you could get a Tube ticket and go up and down on the Central Line in warmth and comfort playing game after game until it grew late, when we could get off at the stops nearest home. I sometimes stayed at Barry's place until we got a place of our own, first in Holloway and then in Chelsea where it was still possible to find cheap bedsitters. King's Road was just an ordinary shopping street, except for a couple of art shops and a café called Picasso.

I had moved back home, temporarily broke, when I saw Helena at a party. She was wearing a horrible tweed suit and was sitting smoking, hunched over the fire, but I was struck by her astonishing beauty, what I called postPreRaphaelite, an ideal of English beauty from a '20s fashion-plate, with her pageboy haircut swinging in the firelight. Love at first sight. Racing heart. Untypically aggressive. Adrenaline rush. Get behind the adrenaline, talk to her, make her laugh, make her stay, meaning that for the first time in my nineteen or so years, when she started to leave with friends I said: "You're not going!" and she turned and came back. There were few complications except every friend I introduced her to asked eagerly if we were 'serious'. We were and I was prepared to put my actions where my mouth was. Giving her priority over my mother was one for a while. My mother continued her manipulations, of course, by finding us wonderful 1930s flats in Streatham. My mother-in-law preferred Clapham, closer to her on the bus. Helena and I hated both and needed to stay North of the River.

Recently returned from Sweden, where I had been mountain climbing and playing nightclubs, I had only casual girlfriends. She had just ended it with her boyfriend, a short, loveable drunk. It took a while for her shoulders to straighten up. For a short while on getting back I was on the dole. She decided to marry me one Friday night when I spent my entire dole money on a slap-up dinner at Romano's. It wasn't so much recklessness as the reasonable knowledge I could write a page in *Everybody's* the next day and be advanced payment a day or so later. Meanwhile, there was always my grandfather's ring which sadly was eventually pawned to extinction. In the late '50s I moved to Notting Hill and eventually, now married and unexpectedly pregnant, to Colville Terrace and then with our toddlers to the epicentres of the alternative society, Ladbroke Grove.

I can see my tiny friend and writing partner Barry Bayley, almost invisible, coming down the stairs with our fridge on his back. It was as if the fridge walked by itself on human legs. I almost expected it to burst into song. We moved all we had, including our toddlers, in the two-seater monster solid steel pushchair I bought in Kilburn. I think it was created by a firm which had made wartime tanks. Fore and aft, like

15

the cockpits of WWI biplanes. Made to survive a nuke. The girls loved it as on Saturdays I pushed them through the busy Portobello Road crowds. They clung to the sides as if on a fairground ride, moving with the flow, the hair on their little blonde heads floating in the slipstream! There's Helena, my mum, the girls, me, Barry, moving by hand. It was only from the Portobello corner of Colville Terrace to the Elgin Crescent corner across Ladbroke Grove. In the middle of everything. Ghosts then. Gone now. No trams. No trolley buses. We had them when I was working in Holborn.

I set fictional Brookgate around Holborn, perhaps the densest working-class community this side of the City. We had our own department store, Gamages. We had a huge joke emporium, Ellisdons, which provided illusions for members of the Magic Circle and blackface soap and advertised regularly in *Tarzan Adventures*. The smell of sweet tobacco from the Old Holborn factory. We had Grays Inn and several other leafy inns of court, where lawyers lived and worked. Behind high walls, the gardens could be closed and invisible, with no-one guessing their secrets. Some had footpaths, ancient trees. I made my first West Indian acquaintance in Brooke Street. I asked how things were going for him. He performed a typical Jamaican shrug and grinned. It was in the hot summer of 1957. The Notting Hill riots. We leaned outside on our door posts smoking. I told him I was really glad his lot were turning up. Just in time. He was surprised. Before you arrived, I said, it was my lot kept getting arrested. Yoof. Youths! We had a laugh but I don't know how the poor bastards stood it in those days. Nowadays someone shouting racist crap is more of an aberration. There are more people on your side.

I had been born with a lot of advantages. I had a supportive mother and a wise mentor. I was not especially self-conscious. I expected to be heard. I was so full of self-confidence I could get arrested and sentenced without it bothering me. That was because of my voice. Because of the schools I attended, I had naturally acquired an upper middle-class accent. Elocution and English were the only classes I had excelled in. At school I was a friendly boy and a friendly youth, always willing to point out inequities and suggesting sensible ways of compromising on issues. I enjoyed debate. I could take a joke and I thought everybody else could. It never dawned on me that I wasn't accepted as an equal of anyone else anywhere, as I'd been raised to understand. All the contemporary public rhetoric about democracy confirmed what I believed. I looked towards World Unity by 1980!

I grew up in the wonder years of socialist Britain, a child of the NHS, priority diets and enough austerity to keep us all healthy as we rebuilt the country to become an egalitarian centre of a great commonwealth of multi-ethnic New Elizabethan nations. A sense that our arguments with the government were serious, realistic, to do with health, housing, secure jobs and wages that Attlee's people did their best to deliver. That and negotiate independence with India and half of Africa. With the continuation of the Spirit of the Blitz and Labour's landslide we felt we were founding a united kingdom of genuine equality in the Birthplace of Democracy. To a large degree my surroundings confirmed my upbringing. Wartime camaraderie and ideals persisted, I suppose. New arts began to emerge. Our narrative was one of resurgence and unity and mutual trust as found in the pages of *Picture Post* and *Eagle*. We did our best to support it. A few exploited it.

I only knew one boss who hated my natural egalitarianism. I'm pretty sure that was what he hated about me. I was friendly to him. I wasn't rude and always ran layouts past him, which he always accepted. I had learned my first day that he had none of my basic skills. I really did know more about editing than he did. He was introduced as Alf so I called him Alf. I quickly realised he had no journalistic knowledge or much else. He had come in from clerical or somewhere! He was a useless editor, a fake writer, his work visible only on forged paysheets, and a low crook of a plagiarist. His only skill was cooking books. Those books still exist somewhere. It would be good to go through them and clarify all the payments for 'written off' stories Alf had pocketed. W. Prout was getting paid long after his death. Rumour had it Alf owned half the houses around Clapham Common. As IPC took us over, and the Union kept its power, he removed our office partitions as an attempt on our morale. We built walls of art-boards. My colleagues were young men with families. They still resisted. We made tiny private caves. He took to prowling in one office door and out by another, looking for absentees he could have done nothing much about in those days. Like others before him, he reckoned without internal phones and friends on the inside. He had no real friends. Just a few accessories.

Next he tried to 'tame' me, I suppose. Suddenly one morning he told me to call him 'Mr Wallace' and, in front of our colleagues, asked me if I didn't think I should show respect for 'my boss'. "Of course," I said from where I sat, looking up at him. "As soon he earns it." He turned red and swung about, leaving. I hadn't expected the victory my friends told me I'd won. He tried to bully me and I defended myself. I wasn't used to his aggression. I lived my life as my grandma would wish, neither looking up to nor down on others. I'd had to live with my mother's powerful temperament and resist it. Her sense of justice was paramount. She also had some distinct Tory tendencies which surprised me. I was, however, happy to fight if that was the name of the game.

Then it became a Union issue with my friends immediately making me a committee member of the National Union of

Journalists because I had just turned twenty-one. I had started as an editor so early, I was qualified in years of service but not of age! I wrote some bad anti-capitalist stories but I didn't join the Trots. In those days, to be in Labour or further left was to be on the side of the righteous. Banning the Bomb, in particular. As I've said elsewhere – I believed the Bomb to be my friend. Party politics would soon pall. Later I saw myself more as Wodehouse's Psmith and I think we merged. I've always considered him and Ukridge as great *schnorrers*. Zangwill was Wodehouse's contemporary. They were part of a flowering of great comic talent in late Victorian London. *The King of Schnorrers*! And *spielers*, of course. Zangwill invented the term 'the melting pot' for the USA. He's in Dover, cheap. Check him out. In 1900, war-profiteers were the subject of *The Mantle of Elijah*. What a page-turner! You can read it free online.

So many stories and they have to fit in to so few narratives. So many ways of suiting the readers. Style can be at least one story of its own. Inconsistent and conflicting narratives, often by the same hand, irritate readers unless you make it clear like Kurasawa and Bergman that you are seeing the same story from several different points of view. More than a few and you're in trouble again. No secret the Wheel of Chaos, drawn on our kitchen table for the end of *Stormbringer*, pointed in eight directions (at least)! Here we go! Memory. Remembrance. Remembering. Memoir.

I am encouraged by my customers to mythologise. To lie. I am not paid to tell the plain truth. At least, not plainly. We are all unreliable narrators. There's not a worthwhile rule in our grammar the Romans didn't make! There is no firm grammatical earth here for we are having trouble describing these visions, you see. Do you see? Aren't we? I have too many stories of time and space and not enough time or space to tell them. Why me? I love this. And I have stories to hear. From

Africa, Arabia, Asia, Alpha Centauri and Atlantis; Australia, America, Antarctica and Andromeda; Polynesia, Persia and Malaysia, New Guinea, New Zealand and New Hebrides. *Have you heard of a certain Dutchman who sails the seas and stars? He's one of the few who knows, you know, to know the moonbeam roads! One of the few to steer a ship into the calm of Ketchup Cove. Oh, he's used enough to the deepest seas and the far far edge of space. But in private he'll tell you he loves neither, as much as the wilds of the Second Aether!* All their epics, stories, their memories, their tribal myths, binding us in one tangled ball, uniting the planet, keeping Gaia together against the odds! Untying the restraints which hitherto there have been on the Inanimate. Other lines encircle the planet, biting deep into the surface, down to the white-hot gases at our planet's core, firing the forge of all our fantasies and therefore all our realities! And what am I? At best, some sort of strung-up tuppenny-ha'penny shaman gainfully employed on creating the crude backdrops to some cheap travelling show. This is my mind on HOLD. Frequently I let a little of it out at a time, oh, time, the waters and the reins of time.

Mai lawds, laidies and gent-elo-men!! I give you!!

PLAYING ON THE BEACH:
TRUTH, LIES AND CONSEQUENCES
And here he is, trying to tell the truth!

I WAS BORN into a world a third of which was pink on our maps. As pink as I was. The British Empire, a cruel and wonderful achievement which left its main beneficiaries baffled hypocrites and spread law and injustice almost equally. But, as my brutal ancestors determined, tall, pale, blue-eyed people with posh accents had authority. So what is the story of the British Empire? There isn't one. There is one. There are many. Too many. I've tried to tell a few of them now and again. Several of my best friends are or were in the same business, also trying out new notions of narrative, looking for a fresh vocabulary, creating new literary tools and perhaps a new literary sensibility for today's world.

When I was young I saw Peacock, Meredith, Stevenson in a tradition. All fond of observations made on long walks, all poets, extraordinary stylists. I associated their techniques with those of absurdists like Firbank. Natural born writers but not natural yarn-spinners, instead brilliantly inventing techniques to suit their quirks. *Imagists*, I called them. Stevenson needed help in constructing his best-loved stories. Their plots, clever as they were, did not come naturally. Most poets have to write narrative for a living, and some have to work hard at it. I used to hear them all, reminding me of my vocation. I had not expected that when we moved so close to the Lakes. I had more hallucinations there than when I was a child. I loved to wander lonely as a cloud but I did not expect to make a living describing how great daffodils are. And of course I know Wordsworth was profound and I love him but I couldn't do what he did in Grasmere in 1800 and pay London rents in 1960. Ballard admiringly saw me as Defoe, bustling about the working city, joining the Liberals as a pamphleteer while a card-carrying NUJ Labour member, willing to tackle any subject for any journal and writing experimental novels on the side. Things like his, which had never been made quite like anything else.

I was learning my trade and was aware of it. I used to claim SF allowed you to learn how to write while selling your mistakes. I longed for the inspiration and talent and time to write lyrical verse, not that it was fashionable, but few of my enthusiasms were popular until the 1970s or '80s. I worked hard to bring fine writers to a wider audience. I countered literary

21

prejudice with contempt. I never tried to compromise. I did not seek to explain anything to the Press unless I was doing a one-on-one interview, preferably with someone I knew. We were publishing for a newsstand audience and most of our fiction was better than anything in literary magazines or commercial fiction magazines. I had edited for years and written commercially since I was sixteen. I intended to make sure *New Worlds* was taken seriously. I was confident we were producing stories and structures which would in the main stand the test of time. The initial response from the posh press proved surprisingly positive. If a bit like a vicar welcoming a motorbike gang into his congregation.

I had a theory that some writers with highly developed visual sensibilities forged stories almost wholly from disparate visions and only produced plots with help. I had no instructors. I copied structures from writers I admired. I copied *The Rescue* for *The Ice Schooner*. Not because it was good Conrad but because it was early Conrad and he was learning from some of the best. I learned from Dickens and popular fiction of the nineteenth century. And by doing it, by editing and analysing what I found wrong with a story. I'd done no university courses. I was self-educated like all my colleagues. Horribly ignorant and widely read. Reading lectures by Walter Raleigh and Quiller-Couch was the nearest I came to a literary degree. They had been the first to teach English Literature at Oxford and Cambridge. Neither of my chosen professors saw writing as a moral science, as Leavis would. Leavis the Disciplinarian, the Inspired Loony, turning up still in his pyjamas to accuse his students of treachery and mockery. He helped, too, with his severe judgements, many of which I agreed with. Images. I saw many like that. Ballard was primarily a visionary, as was Peake. But Peake had stories to tell, not just his own. Peake's was a world of language, narrative and images in equal parts.

His characters came to life as iconographic grotesques. Magi all! Visionaries every one!

Angus Wilson, strange to say, was among them though, in his own words, he could never get out of his causes. In the UK, as a reader for Sidgwick & Jackson, he bought *The Stars My Destination* by Bester, the first and finest of the American SF novels, which lured me into the genre. Wilson is a great, thoughtful writer entirely out of fashion now. Peake was utterly marginalised, never mentioned in the Press in the 1950s when I was reading him and praising him in fanzines. Even when he was featured in and on *NW* he was still in the margins. Now he is part of the twentieth-century literary canon. I was privileged to know several brilliant generations of writers, all with independent ideas about writing. Burroughs and Golding told me to call them Bill. Judy, Angie, Mai, Doris, Susan and Andrea called me by my first name. Perhaps, coming naturally, narrative was an obsession with me and I studied all the great novelists for their technique before their language. I bought writers in serial form, in part-works, like Dickens, so that I could study their methods. And of course I studied Shakespeare because you cannot be an ambitious writer unless you do. And it cannot be said too often how vulgar Shakespeare was considered to be.

My head was full of many fictions intertwining to make more stories, more memories, more fictions. Preparing an ambitious novel was like tuning a guitar with a thousand strings. Heads filled out faces which in turn filled out character. Find the tone for the scene and the overall tone for the sections or the whole book. Impose and be absorbed. Art aspiring to the condition of music. *Tristram Shandy* here I come.

The story of all empires. Expand beyond capacity. Burst all over Pittsburgh, Portland, La Paz, Pearl Harbour, Pyongyang, Paris, Prague and Peckham and Preston. Ghosts of the living and the dead haunt well-known streets and mysterious bayous. Friends who become enemies and enemies who become friends, inexplicable conflicts and conflicting explanations. When I am dead I shall be dreaming another version of your life. Can the time it takes to restructure a dream be counted? Formless shapes precede the reality. I am dreaming or I am dreamed.

There are images congregating, needing stories to make sense of them. A crumpled ice-cream suit and panama hat. No madeleines for me. Just the smell of roses and all the salty wonders of the underground seas where we swim before birth; the womb where curiosity already pushes us towards the light and imagination creates sentience for the stars and bestows divine character upon the elements. How many times have our worlds been born? A magus does not try to interpret the voices of the gods, the magus speaks for the people, finds narratives and interpretations for the people. They draw their power not from gods but from those they represent and so there is mutual respect and we have mutual trust. We are playing for time. Time is what we generally play for. Time is a force greater than gravity and as tenuous as spider-silk.

These days, some magi tend to specialise or work for one tribe. Some are popular and successful intellectuals, well paid for our work. We serve our people, our audience, not some King or Maxwell, nor a dictator nor a feudal lord. We identify with revolting peasants. My friend Alan Moore knows much more about this than I do. John Bunyan is a mutual hero. We come from families of craftsmen.

The shallow seas of memory, the deeper reaches of the mysterious psyche and the currents and shallows we hide from ourselves, the forgotten stories we refuse to seek out, those narratives we avoid with studious cleverness. I had a happy childhood. I was used to speaking my mind. I was scared only of movies and abandonment! Nothing else upset me, even mum's histrionics. (Don't worry, dear, we'll soon be bringing in the airships and the magic swords.) My eldest cousin, Leonard, was in the Foreign Office just across from my Uncle Jack at 10 Downing Street. That was a fact. He was the only one to cross the border from SW to SE London. But Leonard believed my father ran an electrical repair shop somewhere in Sussex. There was a great deal of status involved in these family stories, the strangest of which gave Lord Beaconsfield, the son of Isaac Disraeli, as an ancestor. We were proud of our heritage. I had a powerful sense of Holocaust survival guilt. Yet my DNA shows *only* British origins. The Moorcocks were Yorkshire weavers, solid and relatively wealthy, who moved to one of the great silk-producing centres of Southern England, Wokingham in Berkshire, and later to parts of Oxfordshire and Surrey. They didn't die out. Most changed their name to Moorlock. Wells might have heard it when he wrote *The Time Machine.*

I was expelled from my school at the age of eight or nine for telling stories which kept the others up at night. Because Graham Hall was run by Continental progressives, Rudyard Kipling was not available in the school library and so I went undetected when I retold *The Jungle Books* with myself as Mowgli and my dog Rex as my wolf best friend. I embellished where memory let me down. Luckily, I had read several Tarzan novels before I was seven. I was the wolf-boy. Hear me howl.

Stories explain and speculative gossip fills in gaps until the fable becomes the main story. We often remember our innocent inventions better than experience. We swear they are true. Deciding truth or lies fascinates us. Memory controls us. We control the narrative. We create memory. We say what's true. We embellish. We add colour. We place ourselves and our actions at the dynamic centre, sometimes unconsciously. Many of us go dormant when deprived of social contact. We

25

can't decide what to do. We are not true individuals, in spite of our claims. We *know* as a pack as our *minds* communicate. Not brains, but minds of the kind certain sea-creatures possess. As a pack we absorb and interpret. Through fiction, the stories and experience of others, we absorb and add to the pack memory. When fiction lies too well, it might be said to have failed. Fake views. We are both the pursued and the pursuing monsters.

My mother, in the old Texas saying, would rather climb a tree to tell a lie than stand on the ground to tell the truth. My dear friend Harlan Ellison could turn a very ordinary experience into a lie *as the incident he described was happening*, and then ask you to confirm it. "Side by side we fought our way out of a den of blood-crazed bootboy punks, remember, Mike?" The 'den' was actually *Blitz*, Boy George's favourite New Romantic club, and the 'bootboy punks' were Harlan's admiring fans The Damned. They spoke several languages and so did Harlan but they didn't really share one except written English. Harlan had no ear for subtleties and really only knew Dick van Dyke cockney and Pepé Le Pew French. Two worlds, it turned out, and two languages. The admiring natives appear aggressive to the newcomer. They have strange clothes and accents. The American writer was frightened of a group who could have been his greatest allies. He lost thousands to his discomfort. I'd fixed up an interview in *NME* with my friend Nick Kent, who wanted to do a cover and centre spread which would have made him a name in half the households in Britain at that time. Instead, Harlan reinvented them and himself and fled in confusion away from a mild saxophonist who wanted to know when he was going to write a novel.

I was in the unusual position of having an audience among musicians and the so-called 'alternative society' so most of those I admired became at least acquaintances. With the instincts of a newspaper journalist, I was comfortable in most worlds and when Jon Trux and Bob Calvert came to see me I learned that even imaginative and curious friends had no interest in actually living the experiences that often fascinated them. Perhaps I was too agreeable, too willing to give it a go, to pop the pill or get in the van. "Where are we going?" Pete Taylor drew a cartoon of me at the 1957 Worldcon popping a bunch of black bombers or purple hearts and asking: "What were those?"

In 1956 Alastair Graham, editor of *Tarzan Adventures*, persuaded me to take my first assistant editing job by saying I'd be editor when he left in six months. I gave it a go. Later I would give writing heroic fantasy a go, give *New Worlds* a go, give Hawkwind a go or make records again and revive a modest musical career. Every new immersion for me was a new language learned, a new culture absorbed, a new set of friends, colleagues, skills, co-ordinates and narratives, and sometimes a new friend. Maybe some would stand back to back in a pinch. I prized loyalty in myself and others. At school, I was the one chosen to take our grievances to the Head Mistress. I knocked on her door, feeling my supporters melt away, so that, when the door opened, only I remained, looking up at her sober jowls. But I said my piece and was released.

Harlan had been the same once. Before he took over the rôle of protagonist in his own epic. He didn't remember the time in NYC when he was seen climbing up the outside of a twenty-storey building to reach his eleventh-floor apartment because he'd forgotten his keys. Or when I saw him grab a huge ambulance driver by his lapels, haul him out of his cab and berate him because he wouldn't pick up a sick bum. His close friends had a dozen similar stories, yet to much of the world he was just a great impulsive writer and a liar. Really, he was an undisciplined liar. He knew it himself, I think? "I guess you were always a pro and I was always an amateur."

27

I was his guest. What could I say? I can see his hurt little face in front of me now. A great amateur, a poor pro? Does it matter in the end? I'd say no to comfort him. He thought if he spun enough bull it would come true. A *trumpfahrter*. A *spieler* like half my market friends. Run it up the flagpole and see if it flies. But he was scared. As he got older, it became harder to weave and dodge. He could no longer make his promises come true in time. He had great language but he couldn't weave a pattern or deliver a resolution. He could see it all stopping to be effective as too many people got together to exchange notes about all the lies he'd told.

He wasn't the only short-story writer who couldn't organise a novel. Nor the first with a touch of Munchausen's. But I should really have said 'yes'. If you're charging professional prices you owe the reader professional work. He had started by risking a lie and making it come true in order to get TV jobs and push up his rates. He did a great deal by example to improve fellow writers' advances, conditions and status in SF and the media. Many young writers remain grateful for his patronage.

How do you tell readers the truth when they rely on you for a credible fiction? I suspect that it's by offering every story you know. Impossible? Not entirely. In the '60s I began to develop a technique whereby you put real iconic people, made famous or infamous in fact and books, into a piece of non-linear fiction usually dealing with an immediate situation. An issue of immediate concern, like Diana's crash, the fall of the Towers, and so on because that was what I had designed them for. Public figures or famous characters from fiction brought with them narratives and resonances which required much more space if they were presented in conventional form. Use the trope, use the icon. The less you disguise it, the better it works! The language had to be tight, almost poetry, and the subject had to be pretty immediate; something a conventional story could not easily do with available techniques. John Brunner had said that prose had to battle for audiences with movies, TV, radio. That had impressed me. My first crude attempt was with 'The Deep Fix' in *Science Fantasy*, 1964, under a pseudonym given me by Carnell who got it from the ABC Railway Guide. Another Carnell tip when using British surnames, while the chief saints usually worked for Christian names. James Colvin. After William Burroughs. Then I thought of an international protagonist associated with contemporary events like Czechoslovakia, the Bengali and Burmese revolutions, the friction between India, China and Pakistan. Jerry Cornelius. Ballard refined that technique to his own purposes in *The Atrocity Exhibition*. Wars. Hotspots. Newspaper headlines. Everything we wanted to confront and use for our fiction.

Aldiss, Ballard and I were often referred to as the Three Musketeers of science fantasy. We were the respectable ones the BBC arts programme would ask for interviews. We were together in all the biographical dictionaries, we tended to be grouped in articles or TV introductions. Brunner, too, was a sort of Aramis while in their eyes I was more the hot-headed Gascon and life-loving Aldiss, Porthos. Ballard was close to a perfect Athos, the Comte de la Fère. We were friends but writing independently. We almost never talked about stories we were working on. I was so grateful to publish them in *New Worlds*. We did not share literary theories, in practice at any rate. Those who disliked or felt threatened by our work and notoriety determined we were some sort of cadre with the Trotskyist plans which threatened them in the '40s and '30s. That was how the public saw us, anyway. Barry Bayley remained my closest friend. We worked together. Ballard and I were closest after that. We had children of similar ages and we had the most radical literary ideas.

29

Only John Brunner and Tom Disch liked reading their own work aloud. They were not popular visitors when they turned up with a manuscript under their arms. We had certain literary goals in common. Our political views were radically different. We all more or less agreed that the medium was the message and we needed to invent new techniques to deal with changing times and sensibilities. No matter what, I published them in *New Worlds* and the majority applauded and began to distinguish between what had been one 'incomprehensible' story from another as well as beginning to have favourites among the new writers. That was my experience from working on two previous magazines which were remade. Which gave me a chance to try new, ungeneric material, like Sladek's or Jones's, and trust reader and writer to communicate. Most did. Unfamiliarity was the problem and, once readers began to distinguish between novelty they liked and didn't like, the battle was won.

Meanwhile other 'experimental' writers were spinning thin tales with echoes and repetitions, chess games, card sequences to shuffle a deck of fifty-two into five little narratives based on random events, mazes, randomising. And, worst of all, sequels to classic novels! I met a number of them. Desperate soul-searching men and women given to suicide and madness, the dregs of the modernists, living in bedsits. They were usually pretty awful, but the critics thought they were wonderful. At heart they were decidedly familiar and remained generic to the pulpy core. Stuck in a hospital bed across from B.S. Johnson's publisher, the dying Jimmy Ballard tried to escape the man's civilised drone. The man felt he was bonding with Ballard by talking about the self-deceiving suicide who caused so much grief to his relatives and friends. A friend of mine, who published a poem or two in *NW*, found Brian's damned body. No fun for him. Anyway, Jimmy had fantasies of compromising the publisher's life support. Who would suspect him? But he chickened out and tried to get me to do it as usual, then his girlfriend, Claire. She hesitated. He and I were very passionate about fiction!

Shuffling a deck doesn't strike me as much of an innovation. I'm not even sure about cut-up and I champion Burroughs to this day. Most randomising methods were of no interest to the majority of us. We were looking for disciplined forms of fiction, nothing else. We wanted to make sturdy structures which would take the weight of many narratives at once, without need of rationalisation. Images designed to serve many narratives, which would engage readers without any need for linearity. The neo-modernists, drawing on the same two or three experiences fleshed out with a familiar story or two, some over-familiar characters and a current item of dinner-table scandal stirred them up and called that an experiment. In short, we despised them. Trying to mine fool's gold from exhausted seams. Structure could be achieved through a colour palette and codes, repeated line or certain words, selected rhythms and so on. False alchemists, bad magicians.

Later a new generation found ways of condensing many narratives into one while at the same time expanding their technical range. Alan Moore, for instance, in his literate graphic and graphic literary novels, or Iain Sinclair, with his high punk language, amalgams of myth and reportage, a New Beat equivalent of Northern Soul. You can find us on YouTube, chewing the fat at posh venues. Peter Ackroyd reached back into London's past for subject matter, refreshing old techniques. We all appeared on stage together, part of the same restless agency.

We were of course lazily imitated, sometimes by writers who just couldn't write character or narrative. Our images, our titles, our fundamental ideas were imitated by comics, TV, movies and other fiction, stripping the surfaces of our work and presenting it as novelty. Marvel or DC plundered our ideas, sentimentalised them, perverted them. Our carefully considered images, our symbols, were dragged off to the scrap-yard where we were soon buried under a million xeroxes and I could be told by teenagers that my fantasies used all the familiar tropes of the dark fantasy genre, when there had been no such tropes before Elric, influenced by the nineteenth-century Gothic, thundering with purple prose done for the love of it, Jerry Cornelius, a response to the myths of the twentieth and twenty-first centuries trying to create new language and narrative structures. Few copies had the same resonances. How could they have?

2
Edited Highlights

BLACKSTONE HAD PLEASANT memories of their childhood. They had lived in Richmond, then, in houses near the river, a short tram-ride over the bridge from Putney to Town. His mother and Connie's mother were comfortably close as sisters and remained so after marriage. Their amiable husbands became good golfing and cocktail friends; their children got along well. Every summer they visited the Normandy coast, usually with a day or two in Bon Marché and Samaritaine in Paris. That was how Blackstone came to study French Literature at the Sorbonne, his happiest memories, especially after he reunited with Connie and her friend Juliette, who were doing a year at the Alliance Française. They became inseparable and Juliette had considered breaking her engagement over Blackstone. Connie had talked her out of it. He rather hoped Juliette would not be at the house tonight. As far as he knew she and her husband now lived in the Chilterns. Too far for a quick stay.

Again he began to consider the wisdom of remaining for as long as he planned. He found it extraordinary that people were so insensitive. After all, they had been summoned on important family business, not invited to take a holiday. He would have to go for long walks and read in his room. He might as well give up on the novel and the translation. He had planned to work in Connie's magnificent library. It had come with the house and was very well catalogued. The previous owner had been a philologist, specialising in French. He sipped his drink. Maybe gin would improve his mood. Or maybe some Duke Ellington, the Modern Mozart, 'Take the "A" Train'? He put down his glass on the balustrade and began to go through the record cases. He quickly found the Ellington and, as it finished, carefully replaced the previous record. Oh, it was wonderful! The best of them all. He knew Connie liked it because she was excited when he gave it to her for her last birthday. He shivered. The evening was already getting a little cooler.

There was nothing to do but to turn it up until the carbon danced. From the Mists of Craig Crachan, roaring into blue skies and fluffy clouds and the familiar, ever-broadening, expanse of the Second Aether, boosting his pumper with the last of his Metallica, the captain of the *Now The Clouds Have Meaning* gets his arms through his lead overcoat. "And here goes the tricky bit," rolling his malleable ship down through spiralling clouds soft, multicoloured cotton, dragging the eggshell blue with it, the words flicker and dislocate and then it is formless, raining and *Now The Clouds Have Meaning* is taking a sideroll into the so-called First Aether. Captain Buggerly Otherly makes a quietly comforting landing, switches off his accumulators, downs his MP18 flexiprops, swings clear of the brassbound hatch and limps across the grey tarmac to turn in his papers at Old Mars Station. As usual the domes sweat grey film, obscuring the night stars with permanent recycling rain. Everything here needs a repaint. A thousand towers point skyward, spluttering with Colour K44, pliable, disguised, public and private. Mars is taking a long time to fulfil her early promise. He passes into a shadow. He opens a door. Capstan Charlie, unfortunately, is looking after the office. She is supposedly of

34

a high rank in the CBS. She'd rather sit and watch Worlds End News than finish a game of chess. The company of others discomforts them. Otherly is convinced that we draw closer to extermination but he at least is attempting to do something about it. He is trying to manage his remaining decades. He cared about the cost of cod but he cared more about the vanished haddock. "Where's the catch?" she asked herself again.

"Here's a go, lass." He's looking at the 5Ds on the office console while he waits for his papers to be stamped. "Kid born in Mitcham. Down south! Look at that. Bang straight on the predicted co-ordinates. Did you read that? Everything the *Daily Mail* said would happen and where we should find it! Didn't Sergeant Alvarez warn us this would happen? Assuming it matters."

She shakes her head, her eye on the times. Otherly falls silent. Paper, or something like it, drops to his lap. The *Memphis Probability Examiner* no longer carries hopeful headlines. He groans occasionally. He turns to the *Beale Street News*. They all know what's going on. In this quadrant, the multiverse plays hell with his engines. Is it his fault the Second Aether makes you two-thirds barmy? He wasn't brought up in Bradford to go barmy! After a while, his exit papers still wanting, he says: "Aye, Moorcock. Good Yorkshire name. Weaving family up by Dent. Decent pub up there. Moorcock Inn. My daughter and ex-wife run a midwifery service. Heard it on the omnis. Anyway duty calls. Centuries old. I'm told to join her. Cherry blaze and magenta blue. Not colours I favour for girl *or* bloody lad! Maybe we can compromise?"

She winks. "*Quid pro quo*, no? Born to Chaos out of Law, eh?"

"Now there's a filly for Our Albert to ride! By Lady Xiombarg's quaking bones, I'd stake a thousand camus on that! Here's a fine young recruit for the Squad. He'll take the rear-gunner spot in the ATC. Rectum Ricardo. Lovely kid. Threw six old strings straight into their torps up on the aft bridge and flattened their peppermints, sweet as young onions. Lucky shot of Disney Firehouse Five directly into the nerve pulser! Virgin cargo. Melted vinyl everywhere. Spraying vinegar into all the cracks and crevices worth saving. For safety. Then we'll sail the old amniotic sea, a world of wombs and wailing light, 220 amps of the best. One for you and one for me. And by heavens another angry face blinks and shrieks in horror before the expression slowly clears. Pah! Don't remind me!"

She refreshed her mouths through some sort of gland, licking her drying eyes. For a moment she had a salamander's thoughts. Her body's chameleon colours changed almost as rapidly as *Spammer*'s. Our Lady of the Waves, Sweet lady of the Planes. Then she was a Phoenix again. "Biloxi Fault was no fault of ours but the result of that material you somehow had working portables. George in Brixton. A lot of veg, enough to feed that monstrous pipe of yours rolling into the rig. Best titanium and now look! And who loosed so much fuel into the river. Gods! No wonder you and the machinoix sank your beliefs into all the brooks and rivers and beautiful bayous and crooks and crannies to hear the glorious crunch of the crispy carapace broken in two by strong pincers after we have the dilyfrost joys, so we sweep and say farewell to hateful complexity."

"How can we compensate for the life that's lost? Howling for the tit, flesh or rubber, greedy and grateful and some extra bond is cemented, no matter how you deny it. That impossible bond. Pah! Pah! 'Mother!' you cry as you die. 'Common experience'?" The machinoix ambassador obsessively shuffling a pack of Unitarian tarots and then pausing to inspect them. "Are you questioning my diagnosis? What did I volunteer for? It seemed easy at the moment, the 18th of December, 1939, just in time for the Blitz."

"Makes yer bloody well think," grumbles old Otherly, doing no such thing. His files were utterly corrupted. She could tell by the smell.

"That little lad is bound for glory," says the captain, polishing his comfortable old omnigraph. "Saint Woody and Saint Bertie will rule his stars. He will sing and tell tales for a living, but don't let him *near* a sewing machine! And, while there are omniphones, we shall live! Orpheus in the Multiverse ... Have I even paused to mention Black Holes? An easy fit, I suppose, in what I call Scale Theory. It's embarrassing how old-fashioned logicians insist what can be true and what can't while our own construct comes together with exciting speed. The Grand Equation? Remember? There's serious scientific courage required for the dance ahead. Oh, the mechanics of it. You can't quarrel with the ordnance. The best we could get you. Which was good. Plenty of Zoot Money and Beatles remixes loaded. Bowie? Check the box. You're going to need your Motörhead and Metallica. Don't worry, they're in the forward tubes. And guess what we got you from Meridian? Jimmy Rogers, Merle Haggard. Every track in the arsenal. But be careful. Some of that country music can be unstable in those new cannons of yours!"

"Jimmy R—"

"They'll help when they release their Streisand syrup, which can gum up your ordinaries before you can say Carly Simon. And you've some good Lynyrd Skynyrd as fine sonic klapbak! They did a lot of damage in the Marmalade Pot Massacre and at the Choctaw Indian Fair, so we won't be underestimating them. Look at these boxes. You have a whole extra arsenal of Hawkwind, Pink Fairies, New Order, Rich Kids, Deep Fix, Charnock's Grumbles. We need them more than Amadis of Gaul. We're up against serious professionals here, comrades. They've got gumups from Schubert to Sha Na Na! They can second-guess our every move and they have an arsenal of boy bands second to none. Not just those Korean outtakes they were flogging a track or two ago. Anyone taken on Freddie Force before? Or Mickey and the Matrixes?" A few limbs raised. "And what about the others? You know this is serious. Those horrible wedges they ride about in, cutting through the malleable multiversal planes, vectors of Law at her most simplistic, can cut through Second Aether space, reducing it to ribbons! Turmoil. Absolute desolation in their wake. Locusts. They'll even slice through some of the tributaries of the moonbeam roads. Destruction for the power of it like children who know there is only death in their future and strike about them in fear and anger like captured prey. What Law becomes when left unchecked. Ruin is what they always create in the end. The devil posing as a lawyer. We need better contacts. More damned power!"

At *New Worlds* we were part of a movement which, threatened by information overkill, found techniques for including multiple themes in linear and non-linear fiction, telling stories which were as complex, yet as intuitive, as the mass of outside information being filtered by our machines, our senses, our minds – our imagination. A lexicon for the multiverse. Increasing our sense of what evil was. Fashion ruled over taste. Complexity was resisted or simplified by art. But, where we were aiming to be laconic and concise, others pumped up derivative work in clumsy imitation or dusty homage, so that we were soon distancing ourselves from any 'movement', from New Wave to Cyberpunk.

That's the way of things, of course. You make a precision tool and someone uses it to chip stone. But if you put story and pleasure first you can hardly complain. Bloody airships! Sodding goggles! So, I'm offering you an honest lie or two as a story; and as much truth as I feel I can deliver or that you can take. Whatever depth it has depends on how it resonates with your experience. It has taken me some time and thought to make very little progress. I would not hurt my children for anything. In the first drafts of this somewhat complicated book I wriggled about, anxious to avoid my version of events without a living contemporary to contradict me. Having tied myself in emotional knots to produce a very bad beginning I had to think about it some more.

H.G. Wells and Brian Aldiss did their best with this. I admire their informal attempts at honest autobiography. I was often around the same events as Brian and I have to say Brian's version of shared moments was often not mine. For a start his accounts were more amiable, generous and friendly than many of mine. He was nicer to you than you could be to him but expected complete reciprocation. Give him a negative review and he stopped being your friend for a year or two. Tom Disch was the same. One mediocre review from you and that was that. I learned only to review the books I liked of theirs and from being a Young Turk, hating almost everything, I am now a respectful reviewer only of books for which I feel enthusiasm.

In his memoir, Ballard, to whom I think I was a loyal and honest friend, remembered incidents in which we both figured but where he almost always made himself the most dynamic protagonist of the story he was telling when often I remembered him as a retiring bystander. No Mary any longer to say, "that's not *true*, Jimmy!" A familiar cry at our many meals together. This phenomenon tends to be common to couples and old friends and rehearsed, honed and retold until either party will swear to its veracity. Rationalists or not, our whole existence depends upon belief. Phil Dick and Alfie Bester understood that and their readers accepted it.

Where I could I've checked my memory with contemporaries

like David Pringle or Charles Platt. Both have written accounts of the years I describe. Judith Merril published a memoir in Canada, having sworn me to everlasting secrecy about it. Some of us create strategies to avoid award ceremonies without giving offence. Some are conscientious recorders, even if I don't always agree with interpretations of my motives and intentions. I do my best to be honest, even accurate where possible. I'm pretty sure I know where and when I was born because it is on my birth certificate. Both my earlier wives are dead. Almost all my lovers are dead. Most of my friends, made since the '50s, early '60s and '70s are dead. Tom Disch, John Sladek, Charlie Naylor, Joanna Russ, Mervyn Peake, Brian Aldiss, Robert Nye, Andrea Dworkin, Judith Merril, Daphne Castell, Maeve Peake, Bob Sheckley, Sebastian Peake, Fritz Leiber, Mai Zetterling and David Hughes, Harvey Jacobs, Mike Dempsey, Ronnie Scott, Freddie Earlle, Eduardo Paolozzi, Angus Wilson, Jack Trevor Story, Kate Wilhelm, Alfie Bester, Gerald Kersh, Ted Tubb. Ken Bulmer, Angela Carter, Arthur Clarke, Carole Emshwiller, Jimmy Ballard, Jean Rhys, Harry Harrison, Doris Lessing, Bill Burroughs, Pete Taylor, Jim Cawthorn, Bill Golding and so many outstanding men and women who brought something new and enduring to the world, even if only a little. Drops of rain soon make a lake, as Grandma Taylor used to say. Good company, most of them. All powerhouses of imagination. Doris, of course, was the Matron, such an amiable, quick-witted, no-nonsense dame, like Rebecca West. I only met that formidable ex-mistress of Wells once or twice at Emmie's parties. Sometimes in London Judy Merril, who lived at her flat, stood in for Doris, who had another place, so she could leave and live in her own spare room if it got too much.

I still have a few close friends who remember the '70s as I do. Jean-Luc Fromental, Mike Butterworth, Pete Pavli, John Clute,

Graham Charnock, Steve Gilmore, John Coulthart, Charles Platt are unlikely to mythologise me or the times much. Lang Jones, one of the closest and most beloved, died in his sleep. Always told the truth, however reluctantly, or held his peace. Few musician friends remain. Lemmy and Bob Calvert are dead. Ginger. Graham. Martin Stone. Huw Lloyd-Langton, Martin Griffin, Mac McLagan, Nik Turner and more gone. Dave Brock is hanging on. Others I lost touch with or ceased to be friends with. Neither wife talked about me to anyone still living. As I once told a *Times* obituarist who should have checked his facts about Jack Trevor Story, the true story 'now depends which of us dies first'. I do not deny the love I felt for them, especially for my first wife. They were of a generation of women facing pressure to be five different people, none of them herself, and even sympathetic men thought you could solve that with a bit of moral support, picking the kids up occasionally and doing the odd stir fry. Helena was just a poor organiser, as bad as me for having her head in the clouds but not as quick as I was to respond to emergencies. Jenny was prompt, naïve and too young for me, but old married men was all she'd known. They were both passive-aggressive. I was a bit more direct. If there was a problem I wanted to confront it and fix it. Saved time. And that's awkward, too.

To the world in general one woman was a saint and one was a bit manipulative and irresponsible. At different times in their lives either term might have fitted either one. Helena's Newnham friends warned me she was a *femme fatale*. Not when we were married she wasn't. Even after we divorced she was loyal to me as I was to her. But there was no doubt about her duality. And how swiftly she imposed her own story onto our common memories! Her character was contradictory. She combined a Cambridge-educated moral rigour with an underlying fear of abandonment which she worked hard to bring

41

about. She hated analysing character yet imposed a character on so many of us, including me and her children. After we were separated she was forever expressing her surprise when I did something I normally did, like visiting a sick friend, as 'not like you', which presumably meant I was not the character she had created.

I was characterised as the philandering husband, yet for all of our life I loved domesticity. She wasn't sure about it. Like many intelligent married women, she had periods of intense hatred for men. Her ambivalence was her most familiar characteristic. Helena could be unbelievably vicious, attacking with reckless lack of concern for consequences. She could brood for days like Ivan the Terrible. Then strike. Or not.

Jenny was naïve and basically a mess up, having chosen to be a groupie at the very moment she won a scholarship to the best girls' school in London and a straight run at Oxbridge, winding up as a receptionist for Parlophone, as musician bait; the ex-mistress of three married UA executives before she was twenty-one. She knew a bit about sex and nothing about the drugs she took so recklessly. She didn't know the difference between heroin and cocaine. Everyone had lied to her. She had great taste. An exceptional draughtswoman, she lacked any focus or confidence as an artist. She'd come out of an S&M relationship with a sleazy Cypriot 'art' publisher whom I knew from his unpleasant reputation and his advances to a friend's thirteen-year-old daughter. He did high-end naked-children books I found nasty but she found romantic. Victorian kiddy-porn. Too icky for me. She wanted me to play parts in S&M scenarios I simply found funny. I didn't know how much self-demeaning romantic predatory folly was involved. I feared for my own children and, for a moment, rightly. I had every reason to accept responsibility for imposing my own ideas on her. I had wanted to help her become self-confident, to provide her with a base on which to build self-respect. I had no real idea what I was dealing with. Games were meaningless to me unless they involved a chequered board or cards and cash. I wound up functioning as her father, just as I had for my mother. I was born to hug. To pat a trembling hand. But not to wield a whip. Thank god I left that behind!

Langdon Jones remained one of my most talented, self-demanding friends. Expecting no reimbursement, he single-handedly restored Peake's third volume, *Titus Alone*. He was a superb composer, editor, writer and musician. He discovered and worked with some of our best new talent on *New Worlds*. You can hear his lively piano on *The Entropy Tango*. He put enormous verve into Schoenberg, whom he loved, and would only play for children's parties if they fitted him with a King Kong suit. His musical setting for Peake's *The Rhyme of the Flying Bomb* is one of my favourite contemporary compositions. It's very hard to play. The last time I saw him he said that when he gave up editing, he felt a weight lift. When he stopped writing, he became happier. When he gave up playing and composing, his moods improved. "Every time I give something up, I feel better!" I know what he meant. You get older, your skills improve, you get *more* self-demanding. There is a heavy responsibility in creative work and the better one gets at it, the harder it becomes, and the more an audience expects – or rejects. *Behold! I retire!*

So here we are aboard the *Compromise* bravely heading starwards. Earth is troubled. Food riots and banditry everywhere. Our mission? To make new stories, think about a couple of fresh ideas and a couple of old ones, refresh some, to pluck the skirts of the infinite, to create fresh wonders and further examine familiar characters (or characteristics, anyway). Human nature. Social mores. A whole series of middle-class nightmares. What if my child were abducted? My identity stolen? My wife

43

betraying me. My husband betraying me. Secrets of the Black Market. As I write there is a fear of war in the air. Why do people do that? We all know the consequences. Another horribly irrational and cruel solution to a problem. We know what war does. Yet we drift, masked ghosts, perhaps already dead; unasked gusts, passing guests of the infinite; scale upon scale, the same traits scaled up and down. You must see them, even you with your melancholy walls, from the corners of your eyes, the little receptors which bring despairing laughter. The same characters. The same plots. Too late. You are nothing without the crowd. You have no reason to think for yourself. Fate is so rarely these days our friend. But pity the conscious creature aware of its doom. You make further attempts to embrace your fall but that defies logic. There is no escape from the mighty rockets above and the mob below. You trip, discovering that you are too fat to tie your shoelace and you lie there out of breath, bewildered by this twist in Act Three.

At least I'm wearing comfortable clothes. Manual work, however, is beyond me. I can barely hold an instrument. But I can still play the old songs. *"Lou, with your long hair ..."* I first played it to an audience at the Roundhouse in 1979. Pretty much a wake for those of us who had survived all the suppressed revolutions of our day. Calvert and Alex Harvey and even old Ginger Baker were trying to find an honest wage for a good day's (or night's) work and had chased my attackers! So the six made temporary camp nearby, careful not to show favouritism to either side. Everyone was respected and a Prince and Princess of the Forbidden Marches elected. We had, inadvertently, found ourselves on leave in the Paradise of Lost Dreams. Don't worry, it's an easy fix.

Please assume I'm happy. I was born, most would agree, just after Chamberlain had issued a sad declaration of war against Hitler for invading Poland. I lived through the Blitz to hear the Vengeance rockets coming down. I can still catch their distinctive noises when they fell. V2 was worse. You only heard it when it hit you. My mother said that everyone thought we were trouncing Hitler, though we didn't seem to be getting very far. France was in. They had the Maginot Line. So this time we were pretty sure we were the good guys and could sort Europe out with our quaint old weapons and strategies. But the rules had already changed. No friendly Boxing Day soccer with the SS over a pint of blood that year. A quick trounce, save Poland, get rid of the Nazis, hang Hitler, put Uncle Joe in his place and home by Easter if we're realistic. Bugger Miss Liberty if she didn't want to join in the scrap.

Was that Polly, lost amongst the colours of a vivid vision, blinded like him by glaring, heavenly beacons! All farting in the wind, those Yanks! And bugger Generalissimo Franco if he wants to remain on the sidelines, picking up scraps. Well, all that changed for often- and over-analysed reasons and round the old whirligig goes again. Ka-boom, etc. What a world it was. So speedy. So exciting! *Ker-lank. Polly! Kettle's boiling!!*

Anti-aircraft (ack-ack) guns erected all over the common. Kettles boiling everywhere. Five million cups raised to stiff, British lips. Everyman and Everywoman refusing to show fear to the children! Look, love! Look at the pretty lights. As the Battle of Britain drifted to the east. Going every night for weeks.

"Lights. Bound to attract the enemy. Spare lamps in that stowage. Shells in the other." Rubbing with his sleeve to wipe condensation from his visors. "Supposed to be a big one tonight, lads. They're said to have extra tanks of Como, PPM and Schubert to gum up our shock phones." He bent to flip his toggles. "Eh?" Rising from his scope. Drifting to the main 'phone through crowded cables and hoses. "Oh, for old-fashioned brass!" He paused with delighted surprise. "Pearl? Pearl Peru?" Tilting his grizzled head for better reception.

"Look at that, Skippy! What do you see? You see drifting dangerous housing black with injustice to have clashed with the National Guard by required practice and intention. So we hold it high, this child, above God Itself! It is symbolic of Justice!" Pearl bared her sweet, melancholy soul, "Oh, where shall we trade when this madman has destroyed all our treaties and pacts?"

Buggerly Otherly grumbled over his high-tuned, responsive engines. "She's ready for anything, this old girl. By 'eck, she's beautiful! Listen to that Beethoven 7th! And you should see her holding big and steady on the Wagner when we get into a real scrap." He was gasping at the glory of it. He had clarity in both cans. "But you must hold steady." He became serious. "These are horrid times and you are charged with defence against the Grey Hole, for they are demanding their right to be easy and go where they please. You know those 'arrow heads' they fly – designed to rip through layers of the multiverse and do unimaginable damage to our environment, not to mention the splashover into the First and Third Aethers. They are reckless and full of certainty, these Know Knothing Klub people. So much noise. Is there any way Daniel Boom and his Black Tunnel Boys can help? It was our last hope! What can Martini rifles do against clam-coopers? Someone is smuggling clarinets to the enemy, saxophones of most keys. Well, we can forget the tubas and French horns. Unless we're very lucky!"

Under her plexiviz and lying on her back on an air bed, Contessa Capona turned her attention from the glaring blue-white of Krishna 7 and wondered why the captain was giving so much time to getting the crew off. One fell onto the hull, held there by the ship's gravity. Two swift rupsters took it off to the infirmary and returned to clean the site until it smelled and looked relaxed. Jumkin billowed down from The Chopper Shopper and into HRT mode, readying herself until Manners

46

reached the sharp end and got antsy. "We were briefly humiliated but we took a single arrow from their prized flag of Law and they had nothing better to bring against us. The sea offers us our weapons back! Let's get busy. Must we face a massacre? I say there's a mistake in our calculations!"

Frantically Old Brian, the navigator, scratched his helmet and consulted his almanac. "The plan is to rescue Our Lady who, as we understand it, was captured near here by Norse pirates who in turn sold her to some Irish slaver, a Barbary pirate who raided and captured an entire Christian village near Kinsale in Ireland one night, and was never caught for it nor were more than three of the villagers ransomed back. Those who returned had strange stories to tell. Not just about the Northmen but also about the Barbary slavers and mysterious seas no earth-born sailorman has seen."

"Then our plan," Otherly grunted, switching to Notes. "And before we begin I would really be grateful if the Pale Company would give notice if they have something they need to check. You really should remember that your safety, as well as ours, depends on it." He sat back, looking towards his co-pilot.

"And if we can't deliver?" Quelch was a right-wing radical and aggressive in these squabbles. He sat down under a tree. "What then?"

Heads float about me. They have haunted me all my life until I had an intuitive barrier against them, a way of resisting if not defeating them. But even speaking of my psychic sensibility I have to pause and protect some things. My mind, not my brain, but my *being*, the individual essence in the construction of the Great Masterpiece. Take these upstairs, Frazer. They need to be framed. I will act against the rules. Of course they asked where Penny was. I didn't know. Pass the pepper will you? Good girl!

"Ready?" They locked in as the sounds of Duke Ellington

rose from the starter tubes and with a sudden jerk they rolled sideways, then nose down, then rose up again as 'Take the "A" Train' took them quietly into the Hardly Ever and from there into the Second Aether. "Here's a note. Anyone know a place called St Michael's in Northern Ireland? Derry Down, Derry. No. My mistake. Anyone know a place called Mitcham in Surrey? Semi-rural suburb, about twenty minutes from London. Stinks of lavender and butter. You don't see these old trades any more. And for Christ's sake we can't go to Rowntree's yet. I knew I had a solution to the problems. But what's this ring?"

"Springsteen," she said. "In case you need it. Just turn the inner circle."

For a moment my mother panicked, I think, and we went off to Wales to escape the bombing. She couldn't stand it. She came back in a week complaining they'd charged her threepence for a stale crust she'd asked for to help with my teething. We remained prejudiced against the Welsh for many years. Now, one of my best friends is Welsh. Then I was in Devon with my dad's people briefly, near Exeter. I loved that. I think I was the only nephew then. My great aunt kept a tribe of cats in that old red-brick lodge, behind a wall around an orchard smelling of apples and all the unpicked fruit fallen to the ground and mulched by our feet or gobbled up by the pig. Undulating seas of cats, answering her calls to eat the scraps with which they supplemented their catches, semi-feral fur and the smell of baking. In a world where everybody called you 'my love', the cats were 'my dears'. Her husband, Mr Brown, had been a chauffeur to the big house and they'd let him keep an old limousine. I don't think it drove any more. I used to pretend to drive it through the orchard where it was parked furthest away from the house in their idyllic smallholding. I can hear their old-fashioned West Country voices coming through the blinding light of a setting sun. "Bedtime, my lovin'. Bedtime, my handsome." Sweet Miss Susie Elizabeth Brown, her unmarried sister, adored me with my big blue eyes and mop of near-white curls. The warm, late-summer smells of a wheat-rich, cattle-heavy, sheep-wealthy West Country which was only visibly at war when you saw the barbed wire on the empty yellow beaches. Once, changing trains as you did interminably in wartime, we saw parts of Bristol Zoo on the move, with giraffes sticking their necks out of goods wagons and lions grumbling. The smell was pretty strong. My dad wouldn't take me to look at them. In the end a porter picked me up from the platform and carried me across the tracks to see through a little sliding window a weary and defeated tigress. "Ain't she a beauty?" She was. She seemed a sad beauty to me.

But I digress. Most of the time we stayed in London, in and out of the Anderson and Morrison shelters as the Blitz got worse until the buzz-bombs and the rockets almost broke our spirit, and then we were jumping over bonfires with Hitler and Göring burning in effigy, their smoke drifting amongst the early-summer hedges and flowers of Dahlia Gardens, and they bulldozed the public shelters down. I'd become used to the flying bombs, the disappearing buildings, the piles of rubble, the sudden sight into someone's private life which was pretty much the same as anyone's living in the English suburbs. Empty prams. Turned-over trikes. A bathtub or a bedstead hanging through a wall, sucked from the side of the house. But the price was worth it. No infant school. V-Bombed. In the night. Nobody hurt. Then my dad disappeared and my mum couldn't take over the rent, being a woman. Her brother Stan and his wife moved in. Stan was a wounded veteran, a telephone engineer who worked for Bell. His wife was his nurse. My mother thought she was bossy. The women fought.

By now my mother had a manual job in a nearby factory.

The boss, a sensitive Austrian scientist back from internment, unable to use his degree, offered her a job as book-keeper in the office, and, as a temporary home, an asbestos shack known as 'The Cottage' which had no electricity and was lit by gas. Heating and cooking by Rayburn wood stove. And a flush toilet about twenty or thirty yards away down a track between old elms. That first winter I had to walk between banked snow twice my height to get to the toilet. Noisy rooks nesting high overhead. The remains of a stables attached to Norbury Manor were now in ruins, surrounded by more sickly elms and, in one corner of the timber yard, 'The Cottage' had belonged to the gardener/stableman, then used for storage. It was basic, ugly, relatively new, fairly dry, cheap to heat with our stove and paraffin. Nearby the ruined stables had four stalls either side, still smelling of straw and manure. Time could be so comforting.

The Cottage had rats from the nearby timber yard. They were bold, inquisitive, but they never attacked. We never found droppings inside. They lived in the sawdust and foraged where they could. I came to like and admire them. For a while our rooks were joined briefly by a talking jackdaw. It had escaped from whoever taught it to speak. Perhaps it went home. I was miserable when it left. Every day was filled with the productive sounds and smells of sawmills, frequently recycling timber from beer-crates and ruined houses. Mum was pretty, vivacious, smart, trained and naturally friendly so that no doubt the boss saw her qualities of loyalty and intelligence more quickly than he might have done. Most of the other women hated her. She was a book-keeper at David Gregg's grocery in Streatham before her first miscarriage. She took over the timber firm's books. Fairly quickly she was promoted to the office, being a useful book-keeper and strategic director to her new firm and would be promoted to the board in the 1950s.

I found the Austrian's letters. Beautiful, old-fashioned Continental writing. He was helplessly infatuated. She frustrated him. That fool was the wisest mentor a boy like me could wish for. He valued imagination, being a convert to Rudolf Steiner's Christian mysticism. I owe a great deal to him. We both did. He cheated on his family for us. Perhaps I should say he *planned* to cheat? I can't condemn him, nor my dad, who had the grace to slip out of the picture leaving nothing but a few ERB novels and my mother all to myself. And the well-read Continental as his part-time replacement. Education: wide and unusual. Ego: fired up. Imagination: Valued. Ready to go! Talent? Who knows? I could have done with a slightly more ordinary name, but otherwise it was all good. My young dad, with sunny grin, white shirt and baggy flannels beside his sports car in the West Country, where his dead mother was from, forever enjoys his active youth. My mum smiles beside him from under her Gainsborough hat, on his arm, wearing her summer frock. My arrival wrecked all that. Not an unsuccessful manoeuvre on my part.

This apple of my mother's eye, I enjoyed an imagination more active than hers, better-encouraged, better-informed and better-disciplined. My mother's family were clever but exhausting talkers. My cousin Leonard wrote to me recently, reminding me that our grandmother was a great raconteur. To put it another way, maybe, they couldn't shut her up. They all told stories. My mother had her repertoire and would be asked to recount favourites, and, when she could not, I learned to read so fluently that infant's school with *Dick and Jane* was boring, setting a pattern for me. If a subject interested me at school I would read about it until I sometimes knew more in some ways than the teacher. Almost everything I know I taught myself or learned by example. I wanted to be taught and I wanted to debate but those employed to teach me did not want to discuss subjects. They taught from standard textbooks. Few knew more than was in the books. They were embarrassed and therefore sometimes angered by my questions. Teaching went from the book to our ears in texts written by civil servants and doled out to hastily trained women who had taken over from the men who were in the Force. I was surprised, maybe because I was already trying to reconcile whatever others claimed as truth with the contradictory stories my mother told of wonderful travels abroad (she was actually terrified of sailing or flying). I genuinely wanted to know what the teachers had to say.

I began a habit of fact-checking all I could, not to confront anyone but to see how quickly people's stories could change. I started to judge those I knew by their actions, not what they claimed to be, believing only what I could verify. I was far from mistrustful, but I did want to know all sides. When I grew older I bought newspapers of several different stripes in the hope they would help me find a balanced truth; older still, I moved to Texas to understand American conservatives, listening to the radio stations of the certifiably barmy, ready for the rise of Trump. I was doing something against my mental well-being! If people don't chant slogans I'd like to hear their arguments but if it's over-familiar, left or right, I get bored and more interested in the forces driving them. Their opinion interests me until it strikes me as impossibly intractable. These people have far more in common than not. What a waste of time. And who are all these anti-democrats who wave flags and plot to form an autocracy, like Iran? Iran the Ironic. Full of wealth and losing money. In time-honoured fashion the shaman comes to exchange wisdom with these others but typically they turn on him – scornfully because his opinions are not theirs. His visions are a little different. His magic is bad magic. They can't understand it and why should they?

It's largely impossible for an empathetic person to imagine an unempathetic one. What is it? Neanderthal and Cro-Magnon? A kink in the wiring? You are helpless in argument because they really can't see another point of view. Frustration. What can you do?

Well, you could insist that the Law be consistent in its charging and sentences, particularly if an officer of the law is in the box. You could insist that hunts be charged for their barbaric running of animals to death, with foxes, badgers and hares being most at risk. Then there are all the iniquities and inequities in our Big Cities! The scams, the exploitation, the need to reform our country from top to bottom!

"Ach! What's that smell?" It was Jennifer and she was trying to make herself as long as others looking at the best of the stylings which had been commissioned by Modigliani. I knew by instinct when I was stuck. Shall we go to the Roman dungeons now or shall we make a little picnic on the bench over here? They were now enjoying the recently excavated Roman road, thirty feet wide, garrison and country villas, with some sign that they produced wine in the region, during warmer times and the Graveney and the Wandle flowed down into the Thames. What are we doing about Norbury?

I have been here for over eighty years. In the '40s I had the experience I needed to rid me of any incipient romanticism about war. In the '50s I completed my education in Soho and Brookgate. I mixed with criminals and scholars and had friends who were both. I knew transsexuals and male and female prostitutes and all the misfits Soho made comfortable. Politics and Logic at *The Partisan* (with chess and good grass on the side). Music at the *Gyre and Gimble*. Rhetoric at *Sam Widges*. I learned *Literature* at home and Fleetway. *Practical journalism* in Farringdon Road. *Physics* at the Globe. *History* at the Westminster Library. As at Whitehead's, everyone in Soho and Fitzrovia wanted to teach me what they knew (although I held back from practical burglary). In the '60s and '70s I was part of a new enlightenment, nothing less. Surrealism and Freudianism and cool jazz had influenced the '40s and '50s. Pop Art, Brecht & Co., Eisenstein, Bergman, the Whitechapel Gallery, LSD. Ronnie Lang. *The Divided Self*. Aldous Huxley. *The Doors of Perception*. Rachel Carson. *Silent Spring*. And a handful of other visionary and life-changing books, including William Burroughs, Henry Miller, Mervyn Peake, Ray Bradbury, Maurice Richardson. Astonishing years for individuals like me, free of further education and finding my own subjects, as the popular arts merged with physics and modern sculpture and painting to bring about a subtle renaissance still largely unrecognised and threatened by a reaction only a little more incoherent. The dawning understanding in so many areas of culture that you did not need to reject one in order to embrace the others. Pop Art. I had gone to the Whitechapel Gallery, during the times I worked for Flexhill and then Gold Brothers, admired their exhibitions from the mid-'50s when the East End was still ruined.

Only now are we fully realising our prescience, as people react against the truth and consequences of our deeper understanding of our dilemma, our appalling destructiveness. Destroying our world as we learned, the way Victorian botanists and biologists shot and stuffed, pinned and embalmed every vanishing species they could lay hands on, I was born out of war and I will die doubtless as a result of war or while anticipating one. Kulaks give power to kulaks. This is no place for a metropolitan. How many are now out there in the gathering darkness? No wonder Stalin hated them. Very bad book-keeping, particularly when they confuse it with morality. Walls is one of those solutions. Are you following, class? How do I offer everyone's opinion and tell a good tale or two?

Bear with me. I'm trying. The story of my life! Non-linear association works extremely well for those raised on Goons and Pythons when absurdism found a huge popular audience from out-of-work crossing sweepers to His Highness the young Dauphin himself. Has anyone noted the irony of Ukraine, with its terrible history of anti-semitism, electing a Jew as the best national leader it ever knew?

Pink flamingoes stand on one leg among water lilies in an English ornamental pond. And I smell rotting leaves again, rich, fresh earth. The graveyard. The company of the recently dead. Autumn in Kensington, Brompton Road, Putney, the River. Modernist concrete. Art nouveau marble. I strain towards the water, hands outstretched, safe in my baby harness. We were all more fearless as I grew up. How could we not be? We faced horrifying death and loss every day. We knew what to expect. We demanded little for ourselves. The spivs preyed off their fellows to profit from the Blitz, the shortages, the lesson. They were not popular. Some of them died, often by strangulation suddenly in East End basements, and others were mysteriously killed by shrapnel cuts to the throat in the West End. Some went on to be magistrates. Some were the Krays who scared the crap out of me. They killed, and they were cruel. One of the twins really enjoyed hurting people. It didn't stop with the war's end. It never does. The racetrack gangs became black marketeers and morphed into Ted gangs, fighting for territory all over South London. Not the happy Johnny Ray-loving jitterbugging crêpe-soled rockers of urban myth. Razor gangs. A couple of my friends at Fleetway were Teds, Brixton Chain Gang and Balham Blackshirts. Violence is a habit you have to wean yourself off. My mum was a manipulator, not a threatener. I was lucky to have the father whose 'engineering war work kept him at the office' and eventually ran off with that same office, an unremarkable, pleasant woman pretty much the opposite of my mum. Most of my closest friends were raised by their mothers. Giving comfort is also a habit difficult to shake. Others of us learned that comforting or being comforted can't be that bad. Talk about interdependency! We are enslaved by the peasant drives of others. The kindly kulak gives you the shirt off his back, then turns to slaughter a Jewess in front of her own children. Better not let on you're Jewish.

Like my mum, but unlike some of her sisters, I was never much of a conventional snob. Together, most of that disappeared and they were soon yelling with laughter by the second cup of Darjeeling. Any snobbery I had, I cultivated by reading Whistler and Wilde. My background had taught me to question many assumptions, especially class distinctions, and my mother had been pretty firm about 'not judging a person's character by the colour of their skins'. My family spread through the social strata. My experience and confidence were wide, thanks in particular to my mother who worked to send me to a public school which gave me a posh accent and an unusual way of teaching myself through solitary reading. I remained otherwise highly sociable, as friendly as a happy dog and as willing to learn. I never questioned anything the teachers wanted to suggest. If they had another way of doing things, well and good, but I didn't want to be forced to do it their way when I knew my way worked. Graham Hall taught me to love many subjects, including world mythology. I loved algebra, which they taught seven-year-olds at Graham Hall. Little kids love symbolic logic. I was mocked when I put up my uniformed arm to ask the arithmetic teacher at Belmont when we were to begin algebra classes. First things first, they said. But I came to think they didn't know how to teach it. So if I wasn't getting the education I was promised by the State or indeed the private system, why shouldn't I seek it from a different direction? What was wrong with reaching a logical step by another route?

There were precedents. Tarzan had done well when his parents were killed in the jungle and he had only their books to teach him. Writing in English, but speaking sophisticated French, he greeted newcomers to the West African jungle, the Kingdom of the Waziri, with the courtesy of the mangani, the apes of whom he was king.

I grew up in solitary diversity, in a world first destroyed before my eyes and now reviving. I read old magazines and, not liking most comics except *Eagle*, bought *Champion*, the last text weekly, even though it was a shadow of its former kind like *Union Jack*, *Thriller*, *Magnet*, *Gem* and *Boys' Friend Library* which had flourished until wartime paper shortages. I bought those by the week, but twenty years or more late from specialists in prewar story papers. By buying issues in order I could follow the serials. The beautiful adventuress Mlle Yvonne, the Criminals Confederation, The Bat, Dr Huxton Rymer, Plummer, Wu Ling and Marie Galante, the Voodoo Queen in *UJ*. The master-crook Zenith the Albino appeared in the same paper and *Detective Weekly*. Monthly, they regularly turned up in *Sexton Blake Library*.

Independent heroes, many from simple beginnings, their experiences were as close to my own as Tom Merry's and especially similar to Richmal Crompton's William Brown, who became my hero. The fictional boy I identified with the most, 'Just William', whose long series of books ensured my sense of justice and entrepreneurship! And Sexton Blake's other super-villains like Waldo the Wonder Man or, in books now in our public and private libraries, the other stories of Edwy Searles Brooks who lived a few leafy suburban streets away from our home at 36 Semley Road, Norbury, London SW16, and was no stranger to Lost Races or Giant Squids. He would invite me to tea with his wife and happily answer my questions about his work on *Sexton Blake* and *Nelson Lee*. He was by then a respectable crime novelist published two or three times a year in Collins Crime Club. It was much better money, you got royalties and they 'didn't mess about with your stuff'. Modest, amiable and rather tickled by my schoolboy enthusiasm for his prewar Blake and Nelson Lee stories, he gave me a lot of his time, even though I was mystified by his failure to display his work in his office. Most of his copies were in storage. His manuscripts were immaculate. I still have one. His wife was his typist and editor and sometime collaborator and a sweet lady.

Mr and Mrs Brooks lived a few doors from my Auntie Connie in a pleasant house much like ours, but in the peace of a cul-de-sac formed by the small Pollard's Hill park at the top of the road. That was how I discovered that most successful authors were about as well-off as the local doctor, if they were lucky, and only the rarest had yachts or villas on the Côte d'Azure. But money and fame were not part of my ambition. I wanted to write stories as good as Mr Brooks's and have them published as the half-crown paperbacks you could buy at W.H. Smith's bookstalls. But I still liked the idea of being in a group. By now I had a guitar! I sold my wonderful toy soldier collection, based on my father's, for £2.10s. to buy it.

3

Music, Muses and Melancholy

"WE NEED A meritocracy, not a democracy, with the franchise permitted to those who can prove in a practical way that they have qualified to vote, rather as one must now take a test to prove one can drive a motor. Not property! God, no! You know, reading ability, rhetoric, logic, general knowledge."

"Oh certainly! Just as they get at the average state school!" She was sarcastic. They were discussing how democracy had elected dictators. Connie accepted a cocktail from Harold. The reception room was large enough for a modest ball, with Adamsesque fireplaces at both ends, a lovely crystal chandelier sparkling in the shadows of a ceiling after Rubens's Whitehall Banqueting House. Moat Hinton had been redesigned in an early eighteenth-century nostalgia for the days of the Glorious Revolution. Portraits of bewigged gentry were everywhere, some of them not original to the house. Connie had preserved almost everything when she had bought the place a decade or so ago. "You had the tour last Christmas. I'd had it all done up by then! Cost more than the bloody house, darling. And the land. Come on. Thank God for pa's job and ma's canny nose for property! I'll talk about the other thing later." She had traces of that finishing-school accent most girls had started to pick up, especially if they weren't from London. She lifted her head and winked. They moved back to the sound of chattering as her other guests congregated outside on the wide terrace above the moat.

Harry was surprised. He had not expected to find quite so many of his relations here. Not all of them had dressed for dinner, so perhaps some were passing through and would leave later? These days, of course, it was not always possible to tell. He could be pretty informal himself. Connie guided him through the French windows and out into the crowd. The smoke of cigarettes irritated his eyes. He opened his case and offered it to her. "Sinuses. Best thing's a hair of the dog! Want one?" Her slender, manicured hand carefully selected a Turkish Balkan Sobranie from under the gold band. His prominently proclaimed twenty-first birthday present from his Uncle Barbican, who was something, he thought, in the City.

Most guests were looking towards the west, admiring the view over the oaks and beeches of the small park. The usual lot of faces from familiar to vaguely familiar. Family conference? Everyone! Some were engrossed in conversations that had been going on for decades. Connie took him by the arm. "You know pretty much everyone, I think. Jack and Dolly, of course."

His cousin Jack was something in the Foreign Office, a tall, vacant young man in an unbecoming lilac summer suit which clashed a little with his pink complexion. His black hair was pasted down and appeared to be a toupé. His wife Dolly was vivacious and pretty, with calculating brown eyes, close together. "Harry, darling!" She sprang to embrace him. "Hasn't it been ages!" Jack lifted an amiable glass. "What ho, old boy!"

"They're dead, too," Connie said from behind him. The responding laughter made him a little uncomfortable. He turned. She was talking to a man in a clerical collar. Probably his cousin

Jimmy, who had always been a little religious. They were children the last they met. Apart from with Connie, he really had little in common with anyone here, whereas he and his cousin kept in touch, celebrating the slightest occasion together. He consoled himself that most had cars, so would probably be gone by Sunday evening. The relatives he really loved would remain, while with luck the rest would leave.

"Oh, look! Isn't it lovely?" he heard Dolly say. They all crowded towards the wide low wall to watch the sun in its pretty descent behind the oaks, its ruddy light reflected in the terrace's warm buttery stone. That light made the world almost cosy; but really, thought Blackstone, we are all descending, dropping into darkness. Just darkness. He imagined a fleet of bombing aeroplanes appearing over the trees. This English moment was precisely what, for Blackstone, at any rate, the enemy attacked. Was it envy? As well as contempt? Who were they hoping to scare? The French, perhaps, but not the English! The French were once the serious enemies. Only a few years ago they were beating the world, defeating Germany. Now they were bound to do it again!

He wondered what danger this house once faced from those seemingly gentle hills and the tranquil sea beyond. For now, he realised, he felt emotionally if not physically safe, in a kind of fugue, and veiled against the world. Did some watchman once spot the striped Norse sails on the horizon and begin the frantic tolling of the warning bell? Blackstone found he was savouring his drink, analysing its flavours. Her new chap — who was known by his Christian name 'Brian' — Harry was bound to admit, mixed a very good cocktail. Gin, of course, with a touch of Pernod, not too much vermouth. Outside, he remained close to the house wall where he could not be approached from behind. Certainly nothing wrong with the view! He took a deep, relaxing breath. Suddenly all he could smell was the almost overwhelming scent of roses. Some woman's perfume? He could see no-one nearby who might wear so much scent. He paused for a moment, not wanting the illusion to be over! He could barely breathe, as if his throat filled with soft pink petals, yet the scent was not some terrible cheap Woolworth brand. He could not remember a nearby garden with the scents of quite so many flowers so late in the summer. The intensity reminded him perhaps of when he was a baby in a walled rose-garden in the hush of high summer one drowsy midweek Early Closing Day when even deliveries ceased at noon.

On the far side of the French doors, in the space behind a buttress, the gardener had set up a gramophone. Cheap, cheerful music quickly had Dolly dancing with Jimmy, who was trying hard to be modern. Soon most of the others joined in. Blackstone stood back, a thin, self-protective smile on his face. They danced with unspontaneous gusto. Only Stanley and Dyliss Russett appeared to be enjoying themselves thoroughly, but they were excellent dancers, no strangers, he knew, to the Locarno and the Café de Paris. They encouraged the others and soon most of Connie's guests were dancing in the scarlet light of the setting sun. Their hostess was in the thick of them, her amiable whinny counterpoint to the *Saint Louis Blues*. Was he, Blackstone wondered, on a fool's errand? Had the mysterious business merely been a trick to get him here to meet someone utterly unsuitable?

Blackstone went to sit on the low terrace wall above the depths of the grassy moat. He nodded to his maiden aunt Emmy, whose current religion forbade dance, and to three other bachelors who acknowledged him sardonically as a fellow failure but made no real attempt at conversation beyond some laconic bit of mock self-deprecation. They appeared to know no-one. The greyest clearly walked on an artificial leg.

All three were about forty and Blackstone could imagine how they loathed the idea of another war. " ...used to call us 'the three musketeers'. Remember?" one was saying, "Porthos, Aramis and Harpo, I think."

Blackstone wondered if he could feign illness and return with the new thriller, bought at the station bookstall for his train, to bed. Connie's beds were *horribly* comfortable. And Mr Skene's new one was proving to be a galloping page-turner. The opium-smoking albino was all the publisher promised!

He envied the few whose enjoyment of the dance was not entirely artificial. Stanley, a distant cousin, had married Connie's vivacious younger sister. He was a country solicitor, tall and substantial-looking, but Blackstone thought he resembled a successful bookmaker who had acquired a bit of taste. The man worshipped and enjoyed Dyliss with a rather touching relish. Blackstone had a soft spot for them both. They had been particularly kind to him when his father had died so unexpectedly two years ago.

After a while the air grew chilly, rich with biting insects as darkness fell and the music stopped. Soon only the most courageous remained, their cigarettes now dying suns beneath the emerging nightscape. He was beginning to have melancholy ideas again. He strolled back to the French windows, inclining his head as he passed a newcomer. "Paul." Paul made a helpless gesture back, mouthing 'Later' and pointing at his watch before returning to his audience. Gathering back around him, the resting dancers laughed excitedly at his older brother's jokes.

Blackstone went to get another cocktail. If he disappeared now Paul would assume he was being snubbed. On his way to the bar he accepted a tiny pork pie and popped it into his extremely hungry mouth. Did it have jalapeño in it? He began to cry.

Out of the Scaling Station, a few planes away, Fleet-Admiral Merimée Bland had it in for claws and shredded wading gear or whatever they were serving it up as, these days. Ketchup Kelp was what she'd called it in her midshipmate days when she served as a young potoreen on the Mauve Continuity run and following her own backside to hell. She was not in the best of moods.

"We lost a fresh gnarling out there last night," she told the devastated shipping clerk. "Ever since the machinoix gave up financing the Law our place has degenerated. And this time I'm going to insist on a whitey. I want a new New Orleans Billy Mafoix and I know you know what I mean. Hey! Where you going?"

"Off to old Paris to follow your hopes and dreams, dear captain. For you are our leader until you fail to charm us. You should not rely on these people of god and family. They are here *precisely* because they are untrustworthy in the home stretches down where the densest colour meadows are known to bloom. I am inside the book and flipping its pages. Try it! New idea of someone's. I am ignorant of their backgrounds and personalities, Copcop?"

The gulping clerk made ugly notes all over her frock. "Cop! B-but what of Sicky Green Residue? We promised Hi—"

Something was going on.

"And if you're marking to scale, you had best scale out near Cucumber Canyon to avoid a mess. News? *Spammer?*"

"Lost, still lost, captain." Queenie Xiomby shed an expressive wave and coughed mournfully, spraying rainbows. "She's taken. Taken. No ransom asked. Raped? Who would dare? Ominous, hm? Politics! Parp! Parp! Only the Merchant Venturer Pearl Peru has the ear and the spiritual beauty to succeed."

"Aye, well, Get cracking ya lazy lycra-loving peroxided stereotype!"

Merimée gasped. Buggerly Otherly had joined the team at last. He bustled into his Bigginga-chair, strapping in without a thought, over and click, round and click. You could spot the vets.

"Tom out a spliff and add a high note or two of the good old spellicans," she cried with tentacles a-tingle, "and put some Kingsize Taylor on the *Ogoshophone* before the grey ceiling cannot be crack'd. This could be the night, pards, win or lose! Remember. Stay true to the music and the music stays true to you. And I am Talking Kingsize Taylor! There's yer bloody Northern Soul, missus! Yes, I am!" And off they went at a reckless lick. Into the Suprexistential Bargain Basement. No compromises, more's the pity. Not when the Void licks Its chops.

The great local heroes of Soho soon returned to obscurity or safe jobs. Chas McDevitt's Skiffle; Chris became a producer, I think. Jean Van den Bosch of The Vipers seemed to drink his meagre fortune. I played washboard for The Vipers when their usual boy couldn't do a session. Tea-chest bass with Les Bennett, one of our best guitarists with a massive Gretsch he kept blanketed like a baby. His group was Les Hobeaux. His hair was a blonded ducktail and he wore a powder-blue suit. Good musician. He wound up doing Lonnie Donegan's guitar solos for him, behind a curtain, when they were touring. If we'd learned piano we went into jazz and blues. If we had no particular instrument, we skiffled. Skiffle appealed to us for the same reason it appealed to its poor African inventors. A cheap banjo or guitar, a snare drum or two, a tea-chest bass. Enough to get us free food and maybe a few bob extra. Interest from girls. At fifteen, we didn't get free beer very often. Our name was accurate but unromantic: The Greenhorns. We made an appalling demo at HMV and broke up. At the end of that particular road we were the Popular Music Ensemble and not much more successful. Out of austerity comes forth ingenuity. But not necessarily anything else. There are acetates and cassettes out there of our spoof *Suddenly It's the Bellyflops*, but we never sold any. It is truly bad. A spoof, but a really bad spoof. My real musical breakthrough came later with the invention of the electronic tuner. Leaps and bounds after that. The electronic tuner brought the end of punk as we knew it. I was composing tunes and songs from the age of eight or so. I was twenty or older before I could write them down.

With music or acting, both of which I considered as reliable alternatives to making a living, I was comfortable. I enjoyed them all and I had received a decent and appreciative audience for them. I really didn't need approval. The feeling of performing or otherwise creating a piece of work is the same athletes talk about. Self-approval, if you do a good one. But apart from local gigs our bands didn't attract much of a following. I still had a preference for long narrative songs and thought short songs were clipping the public somehow. I expected the tunes to become stronger but they rarely did, even cool jazz songs. But my efforts to express what was in my head were completely hampered by my lack of skill. I could always tell when I was out of tune but I was terrible about getting into tune. Depression followed, mixed with self-disgust.

Musicians who liked my work were baffled by my blind spot. The electronic tuner, at first a fairly large thing, but soon small enough to clip on the guitar, solved all that, to the relief of my band partners. The electronic tuner, ironically, developed at about the same pace as the neuropathy which ultimately deprived me of the ability to play! When Hawkwind asked me to perform with them I was just beginning to have some new musical ideas. What I began to do for Hawkwind – declamatory rhetoric like 'Sonic Attack' and songs like 'Coded Languages' – was not like the more conventional tunes and songs I did for Blue Öyster Cult or the *New Worlds Fair* album, or *Live at the Terminal Café*, or the modernist atonal music Pavli and I produced for *Gloriana* and *The Entropy Tango* (demos of which *were* eventually released!). I learned my craft as an R&B musician and I never lost my love of the blues, but at home I listened to classical music from Mozart to Schoenberg.

Writing remained my first love. I read Camus and Conrad, Beckett and Ballard, Aldiss and Aldous. I learned my trade from everyone, including Fleet Street. Only comics taught me more about creating complex structure beneath an apparently simple story and also when the wrong structure can stifle development of scene and character.

I made good friends at Fleetway. They had all started at the bottom and were now fully qualified Union members. Almost none had university degrees. My generation was the last of that kind.

Happily my work was going well and as my family grew so did my popularity with the public. My books, like rock-and-roll psychedelia, were hitting the mood of the newly rich kids who bought records and paperbacks with their pocket money and began to have high expectations of the popular arts and of themselves. I said it was the beginning of a brief Golden Age. It couldn't last, could it? Even Jimi must one day pass. And then, perhaps, a sunset for our wonderful, terrible civilisation. From 1965 Jerry Cornelius appeared to celebrate the ambiguous end of the world. If you couldn't change it, at least you could enjoy it. Nothing warmer than panda skin for the new Ice Age! I would continue to respond to current events with Cornelius stories of the '70s, '80s, '90s – and several people as well as me are writing them in the 2020s. Who believes the gods don't travel, swap notes, that Ganesh drops in on Anubis to discuss the relevance of Buddhism in all this? I do. "I don't get it mate," says Ganesh, "we had a perfectly decent system going. Everything nicely balanced. Why rock the boat?"

I would not return to music in any serious way until Liberty asked us for a Deep Fix album in 1974. Before that I had lived a very full life or two and was beginning to understand the psychic advantages of occupying parallel worlds. My work was appearing in book form and receiving good notices. Lancer and Ace in the USA and Jenkins and Allison & Busby hardbacks in the UK. The difference in the reception of *Behold the Man* in Britain was that the book was not published as genre in London whereas it was firmly categorised as 'scifi' in New York. Also in 1965, a story in which I named the Multiverse and described it as a visible and measurable phenomenon, not merely an abstract idea, appeared in the same year as my novel *Stormbringer*! The SF novel was called *The Sundered Worlds*. It was something of a shambles, in two parts in *Science Fiction Adventures*, but Carnell and his readers liked it for its ideas and images! I had a very smart wife and two lovely children and *New Worlds* was appearing regularly with rising sales, reputation and new writers at last emerging. We had a nice-sized home and garden. Low rent. Good friends. A pretty good life. So I looked around for ways to blow it.

I am not cut out for casual affairs and I generally feel guilty, awkward and responsible for everything which went wrong but I also hated seeing people I loved lose their judgement because of my lies and look in every direction but the right one for the source of their confusion. I was so bad at it! Trevor Howard in *Brief Encounter* was Lothario compared to me! Helena decided to remain in Bristol with the girls, staying with mutual friends. I went home to London and two nights later at John Brunner's regular soirée met Katinka van G., the Mata Hari of Moscow Road, and within hours felt the monstrous weight of guilt bearing on my shoulders. I had become The Cheating Husband.

A week later Katinka had returned to Amsterdam, her three children and 'nasty' husband she was determined to divorce. I was prowling around our ruined marriage with the air of a man who had forgotten to wake God on the Seventh Day and didn't quite know how to tell Him. Causing Helena to ask what was wrong, causing me to lie over and over when I assured her everything was perfect. Letters arrived via a complicit friend. So now there were at least three of us in the deception. I felt self-disgust settle on my skin; a palpable patina of the city's moral filth. No pleasure in that at all. I took to drinking too much and walking the streets and wondering how to tell her which I did while taking a bath, the most vulnerable I could be. I had fallen in love, I told Helena, and I couldn't bear her to look so miserable. Pretty much it. All my fault. I had given in to an impulse and now I'd promised to appear as the co-respondent at her divorce hearing in Amsterdam, to give her moral support, whereupon Helena burst into laughter and said: "Well, I suppose you'd better go, then, hadn't you?" Then I went to Amsterdam with a blistered foot and had a horrible time. That was the last I saw of her, but we exchanged some melancholy letters. I loved my wife and children. Yes, she said, she should have known.

I was doing a gig at the Roundhouse a few years later. Some youngster ran up to me and told me that Katinka sent her love. From Amsterdam. I felt awful. "How is she?"

"Oh, she's better now. She cried a lot at first."

I told her to tell her mother to take it easy and gestured hastily as I turned away from her shimmering blue eyes. I had no choice but to do what I had done and she knew that. Since that time, and Helena's subsequent affair with Jake Slade, we had settled into what felt to me like pretty tranquil domesticity. Helena was writing short stories, most of which were published in *New Worlds* and we had written a sort of modernist

SF novel called *The Black Corridor* which had done fairly well. We no longer succumbed to temptation but had made some good women friends and men friends and friends among our peers. We were respected by them and, through their interest in filming *Behold the Man*, had become good friends with Mai Zetterling and David Hughes who widened our various circles with some of the best film and theatre people of that time. I had already talked Lindsay Anderson out of filming the book, suggesting he do the New Testament instead.

I was awfully arrogant and full of myself. I was tall. My accent made the Prince of Wales sound common. It had a certain authority I didn't hear in myself. I'd rather Mai did the film. As an Independent. I was horribly naïve. Ideas continued to feed more ideas, whirling in my head. I could discipline them, turn them swiftly into narrative. There was nothing to it. For me. I had yet to discover that most people couldn't do it. It was a knack! If we needed money I could write a trilogy in a couple of weeks and still have time off for picnics. My priority was to spend time with the kids and to provide for the family; then to keep the magazine going through any doldrums and encourage the spark of originality which lay within our best writers. That was my mission through my twenties. I wanted to dynamite ways of writing out of granite institutions and conventions, teaching new methods to describe new concerns. The old guard, some quite young, were frozen between the prewar radicalism and a new conservatism. Meanwhile, to spread our notions of finding modern multi-dimensional interfaces between technical outer and spiritual inner worlds, we blasted new routes with new tunnels connecting old tunnels creating a hive, a logical maze of new narratives, a presumed level of literacy in the reader. As the demand for complexity dropped amongst critics, if not some readers, we created increasingly complex ways to tell stories. We had heard the booming roar of the mad cavers driving dangerous and illegal routes beneath our Yorkshire house, but no effort was made to catch them. Similarly no-one much knew how to challenge us, and some of the Elders now enthusiastically defended us! So we must be ignored as aberrations. On one hand we were lowly generic writers, on the other we had enviable sales and some good new ideas. So good, they hardly understood the use of the tools we had in our deconstructed sheds. We hung out with the aristocrats of the blended arts. Our heavily illustrated magazine was in doctors' surgeries, well-thumbed. Our names were in the reference books part of the brave new narratives. *The Times* referred to us as one of the N4 – *Statesman, Scientist, Society, Worlds*. Merchant bankers in flares and Cuban heels sought our cultural-investment advice. We met people at parties whose faces were familiar to us from TV, but we were still inclined to stay at home with a few old friends. We were, in a slightly edgy way, comfortable!

4

Memory, Loss and Sorrow

P OLLY, HIS SISTER, came bustling in, a brilliant parrot, accepting a martini from a tray and knocking it back as she advanced towards him. "Mmmm! Good. Make some more. What ho, Harry? Okay, are we?" She sported the pageboy hair of an earlier bohemia. Her rosebud mouth threatened rather than tempted but it went with her glorious arts-and-crafts smock in apple green fringed by large red poppies. He was her favourite brother. Without pausing, but winking as she went by, she erupted into brother Paul Blackstone's surrounding admirers, delivering guilty kisses on both his resigned cheeks, an apology for a missed appointment. A quick retreating wave, another apology to the women, then she swerved in beside Harry like a rider with urgent dispatches, smoothly turning to collect two more glasses, handing him one. Harry liked to think he watched falling feathers at his brother's feet and began not to worry about getting drunk. He found himself grinning at her caustic observations. Under all that artistic flummery she was sharp as a tack. She saw him as a fellow spirit. They had been allies as children in what had seemed endless games on the yellow sands and green hills of Dorset and Devon when great uncles and aunts wove wool and cotton under yellow thatch, where woodsmoke curled from stone chimneys over spinneys and woods of oak, elm, ash and willow, the ancient hamlets and the lush fields of hidden England upon which the original strengths of her economy were built.

"Corporate smoothies sewing scarlet stripes sweeping down from the Middle Edges." Milton Missy slipped his astonishing hands about the gaffawheel and looked up from his natter-lense, his trellised eyes red with rimless secretions and half an inch of Gatsby gardenias ripping the rivets from his rear plate. "Okay, Jean-Paul bloody Sarrrrtre! How is there a future when all we do is cheese fall? Upstart space-lawyers growling along once-friendly skies and policing the swirling pathways down into where all colours become one? What's this idea of Fate all of a sudden? I'll no doubt have this and form lasting memories or we're prosecuting upscale for always and all time to become nowt but fine powder to blow us all and spuff it sideways to what? No, no, you screeps and scallox swaggering supple-ments of scummers beyond *Spammer*, you name it, girls! *The Kraken Wakes!* No way offo, proffo! We can trace slime like you in any dimension my over-boffins determine. These aren't your leftover mandarin peels, nor the Kra-kra-Koreans forever losing themselves in pastel pallor peaked caps and service sta-tion nostalgia. By hong! These guys know how to fight! Ya hanx! Can you test it by Tuluc? Best bunk. Itherig! Itherig the Unlikely, as I play the fartaroorn sideways! Of course we love you, you old Dutchman! Get the DP! Quick – the ruins!"

"Where is our full-grown Kraken now, if not still in Scandian seas? Rise of the wave and swell of the seed? Rise of the weak to crush the strong. Where are her fishlings swimming, now poor *Spammer*'s gone?" Pearl Peru, ever quick to answer a call to arms, has spirtled a way through from the Second Aether, using synthpop credits faster than butterecall long before our Tomato Tornado owl-jumped his own father and said goodbye to the Future Tomato and lost command of the night. Pearl was sorry to get Vertigo Vinn plugged with the last fig newton, "But whose fault was worth it, so soon as Otherly's mile-high Launch is sic semper and not a silver tootsie left any longer, we'll be a-spiralling the causeways of your mind. Listen! Jackal Joe is firing up his Candy Machine and the pistol is a-poppin'! Oh, yes!"

"Well, it won't do, fellows," jerked Tom Blake, licking his chums as hourly as possible. "We're two rakes short of a harrow. The best we can do is run for it. This is how our japes are recorded! Damn the multiverse and everyone who scales in her, every way but sideways!"

"So pick yer tales, boys! Pick yer scales. And it's all aboard to find dear *Spammer* safe!"

With a smart kick to the FAUX-rockets Pearl whisked away, heading at double-lick towards Peppermint Point and the high dessert as she pretended to call it. Teardrop streak like a star into a black hole!

I took to absurdism with delight. Perhaps it was Firbank who came first, I don't know, or more likely Peake or Lear. Or Thomas Love Peacock. I didn't care for Alice much. I know I enjoyed humour, though. I wrote the odd humorous story. I made up jokes and I loved P.G. Wodehouse, Damon Runyon, Jack Trevor Story, T.H. White. I had asked Mr White for advice on how to write. "Read everything!" he told me. So I did.

Soho had Berwick Street as her core, posh restaurants, rag-trade trims, running down from Oxford Street, through the noisy food stalls, to Old Compton Street, Shaftesbury Ave and a bit of New Chinatown. The old Chinatown, Limehouse, had been bombed to bits in the Blitz. In the mid-1950s I began hanging out at various coffee bars with friends who shared the same interests in music and science fiction. We had the original magazines and books from America. We had the exotic US labels.

We had fairly good guitars. Austerity still ruled and tariffs made imports massively expensive. To smoke an American Pall Mall was the peak of sophistication. Lars Helander sent them from Sweden, disguised in *Svenska Dagbladet*. Regular places we met were coffee bars like Sam Widges which had good food and twenty or thirty of us, not more, as a subculture within a subculture. Then there were the weekend ravers, who came to have a cup of frothy coffee at Chas McDevitt's Skiffle, see the pop stars at The 2i's, jive to Ken Collyer or Chris Barber Dixieland jazz at Bunjies or Humphrey Lyttleton and Johnny Dankworth and Tubby Hayes at Ronnie Scott's. Wee Willie Harris and the rockers would pose around in powder-blue zoot suits in Greek Street and Wardour Street. We were the snotty blues crowd. We wore black duffle-coats and jeans and knew stuff about when Brownie McGee first played with Sonny Terry or what Howlin' Wolf said when they told him they didn't serve chicken at Wimpy's.

We tried to copy Long John Baldry, six foot five, gay white Londoner, elegant in his Italian suit, plenty of white cuff, narrow black tie, the first true Mod, sounding more like Leadbelly than Leadbelly. We adored John. He got Reg Dwight into the music business. Elton passed it forward. Chicago blues began to morph into R&B. Brownie and Sonny and Chuck. Our local gorgeous trannie, Angel, sang blues in a husky husk that was really all husk in G. My fanzines began to feature more rock and roll and less folk, more features on T.H. White and Peake than Conan. I still jammed in blues groups or on my own at the Princess Louise or the Skiffle Cellar where Long John Baldry and Reg Dwight sang some good old-fashioned Chicago Blues, and The Gyre and Gimble, where a bloke called Martin Whitehall sang under the arches in a beautiful baritone by night and broke gamblers' fingers for bookies by day. I got into a fight with him one evening when he wouldn't give me my guitar back. Anxious friends pulled us apart. He was a sneak thief, too. You couldn't put a duffel down at the G without him stuffing it into his guitar case and leaving in a hurry. He stole his own coat twice.

Fleetway by day and Soho by night. Pop music one end with Tommy Steele and Wee Willie Harris. Blues and Jazz at the other where Alexis Korner and Cyril Davis passed their lore down to us, the beginnings of what would become The Stones and The Yardbirds. Money from old smokes as Willie Dixon was overheard saying. I had lunch at the Chinese chippy in Berwick Street, supper at Sam Widges, overseen by the terrifying Scotch cook, Black Angus, who sported a massive beard, glaring blue eyes, black curly hair as well as a wide belt keeping up his sporran and kilt. He was very sensitive about your appreciation of his food. I made a joke about it once and he chased me out of Widges and down an alley until I apologised. I only rarely apologised unless I'd been drunk. I played all the blues venues and some folk gigs. I could do long Woody Guthrie songs with Jack Elliot and pick a riff behind Howlin' Wolf who had once glared at me until I stopped. I bought my records at the Swing Shop near St Leonard's, Streatham, or at Topic, the communist bookshop in Charing Cross Road. I bought 1930s pulps at the Popular Book Centre, Old Caledonian Road. My Soho friends included Pete Taylor, John Baldry, Ronnie Scott, Barry Bayley and a bunch of writers and musicians just starting their careers. Gerald Kersh is the best writer to describe Soho at that time, with her mix of sin and aspiration. I corresponded with Pete Seeger and Guthrie himself! Don't ask me who I was. I was yesterday, today and tomorrow. I was living my dream! And I took it for granted. We played at whorehouse dances for the infamous Eileen Fox, whose 'sex parties' were known from Dalston to Dulwich. We met delegations of Icelandic sailors and Canadian

Mounties at Eileen's dances. QCs, Texas Rangers, coppers on a junket from Barsetshire. Racism, hardly heard in Soho. I took a breath. Nobody had seen my expression.

Science Fiction novels began to bore me as soon as I discovered there were few as good as Alfred Bester's *The Stars My Destination*. On Mr White's advice I read everything. Encyclopaedias. Reference books. Sauce labels. Magazines and journals. Every genre of fiction. I enjoyed almost all of it and what I did not enjoy, I did my best to understand. William Burroughs was another mislabelled absurdist closer to the Pataphysicians than the Beats, in my view. I loved Simplicissimus! Jarry! I loved Vian! In English there's a flourishing line from *commedia* through Peacock to John Kendrick Bangs, then Firbank and Peake and Maurice Richardson in *Lilliput*. I studied everyone's technique and caught subtleties of style, going from *Beowulf* to Shakespeare to Marlowe, Spencer, Cervantes, Molière, Beaumont & Fletcher, Fielding, Smollett, Sterne, Swift, Gay and Austen and the Brontës; Defoe to Dumas, Dickens and the Gothics and all I could cram in between, including serial part-works like *Broad Arrow Jack* or *Knights of the Road* or Conrad, that hard-eyed Ukrainian, and all that comes out of his coat with its brilliant brass buttons and Buffalo Bill beard and where shall we find him, rowdy as you are! Where? God knows we must pack them in, don't you agree?

Now here's a go, says Blecky Oljmeier. Are you sure this isn't vaar?

"War?" Pearl brings down her reality iron pulling in the doughty street surprise. "And Box Office, Mr Pump." They are all kitting up for the big drive down. It got mighty dry and dusty along the old Moonbeam Trail. Was she still on hold as far as the Biloxi Fault and Wisconsin Wendy were concerned? Such a lovely place, such a lovely place. "Somehow I had no interstate at this junction which was how most of the generators went down at the same time. There had been some talk of Quite Still Buntre-Jessop hopping it but no other trades, not in the valley anyway. Existentialism or nothing, usually don't spin any dials. What about Wrong-Way Lindbergh?"

"Couldn't turn on a silver sixpence! Didn't you hear me shout 'Drivers'?" Pearl was unable to do a thing with her new chains. She fussed, sending hissing hitpoles all down the front of her new console. "This isn't MUSIC!!! Don't make me *SCREAM*! Please don't! Where? I'm looking. I am looking." Echoes of Hans Keller and Pink Floyd in what might have been debate.

I've little more to add to what has already been recorded. That period of *New Worlds* lasted until 1970, when I reached the age of thirty. Six years to change our world. Whether it was the zeitgeist or something we did doesn't matter now. It happened. SF writers received literary prestige and literary writers wrote SF best-sellers and off we went on another merry-go-round. I had given myself until then to write predominantly fast-paced fantasy and science fiction stories, weaving themes together to form a kind of continuity. All those many years ago at the beginning of time. After thirty, I could fold back my cuffs and start writing to some of my ambitions. The stories I felt compelled to write for myself, my family and for Dr Emil Jelinek, who had helped many Jews escape the Nazis at his own risk and expense. Survival guilt itched at my soul. Who had given up a kindly relative so I might have wise guidance and sane love in my life! For me it resolved into a terrible fortune cookie question. I could write more fantasy adventures and make enormous amounts of money but instead I had bought myself and my family the time we all needed! Helena and I never seemed closer than when we went to The Priory, the posh bin in Richmond, to see Bobby Pervert watching his girlfriend for fear she would reveal his plans against a right-wing putsch centred on Croydon.

5

Showing Sideways

"THIS IS ABOUT Stan and Nellie, isn't it? Landlord's chucking her out? Poor old Nellie. She sets herself up, of course. Only working men can rent, certainly not single women and parents. He wasn't even a veteran. Can see how she feels. She's such a trouper. Went straight out and got herself a job. In some sort of *yard*! Stan thought he was helping. They started rowing and suddenly Nellie's gone AWOL! Nobody can find her. Connie thought she might come here. Not at her mum's and not at the in-laws, nor the Morgans' in Cornwall but you know how sneaky they are down there. They wouldn't let on if they knew. Let Connie tell you. I'm sworn to secrecy. 'The White Rabbit', you know me! Can't keep time and can't keep a secret."

Her voice had warmed and become more confidential as she spoke. "Always running towards the rim and looking down into the bubbling lava, the red-hot core of the planet! The ancient heart and soul of our prehistory. It's in our blood, dear. It's what we have in common with the living, sentient past. Old stones live and hide old bones. Almost every inch of our ground is soaked in human blood! Those hills!" She gestured vaguely. "The rocks are alive! Responsive to the vibrations of a million spheres."

Harry knew he should have been more careful. He loved everything about Polly except her infernal mysticism and that he hated with a passion. Since the eighteenth century, their family had built its reputation on its rational approach to the world. He felt Polly was deliberately cocking a snook at tradition. They had barely had a chance to become a dynasty! Why on earth had she married that awful Warwick Colvin, making so much money from historical novels and even worse films who was always too busy to come to these gatherings? Nobody bothered to invite him any more and Polly never apologised for him.

Taking a last jar at the Terminal Café, Captain Otherly pushed his cap on the back of his white curls, his bluff, red bulldog face representing the best of British endurance. A clay pipe stuffed with *Meng & Ecker's Unusual Vintage* was already sending its intoxicating fruity fumes across his magnificent green-and-white console. Opium to seek, maryjay to find, acid to explore, meth and coke to sustain. He would soon be back in balance and heading for Uranium Cove. His tanks were bulging with very tasty tunes from Mozart to Messiaen, Johnson to Jeff Beck and even his ballast was discarded takes from The Beatles and Dylan. If that wasn't ordnance, nothing was.

Quelch found it impossible to mock. The organic omniphone extension horns bristled everywhere, pinkish yellow, fading electric mauve, still with their original brass plates, glimmering audio-gauges, long since unreliable.

Pah-Boom! Put some Kirby-krackle on it and we're good to go. K-k-k-rakakatak! (Thanks, love.) She's out there somewhere, lads, and she's our One. We follow where she leads. *Spammer* preserves our safety. Blind trust is all we have to offer at this particular moment and we will get through, though it'll take quite a bit of Flanagan and Allen. "Run rabbit ..."

So here we are. I've grown up with a fair amount of

confidence and experience and, at Pitman's, looped around to try to become a working musician and editor, which I successfully did, and writing fantasy, staying on that comfortable curve until I grew restless again and I remained until I began making records, picking up where I had left off a few years earlier when *New Worlds* needed my attention. The story's mine. Also of course yours, if you bought this. The Beatles offered to back *New Worlds* but after I'd seen the wear and tear on the apple-green carpet after a week at their offices, I told them just to buy some advertising. I couldn't bear to see their well-earned money being frittered by feckless idiots. George Harrison shook my hand. I wished him luck. I don't think either of us could imagine the amount of money they were making. But it kept flowing. James Taylor benefitted. He was a friend of a very good young American contributor to *NW*, Joel Zoss. Another smart singer/songwriter. Perhaps there were more like them who came to London in those golden years when the apples ripened and fed us all. I don't remember too much, other than those.

I knew most of the Liverpool poets and Pete Brown through my friend, the illustrator Mal Dean. Sam Shepard came to Ladbroke Grove to give me his first book of poems, *Hawk Moon*. He contributed lyrics to *The New Worlds Fair*. Most of us lived in Notting Hill or nearby. Chip Delany lived in Paddington Street, I think. The cultural river shifted west to where many artists lived because it was cheap. My mother hated it. Our district was a synonym for violence and prostitution. Every run-down house was divided and subdivided. Half of them had serious structural problems. To her, street markets meant working class. She'd grown up near the big South London markets. To me, they were all the wealth I needed.

Our mothers had worked so hard to move us up a class! They could not see the river of cultural wealth which flowed down past my door from Portobello Road, meeting Ladbroke Grove at Elgin Crescent, paralleling Blenheim Crescent and all with economies dependent on the river of Portobello wealth flowing down from Notting Hill and petering out into Wornington Road and, in those days, wretched poverty, where the glittering antique stalls and fruit-and-veg and doughnut stalls became a dirty blanket on pavements which still mixed mercury and gold and street-filth and gave birth to that last great renaissance when tourists came to see us with our flowing hair and our beautiful clothes and our liberated ideas and they were fascinated by our lives and we caught and taught them with our drugs and jewels and drew them into the circle where the sun never set.

I restarted my live musical career. As the music world and the alternative press drew me in and I went on stage with the bands I wrote for and little girls encouraged my dormant romanticism and wanted to show me how sophisticated they were in bed because I grew so tired of never knowing just a little sentimentality and a chance to rest that I didn't care who I had an affair with any more. First come first served my delicate little Marists. Festivals and gigs. Beautiful hair, fantastic makeup, Pre-Raphaelite clothes, lace and brocade. Rolling joints in slenderpink-painted fingers. Licking them with tender tiny tongues. Smelling sweet as sandalwood, powerful as patchouli. Shampoo and toilet freshener. Roses and ozone bring memories at random. Hash pipes glowing round the fire. Linear memory doesn't work very well for me. I make associations like a patchwork quilt. Like my mother, I seem to be rambling, but I come back to the point in the end. One patch here, another there and somehow the narrative begins to come together. I remember tunes better than words. All the sisters but Ethel sitting around the fire at Christmas, sherries in hand and laughing their heads off, telling story after story. They were like cheerful Norns weaving the histories and destines of Heroes. Only in later life did the posh ones begin to distance themselves from the others. Soon it was Mum and Doris keeping their ordinary personae while Connie and Rose distanced themselves, though not as much as Ethel whom I barely knew. I remained in touch with them and attended all their funerals. Towards the end of their lives my mum and Doris became rivals, locked in a form of mild competition Munchausen's which Doris won by dying first. My mother maintained the rivalry, however, for many years after Doris's death. This was not helped by my cousin setting up a morbid shrine to her while his poor father, a retired headmaster and RAF pilot, remained for his final years faintly guilty for a brief affair he had with another teacher while on a school trip to Switzerland.

Of course, I have written hundreds of linear plots and learned early on in the word factories of Fleet Street how to prefigure, to whet the reader's curiosity, to have a carrot-and-stick approach which drives and guides the reader forward. I made up my own structure owing something to Lester Dent's Master Plot Formula. I always preferred to structure generic stories on a three-volume framework, divided into an introduction, a development dealing with the introduced themes and one prefiguring the resolution, and often a fourth short movement, the coda. Four for Hawkmoon. Three for Corum and several Elrics. I used Mozart as a model. For my Pyat sequence I planned it on a slowly developing and resolving 'Wagnerian' scale, with leitmotifs distant waves at first and slowly growing into massive breakers, main themes. *Mother London*'s structure was influenced by the twentieth-century moderns like Mahler and Ives, as well as Messiaen. I wrote about this in *Death Is No Obstacle* and elsewhere.

Similarly I shared tastes with Pete Pavli, late of the Third Ear Band who had played cello on *New Worlds Fair*. I wrote most of our early '8os music under the influence of the moderns. I used early classical models for *Gloriana*, the novel, but wrote atonally when Pete and I did the music for that and *The Entropy Tango*. I played mandolin and banjo on *NWF*. I played banjo for Eno on Calvert's *Lucky Lief* and twelve-string Rickenbacker for his *Hype*! I enjoyed session work and had the patience for it but if a studio or sessions could not be booked quickly, I started to lose interest in a project. It took the better part of five years to get everyone together for *Live at the Terminal Café*. It's both easier and harder to compose on the harmonica, as I discovered while studying the great Charlie Musselwhite. I love suiting styles to fit the stories. There's a joy in it, but sometimes people quite reasonably don't have time for *Karl the Viking* done in the style of *Beowulf*. Most people don't have time for too many extras at all in their lives. One hobby, one author, one band. Even in their reading they mostly want familiarity. I think I'm a bit of a dilettante. I have lots of ideas. I'm always curious. I always want to pass the pleasure on. I love words *and* ideas! Where are we off to now? Blimey! It's a bit bright down here. How are we going to survive all this!?

I called the bunch of pretty girls around us 'Marists' or 'Quantifiers'. Geishas who were never allowed to work at anything more strenuous than crocheting or needlework. I loved them, of course. We all did. I called them by those nicknames because you could go with them around Mary Quant's big shop below Derry & Toms in High Street Kensington while they looked at this or tried that on and you'd board the bus home and they'd start pulling scarves from here, skirts and blouses from there or strings of beads and brooches from elsewhere. There was Fiona and Jilly and Issy and Melanie and Andy, Lou, Lizzy, Steffy and Marianne and Allie and Wyn and Millie. Many worked as photographers' models, appearing often in *Penthouse* or *Men Only* or sometimes doing a bit of pole-dancing but they had their moral code. It didn't stop most of them from flirting. They did waitressing and secretarial jobs mostly. They shared a couple of flats in Latimer Road. Of course some had babysat a couple of times, so inevitably I became the stereotype who fucked the babysitter. I didn't care. I was angry. I had been tricked, profoundly deceived and betrayed and I didn't think I deserved it. Boo hoo! So at her request I lugged all my stuff back to London and began to work there while Helena worked in Yorkshire. She registered the girls in the village school. Her logic for me going back to London was that if I stayed in Yorkshire I would cheat on her in London. We both had abandonment issues; she believed in the pre-emptive strike approach. I knew she was wrong. I knew that I had been looking forward to our time in the Dales. We would not have so many unexpected guests. I had seen this as our chance to get started again.

My diaries of the day are full of determination to become a better husband and father. With me in the tower and Helena's office in a spare bedroom each could stay out of the other's way while writing and sharing responsibility for the kids. With our baby, I had started to write several new series of fantasy novels in order to support us in the coming years. That had all turned upside down and I had no family. Just a big flat everyone but me wanted to live in. Time had not been wasted. Having told Helena that I had no intention of remaining celibate, I had taken up with our neighbour around the corner, the honourable literary hostess Emmeline 'Emmy' MacGillis, mistress of one of my very best friends, Mike Cornelius, who was in America, I knew, having an affair with a model from Las Vegas called Cassidy. As soon as I was back from Yorkshire, Emmy came round to borrow a cup of sugar. All our French doors around the square were open to neighbours in those days.

When he returned to London, I had to tell Mike that I had betrayed him with the mother of his child, on pretty much all levels. Whatever the context I think he had every reason to call me 'yu huckin astard' through his wired-up lips a few weeks after his most recent car accident. Meanwhile *The Final Programme* had just finished shooting and all the Marists had decided I needed to hold a party and invite my friend Jon Finch, the star of the film, a contemporary heart-throb. So I had given the invitations, but I was deeply embarrassed. Trux and I took a drive to Heathrow whose landing strips were dark, the tarmac silent, so we visited a couple of hospitality rooms and ate what remained of their snacks and, when the security guys didn't want trouble and asked us nicely to leave, we did. By the time we got home the party was cold and most had left.

But there, as a sub-strand to this narrative, Millie the 'baby-sitter' was staying downstairs in the girls' room and Franco, my American publisher's brother, wanted to sleep with her there and I'd agreed with her that she couldn't sleep with anyone in the kids' room. Or indeed in the house! Jane was trying to make sure I didn't sleep with Millie and Millie didn't want to sleep with Franco until her period was over. And then her best girlfriend from Prague, Mucha's son's mistress, turned up and she didn't think my rule applied to girls, so I kicked her and the beautiful Marushka up the road to Praed Street with a building full of models (and shoplifters) and I went to bed alone and didn't even mind too much because the Marists were absolutely full-on generous providers of consolation without any guilt or indeed much expense and Franco came back, slipping into the arms of another without missing a beat, as he told it later. And I didn't see Millie for almost ten years. Good-natured as always, she had come to see me at my Albert Hall débâcle in 1999. She was smart. I think she married.

I wonder what might have happened if Helena had agreed

to my remaining at Tower House. Perhaps it would have been the idyll I'd anticipated. Sheep on the fells. Hill climbing in the summer. Long drives in the sunsets. Trips to Kirkby Lonsdale. Autumn smoke in sunlight. Haystacks and barns, the scent of new-mown hay. Turning out a few sequels. It wasn't so bad. In the end we made a different compromise and that kept us going for a while.

Let's say we decided to take our girls to Paris. What had we got to lose? The mothers would gloat at the notion! Taking train and ferry to France, we established ourselves in a snotty right-bank hotel for a few days. We were toying with the idea of getting back together. I don't think we had voiced it yet.

"Sit tight, sithee!" Buggerly leans forward and with a tendril of moustachio'd tenderness, touches the drive-on button and, shrugging of his shoulders, sets the controls for the heart of the sun. "And remember, brother, don't let it touch your eyes and keep marked, buckaroo, or he'll be moonhawking you by the end of *The Mask of the Beast*! I've seen 'em do it! First act or sooner. Don't look so startled, lad. She'd have yer potted like a shrimp tea at Betty's before ya can shout arse'n-all! to a box of Vestas! They all know me East of Resort Rhubarb. Reds and streaked with red and scarlet, you can sail those streams in certain seasons. Irrrrrup chirrrrrrup, old girls. *Sing to the roses! Sing to the sea! Sing to the wild fells of Ingleton, and sing if you will to me!*" Turning, as his co-pilot slid into his straps and cushions. "What law do you look to as superior? Sea, land or Second Aether, I'd say latter's fairest but then I have no trumpet in the orchestra! Must it always be this confrontational, colonel?"

"If colour's what you want, we'll have to say yes!" Colonel Quelch stuck his scrawny neck out of the wheelhouse for the first time. "Sevens to an albino albatross, hoss, but those odds are a loss! Ask any boss. A rolling stone, after all, gath—!"

"Hardly." She showed him her tattooed wrist. "Would you spike *that*?"

Her glance of surprise did nothing for his ego. "You really are altruistic, aren't you!" was an accusation but "I'd forgotten about multiple orgasms!" probably wasn't. The things we remember! Eh? More confusion. Looking over my shoulder.

I believe I mentioned elsewhere my tendency to hallucinate and not being able, briefly, to distinguish between visions and reality. I seemed to hear that same noise in my head, like distant, sometimes nearby, swarms of bees. I saw classic forms of Jesus. Offering me his heart. Historical figures, like Francis Drake. Offering me the world? I discussed these with an odd friend I made when I took corrected *Tarzan* proofs down to our typesetters by the Old Bailey. I can smell the sour ink as they pulled wet proofs and hung them up to dry. A monk. An old Carmelite or White Friar bustles up to the counter. I had forgotten how small he was. Staring through bottle-glass pince-nez up into my smiling face. I knew what he liked to talk about. We would chat in local tea shops while we waited for an urgent piece of type to be set. I liked to do it myself, partly because, in the time I saved, I got to talk to interesting people.

I developed a fondness for Carmelites. Particularly in later years when I met both nuns and monks of their Order in the course of exploring the Ladbroke Grove area. They were a kindly and charitable lot in the main and I had a soft spot for 'our' nuns who, in the early days, helped get the Notting Hill Carnival on the road when it was still being broached as a market-traders' festival! Brother Xavier edited a local parish giveaway magazine and was honestly curious about the imaginative fiction I ran in what was essentially a pulp for teenagers, maintaining the Edgar Rice Burroughs themes of interplanetary romance and with articles about Burroughs's various worlds and settings. I ran strips by Foster and Hogarth because I believed them the best artists. He saw my hallucinations, my vivid impositions on reality, as being close to his own religious visions and was obsessed with their meaning and reality. He found interested conversationalists in myself and Barry Bayley, who became my writing partner especially for features.

When not plotting 'Danny and his Time Machine', 'The Schoolboy Castaways' or 'African Safari', we would spend ages debating the nature of reality and whether we imposed our own blasphemous ideas on God's pattern. Or perhaps we perceived glimpses of God's myriad worlds, either parallel to our own or each with different narratives of His many versions of Paradise? And, perhaps, Hell? If these were mere tributaries, was it wrong to seek the Grand Highway? Father Xavier's gentle figure trembled at the idea. The speculation was thrilling to him but we were modern agnostics. We had read *The Golden Bough*, *The White Goddess* and *The Perennial Philosophy*. We respected his understanding of the world. I had barely heard of Campbell.

I, of course, saw only images for fantasy stories and developed a notion I had started when young. I called it *The Eternal Champion*, about a protagonist who, as I put it, kept jumping to new worlds after doing terrible harm to them one after another and carrying this on his conscience after the manner of *Melmoth the Wanderer* by Charles Maturin. Copies of such Gothics were often very scarce in a world just emerging from a profound anti-romantic period when cheap waste paper was collected for the war effort and if they could be found at all were either very expensive in good condition or cheap when falling apart. They were unapologetically melodramatic, black and white, like a Universal movie! I made it my business to publicise these books and collect as many as I could.

My marriage had collapsed like *The Hindenburg* and I could not bear the idea of losing them, even Helena, who had proven the utter cowardice which she herself always privately claimed to be the motivation for her kindness. So many took up her time – so many distractions that I began to feel I was working for them all.

My behaviour during this period, where the consolations of fame were freely available, was not that of a mature father and husband. Of course I felt cheated of my youth, of romance. I had stepped up to make sure we had everything she needed! Of course I knew how nerve-wracking this would be for Jenny. Before this went any further, I was trying to get a bit of clarity for everyone. I needed to give explanations and I needed to understand. I owed Helena her trip to Paris, to talk things over and see where we stood. The girls were old enough to be tourists on their own during the day and would be with us for dinner. We could then ask them questions we thought suitable. That's the story we told ourselves.

And so we packed some old-fashioned suitcases, booked our usual hotel, the ever-glad-to-welcome-us Le Grand Hôtel de l'Univers, rue Bonaparte, in the old Latin Quarter (in those days neither as crowded nor as welcoming a Cirque as today) and lay down on feather mattresses and lovely creaking iron bedsteads. We did our best to relax! The girls didn't care. Maybe we had kept things from them too successfully?

6

A Newer Reality

BLACKSTONE FELT EXHAUSTED. Must he stay up any longer? Everyone had more energy than he. He was yearning to go to bed, to sink into the feather mattresses and sleep. Perhaps if he breakfasted early he could get on with his novel before the rest of the house was up.

He edged, inch by inch, towards the entrance of the ballroom. His plan was to beg a sandwich from the kitchen, then carry it and perhaps a scotch and soda back to the peace of his room. But Polly was back with a second wind, drunk, as she put it, as a skunk and raring to go. Blackstone's efforts to evade her were fruitless. Listlessly he joined her in the dances of their youth which she accompanied with inarticulate yelps. Suddenly he was taken back to Christmas parties with his mother and his deep embarrassment at being made to become her dance partner. Her efforts to instil gaiety into the occasion made the occasion more melancholy. He stared around desperately but although several of them recognised his predicament, not one was prepared to save him.

He imagined himself a victim of one of Stoker's female vampyres, his energy being slowly leeched from him. He wished he knew a way to keep Polly sober. She was witty company until she drank too much. "I hear you're tutoring, these days, for Oxford?" A man's voice, friendly and familiar. Charles Conquest! They had been close friends, mountaineering in the Pyrenees and the Alps while still at Magdalen. Then Charles had joined the Foreign Office and all but disappeared!

"Hello, old man!" He felt an unexpected rush of pleasure. Charles seemed equally pleased. "Sorry I lost your address. How long's it been? Hello, Polly!"

"I assumed you were out of the country, of course," said Blackstone.

"Hush hush stuff, eh?" A girlish kiss from Polly.

Charles smiled and gave him a friendly wink. He seemed almost embarrassed. "I met Connie yesterday in the village. She said you were coming."

"You live nearby?"

"Sometimes, yes. I say, if you're free one day why don't we have lunch in town? Let's catch up. I have a dinner I can't get out of. I only popped over to give you my phone number."

Blackstone could see that his old friend did not want to talk too much where they might be overheard and was rather flattered.

A moment later Polly was distracted long enough for Charles to give Harry his card and then disappear back into the crowd.

Meanwhile the varieties of shape-shifting needed to get back on the Ahah Line were straining the old *Now The Clouds Have Meaning*'s sonic adaptors to booming point, never good in a sector that valued silence. "Drop the Boogy-woogies and put a tad more gravity into the beejams. Good. That'll do 'er. Ready with the reverse-cackle, cocky! Okay! G-G-GO!!"

And there, by the seat of his pants and screaming like a banshee Kaprikorn Schultz, who would die for the Original Insect, slid into view with his crocodile grin and his high-crowned hat and, when Buggerly Otherly gave him an 'Uncool' sign, ignored his manners and scraped under the baffle netting, apologising to the glaring Quelch, and sat on the corner of the control bench. "You know the equations as well as I do. I didn't stow away on this creaky old girl for nothing. We have to engage with a monstrous reality-cage and everything we live for is at stake. You can guess who made it, specialists! Is our free space to be brought under an iron hand? Is the Second Aether to go the way of the Third and Fifth? Is symbolic logic shown no respect, these days?"

"Ease off there, pards." Her melodious voice came through the omniphone. "Give it a bit of Evil Company and then bring her round on a Kilmister swerve, Captain Otherly. I'm thinking Charles Lever, I'll meet you at Gelatinous Junction and make sure you get ready for a new jar of preserves!"

"I hear you, my beauty! I'm coming in for a swift Randyvoo, me darling, my gorgeous Rose of all Roses, Rose of the Multiverse, Rose the Sublime!"

"Stow that sub-Yeatsian riff, captain. I have real news. And it has flavour. Meet me at the Junction where the others join us."

"Give us more before we fly, Rose. You'll recall—"

"This time there's no doubt and we must act urgently. There's a spy of sorts amongst us and we'll all slip into Grimville if he isn't buttoned up. Maybe several of them. Don't expect the Revels of Red Liquorice ever again and kiss your Masque of the Itch goodbye, because it's not only visuals flick out when they find where we hid the Limbo machine. Remember the threat of the Eternal Moment? Well, that's what we're facing. Nothing less."

"Crumbling Kierkegaards!" Captain Otherly pushed his cap forward and scratched his greying head. "I'd've bet a de Beauvoir to a bent bitcoin that we're discussing the Existential Apocalypse."

"Some of us had hoped to go out with a sigh and a whisper,"

said the Merchant Venturer Pearl Peru, who knew more about Limbo than most. "Can one child make so much difference? Can it decide on the nature of our existence? On whether we exist or not?"

They had arrived without incident at Continuity Harbour, five hundred free Second Aether ships in five hundred eccentric rigs with thousands of crew, not an eye untouched by that hard, glazing light. They had long since ceased to demand the truth. Now all they required was a consistent narrative. They made Biloxi their central co-ordinate and turned the volume to Full.

Time was settling down a bit at the Terminal Café and the Deep Fix were rediscovering their instruments, getting ready to play. At a nod from Cornelius, they started off with a quickstep. Sounded like a modified Belton Richard number. Jack was glad they had their accordion back. They often featured a squeeze-box and didn't have the same swing without one. They already sang in one of the many parish accents strangers found confusing. Now Cornelius himself nodded to lead guitar Martin Stone, set aside his own Rickenbacker, and, still on stage, began throwing a little girl up and down, making her squeal with delight, before setting her back and picking up another. The band played on with relentless fiddle, accordion, triangle and snare following bass and rhythm. Sunday brunch at the Terminal Café. *Jolie Blonde*. He was popular with the mums was Jerry. They sent their children as surrogates. Their every gesture was an apology for their self-conscious confusion.

Sam Oakenhurst was back in uniform. Scarlet and gold. Everyone here took him for a Mountie. He was looking for Mlle Yvonne Cartier. He was uncertain how to handle their eccentric boys. Too much French for his taste. Acadian all over. He thought injectables and stacked boxes might work for a few hours but one dead young lady and that plan became a disaster.

When he arrived, signalling to the stage, Jack saw him from the wings and started laughing. "You don't need me for this."

Dee-Eff were working, loud and pure, with Stone's distinctive guitar sailing the band from verse to glorious verse. The axe that made The Action famous! If he had lived we would have become Martin's band. No doubt about it. On we went, playing for deeds of valour and deeds of colour for it was all out there if you had the courage to take it and then defend it. Jack had done both and was aiming to return wealthy and sane, surrounded by the most reliable doctors and cleverest thinkers. He had already bought a new pair of boots and a hat. While he sought a fresh colour break, he didn't mind keeping company and he knew why she did it. Una Persson was off near Big Pain Plateau. Paulette de Courcy would be happy to work with him, however, and find them an excellent return berth. As his partner, she would do well. They would take the usual route down to New Auschwitz, change boats, and work their way back. His money assured that. It would be disappointing to die or be sent mad near the culmination of his adventure. While the machinoix were occupied with the disfunctioning scaling stations, they could take advantage of the time saved. He smiled ironically, whetting the curiosity of the watchers. He called to his boy.

"Jake. Jacob! Come on here, son. Get your instrument. We start our play tonight! Here first, then the tables. Your character just came free."

Jake looked up from his booth, his polished horns an introduction of savage nature into the comforting interior. He moved his head awkwardly. He was a blushing minotaur. Beautiful as Lucifer.

"I really am serious!"

So that was my ordinary world, one way or another, for pretty much as long as I can remember. Nothing needed to be rationalised for me, whether it was ghosts or dreams or images or the world around me. I enjoyed it all. I was always interested in why and how. When. I wanted to live where the rule of law is still respected. All I hear today is Chaos using the rhetoric of Law. As the preacher said last Friday, Peace is merely a deceitful cloak for a predatory wolf to wear like a sheepskin in a flock.

"We are in control, now! We won a double round!"

"What about London?"

"We control the multiverse!"

"For how long. To what end?" Jake rose with a graceful flick of his tail. "Something is going wrong." He stooped to swing his sousaphone onto his shoulder. "It's not just the sizes. Not just your bloody Kraken. It's the whole spectrum." He knew it wasn't really God. But it had Jack wondering for a moment.

I was, of course, trying to escape reality, as I so often did, but with quality help. My imaginary sister's brilliant, half-crazed mind fed the logic of anxiety back into creativity. So real, so *present, mi siostra,* my imaginary friend. Or I am hers? I certainly belong to her; to her manifestations across the damned burdensome multiverse. "They hate god for putting Xiombarg in charge. I hate Xiombarg. Full Stop. I have for too long been the conduit for her evil! Yet why should you change your loyalties at the moment when you might think of yourself as all powerful! I know the feeling well! The gods themselves are shadows now."

He smiled in doleful reminiscence. "Until about an hour ago I considered myself a smart soldier, likely to survive fairly successfully in an environment of this kind. I needed anti-depressants and here was salvation. I am by nature solitary. Now it wouldn't be so bad to pose as a single entity."

"Or at least a single gender." He took a deep breath and sighed some sort of acquiescence. At least, I hoped it was that! "Think of it. A single intelligence in a single operating shell." He made some attempt at a grin.

"Goron," he began. "You know only too well that this reality is tenuous at best. Why don't you adopt something easier for us all? Not everyone has the knack for it!"

He emerged from something very like a reverie tipover and continued where he had promised. "The conflicting time streams of the 20th/21st centuries were mirrored in Jerry Cornelius". Look at how great we were when we began and how quickly we came to Richardson and the generic novel! The world grew round and prospered and we looked for stories to explain and expand our broadening sensibilities. Many of us started to evolve.

Our story begins, as it always must, with the great Grimmelshausen, the German Quixote, and Pantagruel, of course. And Crusoe and Flanders, naturally! The grandfathers and -mothers of all our protagonists. Their stories are among the first Defoe and others would sell as truth. The printing press, almost as soon as it was made by honest craftsmen with honest intentions, built to last for centuries, became a means of spreading the insane fake news which fuelled the Hundred Years' War. Mankind's inventive genius used to power one of the bloodiest conflicts in history!

But you wanted to ask me how I had met the Three Musketeers. I'm not always able to remember with complete clarity. It would have been in a pub. You always met people in pubs. In Fleet Street. Originally I knew Claude Duval and his two English friends, who tended to stand in for them in England. They were all cavaliers, including of course Buffalo Bill, Texas Jack and the Heroes of the Plains. As I grew up, I began to adopt the same big hats and boots, feathers and lace. I turned into a hippie prince. I was also allowed to access a place called Alsacia off Fleet Street where my clothes were not considered especially outlandish.

Had we met again by then, I would have fitted in pretty well, although I carried a Rickenbacker rather than a sword.

We were on that same trip to Paris. Marvell had been the travel agent, as usual. They didn't think much of our clothes as we got in the taxis and compartments and prepared to suffer Parisian hauteur and snobbery for a few days. We could counter with British arrogance and irony, after all, and a clear memory of the end-of-day scores at Waterloo, should we choose to defend ourselves. Happily M. Raquin, the owner of Le Grand, was a keen Anglophile, had known us for many years and was delighted to see the children growing. We became immediately at ease and we settled in to those old rooms with the pleasure of familiarity.

7

Legendary Locations

H ELENA AND I had settled fairly comfortably into our life
together. I was still sometimes given to outbreaks of anxious ill-temper when I panicked about deadlines. She still fell
into depressions and snarled caustically from the deep armchair I had bought her after she had an abortion, which had
depressed us both. I could easily anticipate a future in which
we continued to deepen what I hoped was our improving companionship. I don't think I had ever been so thoroughly in
love. With the profound depressions she refused to address, I
still found daily life a bit difficult to live with her sometimes,
but I did my best for her by wheeling the children out to the
park and taking over domestic work. During these periods she
was generally pretty caustic, if she spoke at all, but happily
she didn't go after the kids. And in my own hysteria, I didn't
either.

Although Helena generally did much of the practical child
rearing (we never regretted investing a small fortune in our
Miele washing machines), I would get up first every morning
to cook the girls' breakfast, make Helena a cup of tea and,
when they reached that age, take them to school, by which
time I would be ready to start work.

As they grew a little older I'd put Susie behind me on the

luggage rack and Kitty in front on the handlebars and get them to St James's infants' school by bike in a few minutes until I was caught in a cunning police trap. The PC had been after me for weeks but I pretended deafness to his whistle. This time he had a panda car waiting and they blocked me off at Princedale Gardens, so I was fairly and squarely nabbed. While the girls glared at us all, I had the humiliation of being dressed down by the rozzer about putting my children's lives at risk and could no longer pretend to ignore him.

When I felt they were old enough to go on their own, I followed them at a distance, where they couldn't see me, and checked they were observing the Highway Code and everything I had taught them about road safety. They had become friends with the Richardsons, children of Vanessa and Tony, who also went to school with them, and had several classmates from similar bohemian families around the gardens, so their lifestyle growing up never struck them as abnormal. Mai Zetterling kept them giggling for hours with her animal voices. Peter Cushing never could frighten them. Sir Angus Wilson did great impressions of famous politicians. Sir Eduardo Paolozzi let them climb all over his sculpture. We knew journalists, musicians and painters, all of whom made names for themselves. We shared values and politics which were rarely challenged. Later they claimed we had never prepared them for 'real life' but, as we said, that *was* our reality and, no matter how many warning dystopias we wrote, we had no means of knowing how dreadful the future was to become for so many.

That said, we did everything to ensure they kept their feet on the ground and did our best to prepare them for the worst that could happen. In case they were attacked I taught them how to throw a good punch and then run like hell. For Susie's second birthday I bought her a pair of boxing gloves! Later I got them a good air-rifle and taught them how to shoot. From my friend Peter Phillips, then Literary Editor of the *Daily Herald* who wrote a marvellous story, *He Who Shapes*, about a father who took his son's dreams seriously and helped him practically by accepting the nightmares as actuality, I listened to their fears and taught them how to face them off as I faced off the witches from *The Wizard of Oz* when I was a little boy — 'stare them in the eyes!'. I was determined they should have as many choices as possible. I proposed we give them middle names in case they didn't like their first names and names they could convert if they wanted to. I loved the job I had which allowed me to see so much of them and enjoy their company pretty much every day. They were born so close together they were like twins. Different as they were in personality, they rarely quarrelled and from the time they were toddlers I encouraged them to support each other, if necessary against me. When Kitty came home crying because she'd been mocked by a teacher for saying that pasta came from China (as it had via Marco Polo) I went to tell that teacher how ignorant they were, and when Susie was proud of her gymnastic progress but discouraged by lack of support, I spent hours helping her with her somersaults and jumps. Waiters loved them for their good manners and even their grandmothers remarked on their cleverness. We played all kinds of games, every sort of rôle, went to the West End shops and cinemas, museums, exhibitions, movies and art galleries. The happiest days of my youth. And also, I suppose, the busiest. One year I wrote ten books.

When I was doing a novel I would come back from the school and return to bed every day for three days or so while I thought over the story and sometimes wrote a paragraph or two in longhand, working on a map (Europe for *Hawkmoon*, Britain for *Corum* or invented for *Elric* and others). Frequently I deliberately didn't think about the story at all. I'd think about almost everything else. I called it 'sidling up on myself'. My object seemed to be twofold: to get rid of anxiety and to allow my unconscious to start putting together a palette of colours, a lexicon of coherent images which would give an underlying dynamic to a fairly simple plot with what I thought of as a carrot-and-stick element, something which everyone wanted to find urgently and someone trying to find the protagonists and do them harm. The *Maltese Falcon* formula.

I was an extremely fast typist, averaging over 200 wpm with the latest in writing technology, including, soon, my Olivetti electric typewriter and my own Xerox machine. As I wrote the chapters I would copy them and lay them out in order on the expensive carpet we bought for Ladbroke Grove and which we had christened with a big house-warming party.

I borrowed my sense of structure mostly from classical music. Somehow musical forms and vocabulary helped me to structure best. My continuing friendship with the young composer Langdon Jones, who would become *New Worlds'* assistant editor, gave me a far deeper understanding of music than I had growing up and I remained grateful to him for an education I would never otherwise have known. Lang and I remained friends and sometime collaborators and it's his lively piano that can be heard on *The Entropy Tango*, one of the few singles I ever made.

Once I had the novel's structure, that, in turn, imposed the demands I would have to make on myself. This meant I knew what I needed for the story in terms of dynamics, images and so on, before I ever sat down at my desk. Then I would get up and write steadily for three days, working from 10 a.m. to 6 p.m. with an hour off for lunch, composing directly onto the typewriter, writing sixty pages a day until I finished a short novel of exactly 180 pages. A dramatic event every four pages. Scene, dialogue and narration all added to the dynamic. Preferably, no characters would pause for conversation.

Exchanges would always take place during some action. While I was finishing, Jim Cawthorn, my artist friend, would read the book, checking for typos, spelling and so on without me reading any of it over. On the fourth day I would mail it unread straight to the publisher in New York.

That was how I produced most of my early books and sustained the family and the magazine. I wrote sword and planet adventures, comedy thrillers, science fiction. I also wrote western comics, sports comics and features of every kind. I became an expert on African wildlife for 'African Safari' in *Tiger*. I got to know all about speedway or motor racing for 'Skid Solo, Ace of the Track' and Norse history for 'Karl the Viking' in *Lion*. I wrote one-page mysteries for 'Zip Nolan, Highway Patrol'. I did 'Claude Duval, the Laughing Cavalier', 'The Man from T.I.G.E.R.', 'Timmy and His Time Machine', 'The Desert Island School', 'Moonlight Molly', and 'The New Adventures of the Three Musketeers'. I was Fleetway's go-to guy for historical features and fiction. I loved working with the artist, Don Lawrence, especially when his colour was reproduced in gravure. When I was bored I wrote 'Karl' in Anglo-Saxon alliterative verse. Of course, it got a bit complicated when I sailed Karl off to the Arabian peninsula.

Jimmy Ballard said he admired me for my ability to take on any job, write anything to order. He said I was like Defoe. In reality, I know, he was at once jealous and faintly contemptuous of me for my journalistic skills. Perhaps he thought I wasn't a proper artist. Perhaps I wasn't, but I had an instinct for art and promoted or later published his work as hard and as often as I could. I published the first features about him and as an editor published work nobody else would look at. I paid him the best I could, too. He envied me my ability to feed my family as a freelance and hated having to keep to a dull desk job.

My routines were actually pretty dull, too, when it came down to it. Usually I would work out my novella or comic-strip ideas while I took the girls to Holland Park or to Derry & Toms roof garden. A surprising number of scenes in my work of that time were directly inspired by one of those spots. I found pretty much all the inspiration I needed from my immediate surroundings. Characters, even some conversation, would be drawn from people I met. I always put my ability to work down to those healthy peasant genes and the typing I learned at Pitman's. Apart from migraines, I had always enjoyed robust energy. The only thing wrong with me was the irritating noise in my ears which I had suffered since I was sixteen or so, from around the time I took over *Tarzan*. Doctors could do nothing for me. They said it was fairly common. They continued to diagnose it as tinnitus. I associated it with some kind of anxiety since it had begun so close to when I started my professional career. About twice a year I had a bad migraine attack and had to take to my bed and lie in the dark for several days. Helena ran the flat, looked after the girls and was also writing. By the time they were in school they were pretty much at the same level and went to the same classes. They were rarely apart, rarely rivalrous and continued to be supportive. They were my delight.

Rather typically Helena had hoped for a boy, but we agreed to stop at two. By having them young, we would be able to enjoy life with them as they grew to be teenagers. I would take the children out to give her a chance of a breather, perhaps to do her own work or just lie around reading. Never having ridden in her life, she turned out pony stories for my friend Ted Holmes and worked for *Look and Learn* and some of the girls' comics, like *School Friend*. Ted occasionally chased her round a table. I don't think he ever caught her. I couldn't blame him. She was a beautiful young woman.

BEATLES, PARIS, SEARCHING FOR PAST TIMES

WE HAD MARRIED to 'Love Me Do' and had our children to *Please Please Me* and *With the Beatles*. At one point they had occupied drawers below the Dansette record player. They teethed to 'A Hard Rain's A-Gonna Fall' and 'Blowin' in the Wind' and, by the time *Rubber Soul* was out, they were toddling nicely. We still took the odd visiting weekends here and there but eventually we decided we had to have a proper family holiday. So that neither of us had to do any work, we should go to an hotel. The children behaved so well in restaurants, we could eat out where the food was good. Therefore we should go abroad. It cost about the same in those days, anyway, whether we went to Torquay or Torremolinos but we didn't really want a beach holiday. So, inevitably, we decided to go to the other city we knew and loved as much as our own.

Paris had changed since I spent any time there. I was surprised by the vast increase in the Latin Quarter's tourism and a corresponding rise in prices. Everything was as we hoped it would be. Only when we set off to find somewhere to eat did I get a shock. De Gaulle had created a hard currency since I was last there. The franc was now stronger than the pound.

At that point a saga began where I dragged an increasingly protesting wife and children from restaurant to restaurant, menu to menu, astounded by prices which had risen enormously. I found myself blaming and hating tourists, of which, of course, I was one. Their numbers had also grown considerably. It was not that I couldn't afford the prices. Psychologically I was unable to accept it. My old bohemian haunts, where almost everyone at the tables lived locally and frugally, were now conquered and owned by an alien race.

At last, finding all my old stamping grounds in the 6th out of my anticipated range, we walked up to the 5th before I finally relented and went into a restaurant which by then seemed to serve the most delicious dinner in creation and would have been perfect had it not been for Helena's rather ferocious ultimatum that from tomorrow onward we would eat anywhere that looked nice and was reasonably priced, within an agreed range. It wasn't, she pointed out, 1955 any more.

I began to see sense, though I wouldn't go up the Eiffel Tower or queue to look at the Mona Lisa. Since Helena had never been inside Notre-Dame, we followed the other tourists filing in to the gloomy vastness of a building designed as much to symbolise temporal as spiritual power. I had always loved big churches and Notre-Dame was, as Ray had once described it, the mother of all gothic cathedrals. We joined the crowd entering the gigantic doors without much trouble and went along with everyone else walking slowly around the place admiring the soaring architecture, grotesque sculptures and glorious stained-glass windows. We liked the idea that during the Revolution the new government had rededicated Notre-Dame to the Cult of Reason with Marianne, spirit of Liberty, in place of the Virgin.

I had a habit of getting away from the more public or guided elements of a tourist site and quickly found myself in the shadows, climbing a stair, hoping to get into the upper parts, maybe into Quasimodo's famous bell tower, but I had only gone a short distance before a man I took to be a monk, wearing a pale habit, stepped from behind some stonework and politely, if rather coolly, advised me that this part of the cathedral was closed to the public. He smiled at me in what I thought was an odd way, almost as if he knew me. I made an apologetic noise but he did not respond. He simply turned slowly back to the shadows.

Did I recognise him? I have a notoriously bad memory for faces, as well as names. On several occasions I have failed to identify my closest friends and run out of ways of pretending to remember their names. Yet I continued to have the feeling I knew the man. Perhaps I had seen him in Paris on an earlier visit. Perhaps he had a resemblance to the monk I had known in my Fleet Street days. Only as I walked back down did I realise he had spoken to me in English.

Rather discomfited by this minor confrontation, I didn't have the French to argue. He had, I thought, a kind, patrician face. In the right circumstances I might have been a little more confident and insistent but then I was at a loss. I backed down and re-joined my family who were pretty much ready to go. I turned to look at him again.

The monk was still in the shadows. Now, however, he was deep in conversation with a well-dressed woman whom he seemed to know well. I wondered if I also knew her. She was not in her first youth. She had a dark, exotic beauty, a pile of curly black hair, a slightly military air. I had seen her before, also, in England somewhere. For an instant it occurred to me that I must have seen them in a film or even created them both for a recent novel. Since I never re-read my books, I couldn't be sure which one it might have been. I shook off the notion. I really needed this holiday, I thought. Then the girls found me. They were impatient to leave.

We went by boat on the Seine and took a bus to Versailles. We marvelled at miles of tacky, fly-specked mirrors, tarnished gold-leaf and malfunctioning fountains. The gardens were nice. In those days the French still disliked tourism in general and English tourists in particular. They made no more concessions to it than the British. This was in the days before the ulti-mate commodification of history, when Reagan and Thatcher declared that culture and tradition had to make a profit or vanish. The days before Hilton, Holiday Inn, Best Western, McDonald's and Domino's began to take over every individual hotel, bar and café, when it was still possible for small hotels and restaurants to do reasonably well for themselves in the 5th and the 6th, when the Marais was still mostly artisans, students, tailors; decent people, living modest lives.

We bought the girls delicious and elaborate sweets: Eiffel Towers of spun golden sugar, scintillating ruby lollipops, gorgeous confections: *religieuses* made of choux pastry stuffed with *crème pâtissière* and finished with a chocolate *ganache*, which we all fell in love with for ever. Glorious sundaes, exotic macarons and of course all the confits, offal, soups and stews which were so much better than anything which at the time we could find in London, except at Le Gavroche, Rules or perhaps the Ritz.

We dragged the girls around the smaller museums – Balzac, Hugo, Moreau, Montmartre and others. We took a tour bus out to the Villa d'Este, Dumas's rather lonely, wooded gothic monument to his own splendid imagination, which was very neglected, almost as if Parisians were ashamed of the world's most beloved romancer. We both loved those wonderful stories and had grown up reading *The Count of Monte Cristo* and *The Three Musketeers*. The girls had no interest in the books but loved the place, abandoned as it seemed.

Even Helena couldn't face the Louvre. We paid a bit too much for junk in flea markets and we enjoyed long, perfect meals with good friends, great cooks. Since I was fifteen I had built some lasting friendships in Paris. I knew people like Georges Hoffman, Maxim Jakubowski, Philippe Druillet and Michel Demuth. Ray Nelson, whom I'd first visited in the mid-'50s, had returned to the US with his Danish wife, Kirsten. Only Michel couldn't see us. He made it obvious he didn't have much interest in the full complement of Moorcocks.

Coming out of the Métro on the evening that we saw Georges and some of his friends, I had one of my familiar hallucinations.

No doubt it was brought on by our visit to the Villa d'Este.

In the twilit tree-lined street the majority of people had disappeared but I saw four figures wearing all the coloured ribbons, velvet, silks, feathers, vivid tabards, leather and lace of seventeenth-century military men, with rapiers on their hips and broad-brimmed over-decorated hats. Their hair was as long as mine. Their beards and moustaches were also similar to my own. I supposed these swaggering bravos to be advertising something like a new *Les Trois Mousquetaires* movie. I was impressed, pointing them out to Helena who gave me that familiar 'you've lost it again' look, while the girls were attracted to a nearby shop lit to display a wonder of sparkling, beautifully coloured cellophane and intricate paper flowers. And, of course, when I insistently drew attention to the men, they had turned a corner and disappeared. I couldn't be sure of their reality, and Helena responded with her usual scepticism, suggesting I see an optician when I returned to London. Her response was sympathetic, but I remembered to keep my visions to myself in future. Helena was both concerned for me, attracted to a romantic notion of me as a sort of minor Wm. Blake, and hoping that I wasn't displaying the early stages of schizophrenia. I had grown so used to seeing such things and knew them to be just tricks of my imagination that they didn't worry me at all.

That was a minor glitch in a holiday which Helena and I were now thoroughly enjoying, as were the kids. We'd ridden on the merry-go-rounds and the ponies and watched the marionettes at the Luxembourg Gardens. We'd been to the theatre, the Opera, Montmartre and Sacré-Cœur, and, on our last evening, were visiting the Cirque d'Hiver when the girls, who had been keen to go, complained of feeling sick and a quick check proved they had a degree or two of fever. There was nothing to be done but scrap the tickets. I was a little disappointed but I was sure I would be able to see Caveliero, the last great Harlequin, and his troupe again. He was still a couple of years from retirement.

Helena, as always when she wasn't anxious, grew very sympathetic, insisting on my going. I can see her beautiful oval face framed by red-brown hair, her blue eyes which mirrored mine, her mouth's firm bow curved in a half-smile. "Mike, please. You've been looking forward to this ever since we thought of coming to Paris." I told her I didn't particularly want to go on my own. I'd wanted to go with everyone. Nobody else in the family knew the Caveliero troupe, who had settled in France several centuries earlier. I'd really hoped to watch the whole thing *en famille* as we would enjoy Douglas Fairbanks movies at the Classic, Notting Hill, go to see Max Wall in *Godot* or as Helena and I had done, seen Lenya at the Royal Court. We were catching our last glimpses of greatness as our heroes and heroines faded from the world.

So rather reluctantly I got a bus across the river to Blvd Faubourg du Temple and Rue Amelot, dominated by the great Romano-Second Empire dome of the Winter Circus, established here in the 1850s in a part of the Marais' long association with the theatre. Once this whole street had bustled with sideshows, mimes and mob-wit. I had managed to offload the other tickets on a mother and her two daughters, friends of Maxim's Polish father. Madame Rim was very pleasant and shy. She was embarrassed about speaking little English while I found her mumbled French almost impossible to understand. The Cavelieros were all nearing their last appearances and it was still a privilege to watch them perform the scenarios they had inherited from ancestors who had travelled to France from Italy in the fourteenth century. The closest record of their style and talent can be seen in the masterpiece of French cinema *Les Enfants du Paradis*. And so for a few hours I enjoyed the masters at work, playing out the ancient routines said to be the same which entertained the Greeks and Romans. The equestrians, the tumblers, the wire-walkers and trapeze artists had all played the summer in big tops, arriving in Paris for the winter season.

I was not sure Madame Rim and her twins enjoyed the show much but I did. After I had put them into a taxi, asking them to tell Helena I was walking home, I decided to enjoy an evening drink and a cigar and take a moment recalling the performances of the Cavelieros before I returned to the hotel. The old man had given his best as had his offspring. I also knew that I was close to the Les Hivers district, which I was still curious about.

Rather than stroll directly along the familiar boulevard towards Bastille, I thought I would try a more interesting route home. I remembered a towpath beside the canal just below Rue Amelot and a little bridge which crossed the district known to the local bargees as 'Les Hivers' where the waters began to echo under the great tunnels and where, I had heard, five wide canals came together and poured their waters down on the thirsty souls in hell. The area had once been occupied by a Carmelite convent, whose occupants, affiliated to the Poor Clares, were known for their charity. During the eighteenth century, the Jesuits attacked the Carmelites, accusing them of conspiring with thieves, of offering shelter in return for stolen gold. Investigators found no proof of this. They believed the Jesuits, and perhaps another Order, rivals to the Carmelites, circulated the rumour for several reasons, but chiefly because they coveted their lands and wealth. How the district became known as 'The Winters' I had not the faintest idea. I wondered if the name had any connection to Milady de Winter from *The Three Musketeers*. As far as I knew, it existed long before the circus and might have taken its name from a brothel popular

111

with early Victorian Brits which had once stood nearby and was nicknamed (in English) *The Hive*. Were regular customers 'Hivers'?

The names, I thought, were probably coincidental. Yet very little had been published about the area. The first reference I knew was in *Le Vicomte de Bragellone* but I had heard there were earlier mentions in *Bussy D'Ambois* and even certain *commedia* playbooks. Most famous, at least in France, is the great scene in *Notre-Dame de Paris* frequently cut from translations. Apparently mock trials of those who offended the people were a common event in the taverns of Les Hivers up to the middle years of the nineteenth century; more than one eminent churchman or magistrate had found rough justice at the hands of an offended mob.

The surrounding streets were cobbled, the buildings were mostly half-timbered houses of two or three storeys in the high-gabled late mediaeval style predating Haussmann. Buildings like them were the background to many a scene in *The Three Musketeers*. They had been built for merchants of an earlier century. They were now each one evidently occupied by many families. Clearly little progress had been made in urban development for decades. There was no gaslight. The streets were lit by oil lamps on poles which cast a golden glow, giving glass and water a mysterious depth. You could smell them and not the gas. Descending the steps off Filles du Calvaire I enjoyed the sense of quiet which fell once the sound of the traffic dropped. Boulevard du Temple between République and Bastille could sometimes be unbearably loud. In contrast the atmosphere here, when I reached the towpath beside the broad canal, was almost eery. Something else nagged in the back of my mind. Something was different.

There were no tables outside the few bars and cafés still open but voices could be heard coming from buildings whose lights still stained the cobbles. Men lounging, smoking and chatting inside showed little interest in me as I strolled past. I decided to enter the least cheerless of the bars. The blue-eyed Algerian behind the counter greeted me with a perfectly pleasant *'Bon soir, monsieur'*, and poured me a pretty decent Armagnac which I sat and savoured as I looked out at the starlight reflected in the ebony water. After a while I realised that I had become gradually infused with a pervasive sense of well-being. Indeed, it was fair to say that I was somewhat high. The Armagnac had been a particularly good one but it usually took more than a fine brandy to make me so cheerful. Stimulating as the circus had been, I could not believe that the Cavelieros had managed to fill me with quite such a sense of euphoria. I hoped that I was not drunk. I glanced at my watch. I had best be getting back to the hotel before Helena began to worry. If I saw a booth I would phone the hotel.

Part Two

Divergence

Even the first great book of the genre, *Don Quixote*, teaches how the spiritual greatness, the boldness, the helpfulness of one of the noblest of men, Don Quixote, are completely devoid of counsel and without a scintilla of wisdom. If now and then, in the course of the centuries, efforts have been made – most effectively, perhaps, in *Wilhelm Meisters Wanderjahre* – to implant instruction in the novel, these attempts have always amounted to a modification of the novel form. The Bildungsroman, on the other hand, does not deviate in any way from the basic structure of the novel.

– Walter Benjamin,
The Storyteller, October 1936

8

Drifting Across

I ONLY REALISED the cause of my sense of euphoria as I started walking towards the tunnel entrance: The tinnitus which had dogged me for all those years since my mid-teens had become so familiar that I had pretty much grown used to it. Why did acoustics this far below street level manage to cancel out the effect?

For a minute I thought I was hallucinating. "Don't worry about me, squire." Pearl Peru failed to show her disgust. "It's Candycorn Bay for this old girl, and yes, I guess you should be jealous." Giving in to some classic Ice-T. Did the tunnels themselves have something to do with it? That constant sense of a whispering crowd demanding my attention had disappeared. "*Spammer* will be found and resolution achieved. You forget who steers the story! They like to say 'post-modern'. They say, pard. I does."

"But can I trust you?" I asked the echoing tunnel ahead. I think it joined another, to the Seine. I was too tired for an adventure!

Conscious of the tinnitus' absence, I found myself reluctant to give it up. I had borne it for years, since my time as editor of *Tarzan*, and through the whole of my married life. With its going, I felt a loss. Maybe when the tunnel opened up to the street, I would enjoy the sensation. One key on the piano seemed missing. Suddenly everything was in tune. Reluctant to give up that sense of well-being I lit another cigar. It had been so long! I fought against the euphoria. Reluctantly, I increased my speed, heading towards the single guttering lamp in the distance. Through the misty light it seemed the lamp grew no closer. In danger of walking down a side tunnel and getting lost I decided to be prudent. After all, I had a wife looking after a couple of daughters in our hotel and if I was not back soon she would worry. I would go back to where I had started. I would return quickly to Boulevard du Temple. I needed to find a taxi.

I wheeled round and began to increase my pace, returning the way I had come. Surprisingly, the light behind me had not grown much dimmer. I had misjudged the distance. This was a bad idea. I had been self-indulgent.

Because they raised blisters on my skin, I didn't wear a wrist watch. I looked at my pocket chronometer. It had stopped. I was irritated with myself. I should have gone straight back. Relieved, I broke out of the gloom into the unroofed air. I'd call the hotel and ask them to tell Helena I was on my way. I looked along both sides of the gloomy towpath, hoping to spot a late-night bar with a public phone sign. Everything was shut or closing. It was as well I had not gone deeper into the tunnels. I had emerged onto part of the towpath I didn't recognise. Had I accidentally taken a branch path? The whispering voices had not returned! A consolation. Was I cured? A minor miracle? I hurried on until I saw a building with flickering light in its lower windows. They would have a phone. I started towards it.

I heard a voice behind me. A vibrant, familiar voice. I could not put a name to it yet I knew it well. It belonged to a Geordie. Warm, enthusiastic. Someone from my childhood?

"Master Moorcock! Can it be you? I looked for you in London. Not for an instant did I expect you to follow me to Paris!"

I turned. The voice was familiar but the face was not. Had I heard it on the radio? In those days you rarely heard regional accents and this chap him had a distinct Northumbrian brogue.

The short stocky man with his well-groomed Van Dyke and long wavy chestnut hair stood wrapped against the night's chill in a heavy blanket or cloak. He looked a little ludicrous, striking what reminded me of a posed Rembrandt figure.

"Forgive me, monsieur," I said, "but I do not recollect your name."

He accepted this with a shrug of his broad shoulders. "Come, refresh your memory with a tankard of wine at that tavern, which seems the only one still welcoming trade!"

"Sadly, I must decline. My wife expects me. I am late. I must get back to her." The place looked particularly shabby and had no sign for a phone.

He attempted to disguise his alarm. "I understand." He paused and then with an expression of profound regret looked directly into my eyes. "But just now that will not be possible!"

9

A'voir, Paris

I COULD NOT place my new acquaintance, if indeed he was
new. I was furious with my own bad memory for faces.
Familiar, his voice had a slightly sardonic lilt. If I hadn't
known my friend Jim Cawthorn's Gateshead accent he would
have been harder to understand.

I was irritated by his confidence. "I have to return," I insisted. By now I was pretty sure he was drunk, perhaps
unstable and homeless. Could he be naked under that huge
swathe of cloth? No. At least he was wearing boots. They
seemed to be fashionably high-heeled. I still wondered if he
hadn't escaped from a local bin. Was he dangerous? I cursed
myself for an idiot. Maybe if I let him take me to the 'tavern' I
would be able to use their private phone to get in touch with
Helena, reassure her and ask her if the hotel could send a taxi.
"But I suppose I have time for a beer."

"Good." He took me by the arm. "You are needed."

"I am," I agreed. "By my wife and children."

To my surprise, he walked on for a few doors and paused
in front of a rather attractive tavern, an old two-storey
half-timbered building with one window still faintly lit. No
telephone sign. From behind the window I heard murmuring
voices speaking what appeared to be a mixture of French and

English. This surprised me. Generally, very few bargees on this side of the Channel spoke English. If I had heard Dutch or Flemish I would not have been surprised. But I did not know the area and this rather charming individual might at any moment become dangerous. He might also be setting me up to be robbed by the people on the other side of the door. I had only a little money on me and had left my passport at the hotel. In those days few people used credit cards. There wasn't much they could take. It was more likely I'd be kept talking by a few drunks, make my phone call and get back to Helena later than I had planned. It might even be interesting, something I could turn into a saleable story or at least an anecdote. I let him lead me into the bar.

The interior was comfortable, well-worn and welcoming. An old-fashioned, low-ceilinged French tavern, dimly lit by a few candelabra stuck at strategic places on the walls. Customers sat on benches or leaned on the zinc-covered bar. Doubtless because of its proximity to Rue du Faubourg du Temple, the place was full of actors. From the nearby Théâtre du Temple, by their costumes. Like the man beside me, they were still in a performance of Molière. They greeted us both as old friends, roaring like bravos.

I was astonished! I recognised many of them. But from where? Why did I feel a sudden lightening of all burdens in their company? The absence of the Whispering Swarm, which I had lived with for so long, must contribute to this rather mindless holiday mood!

Everywhere I saw the silks, lace and feathers of seventeenth-century cavaliers or the cocked hats, long waistcoats, stockings and buckled shoes of eighteenth-century gentlemen. The former were the same as those I imagined I had seen in the Boulevard St-Germain, still in their flamboyant costumes. This time I could smell their cologne, their strong wine, the smoke

121

from their long-stemmed white clay pipes, the burning tallow. I could hear the clink of their harness, their beautiful gold-chased rapiers and spurs. This was unlike any dream or trip I had experienced, both in its detail and the extent of its reality. There was also what I would call an under-stink, a pervasive smell on the edge of my senses which seemed to come from outside, possibly from latrines, a flutter of noise made up of many tiny sounds. I immediately suspected that my earlier hallucinations had prepared me for this moment when I cracked and lost my grip on reality. I was alarmed. These people were like the characters in the comics I still sometimes wrote. In fact Claude Duval had paid for this holiday.

At the bar I recognised the distinctive figures of Athos, Porthos, Aramis and D'Artagnan, the four Musketeers. Talking to them, and all immediately recognisable to me, were Jack Sheppard, Tom King and Sixteen String Jack while at the tables sat Claude Duval, the most dandified of them all, a slighter, quicker man than the hero of the comics, like others I had used in stories, including the tall, grave Zulu they called Beetle.

I was horrified! Just when I thought sanity and marriage were saved, my mind had snapped. Was I that ill? Something very similar had happened to my friend Frank Redpath, who had specialised in writing for the schoolgirl 'Libraries'. He had wound up living his life as if his characters were real and babbling his plots down the phone to a dozen editors, afraid his creations would fade away and die.

I fought to keep my common sense. These people certainly had the substance of reality. All I could do at that point was let the illusion absorb me. I felt some anxiety. I must get back quickly to Helena and the kids. They were my solid reality, everything I loved and held valuable. I could not believe I was mad. Madness was banal! It took the most obvious guises.

122

I rubbed at my head. Was I getting a migraine? I was so tired. I was surely just imagining the men's resemblances to penny-dreadful characters. These had to be actors. They wore the costumes so well. But I was already entering that confused state people today call 'brain fog'. My memory failed me, as did my common sense. I longed for this company on some far deeper level.

With a murmured word, my companion left my side and walked towards the bar. He ordered drinks from the barman. I caught a flickering wave, as if something much larger passed through the tavern for a brief moment. Had I imagined the colours sharpening? I was less uneasy. "Excuse me," I said. "Perhaps there is a telephone ...?"

From his place at the table, 'Claude Duval' stood up, bowing, suave. I was astonished. He spoke an elaborate French unfamiliar to me. Was I in a film? He was so real! In spite of my anxiety, I began to feel light-headed, as one does when chronic pain disappears for a while. I looked around me. No discomfort. No anxiety. I felt at home in this place. But what had happened to the man I met outside?

'Aramis' doffed his hat with a flourish and addressed me politely. "Monsieur, my Lady Blackstone presents her compliments and requests your urgent company at her estate."

I heard myself responding automatically. "Lady Blackstone. Is she in England?" I had only the vaguest memory of the name. Wasn't John Blackstone an English imaginative writer? Because of that I began to doubt if I did know the family. Blackstone was a relatively uncommon name, also associated with Northumberland. *Spammer* hammered. It had no context. Pataphysics.

He smiled negatively. "She awaits you with some eagerness. As does Lord John. There is an urgent gathering coming upon the Blackstone Massif. *Spammer* called. You did not hear?"

I frowned. I could only guess. Had I written about these men so often I imagined them as friends? Names were so unfamiliar. Could 'Squire Blackstone' be some cruel land-greedy relative involved in a ruthless scheme to swindle his ward out of her rightful inheritance? I almost smiled. I had the sense of talking to old companions in arms. We had certainly fought many skirmishes and a few full-scale battles together in my stories. Many times, with a pressing deadline, I had pretty much dreamed the stories as I typed. Tonight I was dreaming them again. Like the Yankee in Mark Twain's Court of King Arthur; I had fallen asleep at Cirque d'Hiver and was deep in a dream involving the characters I wrote about in comics. Kit Carson, Buck Jones or Robin Hood might turn up next! Although the name was vaguely familiar, I did not know a Lady Blackstone, yet Aramis continued to speak as if we were all old friends. I never got a chance to find out why the plateau was haunted.

I longed for the dream to collapse into absurdity, but it continued to follow its own logic. Since childhood I had grown used to vivid dreams. Until I began writing for a living, I had dreamed vividly of heaven and hell, of Tarzan's jungle, the Norse gods, of wars between the angels, of Parsifal and the Knights of Camelot, of talking animals, the Vikings and Robin Hood, musketeers and highwaymen, cowboys and Indians. My childhood had been happy. If I knew bad, troubling or miserable experiences, I escaped from them in books and dreams, one feeding the other. I had faced down witches and ogres. As I dreamed, I had forced myself to look evil squarely in the face and done what was sensible. Now I wanted to interrupt myself, wake myself up, but the dream persisted. In fact it deepened and became more persistent. Aramis, for whom I had perhaps the greatest liking of all, removed his gorgeous befeathered hat with a low formal bow and said:

"My dear old comrade! I know why you should question all this, but sometimes we must confront what we fear by subtler means. I cannot express how greatly we have missed thee since our last albeit unsuccessful adventure!" And he stepped forward to embrace me, like a lost brother. As he did so he murmured in my ear: "Our lady sends her compliments and tells me that she will try to meet us when we reach Tangier, if not sooner. I understand your friends to be in great peril!"

North Africa? If it were not the nickname for an arrondissement of Paris, then I had absolutely no intention of going to 'Tangier'. Perhaps it was best now to enter into the spirit of my dream and be prepared to wait it out, to enjoy it for its own sake. No doubt I would wake in a taxi or even beside Helena in our bed at Le Grand Hôtel de l'Univers! All I need do was enjoy the strangeness while it lasted and then tell Helena all about it. Maybe I could turn it into a story for the girls at bedtime! Yet, to my shame, both my children and Helena were becoming, in that awful mental fog, an almost forgotten dream!

I did not wake up. Not immediately, at any rate. The man with the Northumbrian accent didn't come back. Where had he gone? As they gathered around me, greeting me and begging me to tell them all that happened since we had last been together, I began to feel rather depressed. I heard my own voice relating stories I had written! These creatures of my fiction had mistaken me for someone else. I wanted to say I had invented them. Was that insulting? What else could I tell them? What was the truth?

They spoke of ships, frozen rivers, a beheaded king we had failed to save. Hadn't I written a story where Duval and his comrades had saved King Charles from the block and secretly smuggled him off to France? An entire *Thriller Picture Library*. *Claude Duval and the League of the Oak*? I remembered it about as well as I remembered any story written at white-hot speed.

I had given Bob Forrest some good pages to draw towards the end, with pre-Fire of London engulfed in snow and the Thames frozen as far as the Pool. Dave Gregory, the editor, had loved it. He said it was the best thing Bob had drawn. Bob was superb at costume stuff. He had drawn *A Princess of Mars* for *Comet* a few years earlier.

Even in one of my rare dreams, theirs was company I would enjoy in other circumstances but in this more-vivid-than-life dream I felt I remembered it all as having been my own! The dream was in danger of becoming a nightmare.

Dreams of course could seem to last for days while taking up a few seconds of real time but this did not make me any less concerned and racking my memory, cursing the vagaries of time. Helena and the children were not my only anchors, they were my responsibility. But only for a moment did I argue. They laughed at every protest. It did not occur to me that my disappearance would still affect family and friends, perhaps cause them to begin a search. I made one last attempt to stay with what my conscience directed. And then my dearest loved ones, lights of my life for whom I lived, slipped into the shadows and the Musketeers' reality became mine. The last reference to them was from Athos.

"They will be there, *mon ami*," he insisted. "Just as you left them! Why not enjoy this adventure for its own sake as we do? Here, familiar time is abolished. We are defined by actions and courage! Our worlds exist side by side." His smile was a mixture of bravery and irony. "One cannot exist without the other. One enriches the other. Life and death, the Balance directs our destinies."

The Northumbrian had returned to the room. I saw he wore clothes similar to the others. He stepped forward, raising his gauntleted hands to reassure me. "Have no fear for your loved ones, Master Moorcock. No harm shall come to them while you journey. Time and gravity are fields which ultimately bring us to the shores of Paradise."

I barely heard his words as I tried to determine exactly where he was from. My family were secure. I no longer needed to be concerned. "Neither shall they suffer, nor shall they know anxiety, nor shall they be in danger ..."

"All of which will be true because I shall be with them." I smiled back at these oddly dressed lunatics, wondering how I was going to escape them.

The Northerner, however, shrugged and with another elaborate bow indicated the tavern door. "Her need is very urgent. No doubt my Lady Blackstone will find some other way to meet you."

"I'm sorry ..." I felt obscurely guilty.

Then I had a moment's persecution mania. The whole tavern was watching, plotting to trap me and hold me. They watched in silence as I lifted my hand in farewell, stepped out onto the dark quayside and walked back looking for a flight of steps so that I could ascend to the embankment and then to Boulevard du Temple. I found one at last. It took me some time to climb to the top. When I got there I could not make out a single streetlight. Huddled against the skyline was a broken silhouette of low roofs. More like a dilapidated village. There was no sign of the six-storey Hausmann buildings which normally lined the wide boulevard. Instead the houses I saw were mostly two-storeys with crooked chimneys and irregular roofs. Moreover the street twisted away into the gloom, lit chiefly by stars and the moon, with the occasional dim yellow light from a window.

Worst of all the whole area stank like a cesspit. A stink which felt actively aggressive. As if it had a mind and a savage desire to attack me. I had obviously walked much further than I thought. Into some hideous slum. Driven back to the towpath I staggered on until I found more steps. I had reached a dark, twisting lane. The smell was not quite as bad so I continued, hoping to find a sign which would give me an idea where I was. The streets were all deserted. Somewhere in the distance I heard a man's voice crying out while a handbell peeled. He sounded like an old-fashioned nightwatchman calling the hour. What forgotten faubourg had I wandered into? Dogs yelped and yapped from the shadows. I saw no cars, no Métro station, no bus stop. I could not afford to become lost in the tangle of surrounding lanes. This place reminded me of an old country town. Once again I decided to retreat even if it meant encountering the bunch of people in the tavern. With a sinking feeling, I returned to the steps, descending to the canal. I started to trudge back beside the dark water until I saw the tavern's light through mist rising thickly off the canal. Perhaps the Northerner would offer me some answers?

I must admit I was still taking pleasure in the relative silence. That constant whispering was gone. Part of me wanted to sleep, to enjoy the peace. I forced myself to remain 'awake'. If I gave in to tiredness I might somehow never see Helena and the girls again. Fear helped me keep going in this appalling supernatural farce. Or was I now in bed reliving the nightmare? Possibly the noises in my head would come back and that would be a sign I had returned to the familiar world. But it was still quiet, even restful.

When I pushed open the tavern door, the men turned smiling heads to greet me. They had expected me.

For a moment, in the nature of irrational dreams, I experienced a wave of pleasure drowning all my other senses. I felt like laughing and cheering. Was I drugged?

Claude Duval came towards me, putting a gauntleted hand on my arm and guiding me to the counter. "You seem merrier than when you left, Master Moorcock. Now, you will have the drink with us, yes?"

"Of course! Why not?" I grinned and gave myself up to the experience. Perhaps Monsieur Duval would be able to explain all that was going on. I reached the bar and was absorbed by the roistering crew!

Aramis smiled, pushing a pewter tankard of spiced wine towards me. "Do you recall our meeting in London, monsieur? When we discussed the matter of the House of Stuart?"

Of course I remembered the story I had written. *To Save a King*. Thanks to Bob Forrest's wonderful artwork it remained in my head longer than most of the millions of words I'd turned out. But otherwise I recollected nothing of any previous meeting. Not in reality.

I had never talked about the Stuarts with anyone except Helena and my friend and editor Dave Gregory. Yet all these men, as happens in a dream, appeared to know me well, laughing as they recollected adventures we had enjoyed together. While they talked, it seemed I remembered at least fragments of those times. Then I knew why I had thought of Dave. He was editor of *Lion* and *Tiger* as well as *TPL*. He had commissioned a text serial (for *Lion*, I think) called originally *The Stuart Sword* featuring all these rapier-swinging heroes. It had run for weeks. 1,500 words an episode. And then Dave had asked me to turn it into a complete 64-page comic script, originally for Steve Chapman, but Steve was cutting back on commissions, while Bob Forrest was looking for work. I had done the whole book in a night. All these memories becoming more coherent helped me make sense of what was happening to me.

I had often described my working methods as 'dreaming aloud' or 'selling my dreams'. I would sometimes emerge from a long session, having written several episodes of similar serials, with almost no recollection of what I had done, yet editors often praised that stuff as some of my best. To this day

I could barely tell anyone what one of those stories was about. Apparently Rider Haggard worked in a similar way. At that time, in the mid-1960s, I was writing whole novels in a trance.

No point in fretting, I decided. I would soon wake up and either be with Helena or on my way to her. After all I was used to being half-conscious of dreaming and of imagining scenes or events. Since I was a boy I had cultivated the state, sometimes going so far as to electrocute myself, to induce experiences. I would not worry about the identity of Lady Blackstone. I relaxed, determined to enjoy the dream for as long as it continued. If it seemed to last a few minutes or a year. I could relax. Sometimes I managed to make a dream last an hour; a day or even a season!

Meanwhile I relished the luxury of silence and fantasy.

10

A Twist in the Tunnel

THE WINE WAS much stronger than I was used to. I remember wondering if it were drugged. But I drank it anyway. I have vague memories of being helped out onto the towpath and then into what became a cross between a boat, a taxi, a bus, and a cheap hotel room. I was aware of brilliant, rapidly changing colours; dozens of them, like flickering neon, as if I could suddenly see more subtle shades of colour than usual. No migraine I had experienced was like it! I felt no pain and this worried me. Voices assured me I would soon be home. Where was home?

I was dimly aware how the appalling stink of the city slowly became the fresh, salty smell of the sea. The room lurched. I tried to wake, to get out of bed, to see where I was. Were we all going home on the ferry? I could barely move.

Later I guessed I was lying along the back seat of a bus or a van. Yet the particular movement was unfamiliar. I was rocked both from side to side and back and forth. I now know I was aboard a canal boat! By the stubble where I usually shaved around my beard I knew I had been on the boat for the best part of a week. The tiny room was equipped with most of my immediate needs. I was reminded of the sleeping cars on a train or the ship in which as a boy I had crossed from Harwich to

Esbjerg on my way to Sweden to meet my friend Lars Helander and drive on to Eskilstuna to stay with his parents. The difference was that the earlier cabin smelled of vomit and I could barely move. One of my fellow passengers in the bunk above me had spewed up all night and the cramped quarters gave me pins and needles. This tiny room was more pleasant and comfortable, evidently constructed by a carpenter who knew what he was doing. They had added lots of idiosyncratic touches, with a folding basin and table and all kinds of comforts and gadgets. I was reminded of the barge in *L'Atalante*, where the young bargee and his bride lived with the old man.

I was perfectly tranquil until I looked through the tiny porthole over my narrow bunk. Then I was horrified. Convinced I had been drugged. Rather than discover the source of any foul play, however, I was more concerned with how on earth we had travelled as far as the Mediterranean in such a short time. Europe's canal network was famous. So complex, it was said, some parts twisted into the fifth dimension. The waterways certainly did extend from Paris to the coastal waters of the Med. But even a modern motor barge took many days to make the journey.

Had they drugged me more drastically than I first thought? What an earth was their motive? I had no clear idea how much time had passed. I could make out no land. Only the golden blue of the water, the silver blue of the sky.

How far out to sea were we and where were we bound? I had been kidnapped. There was no other word for it. I remembered Duval saying something about Tangier. I had no doubt that we were in the Straits of Marseilles, bound for the Maghreb. The region was called 'the West' because it lay on the NW coast of Africa, opposite France and Spain. Probably, as Duval had said, we were headed for Morocco, most likely the port of Tangier. Surely it would be dangerous to take a

canal-going barge anywhere else. Even that would be dangerous in stormy seas, though this boat was riding pretty well.
Maybe she was designed for it. I hoped so.

Judging by the tightly stowed clothes, the little cabin usually had three other occupants with barely any space between
the double-bunks. I was on the lower outer bulkhead. I saw
few clothes not put away, so had no clue about the men I
shared with. By the untidy state of their bedding, they were
not seamen. From the strong smell of lavender and Eau-de-
Cologne I was pretty sure they were French. Now I had smelled
those outer streets I understood their reasons for wearing so
much scent. In London they would be fops. In Paris those
people were essentially forced to live next to a tannery. There
was something to be said for dreams without a sense of smell.
I was determinedly hanging on to every coherent memory of
the real world, as opposed to this dreamworld. I was still not
sure if I would wake in an hotel room, a prison cell or, indeed,
the morgue!

There was nothing vague about my recollections but it was
as if someone had slipped a sheet of glass between my normal
existence with them and my new life aboard the little barge.
On one side I saw a woman and children and heard the constant noise of that murmuring swarm, to which I was enslaved
while awake. My family was rarely sympathetic, of course.
Did I not need a break from the Swarm, even a temporary sep-
aration from my children? I would be a new man for the wife
and kids!

As soon as I was up I began to feel drowsy again and decided to put my head down for a few minutes, falling asleep
again almost immediately.

I awoke at night to find someone had lit a smelly oil lamp
whose smoke made genii shapes in the orange/yellow light. I
heard voices and footsteps overhead and called out, but nobody

answered. As night went on I explored the cabin further, testing the locked door, seeing if I could finesse it open, but it was firmly secured. If this was still a vivid dream it was thoroughly detailed! I felt I was in a Stevenson novel. He was one of my favourite writers. Had I reconstructed his books in my imagination? I did my best to recall everything I knew of *Kidnapped* or *The Master of Ballantrae*.

This was crazy! I called out again and again but no-one answered me, though I heard voices in French. Then as I sat slumped in despair on my bed, I heard a soft click as the key was turned in the lock. Then booted feet crept back to the deck. I heard voices again, then a wave of easy laughter.

Feeling a little sick, I opened the door and eased it outwards. The short passage was empty. At one end was the companionway up to the broad, shallow deck. The seas were growing increasingly restless. My shipmates, if they were that, cheered when I put my head and shoulders over the edge of the hatch and applauded a little as I climbed on deck to get my sea-legs.

Sometimes wallowing dramatically, the barge was under full canvas and making better speed than I had thought possible in such a vessel. Her square, red sails bulged with the wind, her staysails bellying and quacking like so many mallards bobbing astern and around her stubby prow. She had a rather self-confident air as she made her way steadily forward. I guessed she had made this crossing before in all weathers and conditions and had no doubt she would see port within a matter of hours. I had noted the same characteristics in Cornish seamen and their craft, which they trusted because they had been tested in all conditions.

The Musketeers greeted me as cheerfully as before. I found it impossible to suspect them of plotting against me. Neither could I believe that the blue-eyed rogue grinning in the rigging overhead planned anything more than a boyish prank.

With a flourish Duval removed his feathered hat and bowed from his perch, his ringlets swinging.

"Our wine's too strong for you, I fear, Monsieur Moorcock. You slept all the way from Paris." He was charming as always but I refused to be seduced.

"How did we get here from Paris?" I demanded. "What on earth possessed you all to kidnap a citizen of an allied nation and carry him off to sea? Presumably we are heading for Africa?"

"You are prescient, sir." Duval offered me a friendly wink. The little man swung down, legs astraddle. I warmed to him despite my suspicions of his motives, indeed, of his very reality. "What power told you of our destination?"

"No bloody 'power'!" I snapped. "You mentioned Africa when we first met." I looked around the sparsely furnished boat. What cargo were they carrying "In Paris?"

He threw back his head, put his hand on his hip and roared with laughter. "Aha! And I'm the man forever counselling others to keep close-mouthed!

"Aye, monsieur," he went on. "God willing we reach Tangier by moontide or a little later. Last evening we came to Marseille on the *Sapphire Glacier* from the Jade Child's Pelt. You were drunk, I fear, and even slept through the colour shifts of the rip tunnel. When we left Paris last week the moonbeam canals proved propitiously aligned. We left Marseille early this morning and were under full sail by the time we ate a breakfast of excellent *bouillabaisse* brought to us by our sea-going skipper here!" And he jerked his thumb towards the tiny wheelhouse astern. Peering out at me with tongue lolling, his eyes bright with pleasure as he seemed to steer the barge, was a large liver-coloured dog, his long spaniel ears giving him the appearance of wearing a whiteish ringletted wig on which was perched a wide-brimmed, befeathered hat similar in style to Duval's cavalier *chapeau*.

Only a moment later did I spot the shadowy features behind the dog, and recognised another face from my own stories! Peter Popper, the jolly host of The Romping Donkey, where the Duval band congregated in the prosperous little market town of Witney beyond Oxford. The wool trade made that road rich. For some years we lived in nearby High Cogges. Some said Duval even lived in our cottage for a while, a short ride to the Oxford road.

Perhaps it was true what everyone said about me and I never did stop working. Ideas came and went rapidly. Was I plotting another full-length *Thriller Picture Library*, *Claude Duval and The Turkish Hawk*? It felt like it. I had promised not to do a stroke of work in thought, word or deed the whole time we were gone. Was this my way of breaking my promise? I had to admit I was making a decent job of it. I had never fantasised so successfully. The barge's movements were very real in the seas washing around it. She had a peculiar bumping forward motion and a side-to-side roll. Somehow she combined the worst movements of all vessels in one. Yet she continued to control the waters around her. As I stared at the mud-streaked turquoise water rising and falling, bile rose in my throat. I rarely felt this ill at sea. Duval's own courage had never been less in question as he stood on the narrow deck balancing in the water foaming around his feet, the heavy red canvas bulging above him. Apparently unconcerned by the motion of the waves, Porthos sat on a hatch-cover eating a chicken and drinking deeply from two soft leather bottles. His hat was tied firmly under his chin. Its vivid ostrich feathers rustled in the wind. Meanwhile, Aramis and Athos lounged in the stern, expectantly staring back towards the horizon. Did they anticipate pursuit?

D'Artagnan looked at us from where he scanned ahead. A faint purple line sat upon the sea. "Night comes swiftly here.

So far the gods have favoured us, *messieurs*! Our enemies have failed to sight so small and sluggish a craft. Hidden now in the twilight is Las Cascadas. I am glad we do not have to encounter her cruel ruler, the infamous Abbess De Winter in White. We have no time to dispute her terms. The moonbeam sea-lanes were in near-perfect alignment. We should make landfall in less than two hours. Look! There's the coast of Morocco."

He pointed. On the horizon, and growing clearer by the moment, was a thin snake of land which shifted and twisted and came and went and increased my nausea so that I was forced to turn away: Just as I heard a shout from starboard. Bearing down on us, with the red disc of a full moon now framing her dark triangular sails, her oars rising and falling to the beat of a drum growing louder by the moment, came a graceful Arab war dhow! A massive double-decker ship, her open gun-ports elaborately painted in the old Turkish fashion, ready above the oars. Liveried in black, green, pink and gold, like something out of Sinbad the Sailor, her figurehead represented a merman with threatening emerald trident. A creamy foam broke around her prow and the moonlight shattered silver and green against her shadow.

Where had that magnificent ship come from?

Cursing, Duval ran yelling for the wheelhouse. My friends in the stern hurried to drag canvas from two small cannon. D'Artagnan, the Musketeer, made sure of his pistols, then began priming guns and handing them to his comrades, including me. I stared at the clumsy weapon. With his strong teeth D'Artagnan impatiently tore off a piece of burning fuse for me. Porthos, growling some obscure Southern folksong, prepared another gun in the fo'c'sle. He stuck more burning fuses in his hat band.

"Barbarosa!" yelled D'Artagnan, answering my question.

"The Barbary corsair! That's his ship, *The Golden Rule*. If we're captured we'll all be sold to row the Sultan's galleys."

"What shall *I* do?"

He flashed me a smile. "Well, sir, be sure you are not captured. Can you lay the barrel over something steady, point your gun, light her match with this fuzee and shoot? All in less than a minute?"

I was pretty sure I could, though I had hoped for a more modern weapon.

The barge was yawing dangerously as Peter Popper leaned hard on the wheel, changing course. We were heading out to open sea again.

"There wasn't time to reach port and we cannot be sure Barbarosa's confederates aren't waiting for us in Tangier," Duval told me. "He has more men and a far superior vessel. So we're heading for Las Cascadas after all." He pointed into the deep moonlight. "Back there."

I had no idea, of course, exactly what or where he meant. I understood that Las Cascadas was ruled by some pirate hag I had no wish to meet.

I looked back. A cloud obscured the moon. The dhow's lights were fading rapidly behind us. I hoped that meant we had lost our huge pursuer. Minutes passed while we remained alert. A little later, we slowed down and began to turn. I saw lights rising into the sky. Silhouettes. We were approaching a large land mass, perhaps an island, its high, obsidian walls climbing steeply out of the crashing, creamy waves. "Las Cascadas!" shouted Duval, hooking a newly lit lantern in the rigging. "Now, I fear, you have no choice but to present your compliments to the Abbess."

"Our hostess? She's particularly cruel?" I was nervous now.

"When it suits her, I gather." He grinned.

D'Artagnan chimed in. "You've heard no doubt of the

terrible Witches of Tangier? Well, though she bears a Christian title, she is said to combine the powers and ferocity of all three. There is often a high price to pay for being granted sanctuary in her harbour. Las Cascadas' five gates are narrow and only permit entrance to one foreign ship or a few boats at a time. That island once ruled a mighty empire. Today it is an invisible empire of fear. Equally she can seal all gates at invasion's threat or to keep a ship imprisoned. Cruel? The Abbess has shown romantic interest in a traveller from time to time. That's said to be the cruellest fate of all."

"You've met her? You know her?"

Duval became grave. "She is sometimes called the Barbary Rose, Queen of the Barbary Coast, the Rose of all Roses, my Lady Rose von Bek. Once Mother Superior of a Carmelite Abbey in Louisiana in the Americas, though she ultimately married a German. Widowed, she returned to her calling and is now Abbess of the Carmelite Convent of Las Cascadas. You've no doubt heard of the Welsh slaver, Captain Horace Quelch, the most vicious of all the Barbary Brotherhood. Well, he's her current amanuensis! She forbids ships entering port at night. So now we must find shelter in the shadows of the island. Barbarosa's men daren't pursue us so close to the rocks. Our barge has the advantage of an exceptionally shallow draft. We'll request permission to sail into port in the morning."

"And Barbarosa?"

"Perhaps you know him as the corsair, Redbeard? He must also seek permission, for no ship is permitted to lie at anchor within sight of Las Cascadas during the day. He will set sail for better pickings, or he will lurk about the seas off Tangier after we leave Las Cascadas, hoping to catch us when we make another attempt to reach port."

"If he follows us into this port?"

"It's unlikely. That's why we're aboard a humble barge!

139

We're small fry. In Las Cascadas he will be bound by the Abbess Rose's rules. It's a sanctuary for all. It comes under the Abbess's protection. Her articles. Civil discourse. No drawn weapons. No threats. No insults. No fighting. No oaths. No forming factions. All punishable by painful death. In her fiefdom, peace is enforced with iron and fire. And almost all infractions are punishable by torture, then death."

As I heard the chain rattle and the primitive anchor fall through the clear waters to strike the rocky bottom only a few feet down, I felt increasing sickness as the appalling realities of our situation descended on us. This nightmare, I was convinced, was about to kill me.

Dread, dearest fishling, is but knowledge of our failing, for we are mere cells in a greater organism, tied to our function and our function is our destiny. And if you break free of your function somehow you must discover a destiny of your own or die. And should you survive with a future, you must be prepared to die alone. Ignore your dread, for it is but a frightening reality, and follow your nature. Your death will be less lonely ...

Failing can be sweet with punishment, Pearl, insists Monika Mashie, selecting a mashie from her bag as over the bright red horizon comes a wash of hazy multihued smog as the great metropolis of Rainy Pitts breaks out of that horrible mélange of second-rate colours, but Captain Quelch hides behind his claw-like fingers and sips at them with distant lips. Pearl's stomach turns. She hates it when he's hungry. "It's all abstract here, captain. There might be some sort of cafeteria ..."

"Oh, sod this for a tower of cold pies." *Captain Buggerly Otherly pushed back his hatch, threw out the remains of his nameless pasty and kicked his engine to an angry roar. Having vented his disgust he grinned, adjusted his omniphone and cheerfully wiggled his fins.* "Here's to good old Jarry and off we go with a laugh and a fart!"

140

Wishing him well, Pearl was secretly pleased to see him go. He was happier when he had a job.

Blackstone was rather surprised by his cousin's passion. She was a heavy-boned woman and well muscled. He could not move from beneath her panting body, and now, somewhat to his horror, he was becoming aroused.

11

The Barbary Rose

A T DAWN WHEN the waters of the Emperada della al-'rique
Strait were at their most tranquil, I went to the low rail
and stared at the sun rising over the tiny lagoons shimmering
amongst the crags. The pools would begin to dissipate by noon.
Narrow shards of obsidian and flint thrust through uneasy waters
supported some of the most beautiful architecture I had seen,
from Gothic palaces to Baroque towers, looming Palladian villas
to Moorish domes and beautiful little minarets and fountains, all
set behind low walls in evergreen gardens with rhododendron,
hyacinths, hydrangeas, hibiscus, bougainvillaea, lilac, lavender,
chestnut, poplar, cypress, cedar and fig trees sweetening the air,
delightful to see in their blossoming variety.

Contrary to its reputation the island exuded an atmosphere
of peace. An entire town spiralled down from a glorious white
palace to a pretty outer harbour where certain ships awaited
permission to enter the unseen inner harbour. The outer
'quarantine' harbour was already busy with traffic from men-
o'-war to merchants and fishing craft, all seen through the
bars of those massive sea-gates. Beyond this, unseen, set deep
into the rock, no doubt the crater of an extinct volcano, was
still another port where ships, Captain Popper told us, sought,
amongst other things, sanctuary.

I was astonished. This was my own imagination brought to life! A detailed engraving from 'At War with the Barbary Slavers' in *Harper's Magazine*, June 1876, an exotic feature I recalled with absolute clarity. My Auntie Connie's lovely sitting room in the days when women kept their parlours sunny and quiet. I sat in that room for hours with *The Encyclopaedia Britannica*, and bound volumes of *The Strand*, *The Windsor* or *Pearson's*. Those illustrated magazines fed my imagination. I believed the island Convent of Las Cascadas to be a journalist's fantasy. She was at best a glamorous pseudo-myth, mentioned in *Amadis of Gaul* and many other decadent romances of the late Middle Ages. Yet here she was, rising from the blue-gold waters of the Mediterranean like an illustration by Nielsen or Dulac, an Arabian Nights fantasy made real.

I viewed the tiny island with mixed feelings. I experienced an authentic sense of awe, as if I looked at the Grand Canyon or the Vatican ceiling for the first time. I had always projected visions onto the world and rarely been scared of them. I believed them inventions of my own mind, like a kind of photograph.

Our heavy barge ploughed steadily forward, steered by Captain Popper, poled by the sweating musketeers, with rolled sleeves, and piloted by Duval, in thigh-length sea-boots, swinging a line in the bow. The chilly morning air emphasised all sound: the hiss of spray on rocks, creaking timbers, clinking harness, shrilling wind and clattering metal. Iron squealed as a sea-gate was raised enough to admit our clumsy craft.

To my relief Barbarosa's black-and-gold dhow with her wide scarlet sails was nowhere to be seen. She would not be intruding upon the Sanctuary Harbour beyond the cliff. I had rather expected her to be sailing ahead of us. All that lay in front of our barge now were a couple of scows piled with vegetables and fruit following a trim Normandy trading schooner calling out that she carried sea-cloth from Scotland and fine Huguenot weaving from London. When white-robed monks armed with bows, hanging in the swaying metal boxes above the portcullises, ordered us to state our business, Peter Popper, from his position in the wheelhouse, called out that we sought sanctuary. This brought the second gate smashing down in front of us, the waves striking our startled faces.

Were we to be refused?

"Do you agree to the White Friars' terms of sanctuary?" called one of the archers clinging from a rail overhead. Captain Popper acknowledged that we did.

"From what do you seek sanctuary?"

"Barbarosa."

At this a guard gave a signal. The sharply honed portcullis, bright with dripping weeds and brine, began slowly to rise. Carefully my comrades punted the barge under the spikes. As the gate fell back with a mighty splash behind us, I received the impression that the convent had given sanctuary to 'Redbeard's' victims before. Did they fear the power of the black-and-gold dhow as much as we did? A common enemy? Or did they merely trap us for the pirate's pleasure?

Shadowy guards moved above in the dim light. They directed us to pole between high, ancient channels whose stone walls dripped with slime and sea water. They curved overhead to meet and roof the whole passage. That roof opened suddenly to blind us with the morning's brilliant sunlight. We followed shouted instructions, informing us which of several directions we should take in these narrow, echoing tunnels. Our heavy wooden hull bumped and scraped against old bricks and stones. Slowly, we made our way through a confusing sea-maze. Popper had visited the island as a cabin boy aboard an English merchantman. He told me the maze had daunted would-be invaders for centuries. "The old sultan gave

Carmelite monks permission to build an abbey here in 1240 when the Saracens evicted them from Palestine. He was equally tolerant of Jews during the purges. Eventually the white friars and nuns rose to rule in the place of the sultans. Rome never had much influence here. They continue the habit of granting sanctuary to all. They are also versed in arms. Their wealth attracts every sea-thief in the region."

At last the channel widened into a larger circular harbour. Clearly based in the old volcanic crater, the port was busy with a variety of sailing vessels. A Venetian ketch, two fair-sized war-galleys of unidentifiable provenance flying no colours, a couple of armed dhows showing green Arabian flags were hull to hull. A three-masted Boston topsail schooner must have been towed into the marina through the wider and taller passage we saw on the far side of the natural lake ahead of us. It seemed newer than the rest of the openings. I guessed the quay had been built more recently to accommodate bigger ships now sailing the Middle Sea. I doubted that a large Spanish galleon could ever negotiate her way into the harbour. Was there a secret entrance?

The place was evidently devoted more to merchant shipping than fighting vessels. Wharfs were busy loading or unloading goods of every kind. No doubt the bulk of them were the spoils of piracy or smuggling. I wondered what payment the island would demand for giving *us* sanctuary. Perhaps Duval and the Musketeers knew better, but I thought we had little to offer the Carmelite monks and nuns who gave sanctuary to prey and predators of every stripe!

As we docked at the far end of a mole, I waited rather impatiently for my companions to get into better clothes. At last, feeling a little dowdy in simple homespun shirt, waistcoat and breeches in their peacock company, I was able to tread a gangplank up to the quayside. Glad at last to step onto the slick cobbles of the wharf, I helped my friends tie up the barge and secure her mooring. Above us a massive granite cliff blocked all views of the inner island. The barge tied, I sighed with relief. I had been too long on the water. Dry land of any kind was welcome.

Dressed in outfits drawn from the best of the musketeers' seventeenth-century finery, we were still getting our land-legs when a group of armed monks approached. They, too, wore white habits under silver-chased breastplates with steel-cored turbans of Turkish design. Courteously, they requested we accompany them to where their comrades waited with horses. They helped us mount. We cantered away from the crowded harbour, through picturesque and well-kept streets, towards a stronghold. From her slender towers and minarets, she was more a fortified palace than a castle. The horses carried us through a narrow portcullis, a double bailey and into a cloisters surrounding a small lawn with a fountain at the centre. We were greeted by novices in simple white tabards embroidered with a complicated badge made from several symbols, including a crescent, a star and a cross. This struck a chord in my memory. As I puzzled over the symbolism, they led us through a discreet archway, into a rose garden enclosed by tall sweet-smelling hedges. I was instantly taken back to my childhood; my memory of tranquillity. Why did I recall so many scents?

The gorgeous aroma of roses relaxed and beguiled me. I breathed it in gratefully as we approached a small lawn set with a large wicker table and low chairs. We were invited to sit. Athos was the first to accept. He removed his hat and gloves with a flourish, handing them to the nearest servant. One by one the others followed. I had no hat or gloves to take off. The chairs had deep cushions of oriental luxury. Evidently little had changed here since the great Moorish caliphates ruled the Peninsular.

Eventually uncowled novice nuns arrived to offer us refreshing bowls of subtly scented water and soft towels, mint tea, coffee, sherbet, delicious cakes and sweets which were a bit much for breakfast, though I ate one from curiosity.

Everything was of great subtlety and delicacy. Even the pastel shades of the awning, which kept the sun off us, were finely graded. We ate a little suspiciously, not sure who our host was. Then, as we finished, a tall, veiled woman appeared behind us.

I stood up automatically, as did the others, bowing awkwardly or gracefully according to his character. This was surely our hostess.

My first thought was that she must indeed be a crone. Only her heavily made-up violet eyes were visible above a deep, royal blue veil in heavy silk showing the outline of exquisite features but revealing nothing of their age. Her figure, too, was lovely. She seemed a living embodiment of Nefertiti but I heard Aramis whisper 'Cleopatra' and then murmur a courtly flattery as he took her gloved hand and kissed it. Peter Popper merely blushed bright red and stammered a West Country burr for a greeting. She responded in beautifully modulated French to each of us until she stopped, finally, at me. Her warm scent blended with the sweetness of the roses. I found myself bowing, taking her gloved hand. "My Lady Abbess."

"Good morning, Master Moorcock." She was surprisingly tall. She spoke perfect English with a hint of amusement in the warm, almost Cockney, accent I identified with Edwardian upper classes. This allowed me to make an educated guess at her age, for now I heard a vibrancy suggesting youth. She changed back to French. "I heard of you in London. At our City Sanctuary. I had not expected someone so young. You want us to give you protection from our old friend Freddy Barbarosa, is that right? You trust the brothers under my command more than those who serve old Redbeard? I admit my friars are rather expert in the warrior craft."

I agreed that we wanted to avoid the corsair, if at all possible. I had not, however, expected aid from a group of armed monks, though I knew a little about such men. The Knights of Malta were one of the most famous armed orders.

"We have not met but I suspect he doesn't mean us well." I was taken aback to hear the most feared corsair of his day referred to as 'Freddy'. Natural-sounding enough, however, in her musical French. I had given up trying to decide the chronology of my adventure. I really was feeling like a character in one of my own Fleetway stories! Living in a fiction with its own chronology. "I had not understood my name to be so widely known, my lady."

I thanked her for her hospitality. I had no idea, I said, why Barbarosa should be pursuing us. My companions seemed no better informed. I was confused. She shrugged a little. "The politics of this region have become excessively complicated." She spoke almost apologetically. "Bellies ache. Bargains are struck. Debts are recalled. Marriages are arranged. Armies march. Fleets sail. Sometimes it is impossible to follow so many complications. Perhaps Master Redbeard owes a debt to some monarch who in turn seeks a favour from another." Graciously she asked me to sit. In turn she greeted those guests with whom she hadn't yet spoken. Pleasantries were exchanged. Then she re-joined us, allowing herself to be served with mint tea.

"Tell me." She lifted her veil and put her cup to her full lips, revealing a hint of her subtle complexion. "How are things in Ladbroke Grove?"

What did this glamourous abbess think she knew? With an enormous jolt, I recalled who and where I was, even if I did not know why. Might *she* have kidnapped me? Across time? Impossible! Surely she could not also move from the twentieth century to what was presumably some version of the seventeenth or eighteenth?

Not by nature suspicious, once more I wondered what on earth was going on. I looked anxiously towards Duval. I now suspected he could be in league with our apparent enemies or, indeed, our hostess. Had the dhow been sent to scare us and force us to enter the pirate harbour? If so, perhaps she had arranged everything, including my kidnapping from Paris.

Surprised by every event since I had left the Cirque d'Hiver, I again became more cautious. I also had to make sure of my own judgement if I was to survive, I was sure of that. Suspicion without evidence soon becomes paranoia. I needed firm answers, firm ground to stand on and confront this surreal, mad, world. I was on the verge of depression, barely aware of my surroundings as I struggled to recall my identity, further confused by Duval explaining a proposed theory of multiple worlds and an expedition they might mount. Worse madness!

He spoke of the so-called Islamic 'Black Tarzan' and a mythical African kingdom somewhere within the Lost Atlas. It sounded like a crazy pulp story to me. All it needed was some aristocratic Englishman in 'native dress' to turn up and create a corny John Buchan bush adventure. I could almost smell the rot of collapsing empires. Fantastic or not, there was no denying the sense of decadent speculation which pervaded the Lady Abbess's lavish court. I was becoming overwhelmed by it.

Events took on a still more unreal quality. I was drowning in fiction. I couldn't help remembering illustrations by the likes of Dulac, Nielsen and Charles Robinson or those marvellous films made by Buñuel, Man Ray and Cocteau. That eery quality found in *Les Vampyres*. I was even reminded of the frisson I had experienced reading E. Nesbit's Arden stories.

The entire world and its inhabitants was taking on the

menacing absurdity I associated with Beckett or Pinter. At least the 'Whispering Swarm' was gone. I sometimes waited for it. It never came. And gradually Ladbroke Grove returned to the shadows.

I was beginning to think in terms of rabbit holes, Cheshire cats and talking mice. I barely grasped what went on from moment to moment. I looked around me at the beautiful, sweet-smelling hedges, the gorgeous flower beds, the lawns and fountains. The absurdism of Alice, the surrealism of a dream landscape, the internal logic of a visionary like Blake or Peake? Were they there? For me, the Abbess's exotic island had the air and appearance of one of London's posher mad-houses, like the Richmond Priory.

"Mr Moorcock?"

The conversation was in French. I was day-dreaming in English.

I apologised. I had not heard her question.

As if by instinct, she changed into English when she spoke to me. Was there a code we should be sharing? A joke, even? I still could not identify her. Her accent was of an older educated metropolitan English upper class, suggesting Tory fathers and corrupt merchant banker brothers, but that was my prejudice. She had attended a good English finishing school, almost certainly in the twentieth century. By what logic, however bizarre, had she wound up in this strange dreamworld and become a fantastic creature, the unlikely queen of a pirate isle?

For me, at least, the scene was changing from melodrama to comedy.

She, too, had decided to be amused. Her eyes, at least, were smiling. Not the eyes of a cruel witch, I thought. A warm deep violet, candid and intelligent. It was clear she was used to authority. Pretty evidently, too, she could no doubt have us cut to a million pieces and fed to those horrible oily saltwater catfish which hang around settlements in that part of the Med. I reminded myself that Catherine the Great had also been intelligent and very charming and allegedly a touch more inventive at ridding herself of irritating subjects than Vlad the Impaler.

"Come, Mr Moorcock! Surely you know why you are so far from England?

At which she laughed with genuine amusement.

"I fear you could risk offending Captain Barbarosa by sheltering us," suggested Athos, softly, voicing our unspoken thoughts.

"We are rather hoping he will use his great resources and experience to save us from the monstrous sea-beasts which plague us here at this season," she murmured with smiling eyes. Then, seriously: "But Freddy would never break his word once he gave it."

I was a little surprised, detecting no further irony or sarcasm in her voice. Indeed there seemed to be a touch of uncertainty. It occurred to me that she was deliberately keeping us off balance.

Aramis raised an eyebrow.

I tried to stay on the subject, but she changed it again, generalising about the mythology of sea-monsters and the local fish. Skilfully she did not give me the chance to continue. I could think of no other way of questioning her further, yet I urgently wanted to satisfy my curiosity, to find some means of measuring truth and distinguishing it from this phantasmagoria.

For the next hour or so we made fairly easy small talk, mostly discussing events in the musketeers' Paris, my own admiration for the *commedia* and touching a little on theatrical events in London, until she rose suddenly, all rippling silk and bright linen.

"You must be exhausted, gentlemen. I am a thoughtless

hostess. You need rest after spending so long at sea." She instructed her servants to prepare quarters for us.

"This evening I intend to give a banquet in your honour. And," she was charming, "I warn you. You will all be expected to 'sing for your supper'. I take it, Master Moorcock, that you have shared many adventures with these friends."

I was baffled. Apart from the fiction I had read and created about them, I knew nothing of Duval, Popper or the Musketeers. I knew as much about Popper's spaniel! I had only been acquainted with them for a few days and for most of that time I had been unconscious. Truth and fiction were now completely intertwined. What on earth had I to offer in comparison to the colourful tales and experiences of Claude Duval and the four Musketeers!

Helena would love all this, I thought suddenly. She saw herself in a whole series of incarnations! Many of them came from an intense reading of *The Strand*'s rival, the *Windsor Magazine*, which she received annually as Christmas presents from her parsimonious Methodist grandmother when she was a child so that many of her rôle models were based on the novels of Kipling, Anthony Hope, Nesbit, Barry Pain, Phillpotts, Rider Haggard, Conan Doyle, Robert Barr, Zangwill, Guy Boothby, Pemberton, Cutcliffe Hyne and many other writers who celebrated the heroics and aspirations of the British Empire.

I tried to speak of my family but my mouth dried and I became untypically careful. Perhaps sensing something the woman put her finger to her veiled lips, and in a moment, followed by her smiling novices, glided gracefully from the little garden.

When she had gone, the Comte de la Fère strolled over. Of the four friends he had been the kindest to me. With a chuckle and smoothing his Van Dyke, he sat down. "Your countrywoman is a remarkable lady, *mon ami*. Her reputation makes her a legend in the salons of Paris. I have known few like her."

"And he has known some women!" Porthos stuffed a further cake or two into his huge mouth. When Aramis glared at him, he slapped the count on the shoulder. "My dear friend! You have, you will admit, known one or two ladies of extraordinary – strength of mind – no?" Aramis brushed off his friend's mighty hand. He frowned briefly before recovering himself.

"My dear Porthos, I doubt it's possible for you to tell the difference between an English custard and an Ethiopian courtesan, save by the taste, and not always then."

Which drew a bellow of laughter from the big man before he crammed down another brioche. "Lack of sleep makes me hungry," he added, to excuse his gluttony.

We followed silent Carmelites through corridors and halls of that strange old building of many functions. At a certain juncture, the monks repaired to their evening prayers in the incongruous fortress-turned-mosque-turned-church which still resembled the original palace. It opened up in a series of green-streaked marble arches looking out across the white-tipped waves of the Mediterranean. The sea was splendid with the dropping sun in the far distance. Its dancing light was further reflected by the coloured silks and furs piled on our waiting beds. Even the wonderfully rich Technicolor of my childhood seemed dull in comparison.

Again I wondered if I was drugged. At this I began relishing the affair, including the scenery, remembering the glorious pirate and Arabian Nights movies of the '40s and '50s. Later, as I awkwardly let the novices bathe me and prepare me for bed, I could not help thinking that my fantasies were going to be put to shame by the realities I had shared with one of the most famous highwaymen of the Stuart reign, as well as the legendary four Musketeers and the infamous White Abbess of the Pirate Isle!

But who on earth was Lady Blackstone? Not the Abbess apparently. She sounded like a Dickens character. *Great Expectations*? As I slid into sleep, reality and fiction blended again to resemble a passing dream.

12

Dreaming My Days Away

HALF AN HOUR after returning to my apartments, I grew increasingly alert and then quite suddenly fell into a very deep sleep. I was either drugged or exhausted. Perhaps both.

My recent experiences quickly merged into a disconnected dream narrative in which characters from my own heroic stories of Elric, Rackhir the Red Archer, Erekosë, the Eternal Champion and others mingled with more characters from my *Tarzan* and *Thriller Picture Library* days until Jerry Cornelius and Hereward the Wake, the Saxon rebel, were leading an army of blue men across the inner plains of ancient Mars. The images in my mind had begun to resemble one huge panorama of pulp images, including the Treens and the Therons from *Dan Dare* in *Eagle*, some of my favourite Leigh Brackett, Alfred Coppel, Charles Harness and Robert E. Howard stories. *Startling*, *Weird*, *Planet* and *Thrilling Wonder*!

In this dream within a dream came the clatter of sharp magnetic boots in the great star-cabin. Tall, heavily bearded men in horned helmets and furs handled their controls, while below in the ship's holds fierce Mercurian-bred war-stallions strained in their harnesses, eager to feel the flinty, unstable surface of Ganymede beneath their stamping hoofs. Meanwhile Ulkivar Groth of the Kinan Chain growled bloody vengeance against the Usurper of the Inhabited Worlds and laid claim to every planet of the Inner System. *My fishlings! I despair.*

The colours I experienced were if anything more vivid than the moment they had poured from the presses and onto those brilliant newsstands where everything in the racks or hanging from clips or stacked in photogravure piles satisfied and stimulated your curiosity. The letterpress story papers, pulps and comics, offered exotic escape and glimpses into the human condition. Like my dreams their adventures went on for ever, turning into one incredible mélange of galloping highwaymen, noble savages, laughing outlaws in Lincoln Green! Who were these living individuals?

Individuals? Or merely aspects of my romantic self? In my visions of other, perhaps simpler, realities Chingachgook and Uncas the valiant redmen, father and son, trotted through ancient woodlands; Quatermain and Umslopogaas set foot on virgin forest floors, Buck Jones rode helter-skelter across the plains, Kit Carson crossed the Arizona desert, Buffalo Bill galloped in reminiscent circles, Blackbeard and Long John Silver set sail on the Spanish Main, Karl the Viking crossed swords with Saracen knights, Captain Marvel fought tentacled monsters, Yvonne Cartier brought poetic vengeance on the men who wronged her and all kinds of brightly dressed, romantically dashing and wrong-righting youths of every description from the folklore and fiction of my boyhood, to which I added a touch or two of my own and rewrote as the cheap mythology of the rock-and-roll generation's boyhood. But intercutting these surrealistic *Boys' Own* stories of high adventure and courageous, reckless heroes were memories of childhood pleasures: of Christmas and the garish blues, scarlets, greens, silvers and golds of the panto, the delight I took in various forms of transport, from the little fretwork pony cart we all rode in for picnics from Graham Hall, to the big varnished rowing boats at Mitcham Pond and our sparking crimson-and-brass double-decker trams, so sturdy they had been running since Edwardian times and could last into the twenty-second century. I dreamed of holding up those trams the way Sixteen String Jack held up the Dover Mail.

Clutching the soft leather of my mother's gloves, an animal's comforting paw, as Tarzan must have felt when he held on to Kala, his protective she-ape mother, I moved with her through a jungle as mysterious and full of possible danger as any world could seem to someone at eye-level with the hems of jackets, Woolworth counters and the blossoms of flowers. Huge leaves, lianas, branches filling the skies so that scarcely any blue could be seen, just like the tropical plant house at Kew, the ferns and rain forest trees. I had already read *Son of Tarzan*.

There was, however, nowhere I knew like Mars. Old Barsoom, where the wind blew the whispering red dust of dead sea bottoms through her ancient abandoned cities and grotesque manlike creatures crept from shadow to shadow hunting human prey. Where the stillness of centuries was occasionally broken by the distant hum of a flyer from the unexplored arctic, by the echoing clash of swords as red warrior fought four-armed green Thark. Heliumite against Zodangan in the thin, cold air of a dying planet.

That reminds me, thought Otherly, reaching for his omniphone.

And the smell of burning leaves, gold as buttered toast. And the smell of roasting beef blossoming to its fullest flavour from millions of Sunday ovens across the nation as we all heard *Round the Horne* week after week when the country laughed together, ate Yorkshire pudding together and Britain learned to relax until The Beatles arrived to help. *Wakey! Wakey!* Full bellies and *Stars on Sunday*.

I was four or five. Something was going on. I didn't see my father much. Every Saturday the Lees would take me with them shopping to the Brixton Arcade, a covered market full of pawnshops, pet shops, toyshops and everything I could ever want. The price I paid was to endure lunch at the eel and pie shop. The Lees loved it. They were settled gypsies from Mitcham, primarily totters in the junk trade, and they worked for my mother doing cleaning, odd jobs and babysitting. They were friends. Being the woman she was, my mother made them family. Auntie Mary and Uncle Joe. Cousins Bernie and Bridie. Sometimes I would stay with them overnight and they would let me ride the ponies up and down the cobbled muse where they lived and worked. They taught me Romany words and once I accompanied Mrs Marie Lee when she went to sell sprigs of lavender and lucky white heather at the station, her usual authority changed to the professional whine of the imploring old whore. My mum didn't seem too pleased when I told her, but she let me go again when I was taken all the way to Ken High Street, grinning like an angel to help sell a sprig or two. "Lucky white heather, lady?"

What a gorgeous boyhood, with the war all over and done and a golden future ahead, free from anxiety, free to do and be whatever we chose, filled with the promise of unification, solidarity and one world, one government and one people. The National Health. Free university. World Health. The United Nations. Food security. Free speech and education. Free speech was practical. It kept the powerful aware of the public mood. Would they last long enough to make the Universal Declaration of Human Rights a living reality? Nothing else must die. I reached for reassurance through the fog. There was always a fog. It came off the river and the sea. It settled from the sky. It called its deathly comfort, its shrouded cry, its whispering admonitions to do nothing, cultivate one's allotment, its promise. And was usually gone by noon.

I ran through canyons which were shopping arcades and, as

a crocodile, hunted in jungle rivers which were puddles, was swept up in balls of rattling rain and hurtled down spirals of air becoming shrieking chimerae, claws outstretched to seize me as I gabbled nonsense about the Tarot, simple equations, extinction events, positions and dimensions, bizarrely named places I had never heard of – Moonstrip Empire, Goat Normal, New from the Muse, Sweet-old-beneath-me, Itching Comtesse, Ketchup Cove, Argent Cometh, Tinmen Squared. Ukrainian Uke (five strings), Silver-and-gold Terminal, Shanndor's Long Rule, Old Bailey's You-know-why, Mine is my minefield, Sapphire Easter, Rolling Sunday – and I was so many people – my identity merging and separating as I became a swarm and then hung alone, utterly alone, hopeless and abandoned in a single timeless moment where I knew I was trapped for ever and existence took on a darker and stranger character and I had no idea at all what it signified. I could only survive by imagining the multiverse! And terror lurked behind me now as well as ahead! I heard a distant chorus singing Beethoven's 'Ode to Joy' from his great *9th Symphony*. I remember thinking how the composer's contemporaries had judged him mad for writing it and wished to know madness like that. What if my imagination deserted me? I would lose my parachute in mid-air. And then I slept deeply, dreamlessly.

Refreshed, I woke up having purged myself of my worst ever nightmares. I now found it much harder to recall the details of my early life in London and harder to remember my children or my wife. Had they ever been real? I could carry them all. And she refused. Not just for herself but for all of them.

Apparently telepathic, more servants appeared! They laid out fresh clothes as a huge tub was wheeled through the doorway. I had no embarrassment about discarding my nightshirt and climbing into the beautifully decorated bath. I never knew so much pleasure from a few gallons of hot water! In my sleep I had been weeping. They washed my face. I was hoarse from calling. They put soothing nectar to my lips. They spoke Arabic, I think. Or Aramaic. They knew as much Spanish as I did, sufficient to get us through a few simple functions. By the time I was bathed and dressed I made, I thought, a pretty good and strangely light-hearted Sinbad.

I met my comrades outside my room. Everyone was dressed in the same exotic silks and linens. Even after Porthos had remarked that we were 'guests in Rome' we remained vaguely self-conscious. Together we followed novices back the way we had come earlier, but this time we went down steps to the floor below which opened on to a great vaulted hall of marble Moorish arches. From somewhere deep within the complex I heard distant voices lifted in prayer. I saw no sign of religious rites here, however. The White Abbess of Las Cascadas had already arrived. She wore a mixture of deep salmon pink and dusty brown which perfectly suited her. Each fold of her exquisite costume was like a rippling sky. Her face remained thoroughly veiled. Her expressive eyes were still amused. She asked us all how we had slept.

All had similarly troubled sleep and strange dreams but afterwards enjoyed deep rest. That confirmed for me that our tea had been drugged. If so, for what reason? For the moment at least I gave our hostess the benefit of the doubt. I really could not come up with any sinister reason for drugging us when we were already her willing guests.

As we sat down, another figure emerged through a distant archway and joined the table. A narrow, cadaverous head with deep-set, ice-blue eyes, thinning black hair forming a sharp widow's peak, exemplified the meaning of 'hatchet-faced'. Skin grey and unhealthy, as if it never saw sunlight, was glimpsed through his robe of whiteish rough wool. I could not help recalling pictures of Torquemada from my first encyclopaedia. By his pallor, if nothing else, the newcomer was European. Two others came in. I took them for a couple of the Abbess's local pirate lieutenants. Their gaudy finery was of the kind invariably chosen by successful Mediterranean thieves. Next, some kind of major-domo appeared in a massive green turban and about forty yards of blue silk to make introductions.

The lieutenants were Hamet al Sudam and Ali al Kumeli. The cadaverous European was Monsignor Horatio Quelch. What I took for a cream-coloured Moorish djellabah, I now realised was the working habit of the Order of Carmelites or White Friars. The monks had used the same typesetter as us when I was at *Tarzan Adventures* in the mid- to late 1950s. I recognised the habit now. The same order which had been located in the area 'as long as they shall wish' in gardens created for them by some pious monarch. They had been banished from the sometime Mount of Carmel in the Holy Land where all our Abrahamic religions came to maturity. Should anyone be in doubt concerning his calling, Monsignor Quelch wore around his neck a thick piece of ship's rope from which was suspended a massive and exquisitely made crucifix. He spoke briefly, almost reluctantly by way of greeting. I guessed by his accent that we came from the same part of the world. "You're English, I take it, Monsignor Horatio."

He looked down his long nose at me.

"I am Welsh," he said. "Born and bred."

I was not sure whether to apologise or commiserate.

"Monsignor Quelch was once a famous academic." The Rose, perhaps, attempted to lower any tension. "Before he was honoured by His Holiness."

"Aha!" I murmured vaguely.

He waved this away. "A mere schoolmaster, my dear sir. Nothing more."

161

"But of a very famous school," she insisted. "A public one. Blackfriars, was it not? In London?"

"Greyfriars," he corrected her, "in Kent."

The other two men were evidently not Welsh but steadfastly Moorish. They scowled as they looked on, their lips following an unfamiliar language. They spoke a little Spanish and some French and were altogether friendlier to us than to their comrade in arms. The Lady Abbess was charming, clearly unhappy with the Monsignor's poor manners while we, in turn, pretended not to notice his surly attitude. We did not know why he took against us unless he was airing a simple prejudice shared by our nations. In those days I still believed my Uncle Rhys Roberts, that to cross the border into Wales was to be set upon by thieves, to be stripped naked and left for dead by a bunch of two-faced, penny-pinching Chapel-going choristers who worked from preference in darkness and were utter hypocrites. I felt Uncle Rhys had to know, since he was, after all, thoroughly Welsh.

When another half-dozen lesser corsairs joined us, the Rose was clearly relieved. With those reasonably skilled in French, she was happy to leave them talking to her French guests, but Popper and I were stuck with the monks.

The last diners arrived in a group. They were dressed similarly to Monsignor Horatio in long pale habits and brown scapulars. They acknowledged us with a bow, sometimes a brief smile, before seating themselves at the same end of the table as Monsignor Horatio. After they had prayed for what seemed for ever, our food began to arrive. The Moslems accepted this alien ritual with patient good will.

The Moors and monks did not really contribute a great deal to the general dinner conversation. Monsignor Horatio, it seemed to me, went out of his way to be unpleasant, though never directly rude. His manner was sly, insinuating, authoritarian

162

and unrelentingly aggressive. He spouted what seemed the worst kind of religiosity without a gram of spiritual content. In the meantime for her part the Lady Abbess went to great pains to make up for his poor manners.

"You are familiar with these seas, gentlemen?" my lady asked us in general. Only Duval and Peter Popper knew the Mediterranean, Duval as a passenger, Popper as a young sailor. The rest of us were more familiar with North Atlantic waters and then usually only to cross them. The Musketeers, I believed, had a little more experience than mine.

"So you had no previous dealings with our friend 'Admiral' Barbarosa," said Monsignor Horatio. "Since he sails only in the south and east. Usually he does not come so far west. The monster has been seen. As usual it heralds Redbeard's ship. That was why I wondered if his pursuit of you was personal. As if you possess something in particular which he desires . . ."

"I assure you, Monsignor Horatio . . ." began Porthos hotly, only to be interrupted by our hostess, who interjected.

"Freddy Barbarosa is an acquaintance of ours. What's more, we've both signed the Twelve Articles of the Barbary Brotherhood." The Rose looked suddenly into my eyes. A thrill of desire. I almost gasped. Did she feel the same? Then, as my sensations responded unconsciously, she glanced away and began to answer the murmured question of the Comte de la Fère. God! One cast and she had me on her hook!

"It is said our island was a volcano overlooking the ancient land of Atlantis. In common with others, it erupted causing a huge movement of the earth and ocean which broke down a great natural sea-wall bringing the waters of the Atlantic rushing through. Mighty disasters came universally. Many civilisations engulfed. Centuries later our volcano became a stronghold occupied first by Celtic pirates, then by Phoenician traders, then a Roman garrison, then by Visigoths, then a

Catalan monastery, then Moorish slavers and then, when the slavers were driven off, by the Portuguese.

"The Great Alliance of 1229 allowed the dispersed monks of Mount Carmel to found a monastery there in 1234. They were granted sanctuary by the blessed Sultan Nar el Jhoori and have continued that tradition."

Aramis nodded slowly. "That story is known to us, my lady, but in a slightly different form."

She acknowledged this. "We occupy one of those places where narratives are made and remade. We are the story and we are its tellers; everything the human mind makes from Chaos. And we are balanced on sturdy rocks. Sir James Jelinek called them 'fulcra', the original dramas in the sciences, arts and great endeavours upon which all our reality is built. The rest are mirror versions of those foundations, slowly distorting. But the tales vary only by a degree or two. Nothing is a lie. Nothing is strictly true. All Reality changes subtly according to the vagaries of distant neutrons. I give you the version we favour.

"Originally there was an all-but-impregnable Moorish fortress here. Under Spain it eventually became the Abbey of Santa Maria Dolorosa. This abbey briefly returned to the hands of Moorish pirates until the Portuguese took it. They gave it back to the Church, who gave it to Carmelites under the authority of a Chief Abbot. The Abbot, with his monks and nuns refurbished, created the present buildings making this complex. The abbey, it must be said, fell into rather decadent ways. For a time, the monks' pact with the pirates allowed Christians to find sanctuary from Barbary corsairs, but very quickly the island protected ships belonging to all faiths, letting them hide in their rocky harbour when necessary. Then gradually the pirates came to dominate the harbour. Soon the monks continued their alliance in a subordinate rôle. Under my reign, the island is ruled by myself assisted by the Abbot, Monsignor Quelch. We have an amicable alliance based chiefly on trade. We continue the tradition our London brothers began of granting sanctuary to those who seek it."

It seemed clear to me that, in spite of her apparent good humour, the Abbess had no great liking for the stronghold's present Abbot. Monsignor Quelch's title had surprised me at first. A papal honour. So I understood. No doubt he had received it during some particularly corrupt period of Vatican history.

"If you sail on next Saturday's tide," said the White Abbess, 'You can be sure Freddy won't trouble you. Saturday is the soonest he will safely hear. So you must be our guests until then. I sent a fast sloop with a message this afternoon. I await his promise. And then, Captain Duval ..." A significant glance at our friend and, in this situation, our leader.

At this Monsignor Quelch became alert. "I hear Redbeard has a new gunner now." He spoke in that sly, insinuating voice which so grated on me. "And breaks all earlier treaties." I was sure I could sense real malice in his tone. *Schadenfreude*? Not much doubt. "A fanatic, they say," he continued. "A Puritan who, since the king was restored, serves the Low Church cause abroad. They say he can hit a seagull's eye at a height of over one hundred feet."

The Lady Rose was annoyed by his interjection.

"Remarkable," said Athos. "And who is this supernatural shootist? He cannot be English, if he is a cannonier. A Frenchman, no doubt." (The Musketeer held the view that French light gunnery was superior to all.)

"Oh, no," purred the cadaverous cleric. "No, sir. Not at all. This fellow's a Londoner, I believe. English born and raised. A law officer of some description in a former life. Little chap was in the revolutionary army, apparently, before his exile. The king's justices put a price on his head. He'll be hanged, drawn and quartered if he returns. So he has little to lose." Quelch's tone was full of a soiled delight. "He has a special gun of his own which he carries by a strap upon his person. It is twice the size of the largest musket made, with ten times the range and impact. Rifled, I understand. Bigger than a blunderbuss. It is called by a French word, however, m'sieur.' He frowned. "I believe it is *Le Tromblon Tonneron*. Can that be the instrument?"

"Mon Dieu! I know him!' Claude Duval paused with lifted wine-cup. "In England. A wanted regicide! London! A pip-squeak. A pinchlip. A shake-spear. A finger-wagger! He tried to take the Alsacia. We drove him back. Remember, comrades? 'Tis the Runner captain, Jacob Nixer. He was Cromwell's Chief Intelligencer before the Restoration and was sentenced to the full English – hanged, drawn and quartered – by my late master's father." He paused.

A poor aristocrat and younger son, Duval claimed he had been James the Second's valet before he took to the road.

"By the Merrie Monarch himself, eh?" I said. That had been Charles II's nickname. "He escaped?"

"Mysteriously." Pleased that I reminded the company of his past association with royalty Duval replied. "Master Nixer fled to the Low Countries and later sailed with Van Dam under the Dutch flag in the American Indies. They say that's where his gun comes from."

"Oh, gentlemen, it's quite barbaric! Disgustingly pagan!" Quelch spoke with squirming relish.

He was about to continue when Athos interrupted. He spoke quietly and with authority. "I know the gun. It was made for him by the infamous Jean-Baptiste Lefleuve, a native gunsmith in Haiti. He forged the weapon with steel treated by *local magic*. He calls the thing his *Tonneron*, from some barbaric French he heard there. He has done something to the inner barrel to make a ball fly faster and with greater accuracy. Such a weapon might have drawbacks but it has considerable value to whomever commands it. His nickname for the horrid weapon is *Fere Noir*. Master Nixer, I understand, rarely misses."

Quelch continued to enjoy our supposed discomfort. "While he might not wish to offer offence to the Lady Rose," murmured the cleric obsequiously, "Frederic Barbarosa could, however, decide to ask his friend the Grand Turk to throw you in prison until it pleases him to have you released for ransom. Or sold for galley slaves."

"It would seem an unnecessarily complicated plan," murmured Athos, who had Monsignor Horatio's measure and studied him through amused, hooded eyes. "Such redundant complexity seems more the invention of the serpentine Celtic brain. The kind we encounter in Brittany and elsewhere. For a Welshman, the Monsignor seems oddly prejudiced against his fellow Celts."

Quelch smirked. "You envy the ability of we dreaming Celts to understand the cosmos and follow all the twists and turns of the Tarot Path, puzzle the mathematics of the multiverse and the moonbeam roads, read all the charts for the First and Second Aethers, to travel alone, naked and on foot, together with their feline familiars, and know the sound of horns echoing the trails and deep forest-ways of our ancestors, who knew all these things before we forgot them and had to learn again how to be ourselves? But you must not fear, my dear sir, because the time will return back when you will recognise your masters as will everyone and be grateful to follow us wherever our subtle minds lead. For do we not know the great highways and the tiny pathways which connect, to take the adept through the worlds we know and the worlds we must learn to know ...?"

Everyone responded in their different ways to this strange, almost compulsive, statement. I barely understood it. Peter Popper scratched his head and even D'Artagnan fingered his chin as the Abbot continued.

"For it is those unnecessary complications of mind and spirit which make Celtic people so close in blood to the Pictish folk. The world's oldest humans, intermarrying with you all so that some of our memories and dreams are everyone's. But a few remain, my dear Comte de la Fère, only for the pure-blooded members of our race."

There followed a long silence, as if Quelch had dragged all the air from our lungs.

At last Porthos, who had consumed all available food, gestured towards one of the screens illustrating scenes of Far Eastern mythology. "Those are the folk, are they not, who believe sinners are born and reborn until their sins are redeemed?"

"Something of the kind." The Abbess was relieved to change the subject. "I think you refer to the heathen Hindoo, do you not?"

"I do, I believe. It is called re-re-birth, no?"

"Re-incarnation," dryly supplied Monsignor Quelch. "I fear such an idea is a heresy."

"Oh, ho, ho, sir!" cried the Abbess, suddenly animated. "Heresy, is it? Heathens, are we?" She considered him a fool.

I don't think he blushed.

"And you, Master Moorcock, are you familiar with the notions of the Hindoos."

I had read a few books of ancient Hindu mythology and folklore. "If the Hindu notion of Time is cyclic, what if reincarnation itself is random? That is, if you do, let us say, steadily improve by living the best possible life, do you move from the moment you die to the next moment in linear time?" She frowned a little. "Or do you transfer at random? If your life is exceptionally evil, are you next subjected to the most evil tortures in History? Past. Present and future being all one."

She laughed spontaneously, clapping her hands. "So, if we behave well in this life, we are yet punished for an eternity of sins no matter who was saved. I cut off the head of the Foul Ancient and leave the way clear for the Refreshed Ideal, but still I am given no allowance for the good that comes from the deed? What's more, if we are wicked in this life, are we consequently returned to the time of the Great Foulness?"

"Whatever that is," I agreed. "It sounds pretty nasty."

Monsignor Quelch steepled his long fingers, an experienced bore. "But what do we mean exactly by this word 'heresy'?" By this strategy he recaptured control of the conversation. He embarked on a long-winded disquisition concerning the nature of heresy and all the different forms it took, first in the Ancient world, then in the Modern. Soon I had to force myself awake. The two corsair captains were slumped in their seats, utterly supine until jerking up wide-eyed and looking about them in desperation. I guessed they had heard the Monsignor on this subject more than once. As with all his little lectures, this one was heavily peppered with Latin phrases. At this rate I would sleep away my stay here!

By means of his pedantic and rather baffling monologue Monsignor Quelch silenced us all. This schoolmasterly exhibition had plainly embarrassed our hostess. A pirate was permitted to be cruel, sardonic, pathologically inclined, sadistic, to have bad taste and worse breath, but under no circumstances was he allowed to be a bore. Though technically perhaps not wholly a pirate, Monsignor Horatio was sitting at a pirate's table and commanding a pirate's crew while his demeanour suggested to us all that he was at least a part-time corsair.

The White Abbess was the first to break the embarrassed silence.

"Gentlemen, should you not return, you must see our great orrery before you go. The core of this particular fulcrum. It was but recently presented to us by our co-religionists. The creation of two of your countrymen I understand. Our cousin Prince Rupert van der Rijn and a Master Tompion, I'm told. It is a wonder, our fulcrum! It unites our various establishments through the scales of Time and Space!" She leaned towards me. "I will make certain you, in particular, Master Moorcock, shall have the opportunity to observe it. My astrologers are completing the adjustments and I'll have it ready shortly. I take it that you are curious."

I had no idea of her meaning but I thanked her.

She turned again to the boorish Welsher. "But surely the most interesting idea, Monsignor, is the question of Time and whether it moves in a linear or cyclic mode. Some other means? You are full of enviable information, my dear Monsignor Horatio. I so admire the academic mind. You must give us further instruction after we have taken refreshment." There was an edge to her voice which could have cut off a man's head and him not know it until he nodded. Turning to her guests: "Perhaps you are now convinced that, before he took to the High Seas, Monsignor Horatio was, *indeed*, a schoolmaster, in Kent."

"I believe you have, madam," said the monk quickly. "Greyfriars was once the best-known school in England. *Tempus fugit*, eh? And, I must admit, *amari aliquid*. A simple D.D., I became a monk, received this calling from my order, was honoured by His Holiness and now, for my sins, I am lieutenant to a corsair. Perhaps worse!" He darted me a poisonous glare. He was an erratic, thoroughly evil soul and I was very glad that I was not in his power. Yet he had made me curious.

170

His story was an unusual one, to say the least. I knew all about Greyfriars and her sister-school St James's. They were legendary names. Their pupils were legends. Some, like Buffalo Bill, had whole folk-cycles attached to them. Sherlock Holmes and Sexton Blake attended both in fiction. The British Empire, it was said, was founded in the cloisters of Greyfriars. When I was young I thought Greyfriars, St James's and St Francis's were contemporaries. How had a Doctor of Divinity, the housemaster of a school as well known in its day as Eton or Rookwood, managed to leave the profession, study for and be received into the priesthood, become the Abbot of a monastery and turn to piracy under the influence of a woman who used the sanctuary as a base for her own mysterious activities? I could not, however many pints we both had, have slipped such a plot past Dave Gregory, editor of *Tiger* comic!

'But our Great Chapel! You must see it! Now!" Determinedly, the White Abbess stood up and led the way. She refused reluctance with a glare. We were all relieved to follow her. Monsignor Horatio strode, sulking, in the rear.

"What news, I wonder, of Cairo's peril?" She slipped her arm in mine. "Is Prester Johannes any closer to carrying the cross back to Constantinople, Mr Moorcock?" Her voice was amused, warm, intimate.

I apologised. I told her that I knew nothing of Middle Eastern politics.

"I forget that you are fresh to our adventures, sir. No-one knows," she said, "though many affect to. Traditionally, of course, I am Catholic, I find it inconvenient to adopt a single religion. I am less confused and make fewer enemies. That, I suppose, is why I was eventually forced to leave my husband."

"Your husband, my lady? An unfortunate man, to lose you." I was picking up some of the cavaliers' courtly manners. Or, at least, so I thought.

"Perhaps." Her eyes flirted in pleasure. "But he was a Catholic, poor man, and a Prussian. Torn in so many ways! And, by consequence, a hideous dancer. Inner turmoil is so frequently revealed in the Rhumba. He could not for his life learn those steps. And as for the Tango, I didn't even attempt to teach him. It would have been torture for him and caused me the deepest embarrassment! He was tormented by his conscience and unhappy in both body and soul. Or, at least, uncomfortable. Von Beks, you are no doubt aware, come in distinct varieties from distinguished soldier-statesmen associated with the most progressive politics, to utter rogues, given to over-imaginative lechery and unimaginative vice. Either way, they tend to become boring very rapidly. Have you ever visited Wäldenstein? Our transepts compare with Saint Vladimir's."

And so we admired the chapel, a large, sparsely furnished and decorated hall resembling a mosque more than a church or a synagogue. The ceiling was high, cool and curved. The air was cool and peaceful. A few monks kneeled here and there in silent prayer while two old deacons went about their routine business. For a while we stood in an uncomfortable silence, feeling the tranquillity but at that time unable to appreciate it. And then that most poised of us, Aramis, the Comte de la Fère, fell to his knees, as if in prayer.

The Abbess turned abruptly and led us out of that place of worship.

13

The Fulcrum

THE NEXT TWO days were a kind of holiday for all of us as we explored the great palace with its libraries, reception rooms, laboratories, theatre, observatory, kitchens, chapel and many places where one could sit reading or in contemplation, often with views of the tranquil Mediterranean. For me, it also became a kind of transition from one reality to another. I began, if not to relax, to search the library's books for some clues to my situation, but there were few printed volumes and most of those in older forms of language than I was familiar with. We saw the Abbess at meals and passed her in corridors or halls, but she was a charming deflector of leading questions, telling us that the mysterious fulcrum would answer all our questions. The day before we were due to leave, the 'Queen of the Pirate Isle' (as I privately called her after a Bret Harte children's book) told us at breakfast that the orrery was ready for visitors!

I have to admit to my curiosity. She had whetted our appetites very well in the preceding days.

Through hushed passages I followed, also in silence, until the White Abbess paused before a great iron-bound oaken door. Barred and with a large key in its lock, it could withstand anything. Clapping her hands again, she signalled for her servants to open the door. She led us into a gloomy high-ceilinged chamber. Initially the servants made no attempt to light the flambeaux around the stone walls. At her direction we seated ourselves around a massive mahogany table which all but filled the great room. I saw the shadowy outlines of some large machine resting on the table and once again had a sense of déjà vu. Where had I seen those circling bright brass rods and moving globes before? The Science Museum? Nothing seemed physically attached yet all were interconnected. I looked up into the gloom. This was no conventional orrery. It represented something vaster than the solar system or even the galaxy. To me it could almost be the universe in miniature! Clusters of tiny jewels seemed to hang weightless in the air, revolving slowly, without any sign of a mechanism. First it appeared to revolve before us and next we seemed to be revolving around it while the great slab on which it was mounted remained still. I was reminded of being on the old Wall of Death at Mitcham Fair except there was also movement behind me. Shadows. Yet not shadows cast specifically by the machine I saw before us and no shadows of our own bodies as far as I could tell.

Only the White Abbess was in that room with us. Neither Quelch nor Popper, nor any other monks or servants had been admitted. She was illuminated by light which sprang from elements in the machine itself. Her face was serene and still, but her lovely eyes regarded us, looking from face to face.

Duval was intent. "You say the Prince sent this?"

"From the Low Countries where he is chiefly at work. You know him?"

"We fought for the Old Cause together, when we were young. I thought he'd returned to England with the king."

"I understand he concerns himself chiefly with philosophy and certain forms of manufacturing."

Half-mesmerised by the circulating spheres and clusters, I

174

knew that, somewhere, I had seen all those strange mechanisms before. Yet I had physically never experienced anything close to this. Not a universe but the 'multiverse', a word I coined for a story in 1963 for Ted Carnell. At once, my protagonist saw the whole of existence. Normally hidden from human senses, my multiverse was a jewelled tapestry. I was overwhelmed by the beauty of it all, turning, swirling, rising and falling, rhythmically beating upon invisible surfaces. Washing across unseen shores. Pouring from huge, invisible mouths like caverns that were billions of miles across, which could only be sensed and never seen. Monstrous lagoons, endless cliffs, measureless distances in which I drifted like a speck of dust, without direction or purpose.

As I sat there I grew to see less and less of the rods and globes and increasingly more of the glittering clusters of multicoloured jewels as if something were filling in the black areas, almost *eating* the darkness. I had almost no sense of the Abbess controlling this, no sense of my companions being present. Instead I felt a sublime love for everyone in Paris, in London and the 'real' world from which I was abducted. I felt no resentment of Duval and the others, though they were the agents of this experience. Indeed, at that moment I felt no urgency to see my family. But I relished the knowledge of their existence, somewhere in that populated vastness.

I turned my head, looking for the Abbess but now every horizon was full. I saw neither her nor the others. Swirling pathways of shimmering jewels curved away in every direction. Greens and reds, blues, yellows and a hundred million shades flashed against my eyes, drew me in, became me, expanded me and compacted me until I was the essence of all that existed.

And then her face was there, smiling, understanding everything. She was showing me infinity. I tried but was completely unable to express it in words. How had I imagined all this before? How had I experienced all this, so that I could write it in a story at the age of twenty-two or twenty-three? If it had happened before I could not remember. I wanted to ask her a question but did not know how?

"The machine is also a fulcrum." She spoke carefully, anticipating my question. "It is one of a number. They exist layer upon layer in all the planes of the universe. Each has to be balanced. We believe, when *all* are balanced, some kind of resolution is achieved. Some have the means within them of creating a special harmony. That harmony exists for a moment or it exists for an age. Why? we do not know. How? we hardly know. It is achieved through certain actions taken by certain individuals. We only know how to set those actions in motion. We do not know, always, who those individuals are. We understand there are stories, storytellers, protagonists. Some of us are perhaps slightly conscious of our rôle. Some of us are utterly unconscious. Some refuse that consciousness. There are still others who wish to become conscious but are unable to achieve that condition. This can make for some terrible conflicts between protagonists and would-be protagonists. It can produce terrifying internal conflicts." I remember her saying all this, but have no idea how that is possible.

"I think, as a storyteller yourself," she continued, "you must be aware of such narratives and characters. You are still young, still not fully able to understand in any sophisticated way what really goes on. I have chosen to let you know this because you have been brought here not by chance. Perhaps according to some undefined purpose even I cannot imagine. And by the same reasoning I have decided to show your friends something of the purpose they share with you. This is a fulcrum. I believe you will find others in time. Through your stories, your own life, in your friendships, as well as your enmities, you will create resolutions, achieve further resolutions, begin fresh narratives. These will in turn lead to other resolutions. These will lead others to achieve further resolutions, each one helping to maintain the Balance which guards against chaos and the condition of non-existence. The absence of consciousness. Which is the absence of life."

I realised that I was merely staring at her. I could not then take in what she told me. I don't think I wished to take it in. I certainly did not want to accept the kind of responsibility she inferred.

The light now began to dissipate. The orrery in all its parts became visible again. My friends had been asleep, or at least mesmerised. They, too, seemed to be waking up, looking around, frowning.

"So," said Duval, "Prince Rupert's mission to build his web across the world comes to the Abbey of Las Cascadas as well as London and Paris!"

"You have seen one of these before?" I asked him.

"The fulcra?" Duval sighed. "I have served the House of Stuart for some years and Prince Rupert of the Rhine in particular. He has an interest in ethics and natural philosophy. A taste for invention. Some believe these traits stem from his German ancestry."

"Now," declared the Abbess, rising from her chair. "We can retire to the balcony and talk further."

She clapped her hands. Servants entered to attend to the flambeaux and the orrery.

Already I felt I was waking up. The saliencies stayed with me. Why had she had shown us the machine? Did she plan to trick us? To aid her in some complicated scheme of her own? I had been told she was to be feared. Her reputation was not entirely savoury. Had she hypnotised us for some purpose? Was Duval scheming with her to deceive us?

We followed her through the abbey's high rooms and galleries until I smelled the rich ozone of the ocean.

We reached a great alabaster balcony overlooking the blue Mediterranean. She clapped her hands again. Her perfume became suddenly more intense. At her command yards of gauzy silk were drawn back revealing the rest of the balcony. Servants offered us sherbet, coffee and silver dishes of glittering sweets. Again I felt as if I were visiting a set from one of the Hollywood Arabian Nights extravaganzas I had grown up loving. This had to be in part a fantasy from my unconscious. I began to enjoy the eccentric narrative like a surrealist movie. Besides, I did not desire to return to reality, whatever it might be, because that terrible whispering no longer filled my ears as we were joined by Quelch and Popper.

Soon we were all stretched out like so many decadent sultans on comfortable divans, continuing our conversations in conditions any reasonable person would find delicious.

Aramis was enjoying the debate. He had travelled in the service of the Grand Turk. "As a youth I was sent by my father upon a series of adventures," he told us, "and that was one. But I had heard the priest-king takes his banner to Jerusalem to free the Holy City from the Turk's control." I think he tested the pirate's sympathies.

"Either way it is folly to march against the Ottomans with so few resources." Only Quelch shifted uncomfortably in his cushions.

"Like ancient Hannibal of Carthage, has not this soldier-priest a thousand great war elephants at his command?" Peter Popper's wholesome English brought a hint of common sense to the proceedings. Nobody but his friends suspected his erudition. "Only recently I learned that Equatorial Africa is a land of Christians, converted in the years of Our Lord's wanderings, and that a million warriors, many of them Moorish converts, serve his holy standard, waiting only for him to lead them into battle against the Infidel." Peter hesitated. "At least" he added in some embarrassment, "that's what they say in the pub."

The Abbess lifted her veil and sipped her sherbet, her lips curved in a slight smile. "I take it you have no interest whatsoever in finding the Blackstone Escarpment and asking Lord Blackstone to lead you into the Original Country."

"Madam?" Aramis, like the others, seemed genuinely puzzled. Was she stabbing in the dark in hope she would spear a secret?

Her eyes were merry. "I believe your ultimate destination to be the centre of the world."

"Jerusalem, madam! Why should we wish to go there? And become captive, no doubt, of the same Grand Turk." Porthos uttered a throaty chuckle. "And eat dogs and cats for the rest of our lives." He made a face. He had a strong opinion of the world's great cuisines. In his day French food was generally considered to be abominable.

"I assure you, your reverence," Claude Duval fingered his beard, "I am as unfamiliar with that country as I am with the rest of the continent. May I ask who is Lord Blackstone? And what is the Blackstone Escarpment? I must admit, madam, I have travelled extensively, yet have not even heard the place whispered."

She ignored his question. "I understood there is a map."

Later the mouthpieces to several good-sized pipes were flexibly attached to large, elegant hookahs and we smoked a mild concoction of hashish, laudanum and tobacco until I became even more light-headed.

We relaxed again, as our hostess evidently intended. For, not an hour into some conventional small talk, she again raised the subject of a map.

"*The Carta Atalantaea*. The lost map mentioned in the third

Pliny account. It was supposed to show the entrance to what remained of the ancient Atlantean empire." Then after some silence she added, "It purported to reveal the oldest trade road known, now long buried beneath earth and waves, with no contact with the old world. Mythically, an underground route from the Western Sahara to the supposed birthplace of mankind?"

"A tunnel, madam?" enquired Athos. He had the manner of a man grown weary of tunnels. "Some catacomb?"

"Oh, much larger than a tunnel, I believe." Quelch broke his own sullen quiet, too eager to show off his scholarly expertise to disguise his pleasure at his superior knowledge. "A world, of sorts, I think. When the earth opened, swallowing some parts of the Empire of Atlantis and covering up others, making fresh mountains and lakes. If it is the map I saw, then it shows the great canyons and peaks to be found there. The land of Mu-Ooria, some name it. Ptolemy claimed the gods fled there. Ptolemy, of course, makes much of Mu-Ooria in his treatise on Atlantis and the Island Empire of Moo, which unleashed fire upon Europe and Africa in punishment for their aggression. Not to mention their decision to ravish the earth of all her most valuable treasures."

I could not help expressing my curiosity. "What treasures were they?" I was a little bewildered. "I thought Atlantis drowned."

"She is. She did." The Abbess replied quickly. "She first exhausted the earth of her wealth, visible and invisible. So much so that the very ground she was built upon began to crack and fragment. They say she gave one vast gasp and vanished beneath the raging waters of the Atlantic Ocean. Gone for ever into the deepest pit, punished for her failures of stewardship and sins of acidie and rapine."

Boorish Horatio interrupted yet again. "As we know, legends

say that Las Cascadas is the only remaining fragment of lost Atlantis. She will rise when the sins of men become intolerable to the gods. The last of Mother Earth's defenders shall rise against Chaos and Old Night. We shall defy the Breakers of Bonds, the Exploiters of our Disunity!"

I did not listen carefully. I was highly sceptical of Atlantis legends and the prophecies which so frequently went with them. Since I was very young I had understood them to be nonsense. Every crank in creation had a pet theory. As a teenager I had gone out with a girl who had been morbidly involved in all that Egyptian and Atlantean stuff. I think she also joined the Flat Earth Society. I preferred the story I had first read in *Eagle* which said the Atlanteans were descendants of Treens, a race of Venusians. I didn't believe such stories but I did expect to be entertained by them.

The Abbess sensed my disbelief. "You show a healthy caution in your receipt of my story, Mr Moorcock. Most travellers I entertain are usually in pursuit of some tale of treasure and ancient wisdom. You are not here to hunt a myth or find lost treasure. Are you merely travelling, rather as Don Quixote of old, in search of a Cause, or you are travelling from curiosity?"

"Believe me, Lady, I did not volunteer for this adventure and will be glad when it is done. I have no motive. I seek nothing, unless it is a swift return home. I remain convinced that I am involved in a complicated dream. Which is probably the result of too much good food and wine, too much visual stimulus and an excess of imagination."

"Aha!" she exclaimed, enlightened, "you are upon a substantial dream-quest, as am I! And we may not speak, I think, of what we seek. Then, since we are not in rivalry, I'll *guarantee* you safe passage and protection from Barbarosa. In Tangier Isaac-ben-Wahood will help. But you must do something for me in return."

"Gladly, madam," Duval spoke swiftly, before I could reply. He was taken aback but unwilling to lose us an advantage. With an inclination of his head he suggested a world of gallantry. "We are Musketeers and the comrades of Musketeers. We are at your service!"

Duval was either engaged in a complex plot in which even the chief participants were only dimly aware or he was in love again!

Or both.

I had not the slightest notion what she meant by 'dream-quest', though the word was faintly familiar, perhaps from the title of the Lovecraft story I had seen. What was its association with the Second Aether?

14

The Coasts of Africa

I DID MY best to stop looking for logic in this world. I believed I was in an absurdist epic by Carroll. Perhaps the story was a little more like Peacock, the situation closer to Jarry. Maybe the Rose and I had in common the fact that we did not belong here at all. Perhaps every person I met was dreaming a slightly different dream! How could I put this to them?

I desperately wanted to learn more but almost everyone there became cautious in my presence. Soon our conversation ground awkwardly to a halt and we all rose, making excuses to retire.

That night my dreams were oddly prosaic. Daily routines and domestic crises. Perhaps as a result, I woke up much refreshed!

Next morning we found our familiar clothes awaiting us. I would have preferred to wear a light djellabah or some similar robe. When I suggested that Moorish dress would suit the climate better, I was delighted to receive a selection of clothes, including a grey-striped djellabah with its useful hood and a belt and some sturdy sandals. My hostess had also seen fit to arm me with a beautiful, slender curved scimitar of what I took to be Damascene steel. Near the hilt was an engraving in exquisite Arabic calligraphy. When I joined my friends I found them, all but Peter Popper, wearing their own choices of local dress over their familiar uniforms, with hats, muskets and swords carried in long bags over their shoulders. Popper had refused to exchange his shirt, britches and long, inn-keeper's waistcoat for anything more comfortable.

"Pardon me, gentlemen," he said, "but I am English and an Englishman is considered mad if he chooses to go native. No disrespect, gents, I hope."

We reassured him that we were not offended and prayed he did not die from exposure too soon.

And so, in better spirits and well-breakfasted, we made our way down to the harbour. The beautiful sword on my belt gave me, I thought, a certain swagger. The weather was peace-ful and bright when we started. Even after the sky clouded and a fine rain began to fall, the Abbess herself decided to accompany us. A soldier on a skittish pony led us, while the Rose, still veiled but evidently in high spirits, sat a well-behaved grey. The rest of us were on foot. Quelch was absent. I was not sure what bargain had been struck with the woman I still privately thought of as the Pirate Queen. Only Duval seemed to be clear. He assured me I would understand when the moment came. There was too much to explain while we were travelling. Suffice to say, he concluded, we were unlikely to be inconvenienced by pirates. At least, not by Barbarosa. He feared he could not speak for pirates who had refused the Articles of Brotherhood. They followed no code, accepted no leadership.

I still did not know what bargain Duval had made with the Abbess in return for her protection. I hoped it involved no betrayal of our little party.

I knew Duval must have made some agreement, secret to all, save the two of them. To what had Duval committed us? Were the Musketeers involved? Was I the only one unaware of a crime we must commit? I was again suspicious of everyone.

Reaching the harbour we saw that a ship was already preparing herself for the open sea. Her ivory hull shone like gilded porcelain and her sails were spidered silver. Red-jacketed sailors flitted about her rigging, looking like a cast from *Peter Pan* save for faces which had evidently seen and practised every vice. Three tall mahogany masts carried the configuration of a fore-and-aft rigged three-masted schooner, an elegant ship which looked as if she could cross the Atlantic in a day. I admired her. She sported a dozen big cannon port and starboard and was festooned with smaller guns and a puzzling variety of flags. She was the *Only Connect* out of Penzance according to the legend under her name which was carefully emphasised in navy blue and gold. Her copper and brass was impeccable.

I saw an officer in a wide-brimmed Quaker hat and a big, brown sea-cloak climb the companionway to the poop deck and with arms folded regard the working men with a grim, disapproving glare. At his left hip he sported a massive flenching cutlass of a kind used by whalers, but in his right hand he held a willowy foil favoured by effete Spanish courtiers. Monsignor Horace Quelch. Schoolmaster, priest and pirate. Why did he choose to sail when we did? I suspected a man like him. He might already plan to disobey his mistress's instructions, sending us to the bottom with a single fusillade. Suddenly Quelch turned. I saw his glinting pale blue eyes staring directly at me. Even from that distance I felt his malevolence!

We found our barge with sails neatly furled, in good shape and thoughtfully cleaned up. Her heavy red canvas was mended and fresh-scrubbed. The barge had been generously restocked with provisions. Even her bunks had fresh linen.

Peter Popper was especially pleased as he patted his grinning spaniel, Rufus. "I've never seen my wheelhouse so shipshape!

My old girl so pretty! I'll be pleased to show her off when we're back Thameside at last!"

From the quayside the Rose regarded us through veils which barely disguised her expressions.

"And will Captain Quelch accompany us to the mainland?" I asked her as innocently as possible.

Her eyes smiled again. "His errands take him in pursuit of a fine American merchantman. She's riding a little too heavy in the waters and is thus a danger to herself and all local shipping." She avoided telling me directly that Quelch had a bigger fish in mind than us. I had no choice but to believe her.

With little ceremony we said goodbye and set sail for the sea-gates and tunnel ahead. On all viewing points above and around us we saw people leaning over their flower-draped balconies, waving and calling to us as we moved with all the grave, superior dignity of musketeers, into the open sea. I could not tell from the distance whether they shouted encouragement or jeered at us, knowing we sailed to our destruction!

Not long after we left Las Cascadas behind, we made out the faint line on the horizon; a glimpse of the coast of Africa. My feelings were mixed, to say the least. It gave me a serious thrill to know I was looking at Africa. Everything was not only real but a kind of hyper-reality. I remembered a story by the guy who invented Dianetics, Lafayette R. Hubbard. *Typewriter in the Sky* had made an impression on me. A hack writer, working at speed and clearly based on Hubbard himself (he had a reputation for rapid delivery), becomes trapped in his own illogical narrative. He can hear the typewriter clattering out his inconsistent plot somewhere in his own universe. Guns would suddenly appear in villains' hands or swords disappear from the hero's scabbard. A pirate story, I think. Naturally I saw the irony of being similarly trapped. Two of my favourite

186

children's books were by E. Nesbit. Less well-known than *The Railway Children* or *The Treasure Seekers* or the other Bastable books. The two I enjoyed most were usually called the 'Arden' books, written in 1908 and '09. Although they used magic as their rationale, they were about time travel and discussed ideas in advance of her friend and fellow Fabian, H.G. Wells. Events which took place in one book were seen from the viewpoint of characters in the other. Being a Fabian, she managed, in *The House of Arden* and *Harding's Luck*, to talk about social injustice, industrial filth, metropolitan poverty, cynical plutocrats and utopian lost cities while offering the odd history lessons, all on the framework of a romantic page-turning plot. She was a fast, sometimes careless, writer but she told a great story and I read her still. Noël Coward became her friend. When he died, they found two of her books on his bedside table. I knew a kind of delight, appearing in an exotic adventure which reminded me of her. The only difference was that, in a children's story, you were almost certainly going to come out alive and happy.

Within a few hours the coast of North Africa came into view again. I could see the dazzling blue and white of the fishing villages. Their little square houses were clustered one on top of another in narrow, crooked streets, rising on terraces around the harbours. All the villages had at least one minaret showing where a mosque was built. Once as we sailed past a particularly beautiful minaret, we heard the muezzin calling to the faithful in a voice so full of joy that I found myself weeping.

Half an hour later we sighted Tangier. She was known as the Alabaster City because of the gleaming whiteness of her buildings, visible from afar. Rufus, the spaniel, began to wag his tail as he climbed into the bow. Peter Popper steered his barge a little diffidently through her busy harbour. Our craft, so clearly built for inland European canals, was the object of some curiosity. We were unique amongst every kind of shipping, from simple dhows to tremendous men-o'-war. Most of the larger ships flew English colours. Duval sneered at the 'cowardly brokers' who had made treaties with the corsairs. He told me that the English traded openly with the Moslems while the Dutch even converted to Islam to make their piracy more effective. "Have you not heard of those infidels Zymen Dansiker, Jeremy Cornelious and the kind?" I was bound to admit I had not. But I was rather disgusted to hear of English captains engaged in slavery. I looked to Peter Popper. "Are you not ashamed?" He shrugged. "At least they offer good prices for Christian slaves so I hear. The Dutch care nothing for such wretches. Sometimes Dutch and French monks come here and they, too, buy Christians."

Ah, darling fishlings!

Then we saw her! Her great scarlet sails furled, she was unloading a massive brass-bound crate at least the size of a London bus. Slimy seawater dripped from it. Muted, high-pitched voices whispered and cackled. I could not imagine what the crate contained, though I believed I heard other peculiar sounds coming from it, almost cries of pain. Duval shaded his eyes to see it better. "Have they captured her at last?" A mermaid? A dugong? The Kraken? I had no idea what he meant. "What now? Barbarosa swore he would dine off the monster's flesh when he caught her."

I wanted him to explain but he turned away, busy with ropes. Was this the sea-monster Quelch had mentioned? Hundreds of dockers were gathering around the crate to steer her down to a Brobdignagian flatbed truck drawn by teams of equally huge shaggy shire horses harnessed six across, each wheel tended by teams of workers. The smell of brine was powerful. There were other scents. Blood? Something thoroughly strange made me sense colours that turned my stomach.

Barbarosa's galleon stood at one of the harbour's choice moorings. We recognised the familiar livery and hull of that massive three-masted bireme. She was registered in Constantinople as the *Golden Rule*, but now a banner was draped over her impeccably shipshape bow and stern. I could not read her name, for the whole thing was in Arabic.

Athos inspected the words. "Typically vulgar!"

"What does it say?" I asked him.

"He's calling that floating whorehouse *El Baracuda*."

"So this is Milady Abbess's word!" I swore. "She said we were safe at sea but said nothing of the harbour. We're betrayed. He means to take us here!"

"I'd have laid Lyon odds she could be trusted." Porthos pouted to himself. "What's bothering you, young Moorcock?"

"That!" I pointed at traditional food-and-drink purveyors. Bearded men, children and youths in long djellabahs holding up their fruit and fish, their yams and sweets, trying for custom from the big merchantmen. "I'm starving!" Small boats shot everywhere, calling their familiar cries in a dozen languages. A few veiled harlots trilled enticingly to the newly arrived sailors. "When shall we eat?" I asked D'Artagnan. He patted my shoulder.

I apologised to him. "I've been spoiled at Las Cascadas. I've not been myself since I woke up on the barge." He grinned at me without concern.

"I smell heavy magic. New to me. Mighty powerful weights of it. I have to admit, I am unused to it. What allies have we in these parts?" Surely Popper's spaniel had not just spoken to me! He looked at me as if he had, then turned his head away. Peter, of course, expressed his discomfort in his troubled West Country tones.

I glanced around. I could see no other contemporaries. No help there. Athos and Porthos paused, somewhat concerned. I begged them to ignore me. Did I seem crazy to the men with me? Or was there just something in the air of Tangier?

I became alarmed. According to all accounts I had read in *Golden Fleece* and my favourite adventure-story magazines, Tangier sheltered the most savage of all the Barbary corsairs. With legendary Chinese pirates, they were the world's masters of refined terror and humiliating torment. We prayed to whatever we believed in to save us from the notice of Frederico Barbarosa. By all accounts, he was by no means the worst of the Mediterranean corsairs.

With luck, at this moment, the colourful figure on the distant bridge of the *Barracuda* was giving all his attention to the massive crate. What could it contain? And who was the dark woman, her face obscured by scarves, standing beside him?

Hanging in the rigging and over the sides of surrounding craft, the sea-thieves stared at us through bold eyes of every colour. They, too, were curious about Barbarosa's cargo. The sailors were amiable enough. They made no effort to come between us and the main harbour. Slowly, with a kind of clumsy dignity, we steered our way towards the mole where small boats like ours were tied up. I could hear indistinct sounds in my head, almost voices. I was scared. Was the Whispering Swarm threatening to resume?

At last I began to believe the Abbess had kept her promise. She had used her influence to let us disembark from the barge in safety. But we remained cautious. I knew I had to exert the firmest discipline on myself if I wished to continue. *I could see them dancing through the land, following the great dread ...* I had to keep every aspect of my body in balance upon the moonbeam road. I could understand how it would get onto the deck and begin that fatal flickering, losing children just as you seemed at your closest. Where were my friends? Turning with extreme care I inched my way over silver boards. *My girls needed me.* If I wished to see them again I must remain focused. More than ever I had to remain in this *glett*. I had no choice. I had my back to the deck. *I could not return to that kaleidoscope knowing I would fall into countless fragments, each one a smaller and smaller version of myself; each one a larger and larger version of themselves. A bad trip! We must steer an intense and accurate course. Or this whole delicate enterprise is finished and Spammer's mighty dream is ended.*

I fought to keep my senses. Harmony was always my goal. Harmony was what I yearned for. Balance. A rock on which to stand. From the very beginning.

The state of mind in which I found myself was vaguely familiar. How could I have experienced it before? Where had I experienced it? I was both attracted and horribly frightened by it! Perhaps in my deepest dreams of which, on waking, I remembered absolutely nothing. *Spammer?* What kind of name was I hearing? And at the root of this notion, this uncertain destiny, was a raging idealism as we fired the desire to make worlds and stars and galaxies and universes. Law and Chaos swinging wildly in the winds of limbo.

Then comes the path that leads only backward. Five of Swords. Donblas, the Justice Maker; my particular nemesis. What I could smell pouring from the head of the rearing rider was lavender. The elephant god with his burning pale largesse. He carried a fanciful and obviously impractical instrument, a weapon, and began to spin. Stop him for the sake of all souls. Are you with me, Vivienne? And Pandora? What? Lavender. Deadly Syrian lavender!

Syrian lavender. Breathe deeply my children. Sleep the sleep of pain. Everything was coloured. Every gasp and breath of air. *Oh, God! Oh, coherence. Could they not grant me mercy? The mercy of understanding where I was, which path I had picked.*

191

Captain, spare me this dreadful failure of knowledge! And do not let more innocents die. Do not let them die.

Oh, captain grant me mercy. Oh, captain grant me pain. Oh, captain swing your hammer. For the soul of *Spammer Gain*.

Coherence! My prayer might be answered. Music. Sublime. Vaughan Williams. Meredith celebrated the spirit of the lark. Oh, please! Some small sense of order! Perhaps. Fear. Fear. Fear the Original Insect. Oh, there is no pity. No mercy. No justice. Nothing can save us. Only that fierce, avenging beak. *But is the Kraken dead? Or did the Kraken never live? Can she save her children? Or are we unsaved? Are we forever deceived by the scent of lavender and roses? Who shall smell the tender flower? Who shall die and who shall live? All the world shall turn to ice. For whom the universe makes sacrifice. How can we tell if she is our mother or our devourer? Or both?*

The Lark Ascending. My favourite nineteenth-century writer with a fine Welsh composer. She stood before me, smiling. Was she truly benign? Iron and silver/silver and iron/these are the metal which they shall lie on ... There were many worse deaths than the axe.

Had she given me Meredith? His larks, his woods. His woods of Westermain, on whose calm, sweet intelligence I relied. *Beauchamp's Career*, so likely, so near.

The music grew softer, replaced by wild bustling, cries and curses, the clatter of tackle and the crack of canvas, all rolling and smelling sweet or seething on busy water, its waves crested with dirty, yellow foam, as the ships and boats, dhows, galleys, nautilicos and every other kind of water-riding vessel from gondolas, punts and single-sailed dhows to high-decked Spanish galleons, all blazing scarlet and purple picked out in rich gilding, sleek French schooners, filthy Libyan galleys, Greek merchantmen, well-scrubbed English sloops and Moorish biremes, all crowded together, jostling and scraping, groaning and squealing while their crews screamed insults in a profusion of Arabic dialects and African or European languages and patois. The vivid blue sky was filled with flags, rigging and sails of every colour, green predominant, waving in the breeze from the sea. Gulls and big gannets circled above blood- and brine-washed cobbles, and brown-necked ravens circled the waters while vultures with huge wings squabbled on cobbled quaysides and wooden wharfs and a huge variety of sea-wolves, sailormen or fishermen, of all the colours and subtle shades and shapes of mankind, swarmed the rigging and decks, armed with weapons created by the ironmasters of a hundred nations. Figureheads represented the myths of every land.

And there we were, lowering a gangplank and tying up our own craft like common fishers save that all but Peter Popper wore a mixture of the Rose's beautiful silks and satins, the full pomp of an eighteenth-century exotic Oriental pantomime over their usual pomp, so that to my eye they resembled so many overweight clowns. Not exactly working sailors' clothes. Only Popper looked like an ordinary seaman, but he, I learned, had no intention of remaining with us. After he had let us tie the barge up loose enough to get us all ashore with our meagre luggage, he shook the ropes away, whistled to Rufus, and jumped back aboard his barge. Waving us a regretful and affectionate farewell, he steered his vessel out from the creaking wooden wharf so sharply that D'Artagnan was forced to leap clear over the running line or be cut off at the knees as a Moor in a brown-striped djellabah ran up to us grinning widely, if unconvincingly, and offering us a parcel wrapped in dirty white cotton. We waved him away but he was insistent, pressing closer and hissing at us in broken French.

"Infidels and dogs of Jews, accept this gift thou gibbering cretinous whelps of Christian whores." He paused as he took a breath and considered some fresh insults. "Cowardly fops!"

Duval understood first and accepted the package, handing its contents out to us. I had an uneasy feeling that we might not live through the coming day as we pulled brown, hooded djellabahs over our brighter costumes and slipped caps and turbans in our overstuffed bags. Now, at least to the casual eye, we were like half the plumper occupants of Tangier and could waddle unnoticed into the narrow streets of the most cosmopolitan port in the world while, almost unnoticed, Peter Popper turned his lightened barge into the wind catching her thick red canvas and sent her, suddenly pregnant in the brisk nor'westerly, scudding into a bright morning sky to vanish in the halo of the sun. I watched him go, unable to call out *bon voyage* and risk discovery by those who wished us ill.

We followed our guide and stopped at the opening of the first narrow street leading into the city. This frustrated Porthos and Aramis, who wanted to get clear of the harbour and merge with the crowd as quickly as possible. We at last entered Tangier's ancient medina, heading for the old Jewish Quarter, the *Mellah*, seeking the house of Isaac-ben-Wahood. All being bearded, we enjoyed a certain amount of anonymity. I was confused by the voices and the language, the warnings and the promises. What was I coming awake to? I was glad to leave a dream behind, but in my dreams I might find answers and solutions. I was frustrated. I merely moved between an absurdity and a paradox.

In all her glistening whiteness, Tangier was the noisiest city I had ever visited. A thousand dialects of a thousand languages were spoken by a thousand races of every mixture. The beautiful richness of East African women's dress contrasted with the severe black of the *hijab*, though more men veiled their faces than women! Proud Berbers in indigo robes, armed with long spears and shields, masked against the dust, led their horses and camels through narrow lanes. The scent of a hundred spices mingled, from saffron to Turkish tobacco, coffee, mint, frying *merghez*, cous cous, stewing vegetables and roasting meat. And everywhere ran cats of every shape and size, many with missing tails where the butcher's cleaver had caught them escaping with a titbit.

Pushing our way through crowded, serpentine streets, which often seemed to wind back on themselves or into different dimensions, we moved deeper and deeper into a city crowded with the towers of mosques, pale houses with crenellated roofs, heavy doors, green courtyards glimpsed in passing. Again I felt I witnessed scenes and events in a kind of super-reality, a world I had always found in dreams and visions. Scents, sounds, colours were as intense as anything I knew from the world of so-called psychedelic drugs. I trembled as the blood pulsed through me. I was nauseated. I was profoundly excited. The whispering still had not returned. Indeed it had completely disappeared since the Cirque d'Hiver. And, much to my relief, so had the more recent frustrations and hallucinations. I had begun to think that perhaps my voices had given way to worse, to more sinister visions, but for the moment it was not so, at least up to now. I decided I could accept the occasional hallucination if they came infrequently.

As I followed Porthos, Duval and the others into the twisting twittens, I had no idea why so much was happening, so quickly. For an instant my eyes met those of a boy. I was sure he had been staring at us and I started to call out, to ask him if he had been sent to guide us as well, but he turned and ran off into the maze. I had probably been mistaken.

I fell in with my companions. I was fascinated by the crowds whose character changed as we entered the *mellah*. The word meant 'salt'. As we moved on, Duval told me, it might be derived from the habit of making Jews preserve the heads of the Sultan's enemies after they were cut off. I suspected a less bloodthirsty explanation for the origin. No doubt the Jews, as Phoenicians, had been among the first to trade in spices here. I half-expected to find all the men of the quarter wearing *kippahs* but instead they either had the universal djellabah with its hood covering their heads or the square astrakhan hats which I think came originally from the first *ghetto* of them all, in Venice. I was surprised by the costumes of the wealthier merchants. These also probably derived from those worn by Jews in the European cities of the south. In the main I found it impossible to tell how rich they were or what kind of houses they lived in, because, in accordance with the custom of most Mediterranean cities, their courtyards were hidden by heavy doors offering no indication of what lay behind, though occasionally I caught sight of a beautiful garden or something resembling a tenement building.

At last we paused in front of a slender doorway whose arch reached to a beautiful point in the subtle style I associated with Sufism and which had an inscription in exquisite calligraphy which I at first mistook for Arabic and then realised was Hebrew. I had seen similar buildings before. By its position, the arrangement of its mosaics, I recognised the building as possessing a religious or at least scholarly function.

Duval knocked once. A busy drawing of bolts and turning of keys. Then a bright-eyed, olive-skinned young man with the nervous, but inquisitive, pouch-cheeked gaze of an amiable rodent ushered us into a courtyard.

Were we all here? whispered the rodent. We assured him that we were. We crossed a quadrangle. A courtyard so familiar to me that I gasped. Familiar in both Christian and Islamic architecture, but for minor details, this was a religious cloister with arches and ceiling and windows almost gothic in style.

I had no clear idea if I had seen it before. Déjà vu, no doubt. It was certainly religious in nature. A convent or an abbey more conventional than the one on the island? I must have visited a building of a similar pattern, perhaps in Canterbury or Oxford. For some reason I associated it with London, though I knew of nothing like it there. Fleet Street? The Temple? I was certain I recognised the place. I stopped dead, for a moment unable to move, aware of a tawny face studying me from the shadows of an open upstairs window.

Not the Abbess. However, this was a dark woman of exceptional and exotic beauty! Persian, Greek or Jewish. She drew a hood closer. So lovely and mysterious, so poised! Sargent might have painted her. At that moment I was sure I knew her. Had she stood beside Barbarosa as the giant crate was winched to the quay?

I received the impression that her deep, reflective eyes were assessing me for a part in some dramatic invention created by my other working self as I typed through the night putting, as I used to say, my dreams down on paper. (And taking them to the market in the morning.) It would not be the first time I had fallen asleep while I worked, waking up to discover that I had written a perfectly coherent narrative! I knew others who had done the same. Then I wondered: Was she the Rose's sister? Her face was somehow familiar. Even her aunt or mother? There was a family resemblance, I felt certain, and she was certainly a little older, and, of course, I had barely glimpsed the Rose's face.

Introductions of sorts were made with the nervously smiling hamster-youth as we thanked our supposed host for his kindness in sheltering us. He bowed and on sandalled feet led us across a sun-filled quadrangle. We passed through the sheltering cloister, through a second in which a fountain played, and into the cool gloom of a peaceful room at the centre of which was another fountain not making the sound of water. When I looked closer I saw that the centrepiece was in the shape of a fish, perhaps a rearing dolphin. Or, from a different angle, a swimming octopus. Unconsciously I stretched out my hand towards it and then, embarrassed, pulled back at once.

Where had I seen the thing before? The fish at first appeared to be balancing on its tail. When I looked at it in detail I saw that, rather than a familiar fish, like a carp, perhaps, I was looking at a creature with a number of tentacles woven together to *resemble* the body of a fish. Actually, it more closely resembled a cephalopod. A squid, perhaps? Or possibly a cuttlefish. Even, yes, an octopus!

Cephalopods were clever mimics. I had researched them for a feature I did in *Everybody's* magazine, then edited by my old friend Ted Holmes, the man behind the pocket-size comic-strip monthlies like *Cowboy Picture Library* and the others. He also created *Look and Learn*. Ted had wanted a piece on 'Monsters of the Deep' to go with some wonderful Matania Kraken drawings he had found in the old man's studio. I loved Matania's work, especially since he had illustrated Edgar Rice Burroughs in *Passing Show* before the war. The more I had studied the strange sea-creatures, the more I came to admire them. I now perceived them as beautiful. They were certainly amongst the oceans' most intelligent denizens.

Not every branch of Islam forbade representational art. The Persians made beautiful carpets, paintings and tapestries showing scenes from fables and poetry, as did the Mongols and their descendants in Pakistan. Were Berbers permitted to show animals and flowers? I looked around me. Perhaps this only *appeared* to be a religious building. I saw no writing to suggest it was Christian or Arab. Jewish perhaps? We could still be in the *mellah*.

So what was it, this place? Maybe it had a more sinister function? Were we in danger? Only Duval appeared to know anything at all, and none of us had yet asked him what was going on.

Suddenly the young hamster turned a corner and disappeared into terracotta shadows. Another appeared in his place. This man was definitely a Moor, a handsome old fellow with an aquiline nose and a long, well-groomed black beard, the stereotypical proud Bedouin. Adding to the dreamlike quality of the experience, he did not yet speak. Something menaced us.

"Good day to you, sir," said Duval. "We seek Isaac-ben-Wahood. Do you serve him or—?"

The Moor gave a signal. We heard the rattle of metal, saw steel glimmering in the darkness. We were completely surrounded and the Bedouin made no attempt to reassure us. And then, from out of the shadow, an old man staggered. His robes were richer, a little more European in design and beneath a tall fur hat dangled the ringlets of an orthodox Jew. His large, shining eyes carried an expression of regret, apology, and he stretched his arms to us as he fell slowly to his knees, then collapsed until his head struck the flagstones. He had said nothing, but now blood wept from his lips as he sighed a warning.

"A trap!" cried Aramis, throwing back his djellabah and drawing his épée in a single movement. "To me Musketeers! To me!"

Now my five companions assumed a crouch, back to back and surrounding me as the weakest swordsman amongst them. But I drew the curved blade the Abbess had given me, noting its beautiful balance, the suppleness of its steel. In the silence of a cool, shadowy chamber, I was even more sharply aware of that absence, the lack of the constantly whispering swarm. All I heard were the old Jew's laboured breaths.

As my eyes grew used to the light I saw that the chamber was almost entirely filled by tiered seats surrounding the floor.

They stretched up into the gloom. Neither mosque, temple nor church, the hall was more like an auditorium in the Greek style. For some reason I associated it with an old lecture theatre. Every row of seats held small groups of armed Bedouin, lounging in warlike robes and miscellaneous armour, some of which was rusty and well used. And every one of them was armed to the teeth. Was our end to be an entertainment for these men? With a sickening sense of betrayal, I prepared for death.

Next I heard a woman's voice issuing what I took to be orders. Again, not the Rose. Someone quite as used to command. Her clipped Arabic appeared not to be local. It could be Egyptian or Lebanese from the way 'Imshi' passed her haughty lips. Who was she? Some confidante of Barbarosa, possibly. If not the corsair, who?

The Moor stepped backwards. Leaving the Jew where he had fallen, the men began to close in while those in the tiered seats slowly made their way down. I had no doubt at all that we were to be murdered. Someone had discovered our destination. They had gone ahead of us with the intention of killing Isaac-ben-Wahood before we could speak to him. Whatever this might be, I was convinced that my last moments would be spent fighting these killers.

We were suddenly blinded by brilliant light. I threw up my arm to defend my eyes. All I could see was a white silhouette against that golden blaze, a deep red shadow on the dark terracotta wall, out of which stepped a handsome young man in silvered and gilded brass, fine, steel mail and all the other accoutrements of a wealthy and most exquisitely clad Arabian knight.

15

The Road Through Atlantis

I N LONDON AT the Wallace Collection, I had frequently admired whole sets of war-dress belonging to Syrian nobles.
The Wallace was renowned for its quality. What the newcomer
wore was more beautiful than anything I had seen there! Even
in the present situation I could admire his engraved spiked
helmet with its moveable nose guard. He wore a crescent
cuirasse against his throat, chain gauntlets covered in white
buckskin, a flowing silk surcoat with a discreet Arabic inscription in deep green over his left breast, a curved sword
in a beautifully made silver-and-gold scabbard inscribed with
the most unique and exquisite calligraphy, another, shorter,
curved sword and, stuck in a red sash, one on each hip, a pair
of silver-and-ebony flintlocks.

He made a sign and the Moor, with the help of two others,
stooped to take hold of the Jew and raise him to his feet. The
venerable old fellow was dazed, breathing with great difficulty. They helped him to sit on the nearest bench. Some of
the ruffians in the higher tiers still had their hands on their
weapons, but all watched their leader. The newcomer seemed
amused by their nervousness. I was impressed. I had never
before seen one man take control of so many with such great
authority.

In Europe he would probably have been a military dandy like the Musketeers but better at posturing than the pursuit of martial arts. This nobleman however looked as if he knew his business, just as the Musketeers did. His skin was very dark, setting off his deep blue eyes the colour of violets. Those eyes creased with amusement when he looked at us. Our djellabahs barely disguised the clothes they were intended to cover and were now lumpy rags. Indeed we must have looked like fools. I would have laughed myself had I not realised I looked quite as pathetic and ridiculous as the others.

When he spoke the newcomer's voice was warm and liquid. Like a leopard's throaty growl blended with the sharp-edged purr of a mountain lion.

His voice carried a kind of intelligence I had noted in the Musketeers and which I was coming to identify with certain intellectual soldiers. I was about to introduce myself when he stepped out of the light, closing the door behind him to confront us all. When several of the Arabs made to move towards the door he looked at them so sternly that they immediately regained their seats.

"Je suis Antara-ibn-Sawiyya," he said, expecting to be recognised.

"The Abbess's friend!" Bowing and saluting with his own blade, Claude Duval was glad to speak French and anxious to show that he, at least, knew the handsome Saracen and could match his manners. "You are to be our guide to the Far Oasis?"

"Of course." After a second's hesitation Antara-ibn-Sawiyya returned Duval's salute, speaking in pure elegant French. "First we must save your lives! These ruffians are poor scholars, but at any moment they will likely figure the arithmetic and understand how few we are."

Given he had just rescued us from almost certain death, I could tell that our new ally was a little surprised to be described as a mere guide. With a wry movement of his lips and slight drawing together of his elegantly modelled brows, he unsheathed his glorious blade and, casting a speculative eye towards the cheaper seats, invited us to ready our own weapons. Then he gestured to me to step closer to him, nearer to the door through which he had entered. With great respect, he courteously offered the old Jew, Isaac-ben-Wahood, his arm, addressing him in what I took to be respectful Hebrew.

Our assailants were already inching from the pews to the flagstones, looking to the Moor for his expected orders. There were at least two score of them. Then, very quickly, the Arab knight gestured with his sword. His nearest enemy fell, reaching towards his throat. Blood pulsed from his jugular, streaming down his battered breastplate.

As the next man came at him, Antara kicked his scimitar towards me and engaged him. Instinctively, I bent to pick up the sword and, armed with two blades, went to stand back to back with my panting comrades. Suddenly I felt no fear at all. I had enjoyed nothing like this since a boy, playing with Brian Alford as Robin Hood and Little John battling the sheriff's men! It was exhilarating. Still in a dream, I had no thought of danger just as I had none when I climbed sickening heights and took unthinking risks with my young friends in Norbury.

Astonished at the ease with which the blade cut through cloth and leather, then human flesh, I went into a kind of Teutonic battle-madness, much as I imagined my ancestors survived as berserkers, fascinated by the feel, sights and stink of the fight. I had described plenty of sword-swingers, and I seemed to know what I was doing. I was covered in blood. I think if I had paused I would have fallen, but all those sports and games we played as boys came to my aid. There was no doubting the intentions of the assassins, nor the reality of their deaths, as we backed closer to the door. We stood shoulder to shoulder facing them. The old Jew was trying to speak but Antara silenced him gently. There would be time to talk, he soothed.

I became a good enough swordsman under pressure, remembering everything I had learned in cadets and from a hundred adventure films which Brian and I had re-created as boys. Good enough, at any rate, to defend myself with instinctive skill and distract an attacker long enough for someone else to kill him. *"Can Brian stay to tea, Mum?" "Of course he can, love. As long as it's all right with his mum."* Then Sheik Antara-ibn-Sawiyya carried the attack, his scimitar and long, curved knife whirling like insubstantial silver, a tornado of shimmering light and shattering rubies.

I had read about the legendary Antara, even used him once as a character in a Karl the Viking story. He was the greatest of all Arabian heroes, as fine a swordsman as he was a poet and so fine a poet all poetry was named after him! Also called Antara the Black because of his dark skin, he was a former slave, freed by his clan's Sheik both for his courage and for the beauty of his verse. I remembered hearing how many Arab heroes had named themselves after Antara. He must be one of them, since the original had lived in pre-Islamic times. As he fought, the man continued to sing a powerful, ululating Arabic song. He laughed as he spun his sword, and he sobbed to mourn the coming deaths of those who were foolish enough to attack Antara and his friends, all expert swordsmen, who had fought in half a hundred campaigns across three continents. It did not cross my mind at the time how I could understand his beautiful Arabic, but I was astonished by his fighting skills, as well as his singing. One of those strange musical interludes found in the Indian films I had managed to see.

For a few moments blood sprayed everywhere until even the Moor and the Jew, who were not fighting, were covered with

204

the stuff and the flagstones were dangerous! With a murmured word to Antara, the elderly Jew managed to get between us and the door. Gradually, he inched it open, but we were still not quite able to get through it. The Bedouin were pressing us too heavily. My own arms were very heavy.

Our enemies became more cautious as they, too, tired. Though now only outnumbering us three to one, they decreased their distance as they continually thrust at us. So far we had sustained only minor wounds, but I could tell that we should soon be overwhelmed. Somehow we pulled ourselves together, rallied again and followed the warrior-poet into the hottest, hardest battle I ever knew.

Even while I fought for my life I thought how this would make a wonderful experience for my next historical adventure in *Thriller Picture Library*! I even had a title come to mind. Don Lawrence would love to draw it – *Shadow of the Scimitar*! *Karl the Viking and the Ghost of the Tideless Sea*! What a bizarre idea coming at the moment when every reality, including life itself, was at stake for me! The steel and the blood were bad enough. The taste was now constantly in my mouth. I would never forget the sight of flesh parting in horrible red grins, one after another. Our enemies fell backwards with their throats cut, going down in a tangle of gouting blood, jerking flesh, glittering steel, flowing finery, gasping like landed fish for another split second of life. There is a great difference between real death and fictitious death. Much of it has to do with discomfort and pain. Then there is that endless desire to stop the nausea no doubt caused by one's terror. Finally one descends into acceptance.

Our moment came suddenly. The Bedouin attackers paused for breath and fell back. Instantly, the Jew got the door open just wide enough to let him squeeze through and brace himself, beckoning for us to follow. This we did, one at a time.

Finally, Antara slipped through, slamming the door fast while we shot huge wooden bolts into place. The Jew had evidently come this way, for now his hand went unerringly to a dark lantern hanging on the wall. He took it down, opening a shade to throw light on narrow steps curving steeply left into blackness. To his right, more stairs rose up but when I looked enquiringly at them he shook his head and pointed downward, whispering: "That way leads only to the world we left. You must carry on. To the Land Unknown. To the Growling Gold. There to rally for the Battle Never Lost or Won!"

I wanted to ask him more, for his French was easily understood, but he shrugged an apology and beckoned rapidly.

Sheik Antara-ibn-Sawiyya scabbarded his scimitar, accepted the lamp and, with the Bedouin assassins still thundering their pommels on the heavy door, led the way down into a darkness which seemed to exude its own particular sense of hard cold. I felt we experienced the essence of some deeply alien world. Not an unnatural place, in fact a place of almost quintessential reality, the beginning of all that represented the familiar, yet bereft of every ornament, whether logical or sentimental, analytical or imposed. A massive sucking out of life itself. Such a terrifying coldness! A coldness or perhaps more accurately an absence of heat, for I sensed other absences apart from that one, and they were far harder to identify. Lifelessness. Far more horrifying to know than to recall.

Duval murmured:

"Monsieur Moorcock, if you please."

I accepted the invitation, knowing myself to be a liability to the rest, for they were protecting one far less skilled than themselves. The Jew and I went our separate ways. I heard him murmur some sort of blessing as he turned the corner overhead and I began the dark descent.

Though I went down into dim torchlight, the unmalleable

flames from the brands gave off no heat and cast only black, hard-edged shadows. In my haste to escape the Bedouin, I took the stairs into semi-darkness two at a time. It seemed the circular way had no end. The temperature became colder. The light fainter. And suddenly there was no sound.

No sound at all.

A swift silence so profound I began to long for the Whispering Swarm. I was filled with loneliness.

Was this Limbo? This absence of time, space and memory? I stopped. I knew profound terror. I could not take another step down.

Then, to my relief I heard distant voices following me. Aramis and Athos were coming at a faster pace. In relief I waited to let them catch up. I turned with enormous pleasure to regard them. Both men were panting, their faces flushed in the guttering light of their own brands.

We could still see nothing ahead. The roof above us was rising higher and the air still colder. There was a longer, lower echo suggesting that the tunnel widened out. Aramis made a face and, grinning, raised his own flambeau. "Let's see where these steps lead. Brrr. Cold and ghastly, eh? Does not the ground underfoot seem a little unfinished?" He called back to his friends. "Come along, comrades! Our convent's built over some fabulous minotaur's lair!"

16

Legends of the Interior

Porthos, Sheik Antara and Claude Duval had caught up with us. We had rid ourselves of our disguises. We no longer resembled overfed ducks. Now the steps were considerably less steep and much easier to use. They were wider, more even, as if made by alien hands.

Holding a torch aloft, the Comte de la Fère dropped to one knee. "There's been some effort to smooth out the stone," he said. "Different tools were used. *Almost* – I don't know – *almost* – a different kind of brain at work! I am reminded of my years in the Americas. Perhaps ..." He stood up again, thoughtfully fingering his bearded chin. Slowly he raised the torch above his head. "Once I was taken by an Indian into a forest to a great stone portal like nothing ever before seen by me, nor had I been shown any drawings or other representations, however bizarre! The portal led downwards, also, but more gradually than these steps. Yet eventually it, too, narrowed and the darkness became cold, as this place is cold, and became dark, also like this place. As if darkness itself had consciousness. How can the *absence* of something possess a mind? And the great stone tools used to make the floors, walls and steps, they had created a floor like this and the cavern led to—" He flung up his arm again.

"*Regard!*"

We all gasped involuntarily. We had entered a massive cavern. From its distant roof grew huge fangs of stone and then, as the cavern floor fell away into darkness, it seemed they widened as well, to crush us like an enormous mouth.

"Were you ever in Mexico, Monsieur Moorcock?" Sheik Antara addressed me so directly, I was almost shocked. As if only now he recognised my presence. "Amongst the great people who ruled there, from whom the Atlanteans are said to descend? They are sometimes called the T'Enque'm. They built in just such a way as this. They are more ancient than any living creature in all the world. They have become one with their world more thoroughly than any creatures since. They survived the great extinction."

I did not then recognise the term. It had an ominous ring. Was this place dangerous? I thought the air grew danker. Antara, I realised, was probably trying to reassure me. "The underground parts are almost all lost now, due to the frequent earthquakes. Where water was plentiful, food could be cultivated, metal and minerals could be mined.

"Cities were built to sustain those resources and named for the gods." I still scarcely heard him, I was so surprised by the great soldier-poet's relative warmth towards me. Perhaps he sensed my genuine curiosity. "They sought to build in heaven so that it should last for ever. They constructed cities below ground in natural caverns such as these and vast cities on the very peaks of mountains. See! This is a wall. Or part of one. Each stone placed perfectly atop the other. Then it turns *sideways* to become steps. Here, too, there has been some cataclysm. And also deliberate action on the part of the T'Enque'm. These are the *ruins* of a wall, I think, and then they became steps.

209

It is a philosophical shift in keeping with cosmic events. The intellect is ours and yet not ours. My father thought they were built by a race of great octopus who enslaved us. Stone and flesh grew as one. All was organic. Everything had consciousness. Malleability. You follow?"

I did not. I refrained, however, from telling him.

Panting, the others joined us. Their brands gave stronger light, showing a wide path like a dried riverbed worn in the granite leading down into deeper darkness from which emerged the sharp outlines of huge stalagmites and stalactites marching deeper and deeper into the underworld.

Sheik Antara was grinning. His teeth flashed white against his ebony skin and blue-black beard. "If they've guts enough to brave the stairs, I doubt the dogs will dare follow past the first cave," he assured us. "They think they descend into the kingdom of djinns. Bah! Now they truly know hell is in their heads! They are the epitome of ignorance, the conveyors of all sin." He inspected his scimitar before wiping it. "So. So I address, I presume, the kinsman of my kinswoman, the White Lady of Las Cascadas. Our Barbary Rose."

"Indeed," said Duval a little hastily. "By marriage, rather than by blood." He offered me a brief sideways look as if suggesting I keep silent. "We bring fraternal greetings." I think we all felt rather awkward. An unsettling moment.

Then, without any kind of ceremony, the Comte de la Fère stepped forward. Bowing, he told the Arab what a great honour it was to meet that most famous of Bedouin heroes, Sheik Antara-ibn-Sawiyya. I had read folktales and not much else. The world regarded him as warrior-poet, the finest we had ever known.

His sister, Athos continued, sent a thousand embraces. Across the lands of the Franks, his work was renowned, translated into all the languages of Babel. Every civilised library on our Globe had its *Romance of Antara and Antab* in folio to octavo to duodecimo, with woodcuts after the Author.

I was embarrassed. Was our friend trying indirectly to educate us? Thanks to Rimsky-Korsakov's *2nd Symphony* and the sleeve notes on the back of the record, I knew a little about this most famous pre-Islamic exemplar of the perfect Arab knight errant. He was as skilled with his pen as with his sword, a clever rider and a brave protector of the poor, as generous to the weak as he was severe to the strong. That was the entirety of my knowledge. Antara himself would fill a few gaps in my education. As I followed him trustingly I still had only the vaguest idea who the handsome young warrior was. I suppose my logic was simple: if my companions were prepared to trust him, so for a time was I.

What were his motives in helping us? Unlike the Musketeers and Duval, he had only once featured in a story of mine. He was the soul of desert civility, smiling pleasantly and speaking that beautiful purring French.

"My good friend, the Abbess Rose, bid me care for you as I would care for her, person and in the loyalty of my friends. I am to take you myself to the Great Zaouia Oasis, with which I am very familiar. From there, we hope, our mutual acquaintance, Lady Blackstone and, perhaps, her famous husband await you. They will arrange the last stage of your journey, to seek the Realm of the Balance. There dwells the great Frankish priest-king, Johannes, who, we're told, rules the whole world at least as far as the Western Tides. There, Master Moorcock, you will deliver or receive your message. But we can risk the desert only briefly. First we must go further under ground."

I did my best to control my features. I had no idea what he was talking about but did not wish to betray my ignorance. I had no message unless it was for my wife and children, to tell them I was safe. I was thoroughly baffled and even a little

211

frightened. I stared around me as we followed the handsome Arab even deeper into the earth. I recalled the Pellucidar stories of Edgar Rice Burroughs. But this bleak stone forest bore no resemblance to Burroughs's tropical world at the earth's core. No helpful coincidences lay just around the corner to pull us out of trouble.

I looked around me. Was that a voice whispering from the darkness? *Our stewardship of the earth is in question. We shall next determine whether we eat our mother or do we preserve and honour her.*

If the first, how shall the prize be divided? Which shall restore harmony? If she dies, must we restore peace by the sword?

Whispering voices captured in old stones! A psychic record. But not that old familiar swarm!

I had no idea what the words were or where they originated. The sudden reverberations made my sinuses throb with pain. The wave returned for a second and a third time. None of my companions had sensed a whisper or picked up a sound except the occasional clatter and echo of a disturbed pebble.

Then they were silent. Every stone. As the grave.

A pain. A profound, all-encompassing pain: as savage as news of a beloved child's death, it reminded me how far I was lost to my own children. Suddenly, in an instant, my self-composure shredded. I grew unable to move a limb. I wanted to vomit. To kill myself.

M'sieur Jack don't care how you roll the dice. M'sieur Jack don't cut no ice, and M'sieur Jack don't cut no slack ... Colour come by chance to those who took risks ... Rauschenberg, Lichtenstein, Hockney ... then, quite suddenly, I fell through rainbows bursting into a million fragmenting rays ballooning into a paste of pulsing emeralds and my head separated from my body and something gently teased out my tongue with a two-pronged fork making a noise like chickens cackling and goats bleating. I

was awash with blue bleeding through which a new beast oozing
black blood approached up through my own windpipe and became
an embracing angel whose mother's hug threatened to drown me
in the intelligent tentacles of a giant, scarlet cuttlefish signing to
me and each sign given fresh meaning by the shade of her subtly
changing sound? Was that sound? (Colour?) Sound (yet the fear,
Oh, the fear!) beautifully signalling me, speaking to me of her un-
conditional love orange as flames, indigo as fog, comforting her,
asking whispering warm wordless susurrations, almost songs,
lullabies, sighing like whales as they sing across the miles call-
ing wave after wave and mass upon mass, field upon field, size
upon size, nest into nest, weave through intelligent, complex signs
like Chinese or ancient Sanskrit, The Colour Wells, by means of
subtly changing colour and shapes, calling me back into the Vale
of Vichlen, The Eight Primary Rivers and the noble Blackstone
Shades, the meaning of subtlety, mother, beyond father, beyond
parents, beyond Time itself, beyond and before identity, no ene-
mies and therefore no soul, merely a huge chessboard but with so
many pieces ... single massive back to black fusing one cooling
volcanic miasma atop another, a half-shaped vision between the
beginning and the end of time. Oh, gods! 'My sweet, sweet fish-
lings. Lost, so lost on the moonbeam roads.' Those colours fusing
confusing confounding. Waves. Time shock. Waves. Familiar
music brought order, a choir took me close to tears. Crash! To
tears. Waves! To screaming chaos as my sense of self, always
so strong, threatened, no it was on the brink, inevitably going,
to crumble. How did I get here? Back? Guilt like a crusted evil
on the skin. Pain so concentrated and all-encompassing; pain so
terrible any death would be a better alternative. I understood how
death could be so welcome, so very kind, so sweet.

My mother found us a flat. In Streatham, across from the
Locarno. It belonged to the man who promoted Miss World.
She was pushing strongly for it because she wanted us to live

near her. Mrs Denham didn't mind too much. It was also near her. But Helena hated it. I was in the middle because I hated it, too, but it always took a while to think things through. We all went home on top of the bus. After a couple of stops, Helena leapt from her seat and, without a word, began to walk back to the entrance. I was shocked but got up to follow her, mumbling something to my mother. It was a kind of test. Passive-aggressive girl can't say no until a crisis of self-absorption occurred. Then she acted. Then she spoke. I must choose. Not the first or the last. 'Oh, I wish I'd never got married.' How many times did her knife rise and fall? Shock upon shock. I would do anything to make her happy. I was strong. I was stupid, maybe, but I meant well and I really loved her.

Suddenly we were so small, our worlds so dense, in a radiant universe scaled to near-infinity, each planet so fragile, the stars so unsteady; universes created at a thought by careless wits, universes so many, so venerable and varied, cradles so complex and vulnerable, five, five, the lily-white boys, dress them all in green-o ... How could we continue to live with that realisation? She no longer wished for life's good things, though she shared the hymns, the singing. She could howl but said suicide became the only viable action. Guilt builds us a cage. The guiltless supply the materials. Our hands cannot hold such graceless floods. Pessimism of the intellect; optimism of the will. Where was this Eden for which we searched?

But then these notions and questions began suddenly to fade. And oh hope filled me and grace came suddenly and then was gone. Then was gone.

I heard no further voices as we trudged steadily down that smooth rock road along which I imagined a million sandalled feet of the same imperial Atlantean people had come and gone. Long before all the dinosaurs were dead, long before the ice came. Their armour was as ornate and alien as ever drawn or

214

painted or forged. Some of it was stripped from the carcass of a massive reptile. Strangely shaped oxen, beasts like mules and huge massively hoofed and shouldered horses, and some animals resembling large, slow saurians, their long tongues flickering, scenting. Marching out of historic memory into the world of myth and imagination. Before the Catastrophe and the catastrophes that followed. Before the deep cold. I continued to gawp at tall columns which stretched beside the road in both directions, echoing and amplifying every sound. The reliefs carved into each column showed chiefly domestic scenes not dissimilar to those in Egypt. Strange beasts from some misremembered Eden. At the top of each column I saw a tangle of tree branches, as if they had been placed there as nests by more primitive creatures.

"What lived there?" I asked Antara, gesturing. "A very large bird?"

His only answer was a quick, enigmatic grin.

I heard a fast, deep river not close enough to offer danger. Elsewhere a small animal burrowed in loose rock and overhead a bat flapped itself into wakefulness. Other tiny sounds were harder to identify and after a while I made no effort to try. Listening to the desultory conversations of my friends I fell in beside the Arab and rather enjoyed his soundless company for another hour until at last I realised the ground was becoming level and the air a little sweeter.

"Where are we?" I murmured to that extraordinary knight as he led the way ahead, silent as a panther in his soft doeskin boots. Surely he couldn't hear other voices, too? Could he?

If so, he did not answer me directly. Another voice interrupted abruptly. Almost a whisper.

"That was a dangerous trick, Sir Antara. A reckless and unnecessary display which we were lucky to survive." Equally soft-spoken, Athos came up on tiptoe anxious to make no sound. "How many years we might have lost? Or how much sanity shattered? Souls destroyed?"

"I understood there to be an element of risk, sir. And a certain chance taken by those who chose the quick route ..."

"*Chose*? You took a shortcut through the spheres, sir! An invasion many would call heretical. You threatened all our lives and sanity!" So murmured the Comte de la Fère. Prim as a Prussian nursemaid, "Have you not, in the name of some merry nonsense, spared a thought, sir, for those whose charge you have endanger'd? Just to show us a dead and gone tableau! Where in the name of our prophets are we and why? We made no agreement to come so far!"

Why was Athos so angry and Antara so defensive? Indeed, all the Musketeers seemed reluctant to go further, as if they had tired of the adventure and regretted this strange descent.

I was sniffing at the now hot, musty air. Where had I smelled it before? It drew me in. Even the reluctant Frenchmen appeared to be attracted. "To where do we journey? This was not our agreement. Can we return?"

"Easily, sir. I sought some readjustment. Forgive me if I was untoward, sir. We go to the Great Oasis at Zaouia." The Arab prince raised his own face to the wind, scenting a Continent. His voice was low. Was he warning my friend of something? Perhaps he referred to a secret he did not wish to have revealed. But there was something of a triumphant element, too. Too complex a meaning, I decided. "Forgive me if, on a whim, I showed you what was lost for so many millennia, long before the Flood!"

"Our commission took us to Tangier, Sheik Antara. No further."

"I merely used a curious shortcut, sir. I imagined you had no wish to seek so soon a further encounter with those hirelings. Friends here will help us reach Zaouia. There, I hope, you will meet guides far superior to myself."

"Shall those guides return us to France?" Still murmuring.

"Travellers come to consult the Zaouia'n Oracle and thus determine where they shall next journey. Up, perhaps and on toward Egypt; down into the harsh world of Mu-Ooria's great scholar emperors. North towards Far India and the unmapp'd East. South under the golden ocean of our forefathers and thence West and the barbaric lands of the Franks, which I now understand are your preference. Other roads lead to China and still others to Cochin China or Korea and Niphonia, while one secret path, it is said, takes a brave trader to Further-Asia and the Southern Isles." A glow was suffusing his whole face and his intelligent eyes shone with romantic curiosity.

"Australia?" I asked him, half-sardonically, surprising the furious musketeer.

But he did not recognise the name. Perhaps, I reflected, Australasia had yet to be discovered. I felt ashamed, having made light of his enthusiasm. Clearly he forgave me, had probably not noticed at all.

Slowly we descended into what appeared to be a shallow bowl-shaped indentation in the rock at the bottom of which was a wide stretch of underground lake which shone and was as smooth as mercury. A soft glow, like dawn, sprang from the edges of the bowl and I could think of no explanation for it! Could it *be* mercury?

We slowed our pace, unable to make out the nature of this place. Reflected in the lake were the tall spikes of what I had at first taken for natural outcrops of limestone. And we were still under ground!

Now I realised they were buildings. Rock and mud 'skyscrapers' to house hundreds of people. I was reminded of the tall apartment buildings of Ethiopia and Timbuktoo. Surely the builders had masonry skills matching those of the ancients? They must be related to people bearing a close resemblance to the remarkable tribes who settled so much of the African and American continents. I hated my ignorance. Where had I seen similar buildings? Had not the Queen of Sheba brought her prestige to them? Long, long ago, in legend where a world not unlike this had prayed for a Champion? I checked myself. I was confusing fiction and myth. Dreams and history.

As we came to a halt on the ashy bank of the mercury lake, I looked out on what I took to be an island, and for a moment that scene was obscured by a great, steel triangular sail moving steadily towards us. I lost all my fear. I was thrilled. I was now convinced that I had been privileged to look on a thriving part of the lost civilisation of Atlantis. The world for which explorers had searched thousands of years! Were we to meet the Atlantean sailors?

Such was my great naïveté.

Part Three

Submergence

"You may seem to be making a success of things. I admit it, you do seem to be making a success of things. Autumnal glory! Sunset splendour! *While about you in universes parallel to yours, parallel races still toil, still suffer, still compete and eliminate and gather strength and energy!*"

– H.G. Wells,
Men Like Gods, 1923

17

Lebensraum

To my astonishment spikes of tall jagged rock slowly began to move. Cursing, my companions started forward, unslinging muskets, drawing their swords. But Sheik Antara ordered them curtly to stop. "These are my lady's friends. *Our* friends. They are the Off-Moo. They are the most civilised beings of all, an entirely peaceful and intellectual people. Scholars and craftsmen of great wisdom. Forgive me for that detour. It was unnecessary. Uncalled for. But it was a glimpse of our forgotten and distant origins. These people know of us. They were aware of the possibility of our visit!" I noticed his own hand resting on his scimitar's haft for a moment.

As if carved from shards of limestone, the strange creatures glimmered in the shadowy light. I made out their oddly asymmetrical features. Long eyes, ears and mouths, cut in grey and silver, harshly deep, stern and barely yielding, their eyes shifting slowly to regard us, the planes of slate sliding in and out, resembling carvings of robes. Modigliani might have fashioned them from quartz or slate or fused glass. Did they dine on rock, so adapted had they become to their environment? Most of them were nine or ten feet tall, but unthreatening once we recognised their posture as peaceful. Their smiles were black cracks in cooled obsidian, their hands were starred glass and their eyes were cold, flickering volcanic flame. It was hard to know how or why they were so evidently benign. Perhaps their air of antediluvian wisdom reassured us. On soft doeskin boots Sheik Antara approached them, open arms indicating that we offered no threat. He spoke in what I took to be a dialect of Old French and was answered in voices which reminded me of a sound made by water running over granite, melodious and sharp. Surprised by the beauty of these responses, my companions were beginning to relax, as I was. The nearer we got to these strange beings, the more we were charmed. A wonderful scent, not unlike jasmine, came off them. I was a little overwhelmed by it! I staggered, feeling slightly intoxicated. As I drew closer a sense of well-being filled me and I found to my surprise that I experienced a strong liking for these people, as if I were meeting beloved old friends or family members after an absence.

Antara turned to me. "M'sieur Moorcock. These are the Scholar Perfumiers of this region. Their skills are based on the scent of material things. They offer us the hospitality for which they are famous."

Athos answered for us. "If it is appropriate, Sheik Antara, I think our flesh and our spirits would be revived by their generosity. And then, perhaps, we should discuss any further plans."

The Arab seemed mollified. Like him, I felt no alarm. I was horribly tired and ready to accept the invitation for any number of good reasons. I had no idea what lay ahead of us. What did Sheik Antara expect from the future? We had lost Isaac-ben-Wahood and we needed help. I still didn't know where on earth we were supposed to go. Unless this strange place was our immediate destination. In which case it still made sense to accept.

The scholars seemed pleased by our eagerness and led us towards the nearest of the tall buildings.

We passed through a veiled doorway which made a sound like sifting flour and found ourselves in semi-darkness. The room was comfortably warm and lined with the same rock as the outside except that within the walls shifted subtle colours. The predominant smell was one I couldn't identify. Sheik Antara did not follow us at once, but remained outside.

One of the scholars addressed us in a language I did not immediately recognise. I started to apologise and explain when I realised he, too, was speaking some form of Old French and looked to Duval to see if he recognised it. It seemed he did. For a while they conversed together and then Duval turned to inform the rest of us.

"It seems they received a message. Either from a bat or a crow. It is unclear. They were expecting Isaac-ben-Wahood to be with us. They are concerned about his fate. I told him how assassins attempted to take the Jew's life. How we were in a trap set by armed Bedouin and how Sheik Antara had saved Isaac and ourselves. How had Antara-ibn-Sawiyya spoken with Isaac-ben-Wahood? They have magical paths which allow them to cross a thousand miles in a breath. I assumed that Isaac went to find a doctor. Our hosts know and respect Antara. They do accept his word but cannot to be reassured about Isaac. The Jew was carrying some kind of key. We cannot take the moonbeam route! We must take the long route or return. The scholars say we can stay here for a short time and rest. We cannot proceed directly to the Great Oasis Sanctuary if we lack Isaac's key. Without what that key unlocks, we must take a long and difficult overland route. We can wait in the hope that the Jew joins us, or we can continue without him, in which case we must risk the dangers of the desert."

"I know these deserts," declared Sheik Antara, coming in behind us. "They possess few serious perils I have not over-whelmed. The greater djinns are best avoided. They bring blindness, choking and death. It's my feeling that we have considerable danger behind us. The shorter distance between us, the better position we'll be in. Those men who ambushed you are hired mercenaries in the pay of Barbarosa. He clearly wants you removed."

"Does the scholar know why?" asked Athos.

Duval raised an enquiring eyebrow. The Arab shook his head. "It seems none of us does. Many tongues are known here. Spammers and jammers, as we say. By means of a mysterious messenger, a talking crow, the scholars were expecting only Isaac and yourself. They know of myself and our cavaliers in another context. They agreed to help us but not in the manner they were prepared for. They will debate this while we rest. I fear they will expect us to cross the mercury lake rather than let us take the shortcut to the massif. Our survivors they were prepared for. Without Isaac's key they cannot open certain doors. The key takes the form of a chalice, I understand, shaped like sea-beast, perhaps a kraken. Who casts the dust and creates a tale?"

"We know not even where we are journeying. Nor why. And nor with whom." Aramis fiddled with his lace. "Only you, Duval, seem to possess a clue. I think, perhaps, we should seek to find a way back to France. And leave you three to continue a journey which for us has no purpose, no destination and no plan. Nor, indeed, payment! We are at journey's end for four of the King's humble musketeers who were, you will recall, my dear Duval, recruited in Paris to help you and the young monsieur reach Tangier? That commission has been accomplished. Here we are, actually a little *below* Tangier, with ourselves and yourselves all in one piece. Which of us is wanted where and to what point? Sheik Antara knows and understands the region ahead and seems confident."

"Aye," agreed D'Artagnan, "our work is, after all, completed.

While we would not place you in danger, it would seem you are about to embark on a new aspect of your journey that does not concern us. Monsieur Marvell was good enough to pay us all, including you, Duval, half the advance. So it would seem none of us is bound to proceed beyond this point. While we might be said to have failed to turn our charge over to a Jew, we can instead turn him over to an Arab, which is much the same thing. A pagan is a pagan! As long as he is in one piece, I think, our commission is discharged."

"I suggest we avail ourselves of these stony gentlemen's hospitality," suggested Porthos, "eat a little dinner and learn as much as we can about how to purchase passage on a ship back to Bordeaux, say. And be on our way, perhaps after we have caught a few hours' sleep."

And all four musketeers fingered the big muskets they had shouldered but not yet used, because they took for ever to prime, turned enquiring eyes on Duval, myself and Sheik Antara.

"Since I did not embark on this journey at my own will," I said, "and have even less of an idea than the rest of you, I do not feel I should give you an answer or make any kind of decision. This lies between you, gentlemen, without doubt. You are, after all, my abductors!"

They lowered their gaze. Athos murmured, "Not exactly, young man. Your will figures in this adventure more than you know. Or so I understood."

We were momentarily interrupted by the Scholar Perfumiers entering the room with perfectly ordinary and familiar food – fruits and preserves – which they laid out on a low stone table, gesturing for us to sit on cushions and eat. In that same strange French they let us know that such food was generally preserved for visitors like ourselves. It was both delicious and nourishing. We were soon replete and relaxed. Wiping his

225

lips, Duval next brought up the question of the Musketeers' departure.

"You have no curiosity," he asked of Porthos, "as to what lies ahead in this journey?"

"Of course I have!" the big man replied. "We all have. But we are still the King's Musketeers and we must return to our duties."

"How or *why* were you hired to abduct me?" I asked him.

He laughed loudly. "We owed a favour to our friend Duval. We were short of money and his master had work for us. He was determined to bring you to Tangier. Something to do with a matter of honour. Not our business. We have no great interest in what an English wants to do or not do. We are not your enemies, monsieur. Not at present." He frowned, blinking, as if he did not completely remember why he had agreed to get me aboard the barge. Indeed, I could not remember myself!

"You might have the grace, *messieurs*," I replied, "to tell me what you know. Perhaps I have some kind of work to perform. I've had no hint of it."

"A secret is often more powerful than the truth," said Athos. I believed him to be the wisest of them. I said nothing.

They were silent. Embarrassed.

Sheik Antara seemed surprised and bored. He also made no reply. His deep blue eyes moved thoughtfully from face to face, as if he tried to decide something. Duval merely nodded in agreement while the Musketeers remained with bowed heads, unmoving. The Scholar Perfumiers looked politely from one of us to another, smiling a little, or so it seemed from their gaping stone mouths.

Finally Duval put his fist to his lips. He coughed a little. "Everyone makes fair points, Master Moorcock. We have no quarrel with the substance of your remarks. But what has started must be finished. We have, as my friends say, completed the commissions for which we are being paid. Now for Sheik Antara: while we are grateful to you for saving our lives, I take it from what you have said that it is your intention to complete the next stage of this adventure and therefore you have a plan. If we wished to go back, you, I take it, would prefer to continue ..." As he spoke, he shifted his big match-lock musket from hand to hand.

"It is my duty to return to the Sanctuary of the Saharan Great Oasis. The one known in Babylon's history. I have certain promises to keep, chiefly of a religious nature."

All this discussion without any attempt to illuminate me was a little alarming. I said: "If you return to Paris, gentlemen, perhaps you'd be good enough to let me accompany you."

They grew more embarrassed, looking away.

"I believe I gave my word to Captain Marvell to deliver you to the desert sanctuary," said Duval quietly.

I no longer felt any urgency to return. I wondered what adventures the next leg of the journey would bring and where I was supposed to be taken. I could probably return home from there. I dimly remembered reading something about the Great Oasis at Zaouia. I even had a picture of it in my head. There was a school there, maybe a Sufi university. Indeed, some centre of Sufism? I might find help there.

I also wondered how the Musketeers intended to return to Tangier, given that the way we came was blocked by a good many Bedouin mercenaries doubtless awaiting their return. Even if they were to get back by reversing their route to the same streets, the chances were the Arabs would be encountered there. Without Duval, Sheik Antara and myself, they would be hard-pressed to fight them off, however skilled their swordsmanship. Either Duval and Antara had forgotten this or they were upset enough to leave our companions to their fate. I was not prepared to do this.

"Are you going to face Barbarosa's mercenaries on your own?" I asked. "Should you find the same road back, it seems to me they'll be descending and you will be ascending. What will you do then?"

"Fight for our lives," replied D'Artagnan, puffing out his chest. The other musketeers did not seem quite so certain. Aramis even permitted himself a grin.

Athos answered. "If we hear them behind the door, we'll seek a different egress. But they'll be gone by now."

"Well, comrades," said Duval, "you're all greater optimists than I."

Aramis dropped his gaze and now smiled to himself. "I suspect our Bedouin friends were there entirely on your behalf, Monsieur Moorcock. Unable to capture you, they will have returned to report to Barbarosa. Unless your head carries a good price. In which case they are likely to be a little more assiduous in their pursuit of you. Even so, we should have little difficulty making our way to the intersection where you performed your little trick, my lord. Then dockside we'll find a ship to take us back to France. We will not be in danger. We'll sleep here for a few hours, prevail upon our hosts for something to eat, and then begin the journey home. The main fear is over. You'll not need our help to continue."

I could do little to persuade them. I embraced all four and wished them a safe journey. Then we allowed the stone scholars to lead us to small cubicles where sleeping platforms had been prepared. Although apparently of some rocky substance, mine yielded to my body. No coverings were needed. I discovered that they adjusted to whatever heat I required. I found them extremely comfortable and fell asleep immediately.

Next morning, discovering my own clothes cleaned, I put them on and went to find the public room where I had last seen my companions. Claude Duval was there and Sheik Antara, but

228

the Musketeers were gone. The two men were already finishing their breakfast and signalled for me to join them.

When the Scholar Perfumiers brought me a strangely shaped bowl and an asymmetric stone spoon to eat with, the highwayman let me know that the Musketeers had already left. They had wished us all 'bon voyage' and hoped we'd meet again in happier times and cooler climes. Our hosts gestured and, I think, smiled at me, encouraging me to eat. The bowl contained a kind of blueberry-raspberry flavoured porridge which I found surprisingly appetising in spite of the faint electric bloom on its surface. I wondered where they grew the oats or their equivalent and learned that they cultivated all manner of fungus, including mushrooms of many varieties. We had no time to look at these remarkable fields, some of which I had seen growing on stalagmites and stalactites without realising what they actually were.

The caverns were also lit by types of fungus. It 'gathered light' and was brought in from the surface. I really wished I could have spent more time in Mu-Ooria, either to speak and listen through an interpreter or simply be with them rather longer in order to study them. Although many of their devices blended with the rocks of their strange environment, they seemed as complex as the civilisation existing above ground. They certainly showed us no animosity. Had their ancestors lived millions of years ago and resembled humanity, or did they originate in an entirely different kind of life form? If the food nourished us both then maybe we did have close ancestry?

The three of us were finishing our breakfast when Sheik Antara looked up suddenly. He was alerted by sounds outside. Followed by our hosts, he rose from the stone table and walked quickly to the door. We were behind the Off-Moo as we reached the entrance. The air outside was pleasantly cool and sweet. I looked over Duval's silk-dressed shoulder at a completely unexpected scene! Through the caverns of what seemed permanent silvery twilight I saw figures on the slopes above.

It did not take me long to realise that the Musketeers were returning in some haste. And they had brought company, though I did not think it was welcome. Instinctively my hand went to the hilt of my remaining blade.

Down the rocks above the buildings, tabards flapping, feathers waving and silver glittering scrambled the dandified figures of our French friends. Behind them, however, came about a score or more Bedouin Arabs armed with swords, lances and a couple of bows. Our friends had an air of panic as they scrambled hastily down the loose shale. We heard faint shouts from both.

"Our enemies have found us!" murmured Sheik Antara. He did not say the Musketeers had alerted them. He was grimly aware we had brought savages down on unarmed civilians.

We watched as the Musketeers took positions behind rocks. Then the Arabs launched long-bladed spears at them. A few had bows. Arrows clattered on rocks. The Frenchmen ducked down and raised firearms to their shoulders, letting off a fusillade of shots at their pursuers. Two wounded men crawled off to find shelter for themselves. Meanwhile, the Musketeers began reloading, moving slowly and with discipline back towards us and the lake. We carried no weapons to help them from that distance. Were we to see our friends slaughtered?

Behind us the scholars murmured, clicking and whispering amongst themselves before stepping further away from their house and moving closer towards the still, grey liquid of the lake. Then, lowering their heads, they appeared to begin communicating quietly.

When they next looked up, their eyes were like cracks in

granite, glittering diamonds in deep crevasses. They gestured towards the lake. The surface shimmered. Half-seen shapes appeared to move there, perhaps mere suggestions of creatures, writhing, twisting, falling back again to become amorphous. What were we looking at? I did my best to see what the shapes were but could identify nothing.

A sweet-smelling miasma now formed a thin layer which rose to about a yard from the shore, as mist might form on early-morning water. The sweetness increased until the mist became a tangible form on the surface. I thought the shape resembled a massive butterfly, with rich, dark colours moving sluggishly to make a pattern on the wings.

Antara and Duval gasped as they caught sight of the creature rising silently into the silvery air, the great wings beginning to beat upon the mercury lake, sending sparks and rippling shadows over the surface.

The strong, sweet scent alone was almost overwhelming. The form took flesh! The great wings beat with languid motion and bore the body upward until it hovered high in the shadowy air. Apart from the markings, it resembled something other than a butterfly. It became a gigantic pink-grey manta ray rising into the air, silvery droplets falling from its wings, great eyes glaring. It snapped its massive beak, thick wings cracking the air, long tail lashing below as it moved with slow grace towards us, the wings slapping and hissing in the sweet air.

From our strange hosts came a murmuring hum as they lifted their heads to regard the beautiful monster they had raised from the depths. I prayed that they controlled it, for now a soft chittering came from deep in its throat. Evidently under the control of the Scholar Perfumiers, and with complicated multicoloured veins pulsing, it flew toward the beach.

So absorbed in their conflict were the two sides that they

231

did not notice what was happening out over the beach, even though the perfumiers were gathered there, directing the giant ray.

I think all the Musketeers caught the thick scent of the monster before they noticed its shadow fall across them. Desperately the Arabs screamed and began to stumble back, slippered feet slithering on shale. Our friends had not finished reloading but flung their weapons aside, reaching for their rapiers. Too late.

With sudden speed the great water-beast planed down on them, hovered, shivered and began a slow, deliberate descent. Her sweet perfume grew as tangible as the creature itself. All looked up at once, starting to scramble away from the falling shadow. The Arabs ran uphill, the Musketeers ran down. But it was far too late. With one massive movement of her enormous wings, the ray fell. Frenchmen and Arabs were immediately engulfed. She somehow folded them into herself. Through her semi-transparent flesh we saw them struggling inside her and heard muffled screams. Then the enormous thing flapped her languid wings once and, carrying her horrific cargo, ascended into the spikey darkness of the cavern's roof.

And vanished!

Were they lost to us? Had it absorbed them into its mighty body to digest them? I recalled reading of such things. Where was it? Some penny-dreadful story? I know I had read of other mysterious sea-creatures doing the same. Would it carry all the struggling men wrapped and paralysed back to its lair deep beneath the surface, to be consumed at its leisure? Was that the last I would see of my brave friends?

A few of the Arabs were still above us in the hills, climbing back the way they had come with wild, terrified howls. Somehow they had managed to find us in that wasteland. Could they find their way home? The great ray appeared, banked and descended slowly in the darkness overhead, returning to the lake. Surely the scholars did not possess such a savage streak that they relished loosing such a terrible death? I turned to them as they appeared to watch in complete tranquillity while the ray planed in an arc through the shadows, the men still struggling in its belly, no doubt already being digested.

"Please," I begged, "do not let the creature harm my friends. They were defending themselves! Can't you see that?"

The puzzled scholars looked down at me, perhaps uncertain of the language I spoke or of the question I asked. They turned their gaze back to the dark, jagged air overhead. Another cloud of perfume, this one lighter, more bitter, and the ray vanished upwards before reappearing, swimming down towards the beach.

Duval and Antara beseeched them now as I pleaded. They made strange figures in the air, gesturing towards it. I saw it smack its curved beak. It gave a kind of hissing cough, flying close to the shore. Then, quite suddenly, its belly opened. It disgorged musketeers and Arabs in a tangled heap, like fish from a net. Covered in a strange, cloudy liquid, and slithering about like so many landed eels, the adversaries fell onto the slate-grey shingle. We heard their yells and screams as they breathed fresh air again.

Porthos was the first to find his feet. Sputtering and slapping at himself, he looked around for his dropped musket, not finding it. He paused, raising his eyes to the disappearing ray. His mighty bellow suggested he had challenged the monster from the beginning. He shook his fist at it.

Meanwhile the Arabs were dashing into the darkness, clambering uphill as fast as possible, their weapons abandoned. The Musketeers were now all on their feet, staring at us in some bewilderment. Athos looked out over the lake, glimpsing the disappearing ray. He unsheathed his sword to wipe it on his sleeve, which had already dried, rescabbarded it, but still could not find his lost gun. Then he stooped to pick up his hat, catching sight of us as he adjusted it on his head, bowing as he approached us.

"I take it we must thank thee, gentlemen, for our unexpected rescue. I had heard that men, being taken into the belly of the beast, survived unscath'd! I must admit I had not expected to experience it. Is the creature some pet of our jagged hosts? It seems these gentlemen have powers over both the natural and the supernatural worlds."

I heard the Off-Moo behind us murmuring as if they were amused and, turning, saw them gesture with their long arms. The monster they had either summoned or created now began to glide towards the surface of the lake. I watched it slide down into the mist which folded around it. Then, very gracefully, it sank to become one with the lead-coloured liquid, the mercury-like substance of the lake.

The scholars slid their strange, jagged hands into sleeves hardly more distinguishable from flesh, if flesh it was. With an expression of disgust on his face D'Artagnan was combing out his long, curling hair, but he bowed and thanked the Off-Moo. "I am grateful to you, gentlemen. I gather it was you who sent that creature to the rescue. We were, 'tis true, almost defeated. We had almost no ammunition remaining."

He bent to listen to the scholar's reply. The strange being spoke a hissing, crackling kind of French. Even I began to understand it better.

Claude Duval said to me. "Our host remarks that they allow no disharmony in their land. Neither against *them*, against their *guests* or *between* their guests. It seems we've stumbled upon yet another sanctuary and this one appears not to be of a religious nature! In a world of bloodshed and mortal combat we have need of such places."

"And yet the likes of us would have no employment were that a universal condition," remarked Athos with a sardonic grimace. He reached into his doublet, withdrew a flask and took an immodest swallow before replacing it.

D'Artagnan settled his clothes. "I should note that we began no part of the fight, gentlemen, but acted entirely in self-defence!"

"Those Bedouin?" asked Sheik Antara, "They were waiting for you to emerge?"

"Not all," interrupted Aramis. "We were entirely surprised by them. Like the fools we were! When we reached the doorway back into the temple we discovered the Jew had returned. He guarded nothing. His only company was that talking raven, if raven it were. Some black bird or other. The place was deserted. Even the dark-eyed woman was gone. The Jew was particularly in fear of her. She went by an English name, he told me. He still believed she intended to finish him. He had recovered rapidly from his wounds. That surprised me. But his doctor had repaired him well. He was a trifle weak, still."

"Yet you encountered Barbarosa's hired blades!" interrupted Duval. "Were they lying in wait?"

Porthos answered, scowling. "Our Bedouin friends were gone and appeared to have entirely given up their pursuit. Having recovered surprisingly quickly, Monsieur Isaac reluctantly agreed to help us find a ship – on condition that we took him with us as far as Las Cascadas. There he would await the Abbess when, he said, she returned."

"She has left her sanctuary?" I was surprised. While we knew Quelch had gone on to Tangier and Barbarosa was already there, my impression was that she had planned to stay at Las Cascadas.

"Apparently he sent word of our fate to her and he was able to exchange messages using that raven he had with him," said Aramis. "Anyway, that was his price for helping us. Small enough, we thought. We needed someone who spoke the language and who knew the city. So we agreed."

"And no sooner had we found one of those serpentine lanes out of the abbey's courtyard," continued Aramis, "than we were discovered by one of the Arabs, doubtless left there by their leader to spy out for us, should we return! We hardly knew what next to do. The Jew, too, was confounded! He tried to lead us by a safe route, down to the docks and a Portuguese skiff he knew of."

"But they blocked a thousand twisting alleys in the *mellah*," announced D'Artagnan. "The old man called on the help of every compatriot. No deception was successful! And still the Bedouin countered our passage. Even so, we might have fought our way to the dock had not that wily scamp of a Huguenot and his wife arrived, taking command of his infidel compatriots and forcing us back to the abbey!"

Duval raised his eyebrows in surprise. "Huguenot?"

"The damned English Pagan or whatever he was! A sorcerer I'd call him!" spat D'Artagnan.

"Protestant," said Aramis, for the sake of theological exactitude. "Puritan. Nixer!"

"The worst of that unholy crew. He had his cronies with him. The pipsqueak is now self-exiled from the second Charles Stuart's court. If returned he would find himself hanged, drawn and thoroughly quartered like the other regicides. Who was once Intelligencer General under the Arch-Regicide Cromwell when he ruled in England! No doubt he was forced to flee his native country to find work abroad after the Stuart returned to the throne – in the pay of Barbarosa, presumably."

"A strange master for a pinch-mouth of his persuasion. Remember, we heard he was with the Turkish corsair when we enjoyed the White Abbess's hospitality? We encountered him in the old days. In England, you'll recall. When he stormed yet another Carmelite sanctuary. Still carrying that unspeakably monstrous weapon of his. That tromblon, was it? Well he fired it off at the old Jew and damn near cut the poor soul in two."

"He's dead?" I asked.

"As mutton, I fear," said D'Artagnan. "He died in our service and I regret his passing. Jake Nixer revels in his murderous ways. He laughed as he did it! We retreated to the abbey while he reloaded, sending his men after us. This time we could not block the door. We fought all the way back, convinced we were finished. Happily that monster our Mu-Oorian friends had descend from above was our salvation. But our route through Tangier is blocked. It seems, gentlemen," he grinned, bowing, "that Fate has determined we remain travelling companions."

I found myself smiling with pleasure. Only now did I realise how fond I was of the four dandified swordsmen! In spite of all my concerns I began to look forward to the next stage of our peculiar journey.

18

The Road to the Oasis

AFTER ONE MORE meal to help sustain the exhausted musketeers we were introduced to another tall, rather amiable rocklike individual, who carried a large satchel over his shoulder and whose name, he told us, was Am Sool. He was a Scholar Navigator. His people were unhappy that they could not take us by 'the roads'. Since we must use the surface, Am Sool was going to take us part-way, at least to the 'bright air'. He led us out of the house and down to the shore. There, with his sandalled feet standing in the sluggish liquid lapping against the shingle, he put his stony lips together and began to hum. The vibration passed through my entire body. The sound affected the liquid which immediately became agitated, producing tiny, regular waves threatening to wash over the bottom of his strange gown.

Then, through silvery twilight, we saw a bright triangular sail – the same strange metallic sail I recalled seeing earlier. Moving steadily, towards us, the sail was rigid, catching an undetected wind, but it did not fill. No wind came off the lake! The thing could be sentient but remained silent.

Duval asked Am Sool a question. The scholar replied in that same strange French and Duval showed surprise, turning to us. "The ship is driven by moonlight."

Even I was astonished. I had recently written an article about the so-called 'photon-drive'. I was still unable to imagine how so little light could push the glistening sail of so large a ship under Earth's gravity! They had shown how light was harvested from varieties of fungus and attached to the cavern roofs but how the reflected light of the moon drove this vessel was a profound mystery. Again I was frustrated. I wanted to spend some time with the Off-Moo and discover more about their pre-human world.

The beautiful vessel gracefully slid up on the pebbles with a faint hissing sound, and another grey-black Mu-Oorian, all angles and planes, jumped over the rail to hold the boat steady in fists like boulders. He pulled down a gangplank and we climbed aboard.

There was no cover or cabin in the boat, just long benches arranged down each side. We took our places as we got in. Then the big steersman, his features mere cracks in the rock, grasped the tiller in one hand and the sail's ropes in the other. With swift movements he turned the ship off the beach until it was heading out over the lake again, powered by the same force which brought it to us. The silvery light remained exactly of the same quality, as if following us, or propelling us, into the semi-darkness. In the distance the horizon was a pale white line and above us the thin, pointed rocks were menacing spears, shining with that mysterious phosphorescence.

I could not completely rid myself of the sense that the roof might suddenly begin to quake and bring those gigantic shining spears crashing down on our heads. The steersman seemed calm and confident enough. I did my best to relax and look.

The journey did not take long and was done mostly in silence. Within a few hours a shoreline quite suddenly appeared before us and a black rim of shingle came in sight. Then the wide keel of our vessel struck a beach of round, black stones, stopping at last. We were thrown forward, the boat rising almost completely out of the lake. We could easily disembark.

That night we camped on a wide, flat spur of limestone about a mile from the shore. We ate a good meal of cold food which Am Sool provided from his satchel. Then we slept for a few hours.

We continued to trek steadily upwards along a clearly marked trail, noticing how the air grew distinctly warmer until eventually it began to feel uncomfortable. Suddenly our guide spoke again to Sheik Antara. He took two flasks from his satchel and handed one to me and another to Duval. The Arab knight nodded and told us what Am Sool had said:

"The liquid is a kind of concentrated water, enough to last us, if taken sparingly, until we reach Zaouia. He can get us no closer to the surface. From now on it becomes dangerous for him. Perhaps he fears the climate. Perhaps something else. I am not sure I quite understand."

"Has he told you where we are?" I asked.

"Not far from the surface. Perhaps some distance to the east of Tangier. In the Sahara."

"The desert," Aramis lifted an eyebrow, "was not where Isaac planned to lead us, surely?"

"I gather so. Ben-Wahood was told to take you to the Great Medrasa at Zaouia. Was he not?"

Antara exchanged a few inaudible words with Am Sool.

"I believe so. Shall you continue?"

"Do we have a choice?"

"That is where Isaac-ben-Wahood intended to bring you. I gave my word that I would fulfil his pledge to the White Abbess. That I shall do!"

"Why is that? What bond did you two have?" I was genuinely puzzled.

"We are of the same brotherhood."

"But you are of different faiths!"

"We shared a faith above ritual. That we have always done."

For me, Jews and Arabs had always been at odds. I really didn't know what to think. Yet there was little else to do now. Athos echoed my thoughts. "So we do not have a choice? Or rather we can remain here, under ground, or we can go back and face Nixer and his tromblon." He shrugged philosophically. "So we must seek the Oasis!"

"Exactly." Sheik Antara pointed. "This trail will take us into the desert with which I am of course familiar. I can then lead you south-east to the Oasis. That, after all, is the promise I made to Isaac." He looked away, shading his eyes, as if he had a secret he did not wish to share.

"Will they have any sort of refreshment there? You are sure you know the way?" Porthos was growing doubtful.

"I know the Sahara." Antara did not look at the Musketeer. Porthos had obviously offended him. "I have travelled this desert from side to side and end to end all my lives." He lifted his Bedouin *keffiya*, worn over his bright Syrian helmet, throwing back the two sides almost girlishly. As usual he looked magnificent in his traditional costume. I was again reminded of the noble Saladin, whom I'd written about in *Look and Learn* and whom I greatly admired. Antara had his style, though I wondered how he managed to keep cool in the desert! I think our clothes were much more comfortable. My admiration conveyed itself to him. He collected himself, then turned and smiled at the huge Frenchman. "Don't worry, my Christian friend. You'll be in safe hands!" And he clapped Porthos on the shoulder.

I wondered how we would make our way over the desert without riding animals of any kind. Did our guide have any idea?

Am Sool was saying his goodbyes to Sheik Antara. The Arab responded at some length in the traditional manner. After listening patiently the Off-Moo turned to go back the way we had come. With a lift of a long arm, like animated granite, he signalled his farewell and soon had disappeared into the silvery gloom.

Another hour or two and the air had taken on a distinctly sandy quality. The vast underground world had become increasingly narrow until it was first a tunnel and then a very narrow cave through which we had to squeeze and wriggle. By now we were sweating in the heat. We had no clear idea where we were. Then the light brightened, became blinding. We emerged from a cave entrance which was little more than a crack in the ground.

Everywhere was desert. Dunes rose and fell in an endless sea of yellow, red and brown sand. Sand lined our nostrils, our mouths and our throats. We were forced to tie whatever material we had around our faces. I had a habit of using big silk Liberty head-squares as handkerchiefs and the Musketeers, as well as Duval, also had large kerchiefs, Antara, of course, was best prepared, bringing one side of his *keffiya* round to shield his face. Nonetheless, we were all very hot. If I had not had a white linen cap in my pocket I would probably have known the horrors of sunstroke. I was prone to sunstroke at sixty degrees. As it was, I was quickly grateful for my habit of wearing hats wherever I went. I remained sticky and uncomfortable, plodding through the increasingly unstable sand and was grateful for the water the Off-Moo had left. The stuff was viscous but somehow expanded into pure water when it met air.

We rationed the stuff carefully. A few drops really did quench our thirst for long periods. We found the going painfully slow until at last we reached an area flatter and firmer underfoot. Sheik Antara really was certain where he was going. We no longer had to struggle up one dune and down another. We still saw no vegetation in any direction, nor a single sign that human beings had ever been near this region which covered, I thought I remembered, almost half the African continent. What was it I'd read? That it had an area as large as the USA?

How were we to find our way to a single oasis? Whatever her precise measurements, the Sahara was a vast region. I could not believe that Antara knew every inch. Even a small country like England was impossible to know completely. Here, in the Sahara, without roads, signs or even recognisable landmarks, it required a supernatural sensibility to make one's way from place to place.

I could only hope that some caravan might find us.

I screwed up my courage to ask the Arab knight directly if any part of this endless desolation was familiar to him when we reached a rise. Looking down we caught sight of an extraordinary phenomenon.

I admit that I gasped in astonishment. "What on earth is that?"

The flat area we were walking on had distant dunes on either side. They were almost like mountains. From the northwest between two of these rises emerged what at first sight appeared to be a road. The perspective made it appear to grow broader when it merged with the plain. As we approached we saw how it consisted mainly of two widely spaced, very deep indentations, evidently the tracks of at least one heavily loaded wheeled vehicle. This was strange enough. But there were other tracks. Tracks of a variety of disparate animals. Sheik Antara was obviously baffled as we drew closer to them. He peered up at the sun.

"They are heading for the Great Oasis at Zaouia, as we are. It will be easier for us to follow in these tracks. But look at them! What can they be?"

Tracks and spoor indicated a jumble of different creatures moving with a fairly large wagon. That, I could see, was drawn by hoofed and shod beasts, almost certainly horses. We recognised the prints of camels, of animals that were either donkeys or mules, of dogs with large claws and pads. Others we could not recognise at all. Some astounded Sheik Antara and myself, for they were the paws of large cats and the feet of elephants. I found it hard to convince myself that some of them were reptilian or giant birds, perhaps ostriches. In other words, the tracks appeared to be of creatures which had escaped from a huge menagerie or even a circus! But why were the animals all travelling together in an orderly way? Nothing was running. Nothing was hunting. How were they eating? It was impossible to know what the wagons carried, although it was obvious the larger animals did not travel in it. Judging by the disparate tracks and the erratic spoor, not a single one of the large animals was restrained. Moreover, the signs showed that only one man, wearing boots and with a wide stride, walked amongst other tracks beside the wagon. Apparently the beasts had no master save him. I imagined a ringmaster!

What caused so many different animals to accompany the wagon and the wagon-master and not fight amongst themselves or veer from the selected path? I found it hard to imagine the human being who could achieve such lack of aggression. These creatures who were at best rivals and at worst one another's natural prey. As Antara pointed out, there were deer and antelope in that herd as well as big cats and pachyderms! And of quite different kinds. There were small dogs and cats, as well as large ones. But so many sizes!

Surely not even the harshest ringmaster, animal trainer or beast-tamer had achieved such a thing. We found evidence that lions and goats had slept peacefully together.

Our speculation could not explain the strange phenomenon

we were seeing. Were these animals somehow mesmerised? Were they so cowed they dare do nothing against their master? Sheik Antara saw prints he identified as crocodile, hippopotamus and even rhino, some of the most ill-tempered beasts of the African rivers or veldt, animals which were untameable, which had never appeared in circuses and were relatively rare in all but the largest zoos. And what on earth could they be doing in the middle of the Sahara Desert, moving as we were towards the Great Oasis at Zaouia?

For the first time, I regretted that we carried no readily useful guns except for Duval's single-shot pistol. We had been advised not to use long guns, but (having recovered them) the Musketeers refused to give theirs up. As a compromise they were wrapped in heavy cloth to conceal them.

"They seem to be moving relatively slowly," said Duval. "Perhaps if we catch up with them we'll be able to find some riding beasts to borrow?"

"I am not so sure they'll welcome us," said D'Artagnan. "I am, as you know, not an ignorant man. However it occurs to me we could be about to encounter some kind of witch or warlock, perhaps some master of magic with special power over the natural world, some—"

"Demon conjuror, perhaps?" For all his profound religious convictions, Aramis had a deep contempt for those who believed in magic and wizards and considered his friend, for whom he would have died, to have a drop or two of mediaeval superstitious peasant blood still in his veins.

D'Artagnan was embarrassed. He cared for Aramis's good opinion. "I suppose I should not be surprised. We have already encountered the impossible in some version of Hades, where living rocks behave like men. The desert feels familiar – or at least more familiar than Mu-Ooria. I expected merely heat and risk of dying from thirst. But clearly we are not to find anything even closely resembling the ordinary. Those tracks belong to scores of savage creatures never intended to cohabit, at least not since our Biblical ancestors were expelled from their creator's Garden or Noah built his mighty boat!"

"Miraculous," said Aramis dryly. "It certainly seems that we have entered yet another world of wonders? A Biblical world!"

Porthos grunted, uneasy with this train of thought. "I grow tired of marvels. I prefer wholesome miracles of the vintner's and pastry cook's craft. I'd welcome some of those at this moment. And I think it is quite possible that I could eat a water buffalo."

Athos was amused. "And a barrel of good Rhenish to wash them down, eh?" He ran his tongue over cracked lips. "Maybe two."

The beverage given us by our Mu-Oorian friends was almost gone. We had been well served. We hoped it would last us until we reached the oasis as we had been promised. But Aramis, with so much on his conscience, so many memories, preferred the forgetful properties of wine.

Why was I so familiar with these men's characters? I had, of course, read Dumas as a boy and had written my own Musketeer stories for comics. But I felt I had known the Musketeers all my life. The feeling was a strange one. I had originally enjoyed them in the first film version I had seen as a boy, with Gene Kelly. Since then I had seen pretty much all the versions in English or French, sound and silent, yet these four men were like personal friends. This was especially strange because I had been kidnapped by them on the instructions of the mysterious Captain Marvell. Yet no malign motive seemed involved. The motives of Marvell and others could be idealistic or at least intended to do good. Or their motives were utterly malign and well-disguised.

We fell to following the strange tracks where the wheels and larger animals had stamped the sand down. This gave us greater speed, although we could see from the spoor that we were still a fair distance behind the animals. At one point we came on the remains of a camp. Many of the beasts had lain down around the vehicle and a small cooking fire. One human, sleeping with the animals comforted by a fire. Most of the creatures were not nocturnal. Antara looked at the tracks with profound expertise, reading what I could not. They had, he said, probably taken turns on guard, even sleeping in shifts, he thought patrolling. There was some kind of mutual intelligence guiding this disparate herd. They had been careful to urinate or defecate a distance from where they all slept. They behaved in fact like civilised creatures.

"Extraordinary!" Sheik Antara sat on his heels peering at the remains of the fire, at the faint outlines of a large cat, probably a lioness, where she had slept. "Some of these animals are massive. If this is also a lion, and it seems to be, it is considerably bigger than two others. One could be from the Mesozoic. Others seem smaller than one might expect. House-cats almost. And not only cats." We had no explanation which did not involve unlikely time travel.

He sniffed the air. "That stink. It follows them. It's not spoor. Not just that. More like sweet ozone. It's the smell of unusual power. I have tracked lions in the past, though never this deep into the desert. I am puzzled. Pray our Lord that something enlightens us when we arrive at the Great Oasis and that this strange menagerie awaits us!"

Were the scents which came to Sheik Antara the same? They were not familiar to me at all but they certainly excited my imagination. Strange shrubs and trees. Jasmine? Rhododendron? Baobab? Exotic and glorious. They signalled 'Africa' and Africa was the name of romance and mystery, of heated, musty air, and dark discovery. We had still not quite entered that part of the twentieth century where ignorance and inquisitiveness were replaced by information and respect, with an understanding of the part black slavery had played in destroying many civilisations. The so-called 'Dark Continent' had of course been mapped and settled by successive groups of Europeans. It had been written about by the likes of Stanley, Burton, Lawrence and many others. After them had come the African writers themselves, to inform us further and correct the errors of the explorers and settlers.

For me, Africa was a stimulating mixture of political fact and fiction. It was the Africa of Rider Haggard, who had considered himself something of a native, and Edgar Rice Burroughs, who had never been there. It was about as real as the Red Planet of Mars, with its canals and dusty dead sea bottoms, as Venus, with her steamy jungles, swamps and massive reptiles. The inventions of the likes of Verne, Wells, Cutcliffe Hyne, Conan Doyle and the other late-Victorian/ Edwardian romantics allowed me to escape from the realities of my early disrupted childhood. Those welcome distractions from my dad's desertion and my mother's dramatic narratives, her melancholy singing, her tears and my own baffled failure to understand events, had taken me to John Carter's Mars and Carson Napier's Venus, to Burroughs's various imitators and those inspired by him who wrote 'sword and planet' stories before the coming of the cramped capsules, the flying robots, the great radio-telescopes, increasingly accurate cameras and computers. We had to move to interstellar space to find desert worlds and jungle backgrounds once supplied by mysterious Africa.

The romantic frontiers found in Hollywood's Wild West and the Dark Continent, populated by historical heroes like Buffalo Bill and Tarzan of the Apes, were shifted further and further from our familiar world. But at that moment, just before the Sudan and the North-West Frontier ceased to be the setting for *The Four Feathers* or *Lives of the Bengal Lancers* and became the background for news stories involving our political consciences, it was still possible to be drawn in to a romantic vision of Africa as the setting for innocent – or at least ignorant – adventure. That was what I was smelling, even though I knew the Arab was not. He was smelling experience. And he was a little bewildered by it.

What we could smell in common, however, was the distinctive scent of Africa, of her great deserts and veldts, her enormous mountain ranges, high, fertile plains and jungles. Hot, dry and lush, the continent remained for me, at least, the most romantic of them all. I longed for the Equator. The one place which continued to excite my imagination almost as much as the planets of the Solar System which, in those days we still felt might be habitable, even by creatures somewhat like ourselves.

That evening we camped a little distance on from where the menagerie had spent the night and finished what was left of the supplies the Off-Moo had given us. I could smell the faint mixture of hay and animal waste, reminding me of the Brown family's smallholding in Devon where I had kept my base as a child, sometimes wandering into the village and getting a lift home from the postman.

"Now," said Porthos ruefully as we prepared to settle down for the evening, "we must reach our destination or surely starve to death."

"You must not be concerned for us, dear Porthos." Aramis pinched his old comrade's cheek. "There's enough meat on your huge bones to keep us going for a month."

And, to his grunted protestations, we lay down in the sand and prepared as best we could to sleep.

I looked at the stars, thinking over all those things which had come to mind, enjoying the rich, dark sky and distant sounds whose origin I could not begin to guess. I wondered what lay ahead of us and if Sheik Antara knew more than he was willing to tell.

That morning we began what we hoped would be the last miles of our tramp to the oasis.

D'Artagnan, with his unlimited energy, stumped stoically ahead of us on his stocky legs, his rather bedraggled hat protecting his head, his long waistcoat unbuttoned, blue silk trousers tucked into his old boots, dark green sash flapping about him and into which was stuck a variety of European and Arabian weapons, while his wrapped musket was carried over his shoulder, in common with his fellow cavaliers. He whistled some tuneless Gascon song, slapping his dusty thigh to keep time. He crested a hillock ahead of us and was halfway down when suddenly he stopped. With a degree of uncertainty he removed his rather bedraggled hat and wiped his forehead on his lacy sleeve. Then he peered ahead, shielding his eyes with his palm.

"Mon Dieu!" he cried in a high excited voice, signalling for the rest of us to join him.

"Mon Dieu! Mon Dieu! Enfin!"

"What is it?" I called.

"Mes amies! Mes amies!" He began to perform a kind of jig on the hard-baked sand. *"Nous avons atteint notre destination!"*

19

The Sanctuary of the White Sufis

IN SPITE OF our tiredness, most of us ran with considerable energy down the hardened sand of the track towards the distant oasis! Only Sheik Antara and myself walked rather slowly, he with great dignity and me with a certain weariness. I noticed that wide tracks now began to lead into the oasis from a number of directions. This was evidently a meeting place of all manner of trade roads. I knew of such oases but had not expected ever to be so impressed.

The distinguished Bedouin appeared to be relishing the scene before us! His handsome features became more animated. I had expected to find a conventional oasis, a largish pond surrounded by palm trees with a few tents and some camels tethered nearby. This oasis, however, was worthy of the name 'great'. There was not one pond but a number. Wide, mostly oblong, tanks fed by a series of pools protected by banks of low adobe and stone walls. Palms or shrubs surrounded them. People came and went between them. The tanks were of different depths and functions. Some were for watering animals, some for washing clothes and some for bathing. According to use and the sex of the user, the bathing tanks were walled, fenced or even roofed. All were fed by a series of small freshwater pools which disappeared from view behind relatively high, grassy rocks. There was evidently a large permanent population to service the caravans which came and went in the so-called 'secret' spice roads. Much evidence of human hands at work over many years. We saw an animal market, where goats, sheep, camels, donkeys and horses were energetically traded. They were not the menagerie we had shadowed.

The long tents were of a variety of tribal colours from black to white and with bright scarlets, greens and browns predominating. In some places the palms grew thick with large clusters of dates. Fig trees. Olive trees. Cultivated fields and grassy areas. A fair-sized town climbed the sandy rocks away to the south-west. Everywhere were tethered or gathered in small pastures collections of livestock tended by men, women and children in different forms of traditional dress. Scents ranged from expensive saffron to mint. Dogs ran everywhere. The animals were resting. A few ate the various kinds of fodder. Some scented us, setting up a steady chorus of barks, bleats and moans. With the braying of the donkeys and the whinnying of the horses and the barnyard smell, the place could be a country town on market day.

I saw that our musketeers had already reached the outer tanks and were deep in conversation with a number of men dressed in the white, flowing robes of desert Arabs. Porthos seemed to be remonstrating with them and Duval had come between the big Frenchman and the agitated tribesmen.

By the time we caught up with them, we saw that the pools stretched for some distance to a cluster of two- or three-storey buildings of cool, elegant Islamic appearance, defended by a wall.

"Can I help?" asked the black-eyed soldier-poet as we drew in closer to the arguing men.

"You can tell these fools that we are not giving up our

swords!" D'Artagnan blustered, red-faced. "Why on earth should we do that?"

"And you could tell them that we only require a cup or two of water to quench our thirst. We have gold with which to pay for food and wine!" boomed the exasperated giant.

"Of course." Antara moved between Porthos and the Arab, who wore a red felt djellabah, evidently some kind of uniform of office. The Sheik threw back the hood of his own djellabah, advancing with raised hands towards the Bedouin. Next, he began to speak in low, purring tones which had a certain authority to them, and the Arabs reluctantly bowed, answering him. At first they replied in high, outraged tones, gesturing angrily towards the Frenchmen. They were offended, unwilling to be mollified. Antara was both haughty and calming, apparently a little irritated by their rising voices.

He continued to speak in the same reasoning manner and eventually, little by little, they relaxed, clearly wanting to explain themselves.

Antara turned at last to the fuming musketeers.

"The drinking water is free, but there are protocols to be observed. These men are the official Guardians of the Oasis," explained our guide. "They traditionally determine in what order to serve the water. They are perfectly happy to barter with you or sell you food if you are hungry, but the water is available freely to all who come here. They thought you were threatening with your swords and demanding supplies for nothing. Weapons are unwelcome here and cannot be borne. They must be put into safe-keeping until you leave. The oasis is a sanctuary, used by all and available to people of all persuasions. Civilised debate is welcome. Conflict is forbidden."

Porthos and D'Artagnan insisted they had never intended to start trouble. They had simply been very thirsty. This was translated and all parties began bowing and explaining themselves until Sheik Antara held up an imperious black hand and spoke sharply. They stopped at once. Water was offered with a somewhat forced graciousness and accepted in the same manner. Antara drew a deep breath and the atmosphere became tangibly more peaceful. Men, women and children from ebony Benin in the west to Caucasian Berbers, olive-skinned Egyptians and everyone who had gathered to watch, were dispersing, talking and laughing amongst themselves. Even the various livestock quietly settled down.

Although I was glad to accept water from the cleaned and refreshed cups, I was still chiefly interested in finding the animals and their master whom we had followed for so long across the desert. At the oasis of course all the various tracks had blended. There were no signs of individual tracks or animals any longer. Any spoor was cleaned up by boys employed for the job. So I mustered my manners, suppressed my curiosity, thanked my hosts in imperfect Arabic and drank gratefully from the copper cups.

Recovering from their own thirst, the Musketeers, led by the ever-courteous Aramis, by now understood how they had gone beyond the bounds of good manners. Manners were highly valued in Bedouin society, just as they were in Paris, and we were glad to resume on an improved basis. The Musketeers doffed their bedraggled hats, bowed deeply and went as far to apologise in their elaborate French.

We relished the cool, fresh spring. The water was cleaned by running it through gravel and small weirs into a series of large ponds. The attendants told us that the water flowed from the First Pool. We could see in the distance where the pool was guarded by a white wall, nine or ten feet high, further up the narrow valley. The wall, they said, had been built by spiritual soldiers in ancient times soon after they discovered the spring. They settled after the death of a great Egyptian pharaoh, long before the time of the prophets, before Abraham, Moses, Jesus or Mahomet. The pharaoh had fallen into sin and become a terrible tyrant. The soldiers, led by the king's own sister, who was purity personified, rose up against him. But the pharaoh employed evil djinns sent by the Queen of Sheba. The djinns were forced into the depths of the desert during the struggles. They returned to resist the evil pharaoh more than once until the princess died and they had to flee back to this hidden oasis.

At that time they were not called Sufis. They were just men and women who wished their faith to remain pure and faithful to one vision. Over time they found the truth of the Holy Qur'an but remembered the wisdom of the teachings of those who had heard the Prophet's teachings while he still lived, when Jesus was regarded an important figure, as much as Moses and others. Only later they absorbed Sufism as a framework for their continuing tolerance and understanding. The name meant little to me. I had spent part of my teens studying the gentle Austrian mystic, Rudolf Steiner. I had attended Graham Hall, the boarding school in Sussex which had been exiled from Austria by the Nazis, who loathed Steiner's message of tolerance. I had been impressed by his belief in Goethe's ideas concerning art and spiritual development, so I was in some ways already prepared to hear this.

The Islamic words used back in those days meant very little to me. No more, in fact, than Christian words. Being educated at a Steiner school, of course, meant I had already learned respect for Sufi ideas. Since then I had studied other disciplines and was slowly formulating my own particular philosophy and moral system.

I was deeply moved. The oasis had been founded by an order of warrior monks. They had occupied this site since before the time of the Prophet. The wall was there to protect their sanctuary. It had survived since antiquity in one form

255

or another. "Some say it preceded the Prophet. Founded by Phoenician traders before the Punic wars," Antara told me, pleased, I think, by my interest. "But I doubt it goes back to the time of Ramses as some claim!"

I mentioned the guardians of the oasis and what they had told me. Sheik Antara smiled as we strolled beside the pools. "Whatever those ancient origins, there is little doubt that it was visited and consecrated by the Prophet, Allah bless his holy name. All faiths were studied here, then."

We were walking slowly towards the twin minarets which rose above the wall. Set on the further outskirts of the town proper. Between them was a large domed building. Surrounding buildings all shimmered like marble or alabaster. Antara told me that today this was a very famous medrasa, an Islamic University, mostly maintained by the Persians where all subjects were studied, including science and mathematics, poetry, history and geography, painting, calligraphy, rhetoric, even the culinary arts. He himself had been privileged to study at the Zaouia medrasa.

"It is known variously as the University of the Great Desert or The Great Oasis. It takes students of all religions and all forms of Islam. As a result it attracted the hatred of many different sects of most faiths. It was necessary to make the old roads to it secret and to fortify it further. We have defended it twice very successfully. Except when we are under attack, no weapons can be borne beyond the medrasa's walls. The medrasa has not now been attacked since your tenth century. It remains entirely self-sufficient. A sanctuary for many kinds of outcasts."

As we approached the entrance, a white-robed old man limped out of the open gates. He bowed with dignified politeness and clapped his hands. Two tall, bare-chested Africans appeared behind him. He bowed deeply again and spoke to

Sheik Antara rapidly in Arabic. Antara replied at some length, evidently speaking about us. He handed the old man his long scimitar, and waited while the ancient replied. Antara nodded then turned to us.

"He says that he welcomes you to the Holy Sanctuary of Zaouia at the Great Oasis. As I have already said, you must give him your weapons if you would enjoy our hospitality. So, gentlemen, if you would do as I have done I will be glad to escort you to the medrasa. Our weapons will be returned when we pass back through these gates."

By graciously disarming themselves, the Musketeers and Duval indicated that they had completely recovered their manners. The ancient responded with equal grace in Old French, clearly ushering us through the gates. I understood that we were very welcome to the Great Oasis of Zaouia. I did not, however, understand the rest. It was left to Duval to tell me that the Sufis would greet us in person but were currently at their prayers. Meanwhile he would be sure that the weapons we placed with the neophytes would be returned when we left.

We followed the old man through the impressive gates into the astonishing University of the Great Desert.

I felt at once that I was being admitted into a glorious earthly Paradise. The walls enclosed a very large area of date palms, peach, fig and olive trees shading gardens laid in an order that was both geometrical and organic and divided by a series of pools rippling out from a beautiful central fountain whose cool waters played high into the misted air. People of all ages, wearing *hijabs*, *shalwar kameez* or local djellabahs walked along paths crossing the planted gardens and magnificent pools.

An air of tranquillity suffused the sweet-scented interior. Sandalwood and rosemary. These buildings, typical of the finest Islamic construction, were dominated by the glittering dome of the mosque flanked by two slender alabaster minarets and other equally elegant structures raised in perfect proportions. I was reminded of the great Taj Mahal. I would never expect to find such wonderful architecture in this remote place. The Sahara was so vast that whole countries, covered and uncovered by the shifting sands, could be lost in it. I should not be surprised to find this garden and its buildings at a large oasis, but I still wondered why it was not better known. No doubt it had a lot to do with the wishes of the Sufis themselves. Few Europeans had visited even briefly. I had never seen photographs or films of the place. It was a well-kept secret. Most explorers must believe it to be a myth! Perhaps all the best sanctuaries were that.

The sweetness and colourful variety of the plants, flowers and trees, was heady and hypnotic. The air was rich with insects, thick with the whirring of tiny wings. An abundance of bees flew back and forth to distant hives. I became faintly dizzy as I strolled with my companions along a shaded avenue. The scent, as often happened with me, sparked a host of impressions and memories. The path led towards the tall, glistening mosque and its slender, flanking towers. We followed the old sufi along shady walkways. Men and women greeted us, smiling as we passed them, reminding me of childhood. I became more relaxed, watching the sky and the great dome of the mosque with distant, sandy hills behind turning pink. I remembered an old film I had seen on TV when I was a boy. The lights of the town, the fires, were winking out. I felt so close to paradise. The book by James Hilton had introduced the name Shangri-La to a large public: Frank Capra's *Lost Horizon*, with Robert Donat. That hidden world lay in the Himalayas and was far more fanciful. It reflected our longings, however, much as the Great Oasis did.

That film had certainly increased any sense of loss, of abandonment I had. It no doubt affected many that way, but for me it was personal, again to do with my father's disappearance. Was I somehow reconstructing and compensating for my early childhood? Or was I merely putting a corny psychological gloss on my current bizarre half-dreams?

During my teenage years I had been deeply suspicious of sentimentality. Those suspicions had found an echo in Helena and had brought us together. Because of her mother's widowhood, Helena's own experience of being orphaned and peer pressure at Cambridge encouraged her to remain questioning of others' motives, to associate sentimentality with weakness or threat. She made rather acerbic dismissals of many kinds of romance except perhaps her desire to be the male protagonist of late Victorian adventure stories. Instead, I made her Monica in *Behold the Man*.

What might have seemed strange to others, I often took for granted. For a while I developed the habit of dropping some part of a dream into conversation before realising I was coming in or out of sleep. This led to some bizarre late-night discussion.

While talking about schools, I would say suddenly "—and the parachutes held up well." Sometimes I appeared to use association, particularly with colour and smell, almost as much as I used ordinary speech.

Conversations with myself? I hoped I wasn't mad. What was I actually seeing, let alone saying, in those dreams? Was I sinking into a banal fantasy too crass to pass the blue pencil of the most cynical pulp editor? I fervently hoped I wasn't losing control of my sanity. I was fine, I reasoned, while I kept control of the narrative! How would I do that? Madness was when you started to believe completely banal but unlikely realities. Sentient furniture, for instance. Anything else was hallucination or visionary.

I began to wonder about my state of mind again. Was I becoming less rational but much better at self-deception?

This intriguing train of thought was interrupted by the sudden trumpeting of what could only be a large elephant. Followed by the bellow of a bear. We turned into a path protected by high, green papyrus. The pathway had widened at this point and had benches placed opposite each other in front of the hedges.

A long-faced man at least half a head taller than myself, wearing the kind of stovepipe hat I associated with Lincoln and the middle of Victoria's reign, stood between the two animals, an oversized bear on his right and undersized elephant on his left. Their odd disparity of height was rather disturbing. They appeared to pause as we approached.

Our guide smiled and made a short formal bow. "Forgive us, professor, if we interrupt you. I understood you all to be resting."

"Intended and commonsensical, my dear sir, but not possible I fear." The professor replied with a kindly shake of his head. He removed his high-crowned top hat and produced a huge red-and-white spotted handkerchief from his breast pocket to wipe the sweat from his neck. "A few hours ago we were in some distress. Unsure of our safety. Frightened. We were pursued! Or so we thought. The lost children of all the worlds, you know. We have so much on our minds. Only until a couple of hours ago did we understand someone intended us harm. Possibly. We did not give them the benefit of the doubt. We exerted ourselves in our attempt to reach sanctuary. Safe here! Safe here ... Mmmm?"

The size difference of the animals intrigued me. I wanted to ask him to explain. "I think we were following you in the desert, sir," I said. "We were a few miles immediately behind you."

Duval bowed. "We did not wish to alarm you, sir."

"I believe you need rest, professor," our host asserted quietly.

"Most of us accepted the soporifics you so kindly provided, my dear sir. But young Mr Jumbo here, as well as his close friend Mr Bruno, shared my unwillingness to use artificial means of seeking the arms of Morpheus. We continue our earlier conversation. About Kierkegaard you know. We begin and end with Kierkegaard." His smile was open and what I could only call innocent. His wide-stretched arms indicated many animals who looked amiably on, clearly at ease with human beings. "So we strolled out into this lovely garden to talk a little longer."

"Again, our deep apologies," murmured Sheik Antara. "We found your tracks merely mysterious."

"Aha!" he said. "Well, my dear sir, that's good news, I must say. On our side, what? Not in pursuit! Wonderful sense of relief. Much obliged. So we share a similar goal!"

"I think so, sir." I asked him, "Are you some sort of circus? A travelling menagerie? A show?"

"We find it convenient to travel as one, old boy. Sort of disguise. What? Safety in numbers and so on!" He lowered his long, pink head, regarding me with wide blue eyes, as if in thought. His brows rose and then his candid gaze was quick, enquiring. "You were curious, eh?"

"Exactly, sir," I answered.

The elephant, I thought, was only half-grown and barely the height of the bear, who was larger than most. He stood scratching his chest slightly, perhaps managing to control his impatience. The elephant, I would have sworn, was frowning a little. Both gave the impression of civilised creatures a little anxious to continue an interrupted argument. This, in spite of all our recent adventures, seemed the strangest phenomenon of all! I could not help thinking of my earliest comics, *Rainbow* and *Tiger Tim's Weekly*. The Bruin Boys. They were on the front pages every week: a disparate group of anthropomorphised talking animals who wore human clothes overseen by their teacher and den mother, Mrs Bruin. The best were drawn by Norman Foxwell. These animals were otherwise absolutely real and not, it appeared, dangerous.

"I am Professor Consenseo." His pronounced adam's apple bobbed in his long neck as he removed his hat and with it indicated the animals. "My friends and I are taking advantage of Imam Darnaud's generous hospitality. Most of us are guests in those magnificent stables behind the medrasa. They have a veritable *herd* of thoroughbred horses, yet still found plenty of room to put us up! After all, a Caliph built his stables here so that his rivals could not spy on him. And died, of course, upon coming second in the Empty Quarter races. No Caliph now. What a godsend this place is! I believe I have already introduced Messrs Jumbo and Bruno. Names of convenience, of course. They do not speak English, I fear. Not, as it were, to the naked ear!" And he chuckled a little nervously.

Professor Consenseo wore a well-cut frock coat, loud yellow-check trousers, a waistcoat and high, lace-finished collar and cuffs. His boots were rather sharply pointed. The clothes of a mid-Victorian dandy. His high-crowned top hat reached about eighteen inches above his rather lugubrious head. His chin and nose came to elongated points, his wide blue eyes stared mildly from beneath high, arched brows, fixed in an appearance of almost comical surprise, and his lips, which were long and a little thin, had a permanent and decidedly amiable appearance. Taken together, his features formed an attractive, if slightly comical, appearance. He raised his tall hat and extended a long-fingered hand, shaking first Antara's, then mine, then those of the rest of our party. Meanwhile in his left hand his hat rose and fell with the regularity of an automaton. "I am, my dear sirs, Professor Themus H. Consenseo, late of the Serengeti, where you may find my credentials, assuming the place still exists or has yet come into being." He was apologetic. "Moonbeam roads, et cetera. Bad luck, eh?"

He made a fist and coughed lightly into it. "And then of Fort Astor (where we nearly lost our *skins*, ha, ha, ha). We were all at sea. You understand. All at sea, ha ha ha. Only by luck avoiding a *maelstrom*!" He seemed nervous. "The nature of our situation, dear sirs, is yet to be determined. As a matter of fact, we were just discussing it, Bruno, Jumbo and I. We made some alarming movements through the multiverse. Bit disconcerting. As I'm sure you can imagine. Jumping from one plane to another at great speed. Used to be a time a Sanctuary could help with that. Not so much on this occasion. Desperate times, eh? Disparate, too, what? Ha, ha, ha! And your own situation, might I ask? By the disparity of your costumes and your poor faces, could I venture – and forgive my manners if I err – that our situations are not dissimilar. You are perhaps adrift in the chronosphere? Or possibly *dropping* through it like my friends and I? No?" He studied me for a second as if he hoped we shared some experience.

Chronosphere? Who had said "Time is a field. We determine consequences."? I had always been fascinated by theories of time. The word was completely new to me in spite of having read and written imaginative fiction. I have to admit I would use it later in a song! Time as a sphere? Did that suggest we existed within a kind of cloud where everything happened at once? A speck randomly ticking across a TV screen, creating apparent forward momentum in apparently linear time? Did we somehow choose certain timelines which at intervals intersected with those of others and made it seem as if every particular sequence were fixed? History. Might we be

263

unconsciously choosing our own narratives – our time-paths, if you like – from amongst a number we don't always share? And if we accidentally step off that path do certain things happen to us that wouldn't happen to everyone else on that timeline? I was confusing myself. I planted my feet as firmly on the ground as possible. For a moment I felt I might fly off the planet. And now I had a frightening thought.

Were Helena and the girls carrying along down one track while I walked another? I was trying to understand how I shared my story with a pre-Islamic Arab, some seventeenth-century French soldiers, an English folk-hero, and, from what I could make out, a Victorian animal trainer! Was I as helpless in the chronosphere as an astronaut might be in the spacial sphere? I did not betray myself to my companions. Did this wonderful water garden offer me a map which would enable me to get back on a familiar track? A map of the maze of my own mind!

"We are not entirely *at one* with ourselves, young man – um – Are you, perhaps—?" Another brief, quizzical look. At that moment with those enquiring blue eyes Professor Consenseo reminded me of a gigantic, inquisitive cockatoo.

He paused politely, expecting an answer to his unspoken question.

"Perhaps we are," I replied. "I have to admit I've been a trifle cavalier, as it were, about time in the past. It fascinates me. I've written a little about it. But I can't say I understand it."

"How many of us do, dear sir? How few can, I venture to ask, look Chronos in the eye and say boldly: *I know you, sir. I call you to account!*"

"I don't think, professor ... I'm not sure—"

"Few of us can be certain of anything, sir! I reached this wonderful sanctuary through good fortune. Did you know there is evidence that a city was once built here? A great temple in honour of Atun, the One. Jehovah, some say. The ancient Egyptians, gentlemen! Long before the Abrahamic religions were founded. Isn't that extraordinary? That anything should exist so far from the Nile! We feared for our lives and liberty so often! Of course, once I understood we were in the Sahara, I knew of the legend. I had no choice by then but to look for it. To presume it existed. And then seek it out."

"Then how did you find it, sir?" asked Sheik Antara. "You say you had heard of an Egyptian temple in this vicinity? But had you also heard a legend of an Oasis at Zaouia and sought its safety for yourself and your menagerie?"

"Mena—? Oh, *no*, sir, you misunderstand our relationship. The term's a convenience." He turned to where the undersized elephant and the oversized bear sat patiently on the path behind him as if listening to our conversation. "We are travelling together. No doubt you spotted my wagon and assumed—"

"We've seen no wagon, professor. Only your tracks," I interrupted as gently as I could.

"Of course. Naturally. Oh, no, no, no. It is merely a flag to explain—! Too long. Much too long." He fingered his triangular chin. "Ah, well, ahem. I apologise." Flashing an enigmatic smile. "For some months, since we left London and took ship from Southampton, then found ourselves in America and elsewhere – a frightfully uneven journey, sir, you'll agree – it has suited me to present myself as the proprietor of a travelling menagerie. My friends—" an expansive wave "—pose as the exhibits. But we are far, far, far from such an abomination! Oh, indeed we are. Our minds – perhaps I should say our *mind* – are in harmony, do you see, sir? You'll be familiar with Gaia? They consider the notion madness! We have travelled willy-nilly, my dear sirs, about the world – perhaps I should really say *worlds* – since we left Fort Astor. My adventure began not long after I sought refuge in that part of the City of London once known as the Alsacia. Oh, it has been a long, arduous and I must admit *unlikely* journey, gentlemen. I have already related the most recent part of it. Blackstone, I understand, offers a resolution. Once we reached Alexandria it suited us to pose as a sort of travelling circus, just as, in Amersham, it had been our ruse to pretend to be a small private zoo.

"We boarded the train inland as far as Aswan. Then we went into the desert. Deep into the Sahara, sir. Where unfortunately we became lost in its exceptional vastness.

"Now that we are here and able to reorientate ourselves we dropped the deception. No need for it, of course. We could relax. Be ourselves. Converse as we liked. I have to hope that we are on the last leg of our journey. I am delighted to learn that from here it is not far to the Blackstone Escarpment, relatively speaking, of course. There, perchance, further deception will be unnecessary! We have friends there awaiting our convergence."

"But what do you intend to do with your charges? You are *not* an animal trainer, sir, I take it?" Duval could no longer contain his own curiosity.

"Not at all, sir." Removing his tall hat, Professor Consenseo again drew his large red-and-white spotted handkerchief from his back pocket and mopped his forehead. "Although I *have* taken advantage at times of such presumptions. It is my intention to help my friends return to their various nearby planes in what I choose to term 'the Spectrum of the Spheres'. It is what they have asked of me. It is what Lady Blackstone hopes to help me do. A few drops of my famous Elixir of Energy enable my friends to sustain themselves without recourse to eating flesh or even plants. Thus I travel considerable distances with them."

"You know Lady Blackstone?" Duval perked up a little. "We, too, seek her."

"Unfortunately, sir, I do not know her personally. Some friends of mine, acting as intermediaries, have given me letters of introduction. Through them I was fortunate enough to receive an invitation to her estate."

Duval was disappointed. "So these friends? How did you meet them? Perhaps they are acquainted with the Lady Rose of Las Cascadas?"

"I fear not. My friends are men of the cloth. Rather like those who reside here."

"Men of the cloth?"

"Monks, sir, as I said. Carmelites. They dwell at the very heart of London, that City of Vice. The monks of the Whitefriars Abbey off Fleet Street, well known as the *Street* of Vice. I mentioned I resided for a time in other sanctuaries than this?"

Duval gasped. "Carmelites? Our friend, the Lady Rose, is Abbess of a great Carmelite abbey. And off Fleet Street, I knew some monks, excellent soldiers and very devout. They—" Then he fell silent, chewing on his lower lip. I guessed they were the clerics Duval and the Musketeers had mentioned once or twice earlier in our journey in relation to the villainous Jake Nixer. Had they, too, been intermediaries in our journey to the mysterious Blackstone Escarpment, which the White Abbess had also named? If so, it seemed exceptionally likely that we and this strange showman were in some way connected. For some reason, Duval thought it untimely to mention this. I wondered why. We were, after all, making our way to the same destination. I imagined that we would be safer if we travelled together.

What kind of enormously tangled plot was I caught up in? The size of it was extremely hard to imagine. I felt pressured by it. My mind was under siege. I was not by nature paranoid but sometimes felt I was being deliberately driven mad.

"My dear boy!" Coming from behind Professor Consenseo,

this was pure, unaccented English. Familiar. As if its owner knew me. An Oxbridge don.

Was I growing delusional? I knew the voice. Was this why Duval had said no more about his association with Carmelites? I saw the owner walk confidently between the rather affronted elephant and the somewhat thoughtful bear, then step around the professor.

He was tall, skinny, middle-aged, with bright, pale blue eyes in a pink complexion. His cheeks and eyes were rather sunken, yet he seemed healthy enough as he pushed back his hood to reveal a shock of unruly white hair. Again I was vaguely aware of having met him before. Perhaps in the Fleet Street area? Had he tried to sell me a story when I worked on *Tarzan Adventures*? All kinds of would-be writers turned up at the office which was entered almost directly from the street. Some were hacks 'Sammy' Samuels had met in the pub the previous evening. He bumped into them in the ABC Teashop where he invariably took his afternoon toast. They were mostly sporting journalists without a clue about our content.

This elderly gentleman wore a simple monk's cassock over his emaciated body which was slightly bent, as if he had the beginning signs of scoliosis. Yet he was lively enough as he reached feathery fingers to take me by my hands and greet me like an old friend.

"My dear, dear boy. So you survived the ice! Brother Bertrand assured me you would, but I feared that awful man with his obscene gun had shot you. It has been so long. So long!" He looked beyond me to Duval and the Musketeers. "And your friends! The good lord be blessed. The last we saw of you all in the darkness was the black river swallowing you. Great slabs of ice rearing up in the sleety night. We were alarmed because you appeared to be drowning!" He turned to the nearest of my companions. "Tell me, Monsieur Duval, were the others also saved? Your good friends?"

Claude Duval bowed, reverentially removing his hat. "Not all, Brother Isidore." He smiled softly.

Was I the only person there who didn't remember everyone else? But then I saw Professor Consenseo and Sheik Antara looking as baffled as I felt.

The old sufi who had greeted us at the gate was not particularly surprised but didn't seem to know us all. "How happy a meeting is this!" he exclaimed. "I know how you have spoken so affectionately of the friends you were forced to leave behind in London, dear Brother Isidore!"

Duval cleared his throat. "You do not remember the Alsacia, of course, Master Moorcock! They speak well of you. Nor the glamorous Moll Moonlight, Captain Turpin, Sixteen String Jack and our other comrades of the old Steel Toby! You were never there. Not yet, any rate. You dart about so." To me, his smile was not affectionate.

"Not that," I said, "nor them. Nor anyone else. They remind me of something, but not real life! Maybe a dream." I had written a few Dick Turpin adventures, but my stories were all set in London.

The aristocratic highwayman grew hearty. "We're all dreamers here, my lad!" He took me by the arm. He led me past Professor Consenseo, between the still-wondering Jumbo and Bruno and towards the gates of the great medrasa. On the far side of the fountain near a number of wheeled flatbeds stood a heavy wagon, gaudily painted in red, white and gold. Obviously it was one we had followed. The outer canvas was stretched over its big ribs. The banner bore the slogan in vivid scarlet and green, THE GREAT PROFESSOR THEMUS H. CONSENSEO & HIS EXTRAORDINARY TRAVELLING MENAGERIE and went on to list, in gold and black, the various royal and republican heads of state who had all given the show their patronage.

Around the professor's gaudy wagon stood, sat or reclined a miscellaneous group including lions, leopards, pachyderms, a rhino, a huge wolf, a sloth and two half-grown brown gibbons. All were at peace. A number were apparently talking to one another. Several, like the elephant and the bear, were of evidently unusual sizes. A massive and very grateful hippopotamus was sprayed gently by a small woolly mammoth taking water in her trunk from the pool. Nearby a rhinoceros, also gigantic, lay in the shade of a palm, for all the world relaxing in communication with a tiny giraffe. I had the impression that realistic toys of disparate sizes had come to life. Another childhood fantasy. Professor Consenseo was Noah! The Bruin Boys from *The Rainbow* had also inserted themselves into my waking dream. These, however, did not wear human clothes and also managed to maintain their true animal appearance. I began to wonder about *The Island of Doctor Moreau*, H.G. Wells's terrifying tale of animals turned into a semblance of human beings.

"I think our White Sufi friends are preparing supper for this occasion." Cheerfully the professor rubbed his hands in anticipation. "Having lived on the equivalent of cold vegetable soup and groats for many weeks, I look forward to joining you this evening. They have promised a meal following some planned event. I hear our hosts cultivate the culinary disciplines amongst many others. Until then, however, I must see to my friends' comforts. Many are in distress. Most prefer to dine in the open."

With a tip of his tall hat, Professor Consenseo, with Jumbo and Bruno moving at a dignified pace, took another path between the rippling water of the pools and headed towards his wagon. Professor Consenseo raised his hand in friendly greeting to a couple of massive Everglades alligators who lifted ancient snouts from the water to stare with reptilian eyes. I would have sworn they were actually benign.

The next moment a door in the wagon's rear swung open. A large manlike creature descended the steps to the pathway. When the professor approached it, the creature spoke to him, flinging its long furry arm around his shoulders. The stance of the beast was casually human, with none of the characteristics usually associated with trained gorillas. If it had not been for his size and proportions, I would have sworn I was looking at a man in costume, not a silverback larger than Guy the Gorilla whom I often visited at London Zoo when I simply stood in front of his cage and maintained a rapport with him. I also had a similar relationship, as I saw it, with a leopard who had her own cage outside the Large Cat House and would always begin to purr when I approached her.

I remained suspicious of the Englishman's explanations and propositions. I tended to believe in close harmony between humans and other creatures. I even thought it might exist between all conscious things, with or without brains.

This 'cosmic consciousness' was one of the tenets of Rudolf Steiner's belief-system, which he called by the unwieldy name of 'anthroposophy' and which was a step too far for me. Back in those days he had lost me when he suggested that all creatures, including plants, were part of the Gaia model, that is, the entire planet was essentially one conscious being. SF writers rarely believe wholly in their speculative ideas. That way madness lies. While I had used the notion fancifully in a couple of short stories, I had never seriously believed it, any more than I believed that 'the multiverse' actually existed. Only as I grew older and theoretical physicists produced increasingly convincing mathematics did I develop a tendency to believe in that concept and propose my own ideas based on various theories and their evidence.

I turned to ask one of my friends if they had seen what I had seen. At that moment Claude Duval stepped forward and greeted the old man with considerable enthusiasm. "So you reached the Great Oasis, Brother Isidore! And what of the others?"

The monk beamed. "Some stayed in Amsterdam. Others took ship for America. The rest travelled on and are together here."

"The Abbot? Your 'Treasure'?"

"All safe."

"And Captain Marvell?"

"Yes, yes, I think. I believe he received a pardon from the king. You, too!

"The Father Abbot will be glad to know you have arrived. We feared you had been taken when you did not reach the Low Countries. Soon after we escaped from the Flete Street Abbey." Brother Isidore spoke rapidly with the vigour of a much younger man. "The Abbot is in good health. His wound was not, after all, serious. Our journey from Paris had its dangers, but he survived them. Our Treasure, Rabbi Elias, rarely leaves his apartment, these days. He is frail. He continues his guardianship of our 'Fish Chalice'. He is safe thanks to your considerable courage, as are his coreligionists. Most chose to come here, having too many enemies elsewhere."

Though tiring, the monk continued.

"We Carmelites of Whitefriars are not wholly safe from that ferocious Master Nixer and his ill-advised followers. They claim to share our religion yet show no real enthusiasm for our prophet's teachings. We learned that he pursues us still, but it seems he has yet to discover our current whereabouts. Should he do so, I suspect we are already much safer now you and your fellow soldiers have arrived." Again he beamed like the sun and opened his arms as if to embrace us all. "So here you are! Here you are at long last! Welcome, dear friends, into the Medrasa of Zaouia!"

With a sweeping gesture the amiable friar ushered us into that wonderful building.

THE INTERTWINING PATHS

IN THE SANCTUARY of the Great Oasis at Zaouia, beneath a lattice of moonbeam roads, paths cross and recross. Stories are told and retold. People change without and within. Invisible curtains lie between one universe and another. These supernatural curtains are strung like beads, sewn like tapestries. They carry millions of narratives. There I found one reality and lost another.

I had never consciously sought a sanctuary, never known I needed one. Yet here I was, carried by a combination of narratives, of dreams and realities, desires and events. I had never looked for change or revelation. I never yearned for any other life than the life I enjoyed with my family; yet here I was, incapable of recognising those who recognised me. I had no real idea *where* I was in terms of geography. No sense of *why* I was here.

Who could I ask for help? I seemed to be the only outsider. Who was the Christian monk who knew me well? He referred to events I did not even remotely recall. Of course I knew Fleet Street. I knew Carmelite Street and all the places named for the old Whitefriars abbey. It once gave shelter to society's refugees and became Alsacia, a thieves' quarter. Even the Bow Street Runners dared not attack. Who these particular monks and sufis were, I had no idea. They, like Duval and the Musketeers, knew me, but I was unacquainted with them. Only Sheik Antara and Professor Consenseo did not seem to have known me somewhere before.

273

Had Time, like some tsunami, swept up some of us and left others behind? I found it so hard to think about. No map. No mathematics. I found it hard to work out in my head. While I had loved to do algebra – symbolic reasoning – up to the age of eight or so, I had not studied it since I left Graham Hall. I went on to become a pupil at the more conventional Belmont Preparatory which, I was to learn from my friend Brian Alford, who went to Norbury Manor state school, taught fewer subjects than the general curriculum. My mother had the idea that I would do better in the smaller classes of a private school. I learned French instead of Spanish and German and I was never taught algebra again.

To a degree my essential situation had not changed, I still had to create my own means of understanding this world, fit it into the moral sphere which allowed me to act quickly in most situations without reliance on anyone but myself. My memory was wretchedly unsynchronised with everyone else's. I could barely make sense of it on a day-to-day level. At that moment instability was everywhere. I no longer felt as if I were dreaming. Rather, that I was out of control.

Usually I thought I could in some way *take* control. I had grown up with enormous self-confidence. However difficult events became, I usually had a means of grasping the reins, as it were, and steering in a direction which suited me.

Now, however, I could not be sure of my next step. The ground could disappear in front of me. I could not trust whatever internal gyroscope usually kept me in balance. I wanted to pause, to stop the story, to insist to my companions that we regroup. But I couldn't. For the first time since I had met Captain Marvell on the canal towpath, I believed that *nobody* knew the story, *nobody* had the secret and that not a single one of us was in control of anything! I, however, seemed to be the only one who cared.

The medrasa was beautiful. I admired the white, blue and gold marble pillars and the subtle clarity of its geometric designs, the inspirational beauty of its calligraphy. I decided to stop worrying. What did it matter who or what the professor was, why his animals seemed to be of disparate sizes or from different periods. I was adrift. To preserve my sanity I must remain relaxed. I must let the old sufi and the monk lead me. The gates closed behind us. I must bide my time until someone explained to me what was going on. I was worn out. I was not quite as fit as I thought.

I was taken to a plain, functional room and was told it was mine. There I bathed. Then I joined the others for a meal. I did not take part in the general, mostly casual, conversation. When I had eaten, a young monk led me back to my cell. There I lay down and slept, not caring if I knew any more or less of my situation when I woke up.

Not caring if I woke up at all.

It was as if I fell asleep within a dream. Sometimes I recalled the future and predicted the past.

I dreamed I continued to go deeper into the Sanctuary of the Great Oasis. Conscious but unconscious. Alive, yet not alive. I had no business here. I was a mistake, an unwanted, unneeded passenger. The universe was nothing but blind, black stars without interest or a plan, behaving according to an unconscious order and that alone. Time was a traitor imposing false order upon existence.

In my early Elric stories my hero was influenced as much by Camus as de Camp. We were helplessly caught up in an absurd and uncaring Chaos, thrown this way and that by the tides of chance in an unconscious universe. Steiner's ideas were attractive. But I had no proof, no evidence of his spiritual reality. Currently, a different cold and unsentimental logic guided me, but I had not desired or demanded it. I was obedient. I had no wish to challenge the thoughts which came to me. I belonged to some greater intelligence and knew I belonged to it whether I lived or died. I was at its mercy and it was merciless.

I slept long and I slept profoundly and I was simultaneously profoundly awake. Nothing cared if I survived or was extinguished. I was absolutely without value or meaning. I was every element of the multiverse. I was nothing. I was everything the multiverse wished to become. My past was without purpose. My present and future had collapsed. I had cleared my mind. I had dispensed with a soul. Soon I would dispense with consciousness entirely.

Yet there was a pulse, an ever-present pulse. A slow, constant heartbeat that could never be silenced. It presented me with an attractive alternative. Spiritually I identified it as our creator, our ever-present mother who loved us, loved for ever, cared for ever. Our environment, our beautiful multiversal ma, whose tender arms touched my skin with such respectful delicacy. Never threatening, always protecting. She who was threatened yet did not need defending. She who loved us yet did not need our loving. Who might suffer unbearable pain, yet offered consolation. Who could not be consoled, yet longed for consolation. Oh, how I yearned for our forlorn mother. Our lost and stolen dam. That strange, unearthly name, that resonance, that large, unlikely soul.

Our Spammer. Our all-merciful. Our merciless, our mother and Ourselves. Our own. Our dying cause. Our own dear Spammer Gain.

I struggled to rediscover my ordinary humanity. I had no wish to lose it. Losing it meant I would lose all I had ever valued: My children. Helena. My mother. All Dr J. had meant to me in the absence of a father. He had gone in and out of Berlin and Vienna in the '30s 'buying' Jews from the Nazis, helping people escape across the Pyrenees into Spain and on to

Portugal. He had taken terrible risks for the lives of people he did not know. He had taught me the value of individual life, the importance of empathy. How one life reflected the lives of all. A scientist, he had turned to business at the outbreak of war. He had been a model to me. I learned to be human and how to be compassionate. How to engage and how to step away. When to speak and when to be silent. When to struggle with an idea and when to leave it alone. Now I believed I should, at least for the moment, leave it alone. But Time was rarely a reliable ally.

Indeed, Time was flooding past at an alarming rate! I struggled to remember how things mattered. Then some utterly inconsequential thought would fill my head. Bags of blood. Flannel bags filled with blood. Pillows full of flower petals burst under my head. Their scent quieted my lungs. I had no idea why such a contradictory atmosphere hung over the place like a miasma. Were there perhaps other times I should have taken action? Words, of course, can be actions, especially if they become actions or lead to actions. Few shields deflect malice.

Another bath, another meal. We were not drugged. Our conversations were coherent but brief, for we still ached from our travels. We were indescribably weary. Again, a monk returned me to my cell, telling me that the 'Eldest', Imam Darnaud, invited us all to a séance with him later that evening before dinner. Was the 'Eldest' actually the leading Sufi? Or was it Sheik Antara? Darnaud was a familiar name. I tried to recall where I had heard it before. I hardly knew what Sufism was. Something to do, in its extremes, with whirling dervishes? A mystical Persian branch of Islam which accepted Judaism and Christianity? Even Buddhism? I supposed I would learn more here. There were said to be sites the wind sometimes uncovered, revealing evidence of civilisations older and more sophisticated than Egypt.

I had no issues with my instructions, though my tendency was to go straight to sleep and confront our hosts the next morning, if 'morning' any longer meant anything. But that would not be good manners. I knew how much manners mattered to Arabs. I had to remain awake and alert in spite of whatever was affecting me! Some two days' sleep or so seemed adequate, even excessive for a young, athletic man like me.

Again I decided to get an hour or two's rest until suppertime. I lay down on the prepared sleeping dais and tried to relax, thinking over what had happened since we arrived. Two extreme forces continued to struggle for control of my psyche. My sense of time was under attack, I remembered the future quite as readily as I recalled the past.

I had also become unusually self-conscious and self-doubting. Perhaps that was a good thing. I had never considered myself a superior intellect. Now I feared l might be like H.G. Wells. Someone described him as 'having a mind as wide as the Atlantic Ocean – and one inch deep'. I didn't really believe that to be true of Wells, though I regretted that he came to trust his mind above his imagination or his social observation. There is a gulf, for instance, between *The Time Machine* and *Men Like Gods*. In one, writing quickly for a magazine editor, he was inspired by a vivid vision of the end of the earth. He devised a reasoned method of travelling through time and the effects of entropy. In the other he featured long discussions about Utopia, its possibilities and practicalities. These discussions filled a book four times longer than his first and almost entirely swamped his vision of a multiverse, though he did not call it that. His inspiration became increasingly intellectual and his characters ciphers.

I hoped my intellectual ideas never swamped my vision. I thought my characters lived. Like many novelists, I could assume and discard identities almost at will. Helena was fond of telling me how I would wake up one morning and not know who I was, and she would refuse to tell me. I could manipulate and could be manipulated. Morally I did all I could not to be manipulative. I hoped that others felt the same moral compunction to step back, not to interfere even subtly. I sometimes wondered: What did I hide beneath that first and second layer of skin? There are depths and there are depths, there are layers and there are layers, the sea is deep and the sea is not deep, waters rise and fall. All is comparative. Some things we know by instinct, some by reason, others we never know or refuse to know or are too afraid to know. Sometimes we deny knowing the most profound things we ever learned. Who can we trust to tell us the truth? Not ourselves, surely?

I soon lost track of time in my windowless cell. I recalled my mountain-climbing trip with Dave Harvey a year or two before I met Helena. Summer and we were well within the Arctic circle. The sun remained above the horizon. Without a watch, I was astonished by the speed at which I became confused. Within very few hours I no longer knew if it was morning or afternoon.

I woke up in the sweet-smelling cell. I was completely refreshed. Most of my doubts had disappeared. I was no longer confused. I think the peace of the medrasa had influenced me and I was calmer than I had been since this adventure began. When a young sufi monk knocked gently at my door, I cheerfully agreed when he asked me if I would be good enough to come with him. We were to meet the Imam Darnaud. The High and Eldest Sufi.

I dressed myself in the mixture of fresh linen laid out for me while I slept, and followed him along a short passage to the great garden, whose walkways crossed and recrossed the sparkling pools fed by the many-tiered fountains, shaded by palms and cedars. The big wagon had disappeared together with the animals, but I saw the strange Englishman with the odd Italian name. His hat rose high above the general level of the crowd. He had a more determined gait than usual. We had slept long and well. All the people I knew here were walking towards the tower on the eastern side of the medrasa. I joined Duval and D'Artagnan, just behind Athos and Porthos. Legs rising and falling like a puppet's, the tall, gangling Professor Consenseo was talking earnestly to a courteous Aramis, craning his head up to hear. The mysterious Sheik Antara had just disappeared into the tower's entrance in conversation with a youngish man in a dark robe and hood.

The youth guiding me bowed and left. Just behind my friends I entered the cool shadows of a high-roofed anteroom. From there we continued along a narrow passage. Eventually we reached a door which the hooded man pushed open, revealing a dazzle of stars of a thousand sizes, shining with a million colours, moving in and out of time, disappearing, reappearing, circulating, rising, falling, all of them sounding like all the music of all the world. Flaring, dying down, moving in dozens of impossible directions the spheres spun in their orbits. The only unmoving things were a large round table of mahogany inset with all the rare woods of the world. It might have been Arthur's once. Many Western-style chairs were set around it, not one alike, as if they had been gathered especially for European guests. Another orrery! In modern French, the hooded man told us to sit. There were chairs for all and some to spare. I hesitated before choosing a plain, high-backed pine Windsor, between our host and Athos.

"I expected more guests." Our host threw back his hood, spreading his arms. "I await the Eldest Rose, that last survivor of the Universe of Roses, whom some name the White Abbess. I planned to make introductions, for there are things she can tell you which I cannot. I will therefore prepare this séance without her. I am Darnaud, Sheik of this Medrasa. I am known as the Eldest Sufi or the Black Abbot. I have lived through your time since this place fell. This is not my only incarnation. I have lived through your time since this place was built. On what was then *the only known fulcrum*." His eyes crinkled. He noted my surprise. "Before all the others were discovered or made. That is the linear course of our mutual years." He paused as if fascinated by the spinning worlds quite as much as we were. "This is where the greatest jugador who lived. Who lives and will live. Jack Karaquazian. You would expect them to call him something else. Nonetheless he is known everywhere as El Misrani, the jugador, one of four masters who play the Game of Time."

Sheik Antara said, "Then we are both old, Imam Darnaud. But I was always of the desert and you were not. You are from the West and have experience of the world which I lack. Tell us what the fulcra are."

Darnaud nodded. He was prepared for the question. "The fulcra pass like a great rod through the multiversal planes," he began. "Both separating and uniting them. The planes are all the worlds known to exist. And all those *thought* to exist. They are divided by mass and size. They are either too big or too small for us to see, too dense or too opaque for us to discover with anything but specialised instruments. Almost unnoticeably they change so little from one plane to another that we can measure the difference only by size and mass. Movement between the planes can alter our bodies. It takes millions of transitions to affect any observable change."

Athos made to ask a question, but the Sheik silenced him. "Because you achieve a legendary state in so many cultures and across so many worlds you are among the few able to move between these scales – or planes – some at will. Some even unwillingly! Most of you who gather at this place travel

281

against your will, but all of you know, at least a little, how to travel between the planes. Some consciously, most by instinct. Some can follow linear time. Some are unable to do so but are moved apparently at random by the tides of chance. Time is a series of different waves. Perhaps within a field. I should say that time can often be a wave. It is more than that also, for every dimension has dimensions in the near-infinity of existence. Every wave suggests the presence of other waves. Few things are unaffected."

"Forgive me sir, if I find you hard to follow," Claude Duval frowned.

"If I make no sense to you it is because here I can offer no true comparison. Nought makes sense compared to nought." Now that I saw his gaunt, handsome face better I realised the speaker was probably European. His French was as fluent as any educated Parisian. "If you do not follow me it does not matter. I have followed many of time's directions. I owe it to you, as our guests, to identify myself.

"Welcome to the hall of the Great. My name is Emil-François Darnaud. My father was an army officer serving France. My mother came from the low countries from the city of Ghent. It had been my ambition to become a civil servant in the French Foreign Service. My love of action as a youth meant I did badly in the examinations. So I joined the French Navy. I was shipwrecked on the West African coast. Falling in love with Africa, I joined the Belgian Army, believing I could bring the benefits of my culture to the people of the jungle, but of course I was horribly deluded. I became an officer of the Afrikan Korps in the Belgian army. I was naïve and had no notion of the obscene Belgian record in Africa. I left the Korps ultimately in disgrace because of my conflict with the authorities. I was accused of insubordination. I was dishonourably discharged and served a year in a military prison.

282

"After being incarcerated in Belgium I went to France. For a while I lived a dissolute life. Extremist politics offered the only answer, yet I could not make war on the innocent. Eventually I served as a lieutenant in the French Foreign Legion. My job was to get rid of the Arab slave trade. Brutal but worth doing. During that period it was my privilege to meet and to be of service to the Blackstones. I am today a close friend of Lord and Lady Blackstone whom I still serve. We are among the weavers of your stories." He smiled, seeing that I did not quite follow him. "I returned to France and served eventually in *L'Armée de l'Air*. I discovered this medrasa a long time or a relatively short time ago. From the air. It was some while before I was able to come again. We create the narratives holding together the fabric of existence. Upon those narratives all life depends. I expect you to understand this without explanation. If you need explanation, you should not be here. Our order hopes to map the multiverse. This orrery is a simplified representation. For the moment, I am its guardian."

I was half-mesmerised by the moving jewels, by the intense clouds, some multicoloured, some of deep blackness. White, shimmering rods of light sprang from globe to globe. I heard him speak, even understood most of what he said, and without doubt accepted the rest.

"I have a number of names," our host continued. "Some you have doubtless heard. Imagine me as the man I was when I first found this sanctuary. A simple soldier in the service of a man I now know to be a brute, a cynical and greedy king, Leopold of Belgium, who quite literally bled the wealth out of Central Africa."

I am surprised I remember so much of this.

"We are all here to do some form of penance," he said.

I remained fascinated by the orrery. It was an extraordinarily complex one. I considered everything from the beginning of my life to the end. From the end to the present. From the present to the beginning. I trod the moonbeam roads. Back and forth clicks the shuttle of time, weaving the present into the past and future, remembering, predicting, wondering. And I think of Boudicca. Queen's Cross to King's Pawn. Knight into Daylight. Rook into messaging pawn. The dreams of tomorrow. The discomforts of today. The shuttle clicks and clacks, front to back, weft to woof, floor to roof, all the containments of my life, all the continuities and contentments, all the realities and disappointments, all the weaknesses and strife. The shuttle breathes and moves the threads of our stories into a single tapestry. One complex yarn. Fears and reassurances. Feel the smoothness of the texture! The text, the truth. Dissects and heals. The woof and web. So they meld. So they mend. So they melt and bleed and blend. And memory predicts, created in our dreams and mystic lends trivia the depth of legend.

And as I listened pictures and sounds formed, somehow illustrating Darnaud's comments.

And so we live and lie. We bleed and sigh. We writhe and cry. Our torture never ends.

Comply with me. Come die with me. And cry with me and get high with me so that we experience at last the yearning soul of another in all its death, its nauseated breathing, its pain, over and over and over again. How and why can time imprison us all so greedily? This is how we are kept in the dark. How are we? Kept in the dark. Trying to tell the story even as it ends for us. Still urgent. Still incoherent. The sun runs down our corked hats and kills all that's cool until we melt into significance and become the narrative, glimpsing and glancing the truth below the story, the history beneath the heat of unmannered truth.

We do not fall out of love with those we really love. I could never hate Helena, but I could walk away, stop being the cause of whatever problems they accused me of creating. If there is no negotiation, no acceptance of mutual rights and wrongs, why, then, it is important for the one who has, they say, made all the trouble to step back and cease causing trouble. I did it with Helena and took up with Jenny, and when both Helena and Jenny decided I was still a trouble-maker, I left them both and took up with Lou. For many years now Lou and I have had our ups and downs, but she has yet to say I'm the cause of all her problems.

"My grandma was a vindictive woman," said Helena, "and I am exactly like her." But Helena was brighter and less certain than her grandmother. She became a godmother of guilt, a mistress of melodrama even greater than my mother. Her hands-knees-bucket-and-mop act whenever one of my publishers came to see us was a masterpiece of modern theatre. She could make a damp lock of hair fall over her face and brushing it back with a forearm tell a thousand tales of put-upon womanhood. The kitchen-sink melodrama was learned from the best Osborne and the Royal Court had to give. *Look Back in Anger* was actually preceded by a dozen b&w British films, including *Woman in a Dressing Gown*, to show the true and well-trained passive-aggressive just how to pull it off. It's almost a dead art in Britain and America. "That's all right, darling. We'll soldier on." Got 'em every time. Worked on sons just as well as on husbands. But after my mother's Oscar-worthy performances, it wouldn't work on me. Helena, of course, had learned it from her mother, whose husband had died young. My mother had taught herself after my dad ran off. They had a great deal in common. Jenny was outmatched by them all. She only had a nasty little father to deal with. A living one at that.

Unmannered truth. The lies. The ruthlessness of the story rolling on and begging for surcease below. Reaching helplessly for honesty and revelation. For any scrap of understanding, any frame of reason, any pretence of confident understudying. Please, please, please don't make us cry.

The brave pilots fall from the sky. The brave planes slash the softening darkness of the sky.

What do we lack? Are we brutes, unlearned and unbled? Where are our angels now?

Stretched upon the hardening sky we raise our prayers to unhealing truth.

What is our truth but the tales we tell? The storeys in the House of Resolution.

The storeys in the sturdy House of Finality.

The stories in the Houses of Constant Revolution. Of constant evolution. Behind or before? Where are our peaceful hours of consolation? The balanced Gates of Eden? In timeless Eden all minds that ever were enjoin.

Where are the Gates of Eden where all is peace, contentment, contained in loving resolution? In Eden where love is made and there is no punishment, no consequence, no moment, no glorious revolution. For Eden cannot be made to match our slight, impoverished souls? We are Untasked, we fall away like dying leaves.

In this unfamiliar state, I experience the glory of the Fulcrum.

20

At the Fulcrum

I FIND IT difficult to describe the extraordinary complexity of their 'Master Orrery' and the emotion it inspired.

While I watched in fascination, that machine showed me galaxy upon galaxy and what I now know to be dark matter, dark energy and black holes and then made a mighty turn. A living map of worlds and stars more complex than any planetarium, it displayed the multiverse in all its richness. It opened secrets our human eyes and devices cannot show. I felt I had known it for ever. All the dreams and visions I ever had came together with every drug hallucination, everything I would ever imagine. Every piece of music or poetry or prose or play that had ever stimulated me combined in an epiphany, my first vision of the multiverse.

I still don't know if I imagined it from the stories I had written or if I somehow remembered it. Time and space raced in all directions! Had my vision created the orrery? And there was music. I could not place the composer or the instruments but the nearest I identified was Messiaen and the *Ondes Martenot*. I also heard Mozart, Schumann, Chopin, Liszt, Adler, Ives, Reich, Schoenberg, Alkan, Richard Strauss, Brahms, Beethoven and many others, some of whom I could not identify. And sometimes I thought I saw great paintings, sculptures, drawings, all coming and going, being made before my eyes from nothing. As if they were created randomly from the stuff of Chaos.

My companion appeared aware of my confusion.

"Every fulcrum is a sanctuary and every sanctuary a fulcrum upon which and through which the multiverse is balanced, growing and contracting constantly, in a profusion of scales, of mass, of dimensions; a shaft, if you like, driven like a diamond lance through the planes. To make an axis around which fresh worlds spin. Fulcra upon fulcra. Axis into axis. Creation creates creation, on and on, through all existence. All for one, mon ami, and one for all! Spinning and whirling until the end of time. Eh?"

Imam Darnaud threw back his hood and revealed a small but handsome head with long silver hair, a white pointed beard, a sweeping military moustache. His dark eyes were deep, lustrous and oddly humorous.

"I was instrumental, with the help of my great friend, Lord Blackstone, in wiping out, in one area of the country at least, that despicable trade in human life. When that was done I sought the tranquillity of this sanctuary, which I had discovered earlier at a time when I was badly wounded, abandoned by some whom I had believed to be my friends." Darnaud paused to look through the shifting shadows of the mighty orrery which still made patterns all around us, constantly moving in time to that extraordinary living atlas.

"I was called 'Captain' in the Legion, but now I call myself 'Sheik' or 'Imam'. By the appointment of my peers, I became leader of this particular monastery. I have lived here for many years, both forward and backward in time, and understand our mysteries. Some still call me Captain Darnaud. On occasions, if slavers decide to use one of the roads which run through this oasis, I still make it my business to capture the slavers and dissuade any who seek to emulate them." He smiled. "As a

288

former soldier I suppose I still enjoy the exercise, as do those who once followed me from that profession. During the first great war, when I returned to serve my country in *L'Armée de l'Air*, I gained, I must say, a great love of flying. It is a matter of pride to me that I am an experienced fighting man yet have chosen the ways of peace. Indeed, I have become deeply suspicious of those who choose conflict over negotiation. My brothers of this medrasa are skilled in the arts of self-defence. I will admit that occasionally we still hear of slavers elsewhere in the area and deal with them."

This time Darnaud chuckled. "Every so often we enjoy the chance to exercise our sword arms."

The multiverse continued to swirl around us, albeit in representation, and our companions sat, as no doubt I sat most of the time, hypnotised by the glorious subtlety, the sweet amazement of it all. I thought of the finest and rarest works of art. It seemed that rare pieces of art emerged from the general chaos, until Alkan's wonderful compositions, so few of which survive, could be heard in all their beauty, and I could read Meredith's prose and study Roychowdhury's painting and Paolozzi's early sculptures all at once and suffocate from beauty.

So myth is gone and heroes go.
The summer rain and spring's unhurdled now.
Sipped as if we had a choice.
As if we owned a voice.
As if we'd heard a promise made.
And that it was securely kept.

Father faded. Another's made from the dust of memory: A pair of polished patterned brogues in which we dance to different tunes, a lie, a book, a box or two of cards and paints, a colour we recall as if it were prediction, a story rescued from a dying fire. My poor weak mother finds her strength in the rags of lost desire. She looks to me for comfort, a certain promise, a definite take, a narrative breathed into the clay, the cracking clay of false desire, the memory of a promise kept.

A promise made.

A promise played, perhaps a little crude.

A promise kept.

A promise kept within the sphere of memory. Which is no memory at all but another story which one day comes true.

The materials we use are not the sturdy clay of Eden whatever we are told or learn by reading.

What can we learn from passing lies?

The passing lies which fly from the Gates of Eden. This is all we've left to feed on. We learn to sip the wine of Eden. The flowing wine of loss and grieving.

The feel of a gloved yet comforting hand.

The smell of spice and burning fuel.

The pain of fire. Of bringing fire home again.

Swiftly the sword is carried, raised, presented.

And the child is sliced in two.

One half goes to father and the mother takes the other.

Then, forever after. The child strives to reunite the several parts. And resurrect forgotten Eden.

We watch the spheres, the clouds, the colours and the shafts of brass and silver passing between them. Tiny figures come and go like acrobats walking on wires, walking between the worlds. And surrounded by all this we sit and watch waiting for a tale, some new story which the great Sheik Antara will tell us of his shipwreck and his journey into the gloriously stratified heart of darkness. The black cannibals tell him of burnoosed raiders he and his men will have to kill. I hear the many stories told in the pitiless jungles of the west. There men and women seek revenge or ease from the spite and jealousy and frustration in their loins. When there is nothing else to do but dream and dream and wait. Should we wait or shall we dream? We read the moonbeam roads between one narrative and the next. The gleaming roads give our lives shape, which give our lies their shape. Back and forth we go, never still and always awake, dreaming of escape and no escape waits. Because in the end there is only death. Only death and lies and the long fall down through shining clouds and whirling globes into the dark stuff from which we shape our dreams.

"I had hoped we would all be here today," says the great Sufi, who takes the best from every belief; from China, out of India and from before the sons of Abraham carried one god from an Egypt still ruled by the Sun.

"We must gather here at the fulcrum tomorrow and hope by then all have arrived. She comes, I know. She comes. I know because I can hear her in the desert. A breeze births the hurricane. Then all can leave for Eden. This is how you negotiate the road through the gate ..."

Between the stalls — eights and fours — avoiding the whores — fours and eights — the clouds roll black the raven caws — flapping canvas, eights and fours — threes and nines — dodging the law — the Fool, three staffs — the smell of ice — chestnuts and hot wine — kings and knaves — the Ace of Spades — scales and spears from the buccaneers — twelves and four for the scales of law — twos and eights don't hesitate to the nine of Fate don't deviate as the six and eight the queen shall take to the busiest road of the eight hundred and eight the heaviest weight of all the loads is the load we share on eighty eight and here she rises like a vein under flesh to the flick of a thumb time enough to drive the needle in. I look I see clearly I see the moongleam roads, I see everything at once. Everything. At once. To survive I must narrow that vision to sharp sharp focus, a thin silver rope on which to tread most carefully and now we're on the moonbeam road just for a minute. A tick. A second. The Second Aether, the Black Aether, is open to

us and so are all the worlds and places of the heart, deal another
card and bile rises up but my friends are all through – threes
and nines and twelve of cups – adieux adieux – Four for the law
adieux adieux – Play the Fool, Play the Fool; and Play the knave
two by two and Harlequin the tale shall spin. Weary, we of the
Eighth Degree, finding only the golden scale to bring down the fist
of mail. Weary, weary, we of the Eighth Degree. Rhythm and the
rhythm and the rhythm and the rhythm and the beautiful blues.
Are we that part of God that grieves? That part of God Weeping
as so much knowledge fills us. Skipping from stand to stand seek-
ing to save so much. For how long? And for what? How we must
sadden Him. The feeling is mutual. I resist the lure of fur and
fang. God is good. God has a plan. God is merciful. God is divine.
Find the Knight and follow him. Find the Knight that's all in
green. Find the great green knight and follow him.

Follow the Knight of the Desert whose robes and flags are
the green robes and flags of Islam. Something growls through
the room filling it with cruel vibrations but I am embraced by
knives. Oh God! Are these charms and codes the way we survive in Chaos? With only Mandelbrot to map it?

Sheik Antara looks up suddenly. He is the first to understand where the sound is coming from. His hand sits on my
shoulder. A steadying signal. I stare up into the images of the
stars. Savage evil stalks amongst the distant suns. Can I see it?

Making a gesture, Imam Darnaud rises.

And the room is suddenly black.

It is cold.

It is silent.

From the darkness Imam Darnaud says: "She is near. She is
in great danger. He means to kill again. I think we must go to
help her. O, sweet mistress! Such pain!"

From outside I hear shouts of fear and surprise.

Light shafts onto the circular table as a heavy door opens.

292

Imam Darnaud crosses the room to leave. We hurry after him along the passage. In the beautiful water garden the sun is setting. Long shadows create a lattice across the rippling pools. Terrified people and animals run here and there. Most of the White Sufis stumble back from the mosque, their faces ghastly with fear. However, walking towards it with quiet dignity come two extremely tall, thin, ebony warriors. Knights, from their leopardskin tunics and fine weapons. At first I take these handsome men for Masai, but judging by what they wear and carry, they are possibly Matabele or Zulu. My sketchy knowledge of Africa's tribes is based on an enthusiasm for H. Rider Haggard's Allan Quatermain stories I enjoyed as a boy.

The tall warriors continued to stride slowly along the central pathway. They, too, stared above us at the roof of the mosque. Their gaze was grim and steady. Their shadows were long on the red waters of the pools. They carried oval shields of black cowhide which covered two thirds of their bodies. Their spears were iron-tipped. As well as leopard skins, they wore bracelets of gold or brass on their glowing arms and legs. On their heads they wore crowns of waving white ostrich feathers, nodding when they approached the Eldest Sufi, raising their spears sideways in a gesture of peace which was reciprocated by Imam Darnaud.

Now everyone was looking beyond us and upwards towards the sun. We had to turn to see the object of their consternation.

I heard a terrible sound, deep and ugly, and for the first time since we had come to the desert I was profoundly afraid.

It stood with its feet planted on the wide balustrade, staring at us with menacing defiance. Its dark grey body was framed by the red disc of the setting sun. Its glaring green eyes were slitted with careless menace and its great red tongue lolled over a set of savage white, grinning fangs. The thing was huge, its forepaws balancing on the balustrade's heavy crenellations, its back legs half-hidden by the domed marble of the roof.

As Imam Darnaud opened his lips to speak to the newcomers, his voice was drowned by the beast's chilling growl. Far beyond the nearest walls I saw lines of people walking, running or riding hastily out over the distant dunes.

Then it lifted its great head against the sun's scarlet disc and let out the most chilling howl I had ever heard. Even the Black Abbot raised his hands as if to protect his ears from that noise.

The two tall black knights lowered the shafts of their spears and spoke with clear authority.

The wolf turned his glaring eyes on them, opened his massive grinning jaws and growled again, his voice shaking the surrounding buildings and foliage. He was of an impossible size, far too big for me to understand as a living creature. And it stank like the pits of hell.

Again the two black warriors spoke in tones of sharp command. The wolf turned his head slightly to look at them. There was something unreadable in its slitted emerald eyes. Filth dripped from his fangs. He was a beast of nightmare. I did not doubt for a moment that he was real.

And I was certain that every one of us was about to die a gruesome and painful death.

Part Four

Convergence

Fiction has the capacity to teach you to tell the truth when your natural impulse is to not.

— George Saunders,
interview with Tom Gatti,
New Statesman, October 1923

21

Destroying the Evidence

I WAS RETURNING to London from Yorkshire after telling her
about Jenny. Helena suggested that she was prepared to let
me 'have mistresses'. I said that would not be fair. It would
have to be reciprocal, and I would be uncomfortable with that.
I decided to live nearby. I could be close to the children, share
their upbringing and be with Jenny in the monogamous relationship I preferred. I found a flat across the street which
my former lover, Emma Tennant, bought and which I rented
from her. Almost as soon as Helena came back to London she
took up with a man I despised and whom, she said, she also
despised, an Austrian editor and journalist, an appallingly
cynical womaniser, whom I had avoided since our meeting
some years earlier.

Infamous back-door man Dieter Schnickels had large brown,
bovine eyes. I asked Helena what she saw in him. She said
she thought she saw herself reflected in those eyes. He was
frequently unfaithful to her and they were always fighting.
I know very few details. I did not want to listen to gossip
about them. He took up with an Auschwitz survivor and went
off with all her money. He wasn't the only low-earning SF
person I knew who lived on women and institutions. He was
a Performing Flea, waiting around for a breeze to blow him

from one host to the next. For a while, after I split up with Jenny, I was briefly back with Helena. During that time she told me about Dieter and also how she had been raped by our friend Jack one night after a party at Emma's, who had become his girlfriend after I took up with Jenny. Emma said we were opposites in bed. I was as gentle as he was violent. I was never sure who she liked best. I left them all behind in the end. The gene pool was becoming too small. I went to America and met Lou.

That was one of my dreams of the future which I had at the Mosque of the Great Oasis at Zaouia. It meant little to me then. For the majority of my years I blamed myself for many of the events which turned my life. "You always pay dearly for your mistakes, Mike," said Helena's mother one day. I can't remember the circumstances.

This memory would return. I have no idea why it came at the moment I saw a gigantic wolf on the roof of the medrasa and wondered if I was going to be amongst the dead.

I had learned and forgotten a great deal from Father Grammaticus during the months I spent at the Flete Street Abbey of the White Friars. I knew and then did not know how to walk the moonbeam roads; how to communicate with *Spammer Gain* and how to ask her for help; how to open the doors between the worlds and how to close them. I had learned the Tarot Codes from Innez Malady. Or at least I think I did. Now, try as hard as I can, I have yet to recall who taught me the Codes or when or where I had known them. But I could use them. Something within me knew how to lay out the cards and read them accurately. I had stopped in the days before I met Helena, before I became a father or even a husband. Someone had to teach me. But who? My Welsh aunt, Dylis? She and my Uncle Stan had moved into Dahlia Gardens during the war to help with the rent. When my father left, they took over because mum and dad's landlord wouldn't rent to a single-woman parent. Then there was some sort of quarrel between them all. Probably because of my mother's usual paranoia, since Stan and Dylis were living upstairs. This became a pattern. She came to believe that any noises coming from overhead were deliberate. I genuinely have no memory of being taught Tarot. One of the gypsy women had handled cards, I remember, at the mews where they let me ride the ponies. All I remember is that I determined to give the Tarot up. I have a very dim, possibly false, memory of looking at some sort of chart. Spread them in a circle, put yourself in communication with the one for whom you are reading. One circle for the past. One for the present. One for the future. But there were other spheres. How had I learned to negotiate the dusty backstreets? By reciting the Tarot Codes. How did I learn to move from the London I knew as a boy to the London I came to know as a young man? I knew *why* I had learned and I knew why I decided to stop my readings after my 'fortunes' became too accurate and I put the decks aside. It started as a party trick and became something I feared! I predicted two deaths and my friend told me how, soon afterwards, he had been visited by the ghosts of his mother and father. I had no terror of ghosts (unlike my mum), and was not much upset by the supernatural in which I scarcely believed, but it seemed irresponsible to continue. I was scared of myself. Of my own senses or my own talents? I was no older than twenty-one.

Perhaps, after all, it was the Mitcham gypsies who had taught me the Tarot? Rosie, who used to look after me when my mother worked, taught me quite a bit of Romany lore, though she only claimed to be part Romany herself. She would talk about some of the things she had learned and in return I helped her with her reading. I hated her telling me how hedgehogs were covered in wet clay and roasted alive so that their prickles came off all of a piece when you broke the clay open. She laughed at me. *Soft little gorger.* She knew I found that disturbing. She taught me how to put a curse on someone. When I tried it on her, she didn't think it was funny. She said I gave her spots and diarrhoea. And I owed her a shilling.

She told my mother I had put a spell on her.

"He would never do that," my mother said. "He's a nice boy."

I used to read ordinary packs of cards before I had a Tarot pack of my own. I told stories with them. Rosie taught me rhymes which meant little to either of us as she laid out her well-used deck. She spread the cards in lines along the table then she sprinkled lavender water lightly over them. Sometimes she made up the rhymes or helped me to make them up. I don't think they were always original.

> *Eights and twelves, the straight road falls.*
> *Through time and time and time again,*
> *It's eights and nines and ten and ten.*
> *You can fly high above eleven,*
> *You might find Eden but never find heaven.*
> *How strange the range of picks*
> *Above numbers five and six.*
> *Life, death, sleep and dreaming.*
> *Stay safe a-bed from Satan's scheming.*
> *Don't listen to his bad intention*
> *To make full use of Man's invention.*

> *No wish to cheat and none to 'scape*
> *Ill comes to she who stands to gape.*
> *Be good to stand 'gainst evil's joys,*
> *Honest girls avoid the magic boys.*
> *Honest men stay clear of demon's traces,*

Which show so sweet on maiden's faces.
Spread out thy boards so all shall see,
Thy culminating destiny.

Rosie knew my mother could predict horse-race winners and used to try to trick me to get the names. She would show me the morning paper for the steeplechase races. "Ask your mum what she likes best." The long lists of names and numbers confused me. Rosie's urgency alarmed me. "Show her how good you can read, Micky."

I didn't like her calling me Micky. I only called myself Mickey Mouse when I wrote to mum from Graham Hall. I would get *Mickey Mouse Weekly* before I went to Graham Hall but comics were banned there. I so missed Mickey Mouse and Tiger Tim. I think *MMW* was produced by the same people who would later publish *Eagle*. A glorious comic, printed in full photogravure long before *Eagle*. I loved it for the subtly graded shades of watercolour which I had rarely seen in anything but original paintings. I liked it at least as much as *The Rainbow*. But Tiger Tim and the Bruin Boys never had quite the glamour of Mickey and his pals. I had loved Mickey since I saw his adventures played across that screen on the bedsheet pinned on our living room wall, projected by American flyers, friends of my RAF uncle, when they visited on leave from Biggin Hill where they flew Hurricanes. Since then Mickey had been my hero and I remained a loyal fan, at least until he became middle class, wearing long trousers, mowing his lawn and generally paying his taxes like a well-behaved citizen. In 1929 with the bankers and stock market disgraced, he was a working-class hero, cocking a snook at authority, like Richmal Crompton's William Brown. He was the spirit of the poor immigrant, the exploited worker, the powerless child. By 1949, with the rise of an America which had discovered it had something to lose, Mickey was anti-socialist, anti-populist and had begun his transition out of the melting pot.

Norman Foxwell's Tiger Tim never changed much. He remained an orphan living amongst all the other animal orphans at the school run by the kindly bear, Mrs Bruin. My dad's parents had a soft Mickey and Minnie they had bought for their other son, Gerry, in the 1930s. I clearly remember how they were always telling me how I would have them when I was older. They promised them together with the beautiful Wild West Buffalo Bill books they kept with the famous mice in a glass cabinet. 'You'll have to wait until you're a little bit older, dear', they would say, whenever I asked if the time had come. It never did arrive. I was also promised an old musket which fascinated me. One day, to my surprise, my granddad asked if I would like it. With great ceremony, he handed over the old gun. I had barely got it home before I realised the stock was eaten up with woodworm. My mum made me keep it outside. The stock fell off, but I continued to use it like a long pistol. A radium pistol for John Carter. When my cousins came along, I fell out of favour and nothing else I'd been promised materialised. Everything went to those unseen cousins. On many occasions I had reason to resent my Moorcock cousins. I never actually did. It was never their fault, of course, and I never blamed them. Before those boys turned up, Brian and I had done pretty well in tips of half-crowns and two-shilling bits.

My mother never once told me not to see the Moorcock grandparents, though they frequently quizzed me about her private life. Because of their tone, I had an instinct not to reveal very much, especially when they asked about 'that German chap', meaning the Czech Dr Jelinek. They wanted me to tell them that he was keeping my mother or she had moved in with him. Perhaps so my father would not have to pay his

£2.00 a week child support to her? They were not especially pleasant people, all in all. After my dad died, I saw their will amongst his other papers. They left fairly large amounts of money to their local Methodist church, some to their sons, some to friends in the church, and nothing to me or, I think, to my cousins. But that wasn't what I found disturbing. There was something sour and mean about that will, just as there was about them. Maybe it's ungenerous of me to think that, especially after all those half-crowns, but my mother never received anything from them for my keep. Of course, it's very likely she would have rejected it. Discovering my interest in the musket, Mr Evan Richards, who ran the Residential Club in Semley Road, taught me quite a bit about guns, including matchlocks and old sporting guns and how to fire them. He was an enthusiast and a bit of a bore. We called him the Twelve Bore Bore. My mother thought he was a bit creepy. He never made any advances. Brian and I were the only kids who could load, aim and fire a matchlock, a flintlock and a black-powder Colt 36 which knocked you backwards worse than the Bren they took away from me in the ATC. He also gave me an old single-sheet duplicator and I created my first fanzines on it. The thing was messy and labour-intensive, but it produced the initial issues of *Burroughsania* I sold at school.

Whatever I believed about those somewhat unloving grandparents I can't help thinking of the dog I betrayed. I loved Chum and it was my pride which was the cause of my losing him. I was showing him off. That was why I let him follow me to school. I wonder if that betrayal of the first creature I loved after my mum was the core around which all my guilty betrayals revolved: my betrayal of Helena, of my children. Of Jenny. Did I fail them by promising them all too much?

Or did I promise them enough?

And could I have delivered on any more promises?

303

One reason I stopped speaking to Helena was because, effectively, she made me break a promise I made to my children, that I would always be there. It broke my heart that I wasn't available for one of my girls when they most needed me.

So could I have promised them more?

Actually, I think I could have done. Generally, I have managed to keep my promises when I made them. I have a horror of not keeping them. But then there are the unmade promises, the unconsidered matters of the heart and spirit.

A sufi scout, his clothes covered in thick dust, clutched spasmodically at Imam Darnaud, speaking rapidly in Arabic. Darnaud started to reply until one of the tall warriors looked back from where he stood regarding the huge wolf. He spoke in English. "She is in danger. There is nothing else to be done. We know how to overwhelm this wolf, I assure you, lord. The help we need is here and out there will be no help to you ..."

"But you cannot do it alone!"

"As I said, we will find help." His brother grinned, pointing with his spears. "Go, lord! We have followed the wolf this far. She whom you care for needs your help. *He* needs your help. There are others you must rescue. Without her, we are *all* finished. As if we had never lived. We shall have help to quell the wolf. He respects us. Help her. Go!"

The wolf raised his terrible, dark head and growled again, saliva dripping from his scarlet mouth. He did not appear to respect anything. Who was 'she'? Imam Darnaud had spoken of someone in the orrery chamber. She had communicated with him. That was when he had stopped the great device and gone running from the hall. I was baffled. Had the action of that device summoned the wolf? Did it create a gateway for some grotesquely sized creature from the astral plane?

Must we all go dashing into the desert leaving the two tribesmen, brave as they might be, to deal with the threat? The pair was taking on too much. How on earth could they possibly overwhelm that creature? I was about to ask when Darnaud frowned. He signed to his people, turning to the man who had brought the news. He spoke in French. "Where exactly is she now? I heard her calling to me. Out there?" He pointed off in the direction from which we had come on the previous day.

"Yes. On the Western Road."

One of the black tribesmen spoke. "I know she is there. She was on her way. We saw her when we followed the wolf's tracks."

Imam Darnaud nodded. "I expected her this evening. That is why I began the induction. Then I heard her calling me to say she was in grave danger. She is stranded."

"Yes, Lord Darnaud. Go to help her. We will confront the wolf. If we are successful here, we shall follow you if you need us. If not, we shall wait for you three miles due North of here. Take your soldiers. Help her. She must not die, lord."

"Thank you." He pointed with his thumb over his shoulder. The wolf shifted its feet on the roof and snarled again, its green eyes glared like fractured emeralds. "But he came here for a reason. I have seen the prediction."

"There is a conjunction coming, lord. You must know that."

"Not here."

"Near. The Garden. The tall Englishman preceded us. Is he here?"

"One is here. But the wolf? If he comes for the conjunction—"

"He does and we cannot go against the prophecies. Or there will be no point to you riding into the desert and our Mother will not be saved. The story will have to begin all over again. That will take the lifetime of all the stars. There will be a thinning of the patterns. Then we shall all become ghosts."

Darnaud nodded. "I will instruct my monks to take up

305

their arms." He sighed. "How much power we have and yet no power holds for ever against human rapacity." He became brisk.

"She will need everyone you can gather. Meanwhile, the wolf must be confronted. Yes, lord. You must go out to the desert now and find her. Good fortune!"

Darnaud turned to me. "Do you have weapons, Master Moorcock?"

I shook my head. I no longer carried either sword.

He thought for a moment. "But you can use them?"

"I have done. Quite recently."

"You can ride?"

"A horse, yes. I am not sure about a camel."

"Good. We have plenty of horses in our stables. We'll get you one. Sheik Antara!" He looked around for our friend, who presented himself, his face grim and alert.

"Select a horse from the stables. I gather your friends are soldiers. Just as well! Find mounts for Mr Moorcock and our French friends, I would be grateful." Then, addressing the Musketeers and Duval next. "You gentlemen will need your guns returned, too. We do have muskets but most of our long guns are rifled. There is no shortage of powder. The horns they give you are filled, as are the pouches! You are ready to fight beside us? You know a conjunction is coming?"

Duval shared looks with the others. They all nodded and saluted. "We are ready, sir. All we'll want is a match for a short fuse. But you need us to overcome the wolf—"

The Imam shook his head. "We ride at once into the desert. You'll have your matchlocks and swords. Nothing too modern, I assure you!" He looked around until he saw the Englishman. "Professor, you had best stay here."

"Are you certain you will not need me in the desert?

"Fighting men are wanted in the desert. You will be wasted

there. You have your charges. Take them and follow the others into the desert and pray the brothers can keep the thing from pursuing you!"

"But the wolf," I said, "surely two men alone cannot—?"

Darnaud was already shouting to White Sufis running into the furthest tower. Then he turned again to the Englishman.

"Professor?"

The Englishman was pale. "I rather fear for my friends, sir."

"Of course." The Imam nodded. "I do not expect you to fight. Do as I say. If all is lost, and we live, we shall find you!" He called again in Arabic to his people. They were gathering some distance away, looking as if they had recovered a little from their initial panic. Many were already armed. I was impressed by the balance and workmanship of their weapons and breastplates. Some had helmets and shields. I guessed the monks had been warriors before they took holy orders. I began to feel a little better as I was now fitted with a bronze breastplate and helmet that seemed centuries old. I saw the bows in others' hands and asked for one. Brian and I had been champion archers in Streatham Bow and Rifle Club. Darnaud spoke to Antara, also in his own language. The Arab knight replied then turned to me.

"Imam Darnaud will lead the White Sufis. I will lead the Carmelites. You will go with Duval and the Musketeers. You are welcome to the bow, but take a long gun at least." He handed me a musket, powder horn and bullet pouch. "I understand you are proficient with this firearm. He will call you if he needs you to attack their other flank. My men and I will attack from their rear. Are you ready to take the risk?"

Loaded with weapons, I don't know why I replied as I did, but I found myself saying rather haughtily: "I am ready."

Had I prepared for this moment for years? Since I had first read those books my father left behind, I had loved the tales of Edgar Rice Burroughs and Leigh Brackett about heroes who had risen to the moment! This was my 'playing fields of Eton' swordfight scene I had enacted a million times from *The Prisoner of Zenda*. I felt a tremendous lift. *Beau Geste*! I might be about to die, but I really didn't care. I was invulnerable just then. This was my moment and I was starting to taste it as if it was the experience I had been leading up to all my young life. I grinned like a fool at Imam Darnaud.

I had never been readier for battle. Never felt more invigorated, as if I had been born for it! And one of my initial thoughts was – *How jealous Helena would be of my first chance at riding to war with a group of bold seventeenth-century bravos.* How I wished then that she was with me!

I was caught up in the moment, running for the gates with my comrades where they received their swords and muskets, powder, shot and pistols. Once beyond the water garden, out of sight of the snarling wolf, we were brought beautiful horses from the stables. Before I could mount, someone rode up to me, leaned over to set a gorget round my throat. The thing clattered on the breastplate. I had no difficulty mounting the chestnut Arab even if the saddle and stirrups were unfamiliar. The horsehair stuffing on the leather covering of the wooden war-saddle was not particularly comfortable, but it gave me manoeuvrability. Allowing me both hands free if necessary. I grew used to it surprisingly quickly, settling my feet into the stirrups. When a long scimitar was brought up for me I felt its balance as if I had always known how to hold it. I fitted my wrist through the attached loop. I was given a short, bone bow and a quiver of long arrows which were completely unfamiliar to me. The last thing I received was a coil of very strong rope, like a lasso, but nobody told me what to do with it.

Then, in company with my friends, I rode into the darkness of the desert. I had no hint of the violence I was about to face. I had no notion what would become of the fleeing people menaced by that gigantic wolf. I was pretty sure I was going to die.

The Sufis carried elegantly curved damascene scimitars dressed with tempered copper, bronze and ivory. They had long ebony and silver *khanjars*, thick quivers of arrows and short bone bows. Riding in the same company came a smaller force of Carmelite friars, also in white, under the command of Sheik Antara and similarly armed, though with some pistols and muskets. Duval, myself and the Musketeers, with our long guns, pistols and swords, rode on their right flank. We all bunched together at first. The hoofs of the horses were muffled by the sand but still the ground shook under us as we cantered along tracks made by the professor's incoming animals. We dropped our horses to a walk as we drew closer, fearing that those ahead would hear.

It was now very hard to see far under the few stars. The sun had set and the moon had scarcely begun to rise. I was not aware of the scouts Imam Darnaud had sent ahead until slowly they began to drift in. At a sign from our leader, our horses dropped to a slower walk while the scouts whispered their information to him, telling who and where the newcomers were. In turn, Darnaud passed on this information to Duval and the cavaliers.

Their French was hard to understand. What precisely was happening? All I knew was that the 'enemy' had brought down someone called 'the Red' and that someone's mother was in danger. I remained mystified.

The Sufis were more concerned about that mysterious enemy in the desert than the more immediate enemy we had seen standing on the roof of the medrasa. How were the two connected? Was this a concerted attack? Was the wolf a diversion meant to occupy the defenders while soldiers outside crept in?

My high saddle offered more security than an ordinary English saddle. Over its pommel was my long rope. Darnaud told me rapidly what I should do with it when we reached the big vehicle he expected to find out there in the desert. He was gone again before I could demand details.

The scimitar, a wooden quiver of arrows and the curved, laminated bone bow also had a halfway familiar feel, like the flintlock I had been given. Save for my boyhood fencing and archery lessons, I had no experience with either. I was pleased how well balanced the bow and the sword were. I was used to an ordinary wooden Slazenger bow, which you left unstrung as much as possible. This shorter bow was already slightly bent, with curved 'horns' to which the gut string was attached. It was powerful for short distances but had none of the range or penetration of a regular longbow. Neither did it require as much force to pull it. The arrows, too, were longer and the technique of drawing them slightly different. I could tell how easy they were to use from horseback. Riding with so many others gave me an unexpected confidence. The moon, rising higher and almost at full, provided us increased light. I could see the dunes outlined on the horizon but nothing moved.

Another scout brought our small army to a halt. The scout reported to Darnaud who turned to us.

"There was a fight between two forces before our outriders caught up with them. Then a skirmish in which one of her would-be rescuers was wounded. This was followed by a stand-off. She remains in danger. But the chances of rescuing her in the dark are poor. We might harm her. The great cabinet is damaged." He controlled his horse, glancing about, dropping his voice. "Much of her liquid will have seeped into the sand. She will die if they can't get her to the oasis by morning. Our best plan is to wait for dawn light, then make sure we surround them. We need spotters to report where they are and riflemen to hold them down. Then, under the muskets' cover, we should get her out rapidly. Those who go in for her must get their ropes around the cabinet and ride rapidly for the oasis. The rest of us will keep them pinned in one place." He drew a breath. "We should probably decide now who sleeps for how long, and when. That way we'll be as fresh as possible when we fight them in the morning."

And so we took up positions around deep tracks created by something much heavier than Professor Consenseo's wagon. These ruts bit into the sand, obscuring those made by the menagerie-master's vehicle. I immediately thought of a massive gun. The Black Abbot of Zaouia said nothing of being threatened by such a weapon. As far as I knew, the monks did not have anything much heavier than a few rifled long guns. The flintlocks now carried by my cavalier friends were considered to be rather advanced.

Darnaud disappeared into the night, taking the better part of his sufis with him. They would make the first strike and we would come in as soon as Antara attacked their other flank. Then we must do our best to get hold of the gigantic wagon's shafts and pull the vehicle back onto the tracks left by the Englishman. Darnaud and his sufis would cover us. If the attackers caught up, we would surround the wagon as best we could and defend it until reinforcements arrived.

I felt tension in the air like an infusion of unexpelled electricity. I heard loud voices raised in anger. Another voice bellowed with rage and pain. Mocking laughter joined at least one woman's voice calling out to someone, all in unfamiliar languages, one of which seemed to be Turkish.

Beside me, Duval muttered: "Are you well, lad?"

I think he had sensed something. I did my best to sound brave. Actually, at that point, I was beginning to feel more than a little sick. The adrenaline had gone out of my system and was now pretty thoroughly replaced by a nervous terror.

I was a little reassured by the concerned Duval. "If it comes to fighting, as I suspect it will, and before dawn, too, despite Darnaud's optimistic plan, your natural instincts will return to save you." In the brightening moonlight I think I saw him grin as he reached out a gauntleted hand. "It's hard now to distinguish what's happening. I'd say there's considerable confusion out there. The big, wheeled cabinet, perhaps initially in the hands of Sufi friends, is now held by those who followed and attacked it. Those friends might have come close to the oasis and then been forced to take a stand against their pursuers. At least one of those in pursuit, a man, a leader, I suspect, was wounded. My guess is that he was possibly abandoned by his own people if I understand his cursing. It sounded like a mixture of Turkish and Spanish. Maybe Venetian!" Duval paused.

"Another odd thing is that they seem to have women with them. Two high-ranking gentlewomen, perhaps wives of nobles. Their accents are hard to identify. They might possibly be Austrian. English, maybe? The rest of the ruffians are a mixture of English, French, Portuguese, Spanish and Italian. Men of no special account. Escaped Spanish galley-slaves. Not a decent cook amongst 'em, if I'm right. They seem to be eating a cold supper and are decidedly nervous. They fear intervention from a more powerful band. Led by a disciplined captain. One at least. No doubt they're mercenaries. Sea hounds hired by leaders of an altogether higher rank. Unhappy in the desert. On any land. They were unprepared for the conditions of this fight. Many would go home if they could. There's another factor I can't quite make out. Something terrible of which they're mightily afraid. Some of them refer to it almost as if it were a god. One of those Hindoo things! A Leviathan? A sea-beast? A kraken? A monster? Not likely out here in the desert, of course, unless that's what is in that enormous crate.

It's pretty heavy. A bigger team was drawing it before some-one cut the traces. If we're forced to drag the thing, we'll have a hard time getting it to the oasis. And a hard time stopping it when we do! Especially if we have to fight her escort while we do it!"

He had gathered all this from listening and from what little he could see. I congratulated him, but he shrugged. He pointed out that he had the trained observation of a profes-sional soldier. "Not to mention those of a sometime Gentleman of the Road!" He winked and slapped me on the back.

He went on briefly. "Two of those people I know, I'll swear. One of the women, maybe. And a man. But the man is the one who's probably wounded. Now, if you *can* get some sleep, we'll—"

Then the night was bright with explosions. A flare filled the darkness above but obscured a landscape alive with the thrum of bowstrings, gunfire, shrieking musket balls and wild shouts. Duval patted me on the shoulder, signalling that I should mount my horse. He swung into the saddle of his grey stallion, metal all ajingle, fixed his hat firmly on his long, curl-ing locks, secured his Arab *jumbiya* dagger in his sash, then dragged at the horse's reins to bring him around. He spurred the beast into a gallop. I followed hastily, desperate not to lose sight of him. I remained conscious of the other musketeers around me. All of us headed down a long dune towards the silhouette of the massive vehicle which lay broken, on its side. Some of its many wheels were turning in the air. Was that the gun? We should have to right it before we could haul it away.

Duval's grey stallion was still ahead of me. I made out the faces of other musketeers and a few monks. They were gal-loping, surrounding me, as we rode towards the huge wagon. It loomed larger and larger at our approach! I gasped. The thing was at least the size of a three-storey building! More

313

gunfire sounded from behind us now. The people covering us had been taken by surprise. Which meant the enemy had been waiting for us. Aware of our presence they had regrouped and attacked again!

I heard Duval and Athos calling. They had reached the wagon and were trying to secure it by shooting arrows with ropes attached from one side to the other. They were lucky to be riding such big horses! Athos even stood up in his saddle. I prepared mine, attaching a light cord to the rope, though this was yet another part of the plan I was uncomfortable with. I felt like Pecos Bill about to lasso a twister!

Suddenly again I saw more flashes, felt and heard musket balls whistling about my head!

Danger! And seriously close by!

Coarse shouts! Not one in a tongue I could understand!

I knew fear again!

For a moment I was blinded. Sand clogged my throat and eyes. Then, when I could see again, Duval's grey was nowhere. I heard galloping hoofs, turned my horse to follow them, expecting to be hit by a heavy lead ball!

All at once the musket fire went deathly quiet. I could swear I heard the wind soughing over the desert sand again. There were no more flashes. With the sand stinging my skin, standing in my stirrups, I continued to gallop on. Their muskets must be reloaded and primed. They had fired off all their guns at once in panic at our sudden attack. I was elated. Now we had a good chance of righting the massive wagon and getting it back to Zaouia! I unslung my bow. I felt much more comfortable.

Upon the undulating dunes I saw something silhouetted against the skyline. I had no idea what it could be. It waved like the branch of a sapling. Then it was joined by one or two more. Palms? Not quite. But what on earth was it? Something alive, maybe?

It made strange, whipping motions. Tendrils! My stomach turned! Something very much alive and decidedly unhuman. Unmammalian, even! Surely not reptilian?

Thoroughly alien. Something from another world? From another space-time? I had not observed such terrible, unearthly shapes on anything except the covers of sensational horror magazines!

When I saw Duval's horse swerve radically ahead of me, I was relieved. I had found him again! I was temporarily deafened by fresh musket fire. The sound of fighting nearby seemed distant and unthreatening. I knew, of course, this was illusory but my spirits rose and I continued to follow Duval's grey. I heard him shout, saw him whirl his rope. His horse swerved again and I lost sight of him. I heard a keening like a high wind I had previously associated with tornadoes or typhoons. A shrieking! A kind of unearthly yelping. The sound of six converging express trains. For a moment I wondered if that gigantic wolf led a pack. But the noise sounded far too high for wolves. What on earth could it possibly be? The sound grew into a desperate keening, louder and louder before stopping suddenly. And at the moment it stopped I knew a shuddering thrill of terror. Pure, cold fear. Oddly, however, the fear was not for myself. I feared for all eternity.

Then came silence.

I could hear myself yelling wildly next as I tried to keep up with Duval. Somehow the scimitar remained in my gloved hand, gripped tighter than anything I had ever gripped before. Shouts were still distant. Where was Duval? I turned my horse. I saw no riders. The Musketeers and the Carmelite monks could not be seen. I appeared to be on my own, calling to an uncaring deity in an uncaring universe.

I found myself whispering, begging for sound to return. I heard one word pass my lips, so quietly.

"Please ..."

There was no response.

I would have been grateful, just then, for the Swarm's return.

I wanted to be gone from there. Back to our Ladbroke Grove flat, playing on the carpet with the children, with Helena, even with Pip, the dog, in that comfortable, ordinary domestic world. Could I ever see it again? I no longer cared if I went on hearing that Whispering Swarm taunting me for ever or experienced the irritations and anxieties of ordinary life. Or if I never wrote another word. I just wanted my family, my close friends. I had never valued them more.

I saw a shadow against the skyline. A mounted man. Not Duval.

I began to yell again, swinging my glittering sword, wildly spurring my horse forward.

Another blinding flash. A monstrous roar, like an explosion! I flung up my arm to protect my eyes. Then something hit me full in the chest. I flew backwards off my horse and rose into the air, flailing as I tried to find something to hold on to. I grasped nothing for what seemed minutes. Then I fell on my back so hard that all the wind rushed from my lungs. I lay in soft sand feeling extremely relaxed, so happy that I was no longer fighting. Was I returning home at last? A noble invalid. No. Better. I was dead. And the dead had no responsibilities.

Something was falling on my face. I thought it was rain. I did not know or care why it was raining in the desert.

Sand spattered down on me. It began to fill up my mouth! I felt the fingers of my right hand tighten again on the hilt of my sword. When the sand had stopped falling I turned my head but could see nothing. My left hand was sore and began to ache. I lifted my head and tried to see the rest of my body. Eventually I made out my legs in their white baggy trousers, the tall, leather boots I had been given. Across my chest lay

316

my bow and quiver of arrows. Only the rope was missing. I wondered if I was dying or if I had been injured and, if so, where. Profound silence. I was deaf.

I bent my leg and put pressure on it, bent the other one. Rolling over, I got slowly to my feet. I was hurting but nothing seemed injured. I stumbled forward. I tripped again. I thought I had fallen because of a severed limb. Perhaps that blast had been heavy enough to blow off my leg? A cannon might have blown several people up, myself amongst them!

I looked down. Something actually moved beside my foot. I backed away. I thought it was a snake, disturbed by the conflict. Did they have snakes in the Sahara desert?

I felt a soft touch on my cheek. It was like a young girl's caress, hesitant, gentle, as if one of my own children put her little hand against me. What on earth – or even *off* the earth – could it be?

A snake's skin was dry and nothing like this. Was one of the women Duval had mentioned playing a trick on me? As I stumbled around in the dark I fell again. I could smell something now, like honey. And a sour smell, too, but not especially unpleasant. Perhaps the scent of honey gone rotten. I heard sounds akin to music. A faint mist rose against the moonlight. I had the unlikely notion that someone had been transporting beehives across the desert. That was what had been in the carrier! There was that soft, delicate caress again. For a moment something tried to grip my waist, to drag me to itself. I struggled, broke free . . .

Then I was up and staring at the barrel of a musket. At the other end of the musket I saw an uncouth, grinning face. I knew the type immediately for I had seen it on the Tangier docks. Indeed I had seen it in contemporary illustrations. I was looking at a typical 'sea-rat'. The kind which haunted harbours from Portsmouth to Piraeus. Filthy, poorly dressed, narrow head wrapped in rags, badly nourished, they did any degenerate and disgusting work for a few dirham. I had read about such creatures in Scott, Dumas, Conrad, Stevenson, Marryat, Ballantyne and Mayne Reid and I expected to die at once on the point of a bayonet. My bow was lost. I still had my gun, but it needed priming. Only the scimitar remained in my hand and it came up automatically to block his musket and drive my blade towards his face, actually catching him in the throat! It was a remarkable stroke, nothing but good luck and I had not killed him, but he thought I had. He screamed, clutching at his neck and stumbling off into the night. Quickly, I primed my flintlock, blowing on a piece of fuse to keep it alight. Sure enough three more of the ruffians came at me. The first received a bullet in the head and to the second I delivered a scimitar wound. The eruption of human heads into a mass of bloody bone made me feel sick but my life was at stake. Leaving the corpse of their comrade, the others slunk away. My interest in ancient weapons had saved my life but the recoil of the gun had finished me. The stink of death and freshly discharged gunpowder filled my head and I fell backward against that huge wooden cabinet, slid down it into the sand and lost consciousness.

Dawn woke me. The faint sunlight dazzled my eyes. Fighting still went on but I had no idea where. My back was against the huge cabinet, which lay partly on its side, its wheels angled to the sky. The lid was broken, forced upward. I was staring at the interior. Something shone there, but I could not quite make out what it was. Treasure? Is that what they were fighting over? I stared hard, not wanting to get on my feet in case one of the enemy saw me. For the moment, at least I was glad to be presumed dead.

Staring into the crate I became used to the darkness a little more but it took me time to make out what I was looking at.

Something moved inside, making a wet, swishing sound. Animals? People? The smell was not unattractive. Honey? Vanilla? Lavender? My birthplace in summer. Coalsmoke in winter. Nothing was entirely familiar. Perhaps the gigantic box contained not a gun but prisoners? More animals? What *was* that scent? I felt I really should identify it! The kin of some of the beasts I had seen in Professor C.'s menagerie? What if his caravan had been raided by the likes of the unsavoury individual I had fought earlier? Was this the rest of his odd cargo?

The broken lid moved a little. I squinted, shielding my eyes to stare inside. It glittered. Maybe treasure of some kind? But, if so, why would it be in liquid?

Something moved again. Organic. Shielding my eyes against the growing light, I peered closer. It was a great bowl, I thought. A creature swimming in a bowl? And then I found myself gasping in horrified astonishment! The light went out and came on again! I realised what it must be. The huge orb blinked. There was no doubt about what I was looking at! Or what was looking back at me!

I was peering at a gigantic eye. Not a human eye. Unlike any animal's eye I had ever seen. And that single, sentient eye was peering back at me. Against all my normal scepticism, I could not help but speculate.

That eye was not human nor did it belong to any other mammal. Yet it reflected a true intelligence. Something certainly humanlike and even vaguely familiar. My fantastical reading contrasted with my natural common sense. Surely this was not at an alien creature from outer space? Not even a dinosaur had possessed eyes so big! No animal like it, as far as I knew, had ever walked the earth. Was I looking at some kind of lifelike statue? A carving from an Egyptian monument? A sea-monster? The Kraken? Impossible! Or perhaps not quite impossible in this unlikely world.

As I stared with almost hypnotised fascination at the eye, a fleshy grey arm tentatively crept out over the edge of the box. It moved slowly towards me. I was a bird, held by the stare of a snake. I dare not move. I was afraid our enemies would see me. This was what had touched me so lightly in the night. It had not harmed me then and probably would not harm me now, but there was no doubt about what I saw. Or thought I saw. Or came close to identifying in my ignorance at that time.

Writhing and curling in the heated desert air was the massive 'tentacle' of a giant cephalopod, complete with pulsing suckers! And it was far more convincing than anything out of Jules Verne's *20,000 Leagues Under the Sea*!

For my sins, I had never been able to read H.P. Lovecraft's Cthulu stories, but I was very familiar with their illustrations in *Weird Tales* or *Famous Fantastic Mysteries* where Lovecraft and his followers had appeared. I could be mad. Remembering old pulp magazines. I was used to projecting images onto reality; this resembled a monster from a science fiction story!

I gasped and recoiled. I was back in some dreadful world of my own imagination. Then, almost immediately, I became calm before fear began to wash over me.

Again that 'tentacle' – now tawny, next grey-green, next brick-red in colour, its questing suckers pulsing slightly and very slowly, very gradually snaked over the broken edge of the massive crate and twitched, writhed then carefully began to approach me. It seemed to have an intelligence of its own. For a moment I wondered if the arm not only had independent movement but also intelligence. How had it seen me? Again, frozen with fear, I could not think.

I knew what helplessness was.

As that alien arm inched along the box's broken edge, I opened my mouth but no sound came. Had the creature begun to devour me I could not have screamed. I wanted to run, of course, but I was locked in place, too terrified to move a single muscle. I had the urge to placate the thing, to soothe it. I still could not speak. Even to beg it to set me free. And then, perhaps in response to my need for reassurance, a new feeling began to infuse me, telling me that I was not about to perish. At first it was tentative but then it pulsed through me with vibrant strength! I knew a delicate sense of calm, of affection, even something I could only describe as 'love'.

Completely unexpectedly, into my mind came something like a voice, something like words. I was again reminded of that 'whispering swarm', that constant, terrible sound of voices, with degrees of tone and loudness, like speech, but not speech, for I could never clearly discern words. That sound had become normal to me. It was the 'tinnitus' I had experienced since my mid-teens. The absence of that swarm was the thing I was still most grateful for. I was no doubt paying a price. Now came voices of a different nature, with a completely different emotional meaning. The tone was full of a yearning misery I could scarcely bear. I think I wept. I longed to put an end to that deep unhappiness. I wanted to make her misery my own. Lift it from her. I wanted to make her feel at peace.

And then I knew that this was the 'she' whom Imam Darnaud had addressed the previous evening at the orrery of the medrasa. This voice, not the women I had heard in the darkness, had drawn him urgently into the desert in a desperate attempt to rescue her.

The voice of a monster.

Now those arms, those delicate suckers, roamed gently over my face, over my head, my neck and arms. Their touch was that of a mother caressing her child. She spoke to me sweetly, sadly, murmuring as only a mother *could*. She stroked me as only a mother might stroke me. I felt another arm come from behind, to cradle me. And I wept with that mixture of profound emotions a child feels for its parent. A parent it had lost and now found.

My fishling, sweet fishling darling sad lost fishling, I am here. O, that I could help you, save you, succour you. How many black stones has it taken to find thee? But we cannot help either one for we are here without means. Sunbeam Capture has gone. We have no friends to help. Dear Pearl Peru is lost to us. Professor Pop has popped his clogs and Captain Otherly is gone out. All help from our friends fails as the great conference calls us in. Carbon Lie is gone, and The Provost of Nantes is gone and we cannot find the faintest hope where our old stripes were once deep. The Lone Arrow threatens to overthrow all balance! The flutter of a robe. The Black Monk has gone. Our hopes lie here. But at very least I must have water. Help me find water, little fishling, and I will find my true scale as all shall find theirs.

The voice became fainter and even more melancholy.

Once I was the size of a universe.

The size of a billion universes. I WAS the multiverse. I saw it and I absorbed it as you did next.

Once I swam through space.

And I was the mother of creation.

All reality sprang from my womb.

My voices once brought exultation.

Now Silence takes us to the tomb ... Oh what's that roaring? What's that PULL PULL Oh! Putting mouths to our words. Shimmy up! Movement of God's People! My heads! So many mounting heads! There will we make our stand in that moment in the back of the head. Shimmy up!

The whole time these words sounded in my mind those soft arms, as round as good-sized tree trunks, caressed me, stroking my lips, my eyelids, my cheeks, seeking to sooth me in spite of her own dreadful pain. My questions faded before a gentle flow of answers.

O, sweet fishling, mine, sweet child of the chaotic dark whose pain I cannot conquer, whose help I cannot draw upon! Sweet creation of the mighty elements, of that immortal love. Once I longed for you all to save us. Now there are so few. My egg. My glorious simulacrum. Sweet. Sweet fishling. They run from their burning homes; they fall from their fragile boats; they cry for help, and I can give them nothing. They cannot hear me or feel me. They create imaginary supernatural entities with which to deceive themselves further. Their complex, miraculous, vulnerable bodies are torn apart. I hear them. I love them. Foolish evil is a miasma filling their fishling minds. O, my sweet, frightened children. Where are they gone, your brothers and your sisters? Once I gave birth to so many. Once, those tiny souls illuminated numberless oceans and caverns beyond count. O, my fishlings!

And it seemed to me that her words had the beauty of the great melancholy songs, the aching pain of Mahler's *Kindertotenlieder*, his songs for dead children, one of the most moving pieces of music I had heard in my life. And not only was there a similarity of tone, there was a similarity of theme: That aching sense of loss which had been Mahler's, which it shared with Mozart's death march and Alkan's *Marche Funèbre* or Liszt's *Trauervorspiel und Trauermarsch*. I had never been so moved. I was overwhelmed as she grieved for her children. For countless millions of her offspring. Tiny versions of herself. She grieved for her children with whom, I felt then, we all belonged, whom she had sworn to keep safe. And now feared she would betray.

O, my sweet, delicate, vulnerable fishlings. Those stories, those legends. Those first ones. The beginning and the consistency of all our existence. We must save them. We must not die or let them die. The Balance must be made. He must not destroy it. Where are my lost fishlings? Why has he separated us? Where are my great captains – the merchant venturers – the chaos fleets – the brave, glorious heroes of the moonbeam roads who come together at the last conjunction, who heal our weeping worlds? Where are Thought and Mary Mercy? Where is Kindness, unrestrained? What is it, fishling dear, which drives sweet empathy down?

She wept with them, all her heroic children, the creatures of so many worlds who aimed to heal the rifts breaking the multiverse apart and creating a place without life or memory, a place without narratives and therefore without existence, caught for always in a moment without Time.

I tried to answer her but I could not. I tried to understand and on some levels I did understand, but not as profoundly as she wanted me to. For there was a force more powerful than me which had captured her and stolen her children and put them in another place. It was a place I would never find on my own but I longed for it, longed to enter it and help her, even though I knew I did not have the means to find it alone. And all the yearning in her found an echo in me and was reflected in my love for my own children, the children that were lost to me, separated from me by layers of time and space, by walls of misunderstanding and an-swers that had proven too easy. This massive cephalopod, maybe not even of Earth, not even of my own galaxy or universe, whose chronic pain was offered to me, just a little, in the knowledge that all her pain and all the pain of her children was so great it must destroy me, body, brain and soul. Her love threatened to burst from this universe and was so great it might destroy existence as she wept for her lost children and her lost reason, so tenderly stroking my face, like a loving mother, stroking my body like any mother seeking to protect and comfort one child who was also countless children, her babies, her fishlings, her brood. The child which was so like and unlike her, part of that great eternal con-sciousness which connected all worlds and creatures throughout existence.

And had she been the one to teach me the logic of what I knew

324

as the Tarot, part of the means I had of walking the moonbeam roads, the roads between the worlds, which those who told and taught the narratives used to spin the stories which made up the fabric of that reality we chose to call the multiverse?

We had driven so deep, yet still had only weakened our own strongest and most ancient barriers. Was this clarity real?

I knew that I knew almost nothing. I was no more than a vessel, a chalice among chalices, as those arms gently stroked my face and I was drawn up to her by the infinite sadness in that single, alien eye.

I thought of all the repetitions that went to make originality. I thought of the patterns of what, in 1962, I had started calling 'the multiverse' in a my first SF novel, *The Sundered Worlds*, a two-parter for *Science Fiction Adventures*, where parallel universes repeated one after another, crowded in a blaze of varied colour, filling space, thickly jewelled. 'They listened and learned that the multiverse contained many levels and that their universe was but one level – a fragment of the great whole. That it was finite but beyond the powers of a normal mind to comprehend.' The fragment was a shadow of the whole. The whole contained the fragment. Just quirky science fiction ideas then. I didn't really believe them, any more than the readers did. They were neat notions. Scientists dismissed them. Even the one scientist, David Deutsche, in Cambridge. Mothers were all the same. Mothers were all so different. Mothers made powerful sons and destroyed them, beautiful daughters, and betrayed them.

Behind me I heard a soft, feminine chuckle and, turning, I saw that woman again and now I knew her name.

"Mrs Malady," I said.

22

Insects and Elephants

S HE WORE A dark blue pillbox *al-amira* with a dark blue veil hanging from it. Stirred by a light breeze it only partially obscured her face. Her long swirling djellabah of a lighter blue hung below her knees, covering a blue silk kaftan. Her cloak was also blue but so delicate as to be virtually invisible.

I was pretty certain I had seen her before. And not in an Arabian Nights movie of the 1950s! Her name rang a distinct bell. Was she a friend of my mother's? Helena had no friends like her that I knew. I don't know why, but I thought she was more likely to be the mother of a girl I had dated as a kid. I couldn't remember any girl's mother looking as beautiful, especially one handling a big seventeenth-century horse pistol and sticking it under my nose! She had dark, almond eyes, soft olive skin, deep red lips and slim jet-black eyebrows; one of the most exotically lovely women I had ever seen. I recalled my Greek girlfriend, daughter of a communist labour leader. I couldn't remember my girlfriend's surname, but I was pretty sure it wasn't Malady.

"What did you say?" she asked.

"Mrs Malady?" I said. "That name comes to mind."

She was a little surprised. "You know me? No! You know Moll, my child! And who might you be, young man?" Her questions seemed rhetorical. "So perhaps you only half-know me." She was looking from me to the soft, reassuring arm which was disappearing back into the broken crate. Was the thing afraid of her? Or merely cautious? "Do you understand what that monstrosity is? She's a gentle enough mother, eh? You're her boy, are you? Come to save her?"

She did not put down the huge pistol but changed it to her left hand. "Have you?"

"What do you intend to do with her?" I asked. The creature's arms had now almost completely disappeared inside the crate.

"Initially? Why, to keep it alive, of course," she said. "It will die without water, as you probably know!"

"I did not know. I understood you wanted to kill her."

"Why should I do that? You are confusing my motives with those of Jacob Nixer! He is from a very different time and place. He thinks he relives *Pilgrim's Progress*! I have every intention of selling the beast. It would be a major attraction for any carnival, eh? Tivoli? Vauxhall? Palladium Park? You must know from Duval how much the monster's worth. It can be persuaded to obey. Oh, I shan't harm it as Jake Nixer and his cronies mean to do. I intend to keep it alive," she said. "The *spammaldjin*'s too valuable for one big dinner."

"Jacob Nixer?" I knew that name, too. Either the Rose or the Musketeers had mentioned him back in Las Cascadas. Or at a point when we were at sea somewhere on the Mediterranean. A henchman of some enemy who was following us to Tangier? "He's your colleague? Your servant, maybe? Your friend?"

As we spoke I was slowly becoming aware of more fighting going on around us. I heard the clash of metal, the noise of gunfire, yells and screams, horses' whinnying. Then, to my relief, the battle moved quickly off to the south-east.

"He's no friend of mine," she said. "He shot Barbarosa."

327

"But he caused all this?" Now I recalled the name. "He's the one who *sails* with Barbarosa! How could Nixer shoot his own captain?"

She filled up with barely controlled fury. "Because he's one of those who pretends to piety in order to fulfil his own agenda. Then kills you in cold blood for the crime of keeping Catholic rites. He sails under a flag of peace and reason. A Quaker flag. But he's a Puritan. A natural turncoat, like most of his mealy-mouth'd kind. He sailed with Barbarosa because no-one else would have him. No cause. No city. No country. No captain. Oh, there were many admir'd his skills, but none trusted him. Before he was a masterless man. Then he was Cromwell's Intelligencer General. But when the Protector died and his son showed himself a weakling, the Parliament entreated King Charles's son to return and ensure stability to the Commonwealth. This was done with good speed and now the Kingdom is restored. Puritans punished, banished or fled to the West Indies. I am surprised it has taken so long for the news to reach this remote part of the world! However, all is at last ordered."

"Madam. Forgive me. I do not follow you."

"I was his captain and Nixer his first mate when we took commission from an old partner of his who helped him keep balance in the Middle Sea. I remained aboard to watch his crew for him. Nixer went with him to meet his old friend Quelch. I should have been more suspicious of him then. But the Rose was a woman and so was I. I should have allowed for my befuddlement. Bah!" She scowled in silence for few seconds. "And they say the old stories are fading!

"When His Majesty King Charles Stuart returned to the throne those who still lived and those left behind, who had not fled abroad, were arrested. Commoners like Nixer were seized, given a quick trial then hanged, drawn and quartered.

Not a comfortable fate, to have your own genitalia stuffed into your mouth as you die." She smiled reminiscently. Behind a delicate hand, she licked her lips.

"You think this naïve? What could Jake do? Like so many, if he had remained in England, he would have had no choice. There was little he could accomplish. No Christian of any stripe would employ him. No Jew, either, for he had not proved himself their friend as Cromwell was. It had to be a Saracen! For only they combine the same religious zeal with self-interest. So he sought for a berth with the worst heathen on the Middle Sea. A turncoat Christian like himself. The man who stole the entire village of Kinsale and sold it into slavery, child, woman and man! One with almost as few scruples as his own." Mrs Malady, if that really was her name, looked everywhere around her, as if she feared to conjure the man himself.

"He pretends he is horrified by the *spammaldjin*! He swears that his religion makes him disgusted by the creature. But he is a hypocrite, lad. He'll betray you, no matter what bargain you've struck with him. He's a wicked piece of work and means to sell the *spammaldjin* for meat or to Consenseo's circus if he can find it. And do us all out of a fair profit. He pretends he means to kill it, but I know his real motive. As soon as he gets the chance, he'll betray you, too."

Given what I already knew, I had the distinct feeling that the lady was accusing Nixer of her own plans.

By now the fighting was very distant. Putting down her huge firearm Mrs Malady began to feel about my body for wounds. Finding none, apart from several bad bruises which made me wince, she frowned. "I know he shot at you and I know you were knocked from your horse. But I now believe he put nothing but a good portion of powder into his weapon! And that makes me think you were in some plot together. That's why I suspect he deliberately failed to kill you, and

329

that you two were both planning to sell the *spammaldjin* for a tidy sum! Why else would he have failed to load his tromblon? I mistrust anyone who rides with that scoundrel Duval ..."

"Duval, a scoundrel? How so?" I was genuinely curious. "I know he spent some years as a highwayman. A valet to James, too. But I never saw him break his word and he's proved a loyal enough friend to me." My voice trailed off as I began to realise that I had no reason at all to trust Duval. Indeed, until recently, I had suspected him myself.

Her eyes narrowed and she laughed. "Never yet broke his word?" She was looking around her now, smoothing out her costume as the noise of battle drew nearer. "He was one of those who was first commissioned to take the *spammaldjin* home. You must know something of what's happening here?"

I looked away. "Not much," I said. "I am here against my will."

Her lively beauty was even more apparent as she laughed again. "Duval did not promise you a share of the profit when he sold the *spammaldjin*? I am sure you did not cross the Sahara for nothing."

I shrugged. "I was kidnapped ..." I began.

"For what reason? For profit? You have wealthy relations out here?"

"I don't have wealthy relations anywhere," I told her. "I have no idea why I was kidnapped. I was on holiday with my wife and children in Paris. I was taking a stroll by the canal near the Cirque d'Hiver when—"

"Le Cirque? Near the Convent of the Carmelite Nuns?" she asked.

"I really don't know."

She straightened up, raising her pistol to point at me again. She was smiling as if I had just answered a question.

"So that's why he wants you alive. I was wrong. He doesn't

want an accomplice. He wants you because the *spammaldjin* loves you. Because you are one of her children. You're bait, my dear sir!"

I still had absolutely no idea what she was talking about. I was glad that someone did know why Duval and the Musketeers had brought me into the desert. I had some sort of affinity with the cephalopod. I turned to see one of the monster's arms disappearing back into the broken crate. Had the alien's intention been to protect me? "What's going on?" I asked. "If you know what she is – then I beg you to tell me. I have no idea how I got into this world or why I'm here! All I want to do is go back to my own. If you can help me do that, I'll gladly leave you all to your own devices."

She looked at me speculatively. "I believe you," she said. "But I have no idea what Jacob Nixer plans for you, nor Duval – nor, indeed, the others. He doubtless took you out of the fight with his usual cunning. He means to use you later." Then she turned, hearing muffled hoofbeats galloping towards us. "I have a suggestion for you myself. But if this creature dies, then—?" There was dust advancing. It burned my nostrils. I heard a warning shout.

Cursing, Madame Malady primed her pistol.

I looked over my shoulder and saw Sheik Antara, a scimitar in his hand, a rope in the other, bent flat over his galloping horse's neck.

And behind him rode the Musketeers! They had their flintlocks and were loading and shooting in the saddle at speed.

Suddenly Mrs Malady raised her heavy pistol in both hands, aiming at Antara behind me. I struggled to my feet and flung myself into her. She fell backwards. The pistol went off and flew out of her hand. Then she was up again, struggling to the dunes. Ignoring both of us, Antara and the others worked rapidly, getting their ropes around the huge cabinet. My horse

331

had not moved far. She stood only a few yards away. My rope still hung from my saddle, I remounted as quickly as I could and, working with the others, hauled the container back so that it stood on all its wheels.

"Milady must wait!" Duval was back. Dust everywhere!

The container remained lopsided but most of its many wheels worked so we could gradually drag it back to the well-worn track created earlier by Professor Consenseo. We could hear the battle returning. One last heave and the wheels were steady in one of the ruts. Just as we got her lurching forward, Darnaud and his sufis swept in to surround us. The white Carmelites formed an outriding defence, protecting those protecting us. I was impressed by the skill of Darnaud's military leadership, especially as our attackers continued to shoot at us.

Then I saw a lone sufi on a fast-moving Arab stallion racing in from the left flank, going in the opposite direction. Others were riding the same way, perhaps wounded or hurt. The rider was leading another horse. Hanging over its saddle was an evidently wounded man. He was not of our party and neither was he with the Arabs. His clothes were bright and filthy, closer to those worn by the men pursuing us, most of whom seemed to be the scum of the seas. I had no time to look at him, for now we were veering between dunes, still following the trail created by Consenseo's big wagon, a fraction of the size of the one we now hauled.

Darnaud rode up beside me. "Are you hurt, lad?"

I shook my head and gave him a quick grin, glad to be doing something. He rode past me, swerved his horse and galloped back towards the enemy. I turned my head in all directions, looking for Duval and for Madame Malady, but I could see neither. I did, however, see another rider on the crest of a dune. I was reminded of the powerful pictures of Lawrence of Arabia, wearing white and mounted on a white camel.

Though indeed mounted on a pale tan camel, this white rider was pretty evidently a woman. Clearly not Madame Malady, she was fully veiled so I was unable to distinguish her features. She was armed with a bow and quiver of long arrows and a curved scimitar. I was pretty sure she carried a machine pistol. She rode down the other side of the dune and completely vanished from sight. I remembered that Duval had heard two women talking that night, both well-bred. I assumed this was the other he had heard. Meanwhile, I was not surprised that Madame Malady had completely vanished.

More gunshots. We were riding into an ambush. Several fighters appeared over the dunes. All bore firearms. We had no choice. We had to keep moving forward if we were to get the strange creature in the crate to the oasis. The Musketeers were calling one to another. I could not see Duval. Athos as usual was taking charge of his friends, following Darnaud's instructions. Sheik Antara was at the rear. The Carmelites kept a strong presence around us, mostly using their big horse pistols, forcing our adversaries to keep their distance.

Some of our riders fell. Many had arrow wounds. Our enemies were conserving their powder, probably for a major attack. I spurred my horse into a faster gallop. We could not be far now from the Great Oasis. The big wheeled crate was bouncing between us. Gallons of liquid were sucked up by the sand as we moved. Then I heard a huge boom and everything spurted upwards. They were using a cannon. Could this be the tromblon Madame Malady had mentioned? The one Jake Nixer had fired at me?

Darnaud was calling to his men. A couple of sufis broke away and began to circle the main mass of riders. They, too, disappeared behind the dunes and thereafter I heard no further cannon fire. I assumed the big gun had been silenced.

Athos came riding up. "No wounds?" I shook my head.

"That's Jake Nixer's mighty tromblon! We thought he'd killed you with it last night but it seems he only took you with a blast of powder. He was after you alive for some reason. We sought you out but you'd gone. Someone else saved you. Know why he fired at you in particular?"

My head was buzzing. I barely made sense of anything from the moment when I was knocked off my horse to the time when I met Mrs Malady. But now I was glad to be caught up in the heat of action. "Where's Duval?" I stared around.

"We don't know. We thought he'd saved you. Might be wounded himself."

I remembered the wounded man I had seen. Had he captured Duval? Could we save him? Many of the men around me had bloody clothing. I could smell human excrement and urine mixed with the stink of blood and powder. The smell, I remember being told once, of trench warfare. My terror grew. This was not a dream.

Where *was* Duval? In spite of Mrs Malady's belief in his villainy – or at least her accusations – I thought of the cavalier highwayman as my friend. I had written too many stories about him to regard him as anything else. Of course he did seem to be the chief instigator of my current situation, but it was hard to think of him as the scoundrel Mrs Malady made him out to be. Had he really planned to use me as bait to trap a gigantic telepathic octopus? If so, surely that was not his only reason for kidnapping me from what I now thought of as my home universe and bringing me into this one! He cared for me, I could tell from his kindly, avuncular manner.

And who, indeed, was the villainous Jake Nixer? I had heard all the Musketeers mention him. They didn't seem to like him much. Clearly he was a bigger swine than any other swine on their side! In spite of anything the mysterious Mrs Malady might say, I was more inclined to trust Messrs Athos,

Porthos, Aramis and D'Artagnan than anyone else. Fictional characters they might be, but when I wrote about them for *Thriller Picture Library* they had seemed considerably more trustworthy than Mrs Malady!

All this passed through my mind as I rode helping to drag the huge cabinet towards Zaouia, the Lost Oasis. I very much needed to question Duval about everything the mysterious woman had said to me. Where was he now? Amongst our wounded? I prayed he had somehow made it back to the medrasa. Who else would be hurt before we managed to get there with the monster crate?

More shots sounded, sending up spurts of sand all around us. There was a very good chance that one of their musket balls would hit me and put an end to my questions. The enormous box was extremely heavy. It bounced and groaned with every minor bump in the track. The huge animal it contained had not seemed well to begin with and now I wondered if this hell-for-leather ride were not harming it further.

I saw Darnaud, Antara and the Musketeers, but none of the others. I began to fear that Duval really had been badly wounded or left for dead.

My impulse was to ride back and look for him. I could not do that, of course. I was now responsible for the inhabitant of the crate. If I abandoned it I would not only be betraying my friends, I would betray the 'monster' which had given me solace, which had felt affection for me. What had Mrs Malady called the strange, alien creature? The *spammaldjin*? A strange, alien name. I was pretty sure it was not Arabic or even Turkish. Apart from its need for water, I did not even know why we were dragging it back to the oasis! Or why it had been carried all that way across the Mediterranean and then the desert.

Under Darnaud's direction we struggled down the rutted

track as rapidly as possible, still heading for the oasis. Now we could see Zaouia's tall palms in the distance. We had almost reached our destination when a horseman appeared from the direction of the monastery.

Apart from his wide, white Puritan collar and cuffs, the rider was dressed unsuitably all in black. He was not a natural horseman and was unsteady in his saddle, chiefly because he carried a massive blunderbuss strapped awkwardly under his right arm and across his horse's heavy neck.

He had an unpleasant narrow face. His small eyes were close together. His pale, sickly skin was stretched tight over his skull. His red eyebrows met in the middle under the wide black brim of his Quaker-style hat. Incongruously he reminded me of a bad Thanksgiving cartoon. However, in no way did his face amuse me. Instead it sent a long chill through me. Of course I knew at once who he was! Madame Malady had given him a name and I instantly remembered it. He was the one who had blown me from of my saddle with a charge of gunpowder, keeping me alive but out of the action. This was the ex-Chief Intelligencer of England, Cromwell's secret spymaster, Jake Nixer! What he had against me or planned for me I wasn't sure. In spite of the fact that he had stunned me rather than killed me, I felt only suspicious of him. I guessed his intentions were in no way benign. I was mystified and frightened, certain that he had a private vendetta against me while also wishing to keep me alive, perhaps because, like the woman, he believed I carried useful secrets or had some mysterious power.

As we came to an untidy halt he motioned with his gun. We formed a defensive semi-circle around the giant wheeled cabinet. We could not risk him taking a shot at it with that horrible weapon. As we stopped, I rode in close to the box, concerned for the cephalopod. I attempted to glimpse inside. But I heard and saw nothing except for a faint sound in my mind like the activity of distant radio static. Was the creature trying to communicate with me?

"Stand away!" called that impure Puritan. "I have no quarrel with you as I demonstrated when I shot off Old Thunder here with nothing but powder to demonstrate his power! Did you enjoy last night, Master Moorcock, hearing Jehovah's Voice?"

I didn't reply. I hated everything about the man, including his high-pitched, mocking tone. I could not bring myself to speak. Two other cronies appeared on the dune now, their long guns covering us.

One was dressed very similarly to Nixer, with his dark greasy hair sprouting from under a black, broad-brimmed hat framing a dour, sneering face as unclean and unpleasant as Nixer's own. His companion sported an unkempt Van Dyke and the faded finery of an old-fashioned and dissolute cavalier, with a drooping hat on his long, brown, tangled curls, sprouting a couple of badly dyed blue and purple ostrich feathers shading his face. He had dirty lace at throat and wrists, a stained doublet of green velvet, over which was a wide belt of cracked leather passing over his left shoulder. Lastly, he wore britches of red doeskin tucked into jack-leather boots, folded at the calf to show a tattered yellow lining, and spurs of cheap trade silver. Both men wore swords and had the unsavoury looks of people willing to follow any cause for the best reward. As with Madame Malady I felt I had seen all three before. Riding close and stopping beside me, Porthos murmured that they had not yet had time to reload. He frowned. Turning in his saddle he looked back at our men. All were uncertain what to do. Nixer's massive portable cannon was now levelled directly at Imam Darnaud.

The Sufi leader raised his hand to bring our men to a full halt. His face was grim as he stared back at Nixer.

"You can go on without injury," Nixer called. "All we want is the contents of the crate."

337

"And I've a good idea what he wants to do with it," I murmured to Sheik Antara.

"Indeed," replied Darnaud. "But I shall die before he has his way. Are you with me, gentlemen?"

There was general consent from our men. We began to tighten our ranks around the big cabinet.

"I grow impatient, gents," admonished the smirking ex-Intelligencer.

"She'll die if we can't get to the oasis soon," murmured our sufi Sheik. "Nixer knows that. All he has to do is delay us!"

I was not entirely sure what type of creature the *spammaldjin* was, but it was pretty clear to me that she needed water to survive and the nearest water was at the oasis. I had heard her sad voice, felt her gentle touch and those had brought out all my loyalty. Like my comrades, I, too, was prepared to die for her as a child might die for its mother. I did not know why. And neither did I care why. Whatever power the creature exerted over us, we were all prey to it. For good or ill, we were hypnotised by something. Good or evil? We might never know. Yet we were going to defend her or perish in the attempt.

Suddenly D'Artagnan dropped the rope and with his sword raised above his head and a wild yell spurred his horse into a crazy gallop, dragging a pistol from his sash as he took his horse's reins in his teeth. Nixer didn't want to waste his shot but both his men had loaded weapons. I shouted for my friend to stop, seeing the cavalier lift his musket to his shoulder. I began to follow the headstrong musketeer. Then I heard a loud bang and saw the cavalier's horse rear up, neighing, as a musket ball grazed its flank and it flung its rider into the sand. The horse galloped away leaving its rider scrambling up looking around for his weapon. Nixer turned his own massive gun towards the source of the shot. Another rang out, causing

Jake's Puritan lieutenant to duck and fire his gun at random. With pursed lips, Nixer sighted towards the giant crate and prepared to shoot. D'Artagnan, followed by his fellow musketeers, was almost upon him. Cursing, he spurred his horse and, with a shout to his men, rode off down the other side of the dune, kicking a huge cloud of sand behind him.

D'Artagnan's friends caught up with him. I heard confused shouts. Now the Musketeers were off their horses and prone in the sand as they primed their guns. Sand flew up everywhere. Nixer had brought more men than we had bargained for between himself and our own people. By the time I reached the top of the hill, Nixer had positioned his small army on the trail, blocking our route back to the Zaouia oasis. If we proceeded we would find ourselves in a pitched battle. I could see that many valuable lives would be wasted before we could get the big crate to safety, if at all.

Imam Darnaud now joined me and took in the situation. He seemed desperate and close to weeping. "She will die," he said. "She cannot live in this desert! Either she finds water or she finds aether but if she remains in the desert she'll be finished! It means the end of our existence at very least! I mean this, my friend, as God tells it! There is no tale truer!"

"Who fired that shot?" I asked. "Do we have more allies? Please, sir, let me know!"

"The shot came from yonder." Darnaud pointed. "I don't know. Quickly, lad. Keep your head down and try to find out who it was." He handed me a primed pistol. "Don't let Nixer or Love take you." I gathered that Love was the other Puritan.

I turned my horse and set off back over the dunes, keeping to whatever cover I could. But I saw no gathering, just one figure lying in the sand. He appeared dead. I recognised his clothes from those worn by the wounded Turk I had seen earlier. I suspected he was pretty badly wounded. I wondered why he was on his own or why his men had ridden away without him.

Dismounting, I advanced cautiously, but the figure made no effort either to get away or to defend itself. From what I could see, the wounded man was no port ruffian but some kind of gentleman or at least wished to be taken for one. Rich clothes, including velvets and brocades, with a soft green cap on long curling red hair, a heavy red beard. His clothes were incongruous for a burly, middle-aged man. I began to have an idea who he was. He had evidently passed out. Yet there had been no retaliatory gunfire. I was baffled. How had he been hurt? He sat up suddenly. "Villain I may be, as my country-men see it, yet I'll not stand by and see that turncoat Nixer kill the creature I'm charged to deliver to yonder sanctuary!" He looked surprised.

As I drew closer the man clutched at his breast. I ran forward. Was he badly wounded? I saw him lift a pistol. There was no cover. I put my horse between us but then the wounded man called out in French.

"Are you of the *spammaldjin*'s party?"

"I suppose I am, sir. And who might you be?"

"I was *spammaldjin*'s protector. I am the man who brought her here?"

"You're not one who would kill her, sir?"

"Of course not. She needs water. Her carriage has been o'er-thrown and without water she must die, sir. Nixer wants to kill her. I aimed to kill him but I was never a decent marksman with a handgun. If you love her, you must get her to the oasis. Did I hit him?"

"Nixer?"

"Of course Nixer, boy! Is he hit?"

He had lifted himself on one elbow and was glaring at me from his hard, ebony eyes.

"No, sir. He is not," I said. "But the horse of one of his confederates was and that startled him. Whatever they meant to happen did not happen!"

"She's still alive? The *spammaldjin*?"

"As far as I know, sir. We were trying to get her to water. We were on our way when Nixer embroiled us in a fight. Who're you, sir, if I may ask?"

"Damn you, boy, I serve the *spammaldjin*! I am one of her servants. I aim to serve her, but I don't seem to be making much of a job of it. She's in serious need of water. I need to roll her carriage to the oasis to save her life!" He had managed to get to his knees and I could see now that he was seriously hurt, with a blood stain in his right side which clearly pained him.

I ran to help him to his feet. He stood, gasping. "I'm a fool to have trusted a damned Huguenot, and a skimpin' turncoat one at that. Call me a heathen convert, if you like, but that creature with his Bible-spoutin' purple pieties turns your stomach while he's picking your purse." He groaned suddenly, but talking evidently took his mind off his pain.

"Show me a man who knows every verse in the 'good book' and I'll show you a hypocrite who knows every variation of the Ten Commandments because he's tried 'em all out!" His red beard bristled. "Whatever 'thou shall not' he's done the 'thou shall' of it and added a score each of his own from Arson to Zealotry. I never knew a man who enjoyed punishin' the pagan or sanctionin' the sinner as much as Jake Nixer." Glaring around. "Where's my pretty jacket?" Shrugging it on. Trifle tight. Man and costume had seen better days. "I'll say that for him, he had a fine reputation as a torturer. He could make a widow reveal the whereabouts of her last mite quicker than a quip from a Portugee cunny-monger. But I was a thrice-clapp'd whoreson to trust him on this expedition, I'll say that. I promised the only woman I ever truly admired to get her

341

deity to her destination. Then I let myself be befuddled by a deacon-dodging bible basher and a twist-tongue'd harlot."

"Jacob Nixer?" I asked, knowing the answer. "And Madame Malady?"

"Not even adepts! Took *him* on as master-gunner because he hated the Pope as much as I do – and because he knows his powder and shot. I'll credit him that. Took *her* on because she claimed to be the previous mistress of the boss of this sanctuary we're heading for. Knew all his weaknesses. She was a friend of my commissioner. And, I have to admit, I fancied her." A cheerful spit into the infinite.

"No fool like an old one, eh, son? We got out here not two leagues from the oasis when I discovered they both planned to kill me. She wanted to sell the *spammaldjin* to someone who's offered her a small fortune for it and they fell out because Nixer had some crazed idea our cargo was the Antichrist. He means to shoot our *spammaldjin* and she means to sell her. When she realised his intention, she comes to me with the story and offers me half. Well, call me a double-dealing Turk-toaster but when I give my word to a friend I keep my word to a friend. I'm about to issue orders to clap 'em both in irons when it turns out she's converted half the hands to her cause and he's brought the other half over to his side. So he takes out a pistol and shoots me down but can't get her crew to his call because she's fucked half of them and promised to fuck the other half! I get away on the only decent horse we have and he and she set to scrapping so close to the sanctuary that the Sufis send out riders to see what's happening and the rest you probably know. Now I've no-one to trust and I'm doubtless dying. I'll go to my grave having failed to keep my promise and that means I'll lie in Limbo for eternity knowing that my last act on earth was to break my word to the only damned woman I ever loved or cared to serve! Do you envy me, lad?"

342

"No, sir," I said, "I do not. But I have spoken to the *spam-maldjin* and you must know that all whom I count as friends here, including Imam Darnaud, who is leader of the Zaouia medrasa, are sworn to see that she reaches her destination, which is as I understand it the home of Lady Blackstone. I, too, have made that promise and will do everything in my power to get her to safety. Do not ask me why, sir, because I hardly know."

He was breathing painfully as I got him to my horse and helped him up into the hard saddle. But he paused and offered me a steady look. "It would give my black soul great peace to know you speak truth, lad. I would bequeath all I owned to you, were it to be so. Know you that I have done well from the privateering trade."

"I do not want your treasure," I told him. "I want only to be united with my family. My wife. My daughters. From what she told me I believe the *spammaldjin* will help me get home. If I can help her, too. I don't know why, but I believe her. She talked to me last night and she made sense."

"She talked to you and you understood her plainly? As we are talking together now?"

"Yes, sir. She is dying and I do not want her to die. There's – there's a goodness about her I find hard to explain ..."

"Quite so. If you love your family," he said, "then she will do that, for the *spammaldjin* is nothing *but* love. And family means all to her. If I understand that, then there's hope for most of us. Including my black soul. She represents everything I ever lost since I left my ma's tit."

As I led my horse over the sand to where I had left Imam Darnaud with the big crate, he leaned back in his saddle and dragged my heavy flintlock musket from its scabbard. Looping the reins around his pommel, he began to prepare the thing for me. "I've lost a deal of blood, lad. So I doubt I'll have the

343

strength to level this thing, but I'll hold her ready until you should need her. I'm Barbarosa, by the way."

"I had a sense you might be, sir," I said.

"No need to be afear'd of me," he added. "I'll be dead soon enough and have no followers to threaten you with."

I must admit I had not expected the most dreaded corsair on the Barbary Coast to have this somewhat avuncular manner. The mention of his very name had sent Captain Popper skittering back to his home port. When I remembered that, I also recalled that large crate being lowered to the Tangier dockside! So that was what was going on! Putting two and two together, I could guess pretty much what had happened since we left Las Cascadas.

Not trusting us – or at least all of us – the Rose had commissioned her friend Barbarosa to take the *spammaldjin* to Tangier and from there across the desert to the Zaouia Sanctuary. What the giant cephalopod was and what she represented I still had no idea. I believed Barbarosa and the *spammaldjin*. I had a very poor idea what was going on or why I had become involved. And, of course, I now did not know if I could or should trust Duval. I guessed that the Musketeers and Sheik Antara did not have to be suspected. How many of us would be left alive when all this was over?

The two of us were slowly making our way back up the dune on which Nixer and his men had stopped before. I kept behind the horse and Barbarosa lay flat against the animal's neck. I spotted Darnaud and two of his sufis coming around the bottom of a dune and whistled softly to attract their attention. They saw me and rode slowly towards us.

Whispering, Darnaud said: "We are going to divide our forces or it's a stalemate. We need more men, if we're to have certain success. There is only one way to get her to the oasis and that is by running her through their blockade. We have men behind them who will pin them down. But we must expect to lose many of our soldiers."

"Perhaps not," said Barbarosa. "Can you get me back to my camp, where the fight started?"

"Possibly," said Darnaud. "Why so?"

"Give me two good riders and four good horses. And, before you do that, get someone to patch me up. I need to stay awake."

Darnaud and I returned to where our men were still waiting. The ruffians under Nixer knew that all they had to do was out-wait us and the *spammaldjin* would simply die. The other men, under Madame Malady, were already beginning to drift off, making their way back to Cairo, as confidence in her scheme of selling the huge sea-beast melted. They had no stomach for a fight. They did not believe that the creature would survive much longer. They were glad to keep their lives.

We returned to where our dour-faced men waited. They, too, had little expectation of success. Darnaud spoke with two of them while Barbarosa was being treated by a Carmelite medical monk. The corsair received a reviving draft of medicine. His wound was patched up so that he no longer lost blood. I was surprised by the speed at which he improved. He rode off with two men while Imam Darnaud watched pensively. He did not tell me what was happening, presumably because he was afraid the outcome would not be as he hoped. Instead, he signalled for me to continue back to where we could look down, with the Musketeers, on the other side of the dune. The long carriage containing the *spammaldjin* seemed eerily quiet now. No sound or movement came from it. Our own people spoke little. Some of the Sufis were clearly praying. The Musketeers, with firearms primed, continued to keep watch on Nixer's camp while others below looked towards the tall date palms gently waving in the faint breeze.

I wondered if they were still thinking the same as I was. Even if we eventually made it back to the medrasa what would we find there?

How many of the fellows we had left behind would have survived the attack of that gigantic wolf? Would the whole of the medrasa be destroyed and left in ruins?

I fancied I heard a faint, triumphant howl. I dare not think what we would find, even if we were able to get the *spammaldjin* to the water on which her survival so desperately depended!

23

The Gathering at the Oasis

WHILE I WAITED with him, Imam Darnaud sent his men on a series of errands. I wanted to ask him what was happening. There was no time. He murmured urgent orders. Frustrated, I felt useless sitting on my skittish horse with nothing to do. One or twice I tried to attract his attention but without success.

He sent the Musketeers a message instructing them to pin down Nixer for as long as possible. Within a few minutes one of the young novices returned. He had gone off with Barbarosa, somewhat grumly but now he was grinning all over his face. He said something in Arabic to Darnaud. The Imam replied with a smile. Laughing, the young man rode back to where, presumably, he had left the Turkish pirate. Another cantered up, received his orders, and quickly rode off again. I knew, of course, that battle plans were in progress. Matters were unfolding too quickly for anyone to spare time to tell me what was going on. I hoped to receive orders, but Imam Darnaud told me only to be ready with my rope, now re-attached to the cabinet. I must then be prepared to ride as fast as I could and help drag the massive tank to the oasis.

In a moment Sheik Antara came back. A little battle-dusty, he was a magnificent warrior. Jet-black, aquiline, bearded, with his round shield, sword, spiked helmet and glittering spears at his back, he was the perfect picture of a proud Saracen knight errant. Antara again spoke in Arabic to the Imam, Darnaud. They exchanged a few more words. Antara turned his horse to ride up and down the long cabinet, inspecting its wheels and doubtless checking to see if it was still sturdy enough to continue a further rapid journey to the oasis. When he was satisfied he nodded and began another inspection of the ropes we had already used to get that far.

Next Imam Darnaud rode over to the broken part of the huge crate where, so recently, I had my own encounter with the *spammaldjin*. From his saddle he tried to reach up to a place where the boards were broken. Even stretched to his full height he could not see to the top. It seemed to me he was in some way speaking with the creature inside the cabinet. For a moment I thought the great cephalopod was communicating with the Sufi master and he with the *spammaldjin*. In a few minutes the séance was over. Somewhat concerned, Darnaud resumed his seat on his horse. He trotted back to where I waited.

"We are going to have to be careful, lad. It's a desperate scheme and whatever happens will cost a good many lives on both sides. I can think of no other way of hauling our charge to the water tanks. You should get yourself into position ready to pull the *spammaldjin* to the oasis as swiftly as possible. There's no certainty Barbarosa's ideas are practical or will work out for us, but there it is."

I guided my sturdy little horse over to the gigantic wheeled tank. Darnaud called for the rest of our horsemen to get their ropes around it. Water was seeping through broken timbers and evaporating rapidly. It was clear. Without my being told I knew very little time was left for the gentle cephalopod!

Then suddenly from the dune which looked down on Nixer and his men, the Musketeers began firing with surprising

348

rapidity. I had a chance to witness my friends at their most professional, using those flintlock guns with unbelievable speed, two firing as two loaded. But I still could not see Duval. Was he truly with Nixer and company or had he been killed?

The return fire from Nixer and company was ragged and inaccurate. Clearly the ex-Intelligencer General was reluctant to use his mighty tromblon, since it required a huge powder charge, but every little while there came a boom and sand spurted in all directions, obscuring the scene so that it was impossible to see how my friends fared.

I saw a little of the fighting before Darnaud raised his arm and called out an order. Then we were all riding as hard as we could, pulling the cabinet with us. I had a moment of anxiety when at first it refused to move, but, suddenly, with sand flying, the wheels began to turn.

We rode into a rising sun casting long ragged shadows across the sand. I wondered how the oasis would look when we got back. What was the outcome of the fight between the African warriors and that monstrous wolf? I fully expected to find the oasis and the beautiful water garden totally destroyed by the wolf and his trackers, to see dismembered people everywhere and find the red-fanged monster standing in triumph over the remains of our peaceful sanctuary. Would I find two black warriors, Professor Consenseo and his charges, Father Isidore and the others all dead or horribly maimed? A charnel house of martyrs! I would probably never find out, because Jake Nixer's bellowing tromblon or one of his follower's swords would finish me off long before I reached the settlement. *Or did I have more lives than one?* Not many of the riders, I guessed, would complete this desperate ride. The words of Tennyson's stirring narrative poem came to mind as I recalled a similarly doomed charge. I galloped to its rhythms. *Was there a man dismay'd? No, though the whole world pray'd . . .*

We kept a tight formation around the huge crate. The size of a block of flats, it loomed over us. Every so often it came to a juddering stop and I was certain it would fall and crush us. However, as we hauled on it, it rolled increasingly under its own momentum. I was elated. I was pretty sure I was going to die. But I was still elated. I did not mind as long as the *spam-maldjin* was saved.

I think we all believed we were in great danger of dying as we raced towards the medrasa. With ropes taut we turned between two tall dunes and suddenly the world erupted again! My brave mare scarcely blinked but galloped forward, straining at the rope. I felt she knew, even more than I, how important it was to get the great cephalopod to water.

There came an enormous boom! The ground blew up, high into the air. Everything was suddenly silent. A great column of sand rose and kept rising over our heads. The silence! That terrifying silence. Was there any return to sanity now? Was all Chaos?

Suddenly sound returned. A reverberating roar. And we rode on. Rode towards it, galloping blindly into that yelling bloody wall. The noise was now like a voice out of hell with screams and yelps and prayers rising into the sky. The air was too thick. I could not breathe. Then something horrible struck me across the face.

I closed my eyes to protect them. My horse and I were moving without seeing. I drew up my djellabah's hood to protect myself against bloody parts of men and animals falling with the damp sand. Another column exploded behind us. None of Nixer's men attacked. Something was wrong. Did another savage trap lie ahead?

Without enemies blocking our way, I had time to consider what was happening to us. I was only aware of the heavy rope. Had we left our attackers behind us? I heard more firing and explosions at our backs. I glanced around quickly. Where were my comrades? Some had blackened faces, bloodied skin, missing hair or torn clothing. The horses and the camels, too, showed signs of heavy battle. Luckily none had more than superficial injuries.

The Sufis and Carmelites had grim faces. From relief or disgust? Though Nixer's men had threatened us and planned to kill us all, there was little pleasure in winning one's own life at the cost of so many other human souls, no matter how savage or misguided. Like many monks, I tended not to blame the ignorant for the sins of their leaders. Wiping the blood of a nameless sea-thief from my arm, I was very glad I lived, but deeply sorry he had died.

As the great oasis quickly came in sight, a few shots continued to sound behind us. The oasis was at first sight entirely deserted. Either the inhabitants had fallen back behind the mosque walls or the wolf had killed them. If the inhabitants had rallied to help the pair how had so many unarmed women and children found the courage to attack the wolf? Had everyone decided to go after the monster at the same time? And been simultaneously devoured?

We had seen the permanent secular population flee into the desert. Had the wolf found them?

My answer was a sudden loud cheering and I looked back. I saw all four musketeers mounted and riding to catch us up, waving their hats and weapons like schoolboys at a sports match. I had no idea how it had been done but they were definitely victorious. We were all somehow victorious! Like the White Sufis and Carmelites falling in behind us under Antara, shooting at those few of Nixer's men who continued to harass them before the sea-thieves ran back up the dunes and disappeared.

Antara was laughing with the others. "The survivors will

think twice about attacking someone while leaving their ordnance unguarded. They'll get back to Tangier, if they're lucky, but they won't have any gunpowder with them when they do! We used most of it to blow them to kingdom come!"

We were at the central oasis almost before we knew it. Slowly, carefully, we drew up beside the water. I was mystified. Why was the settlement so relatively undisturbed? The next action also surprised me as I watched the White Sufis busying themselves under Imam Darnaud's orders, erecting a great folding canvas screen from what they found attached to the side of the crate. I heard a splash and an ecstatic sigh. The massive cephalopod had entered the water. For the moment the *spammaldjin* was safe. I assumed that, for the Sufis, the monster possessed a profound religious significance. They believed they protected either her mystery or her modesty.

As we rested, wondering what we had yet to face, Imam Darnaud congratulated us. "I thank you, every one. Few of you anticipated our strategy and you fully expected to die. Yet you went on in good faith, prepared to give your lives for hers." Standing in his stirrups he looked around him.

"You have all made me proud," he said. "You have performed actions of considerable courage and skill today. I have to thank Admiral Barbarosa for his plan. We used the powder he was carrying when he thought his followers were loyal. He needed it to get them all back to Cairo. Now the survivors will doubtless be fleeing to Tangier as best they can."

I understood what Barbarosa had suggested to Darnaud. He and the White Sufis had returned to the corsair's almost abandoned camp, seized the gunpowder and used the barrels to bomb and distract the enemy, allowing us to get to the oasis without further interruption and without, apparently, the loss of a single man!

I asked Darnaud if they had found and captured Madame

Malady. He did not know and signalled to a weary old Barbarosa, bent panting in his saddle. The corsair was still feeling his wounds but he rode up, grinning at me. I asked again after Madame Malady. "Have you seen her?"

"We have not, lad. To tell you the truth, I'm not sorry to see her go. Her forms of diplomacy were better suited to the West than the East. She salvaged what she could of our resources, including about ten men who no doubt guessed their likely fate if they stayed in these parts. And fled."

"You knew her well?" I asked. I was to a degree distracted by what was going on around us.

He shook his head. "I met her in Tunis last spring, as I told you. She persuaded me that she was a friend of both the White Abbess and of Lord and Lady Blackstone and could help with getting the *spammaldjin* home. There was some urgency, as no doubt you know. By the time I reached Las Cascadas, the Abbess had gone. I now think La Malady never knew them very well. She's an adventuress of the kind a man meets in most of our big ports and capitals." He raised his huge eyebrows in an expression of self-mockery. "It was my bad fortune to believe her tale and to take her to bed. At my age I should know better. I allowed myself to be compromised! Still, she'll have an easier time getting back to the coast than Nixer and his willy-jackers. Both will have a harder time reaching Tangier than I will have returning to the embrace of the Caliph of Cairo. I have friends in all those ports. They have none. They'll have to dance a jolly jig or two to find their way home, those who don't wind up pressed into the Sultan's navy to enjoy a little light rowing!" Like many a successful captain, Barbarosa was used to imposing his heavy irony on an uncomplaining crew.

"So it's thanks to you, Admiral Barbarosa, that we're alive only half an hour after we expected to be keeping an appointment with the Recording Angel," said Porthos, accepting a flask of water from a Carmelite novice. He saluted the corsair. "We owe you a case of good Spanish wine at least!"

"You deserve your reputation, m'sieur," said Barbarosa. "I've gone up against French marines many times, but your gunnery is the best I've experienced in a life of making war around the Mediterranean."

"We are the King's Musketeers, sir," said D'Artagnan. He puffed his chest. He was half the size of the Turkish admiral but the two had considerable body language in common "There are none better in all Christendom. Or beyond."

"So I gather," boomed the Scourge of the Middle Sea dryly. "But what of your friend Duval? Was he not with you?"

I looked around for Duval, but he was nowhere. I had a terrible sensation in my stomach. I rode back to ask Sheik Antara if he had seen the cavalier.

"He was with me in our first charge on the pirates," he said. "But then I lost track of him in the dark. I didn't see him fall and at sunrise I couldn't see his body or his empty horse, so I assumed he was with the cavaliers. He's missing, eh? I'll ask Imam Darnaud to send men to look for him as soon as 'tis safe to do so."

Of course I feared him dead. "Why don't I go back and see if he's amongst the wounded? I'd be better employed there, I think."

He shook his head. "You're too valuable to lose, youngster. We'll send a party back when this is all done, never worry. Duval survives." He shrugged his shoulders. "One way or another, legends survive. He's no doubt waking up somewhere with a sore head. He'll come slouching in when it suits him. Probably with his pockets full."

I wasn't entirely convinced, but I had no real choice. I accepted their reassurances. I wondered if I would never see the laughing highwayman again. I took one last look back before

I rode towards the Musketeers. They were talking and laughing, clearly exhilarated by their recent success. When they saw me, they welcomed me like a hero, slapping me on the back and congratulating me on my riding (which was barely adequate) as generously as usual.

It was time to regroup. What had happened in the medrasa? Did the gigantic wolf wait to pounce?

I had little stomach for what we might find in those once-lovely water gardens. I thought it was likely to be much worse carnage than anything I had witnessed in the desert.

Slowly the two leaders got their men back in order. Then all of us began to walk our horses towards the gates of the medrasa, dreading what we were likely to find. The silence was ominous. The silence of death. Not even a crow cawed. I had an image for a moment of all of us become skeletons riding skeletal horses towards the gates of Hell.

That entrance was closed when we reached it. Nothing emerged. Nothing went in. It seemed every living creature inside must have been torn to shreds before that vile wolf loped back into the desert. I could only imagine the carnage we would find. I shuddered. I was already grieving for Consenseo and his friends, for Father Isidore and the older monks, and for the group of rabbis who had not been able or willing to accompany us.

The great gates opened and we rode through. Where were all the others we had left behind? My innards churned. At that moment I was experiencing an appalling sense of dread. I was certain that I was about to see something abominable, unbearable and impossibly evil for which nothing in all my more than twenty-five years of life had prepared me! I think I was in shock.

The trees looked completely untouched. There was no sign of blood or broken bodies anywhere. The marble slabs were unstained by blood. The water in the gardens was cool and clear. All I could hear was the music of the pools and streams. Ahead, the domed mosque and the twin turrets appeared totally intact. There was not, in fact, the slightest evidence of distress. Initially, I knew a sense of anticlimax, a peculiar feeling. Not exactly disappointment. I had prepared myself for horror and encountered instead what I could only describe as tranquillity.

At the Imam's orders we dismounted. We left our horses and camels outside the gate. There was no-one to take our weapons this time. We began to walk up the central path between tall cedars and palms, between beautiful poplars and pines, toward the glittering walls and dome of the medrasa.

As we drew nearer I began to see, around the last water garden, groups of seated people facing the mosque. I reached the final fountain and its pools in the company of the Imam, the Sheik and the four Musketeers. We paused to stare in surprise at the scene ahead.

I saw a large group of Arab men, women and children. They had evidently survived the wolf's attack! What had saved them? I made out the faces of people we had left behind. Old Father Isidore was there with some of the older sufis. I saw Rabbi Henschel and the rest of the little group of Jews who had come to the medrasa. Had the wolf harmed no-one? How had they survived?

An even stranger sight! I was reminded of an audience for an open-air concert on a peaceful Hampstead afternoon. Seated quite naturally amongst the humans were animals of disparate sizes. The water, too, was filled with many creatures! I counted at least five tigers of different scales! As well as the strangeness of wild animals mixing naturally with humans, I was forced to note the tremendous difference in size amongst them. There were large hippos, small hippos; large, medium and tiny crocodiles and alligators; water buffalo, both monstrous and miniature; big rhinos, small rhinos. Other beasts who, in the heat, preferred to wallow. Gorillas, chimps and monkeys. Lemurs, meerkats. Ferrets. Razorbacks. A huge python. A tiny cobra. One hippopotamus the size of a cat. A crocodile had the proportions of a rhino and entirely filled a smaller pool.

Along the edges of the pools were crowded hundreds of animals, all of the sizes, including big cats, elephants, lizards and rhinos, giraffes, zebras, bison and other, predominantly African, mammals. Side by side sat Professor Consenseo, Mr Bruno and Mr Jumbo. The people were relaxed with the animals, perfectly at ease. The two very tall hunters, who had been tracking him, sat in the front on either side of the gigantic wolf which now lay comfortably between them, apparently half-asleep, though a paw would twitch violently at odd moments. What had happened in the time since we left to engage Nixer and rescue the *spammaldjin*?

Imam Darnaud called out a greeting.

While no words were exchanged, the crowd appeared to welcome us. They all gave the appearance of people deep in thought.

I drew a long breath. I knew such extraordinary relief that I began trembling all over. I broke into a sweat. I had anticipated the silence of death and found instead the conversation of life.

I think we were all equally surprised and astonished to come upon such an unexpected picture. The people seemed cheerful enough. They weren't mesmerised. Yet few of us, whether newcomers or not, wanted to express their pleasure vocally and we waited quietly while what I can still only describe as a séance continued. I could not say exactly what was happening. I felt as if we were enjoying a conversation without actually understanding any of the words. If, indeed, words were actually spoken. Watching an invisible play? I had been a small child with pets. I think I knew what I witnessed. I did not know, however, what to call it. I remembered country walks as a boy and talking to ravens and magpies, going to the zoo and being in touch with animals who recognised me as I recognised them. Sitting with Guy. Stroking the leopard. Speaking almost inaudibly. Making her purr. Of course, we couldn't all communicate like that. And we could speak in different forms, sometimes in body language, through eyes, in signs and by a kind of telepathy. Sometimes in a form of simplified sounds – noises and grunts, high-pitched sing-song baby-talk or any version and combination of those things, most in low key and unemphatic.

Once, as a boy, I had come upon a pair of hares fighting in a field. It was March or early April. They had stopped to look at me. I had smiled. They weren't at all amused – their bright, black-brown eyes were serious, angry, glaring, involved in serious business. While they did not want the interruption, they were perfectly understanding. They knew that we were all thoroughly aware of the circumstances of our meeting and had no wish to disturb the other. Mutual respect? They say children understand Nature better than adults but it is true that Nature, or at least creatures, have a good sense of children, too. Insects or elephants, it doesn't make any difference, and there are no real rules. That kind of communication appears to be entirely arbitrary. It comes and goes and is only there because of a certain moment, a drawing together of singular harmonies. That is the way of things in the multiverse, even for those of us who can walk the moonbeam roads, who can stand for a moment or an eternity outside of time and space and see what is there or not there. What might never have been. Might forever be in plain sight. Or forever invisible save for a single moment. That is the multiverse. Only a very few of us are able to peel a sliver of knowing from one of those moments. And then it is gone and we have no notion why. Of course there is logic and some of us create great formulae through which we establish communication and tell complex stories, as I have done, of the Terminal Café and of princes and gods and my people, the Londoners. Who is to know what are tricks of the eye and flickering movements of the moon and what are profundities communicated on sheets of slender steel?

Singular impressions, some coming thickly one upon the next. Scents, visions, emotions; extreme sensations. Then an experience would be communicated. All our heads would turn towards the individual informing us. I could not easily say what I was understanding. I think, together with sounds and a certain amount of facial expression and body language, we were all achieving profound understanding, chiefly from the wolf who sat before us. Intratemporally we were adding to this, handing back something of our own narratives. And there was no confusion, no contradictions. I was reminded of very complex modern music, rather like my favourite Ives. I had no conscious understanding of what was happening in the great water garden except that everyone seemed to be communicating, perhaps using the giant wolf as some sort of conduit. Recalling that moment, I think we might have been broadcasting, too, in the hope of reaching others, the like-minded.

For a moment, Professor Consenseo looked across the water at me and smiled. I understood immediately that after we had set off to save the *spammaldjin*, he and the animals he had saved in his travels around the world, or who had found him here by instinct, had gone to help the trackers and the wolf. The trackers understood that the wolf was seeking a way home. They, too, walked the moonbeam roads, leading lost creatures back to their original homes. They were the N'nata'beli ghost trackers, On'beon and M'natka, from a tribe to the north-east, many miles away across the desert and the veldt in jungle country within the shadow of the Blackstone Escarpment. They had previously visited the White Sufi Sanctuary when tracking the wolf on his way *from* the Escarpment.

Now I knew why the Sufi Sheik had been so unconcerned for the safety of his orrery and the medrasa. The ghost trackers had already been through once, seeking not just the great wolf but a number of the animals now found by Professor Consenseo. He did, apparently, what the brothers did in other parts of the world. Every one of them, human or feline or reptile or any other species, strayed to different 'planes' looking for their original planes, uncertain where they belonged. This story came to us all through a kind of telepathy mixed with body language, some verbalisation. A good deal was communicated by the twitch of an ear or the movement of a whisker, an eye, a tail. A scent. I came to understand the empathetic links existing between those of us who inhabit consciously the planes of the multiverse. What intuitively I had come to understand about all existence, and thought I was inventing for my fiction, was actually simply a small part of the truth my mother and others had come to know. And what some of my children had come to know. What scientists, philosophers, spiritualists and religious teachers also knew, learned through accident or long study, by many different means, including the wisdom at least some of us, including my mother, feared. And sought to escape.

And at the conscious heart of all this knowledge was the creature whose life we had struggled to save out there, beyond the dunes. Who had stroked me and protected me and told me that she loved me, who some called the *spammaldjin*, the All-Mother, and who we had gathered at the Oasis of Zaouia to carry home, so that the multiverse could remain in balance for perhaps a little longer.

24

The Wild Prince

I HAVE NEVER been sure when I became The Wild Prince. The Wild Prince moves the world and the world loves him. But you can never keep him at home. He's the idealist who invests in the human race rather than his family. You know the type. Head in the clouds, hand never on the handle of the pushchair. Rarely and always reluctantly seen at Tesco or Safeway.

Helena told me that, when she talked with her friends at Newnham, they all decided that romance was the only thing which kept the human race going. Without it, they thought, women would never be attracted to men long enough to have babies. I found this amusing when she first told me, but not entirely convincing, because I thought lust was what produced babies. Later I realised that women like Helena and her friends made almost no connection between lust and sexual attraction. Or, as she added, "We're groupies. For someone. Poets. Mathematicians. Musicians. Painters. You name it." She never really told me why. "We link romance and sex," she explained. This meant that they were attracted not by big biceps, mighty thews or other Tarzan-like characteristics, but by men who were clever, talented, witty, moody and idealistic. Sensitive was a big prize. At least until they got a cold. Of course it helped to be like Byron and have an *interesting* medical condition as well as good looks and a certain noble stoicism.

She only once told me, after she had agreed to marry me, that she loved me; hastily, in a pub, just before closing time. "I love you, by the way," she said briskly, glancing away as if she had just admitted a weakness.

I wasn't raised to be English.

I didn't stop loving her from the moment I had seen her at that party soon after I got back from Sweden. I loved everything about her, from her flights of fancy to the way she tripped across the street, calling the dog as she set off to the shops, the hem of her skirt hanging loose. She began to tell me that she wished she had never married me from the morning after we were married. Yet the romance, it seemed, never did wear off.

Of course there were other qualities which attracted her on a more visceral level, but she hardly ever was able to identify them. Our marriage developed problems in the usual way of things. I used to think it was all my fault because of my own failure to pay due attention to her desires. I came to believe her deep unwillingness to discuss these problems was due in part to her passive-aggressive conditioning. Whatever the reasons, we both began to feel depressed. This meant that Helena typically drew into herself, while I tended to leave the house without her, even after the girls were at school. We would receive an invitation. She would accept. At the last minute she would refuse. I would go alone.

I didn't blame her when it involved going to SF meetings at the Globe or going to the pub with Ballard, but she didn't have very many interests of her own outside the home. We went to the theatre quite a bit. She liked to go to the pictures, and she enjoyed having friends round for meals. I couldn't exactly be called a gadabout myself. I worked a lot, of course.

Fiction. Features. Anything to make a living. She was not a music groupie. She didn't like going with Lang Jones and me to The Flamingo to hear the outstanding R&B bands of the day, but she'd sometimes go to a larger gig to see Hendrix or The Who. She said she didn't like to leave the children, but we had lots of friends who volunteered to babysit. Most of my meetings were with editors or authors until I began performing with bands again, so that I wasn't in as much as usual. She was, she said, glad of the peace and quiet. A few times a year I would go walking and climbing with friends, almost never for more than a week. I certainly wasn't chasing other women and I'm pretty sure she wasn't lusting after anyone else.

I suspect that she saw too much of me and grew tired of my self-obsession, a permanent condition of the self-employed. Anyway, because she didn't want to come to events or publishers' parties when we were invited maybe she really did prefer to stay in and be with the kids. In many ways she was a traditionalist, never much of a feminist. She and her friends preferred to talk the radicalisation of Emily, rather than perform it. I looked forward to times when we could go on an adult holiday abroad together, when the girls could be left with friends or relatives without us worrying about them. I thought she enjoyed our one holiday in the USA, but in some ways that, too, was probably boring for her since we didn't do much in terms of tourist stuff. Also we arrived at a crisis in Jim Sallis's complicated love life, which didn't suit anyone but Jim.

I don't think I ever went up the Empire State Building until I took my son during our Grand Tour of America, from sea to shining sea, the main object of which was to draw him out of his teenage introversion. We had started to worry that he was becoming too shy and not interacting enough at school, so he and I went by Greyhound bus from New York to Washington to Atlanta to Mississippi to New Orleans and Los Angeles and back again, via the Grand Canyon. It worked its objective, at least, and by the end of the trip I could hardly stop him talking. It was a good trip. He met, as I'd hoped, adults who treated him as a young man, rather than as the child he was at home. I think it prepared him for college later. But that was another story to be told at another time. I was looking forward to a holiday *en famille*. I think it would have been nice for Helena, the girls and me to make a trip like that together. But we split up, and I took the children on different adventures in the USA and France and elsewhere. I was determined to offer them every option possible.

As the problems of the magazine grew worse I was out more. I drank and drugged more as I tried to solve those problems and I believed that Helena probably preferred to stay at home watching TV, perhaps helpless to solve any of my apparently endless problems or not really caring, at least then. She and the girls stayed in Bristol for a holiday with my friend, the economic geographer Dave Harvey, while I needed to get home to London. Dave and I had met in Sweden and bonded over Mervyn Peake. Because a friend wanted to, I dropped in to one of the Brunners' 'At Homes' where I met a Russian woman, and we had a brief affair. I felt so guilty that I almost immediately told Helena about it. Helena didn't seem too unhappy. Maybe she didn't care. The thing was soon over. I felt almost as guilty about leading the woman on as I did about deceiving Helena. I always swore to myself I wouldn't be like my father.

Next time I went to the US Helena had what she thought of as a retaliatory affair with Jake Slade, an American writer friend across the road. She quickly told me about it. After that was over we both settled down for years of what I honestly thought of as domestic happiness together. Ordinary routines, family holidays and so on. I was surprised to learn quite how much her mother's approval meant.

In 1970 I was paid a film option on my book *The Final Programme* and, at my suggestion, Helena drove with Gala Hill, a woman friend of ours, to West Yorkshire in the Dales. Mike Harrison, Tom Disch, John Clute and I had spent time walking and climbing in the area and it always made me feel as if I had arrived home. My father's family had come down from Hawes in the late eighteenth century. With the film money Helena bought us a house there. Tower House was an Edwardian extension of Storrs Hall, a seventeenth-century manor across from Storrs Common, Hawes Road, above the village of Ingleton not all that far from Moorcock, by Dent, the highest (and poorest) village in England. I suggested she buy it wholly in her name because I knew how insecure her father's death had made her. She was inclined to look on the bleak side. I had always lived with the shadow of Mervyn Peake's early illness and death hanging over his family and seen how it had hurt them. I worked as hard as I could to give Helena maximum security and independence. That was part of my father-rôle. At an early age I became notorious for buying large amounts of life insurance, in case I died prematurely.

Life seemed to grow happier, easier and more ordinary in spite of the anxieties I still felt around each new book. We started going out together more, even if it was to the Mickey Mouse Cinema with the girls or for a meal at L'Artiste Assoiffe in Kensington Park Road. But sometimes we ate dinner with friends. We held a few parties, mainly because someone else made us. We saw Lotte Lenya twice at the Royal Court. We both loved Brecht and Weill. We were keen on Bessie Smith, too, but I could never share her taste for Schubert. We saw a few good plays by Pinter, Stoppard and the like. And did a few P&T events at the schools. Slowly I started to make decent money, especially when the time came to fold the magazine and stop repaying its debts. We looked forward to being able to take holidays together, perhaps to buy a house in London. In 1971 I took my regular business trip to New York, glad this time I didn't have to sell anyone another fantasy sequence, and was seeing an editor who had specifically asked me for a literary novel and was prepared to pay me a serious advance for it.

As soon as I arrived and settled in to the Gramercy Park Hotel, where I always stayed, I phoned Helena as I usually did to let her know I was there safely and would soon, according to tradition, be taking my regular trip to Saks Fifth Avenue to get her some clothes. That was when she told me I had better get her some things in the Empire Line style. I was surprised and at first didn't really understand. Then she explained.

She was pregnant, she said. She had stopped birth control without letting me know because, she said, she felt 'broody'. Of course, it also meant signing up for another fantasy sequence and probably a few more after that. I had hoped to spend the time working on what I called my 'holocaust novel', the memoirs of Colonel Pyat. I would have to set aside the literary novels I was planning. Back to the old grindstone. We both agreed to the principles of zero population growth and 'Stop at Two', but it appeared that she had agreed somewhat less enthusiastically than I had. Earlier that year we had been on holiday to Marazion in Cornwall, a beautiful little town, part of an old coastal mining community where legend said Phoenician merchants traded cloth for tin. It rained so much that the local fête, which had insured against it by so many inches, made a handsome profit. We spent most of the time, when not sloshing around in newly bought wellingtons, with very little to do. Even books were scarce. The only book I had managed to buy was a Cornish–English dictionary. I couldn't find an English–Cornish equivalent. So I read it. By the end of the first week I was pretty well educated in basic Cornish, which became the basis for my Corum books. Although the outline I wrote was for a character named Borem of Purile (which nobody caught) I made him some sort of anagram of Jerry Cornelius and that was how Corum Jhaelen Irsei was born, the only character of mine to be based on a specific English region. I got over my initial cynical depression.

I did my level best to see our whole situation from Helena's point of view. I spent a lot of my time trying to comprehend it. Since she habitually refused to explain her point of view I could only ever guess what it was. Was she trying for a boy? Did she expect to secure an already secure marriage? Had she come simply to expect the worst from me? Had her father's death prepared her to anticipate my early exit? Those were my best guesses. I also did everything I could to look on the bright side. I have to say it was a bit of a blow at the time. My anxieties came back with a vengeance. I used them to fuel a fecundity of my own, as always. But those years were not my most relaxing.

I anticipated that potential future during the period in which, it seemed to me, I explored my psychic past. Yet, oddly, for all that often vividly clear anticipation, I made no special effort to avoid it happening. Perhaps this was because something within me made me hope, in spite of having experienced the future, that it would prove untrue.

We anticipate a great amount, of course, but we rarely do anything about it. In spite of knowing the worst, we still continue plodding along the same timeline. Perhaps we go knowingly into the path of the avalanche or become knowingly swept up by the holocaust because we are primed to avoid anticipation of death. For the largest part of our normal lives we barely think about the inevitable. Only when otherwise depressed do we worry about earthquakes or cosmic doom. All become inevitable. The apocalypse is as unlikely as a car accident, the holocaust might not, after all, engulf us. Why waste time on anxiety? It might never happen. Time itself might change or we'll find ourselves on a different level of the multiverse. Some of us drift. Some of us believe we steer a steady course to certain goals.

So because my marriage was generally happy with only the occasional worry about the next book, I put those memories of the future to the back of my mind. Helena's romanticism was to my advantage and to my disadvantage. I did not anticipate the greater folly into which it would lead me. I did not allow for others taking independent action! How far the person of strong ego (bordering on narcissism) falls! And there is no doubt that I was not the only member of our union to come to that understanding!

In avoiding the consequences of my own actions, I simply created another narrative. Helena created characters for herself. And for me. She was the plucky modern put-upon housewife of her several novels like *Mrs Mack* or *We'll All Have Tea* and I was The Wild Prince or, sometimes, The Enchanter. "You put people under your spell," she said. "You're a controller!" Iris Murdoch had a lot to answer for to her generation. There was also the louche gallant, for which, I suppose, Ted, the Old Murderer, Hughes, as she and Emma called him, was chiefly responsible.

I'm pretty sure I wasn't the aggressive louche poet of her fiction because I really did prefer my family and I supported it. Bills were paid on time and children provided for. If we needed something I would find the money. We were never in debt or late with the rent. I'm pretty sure I was neither insensitive nor selfish, except where work time was concerned. As a rule, I neither struck others nor used physical force on them.

The one time I slapped an hysterical daughter on the back of the legs I cried. The one time I slapped Helena she told me she would have done the same, given what she said to me. Still no excuse. Nor for my drunken challenge to a man older than me. I never forgot my moments of violence. I was physically forceful with her once when I thought she was trying to get me to be more 'manly'. I didn't like it. I didn't want her to like it. I suspected that her fictitious protagonist was probably based on the Austrian boyfriend, Dieter Schnickels, she called Peter Pickles behind his back or sometimes simply Shnickelgrauber. If ever I need to remember why we split up, I take a look at one of her early novels. The world she saw was my world but with a romantic scrim in front of it. Or rather an ever-changing cartoon. If anyone thought her second novel, full of rock bands and alternative society stereotypes, was autobiographical they would have me down as The Wild Prince. The hippies and bohemians she writes about in her early books were recognisably our acquaintances, but were almost never self-conscious.

Not once in anything I read of hers did Helena write about a man who brought her tea in bed every morning, who made it his business to try to take the kids out for as long as possible, so that she could get on with her own work. A man who tried to write at night so that she could sleep through. A man who encouraged his wife to write her short stories and published them. Who fed his baby girls at night so she didn't have to. A bloody paragon, me! Yet these are certainly my memories, just as I remember her, after my breakdown, walking me round Richmond Park to help me to get rid of the largactyl the doctor had put in my system. She bought me perfect, thoughtful presents. After we had split up she remained loyal, just as she defended me against the sneering remarks of French editors declaring how vulgar I had been in paying everyone's bill in a restaurant. She had been there and seen the freeloaders.

I refused to listen to any gossip about her. I lost friendships, sometimes, as a result. Things began truly to go sour after I married Jenny. Helena used my name all her life so I suppose that meant something. Perhaps I shouldn't have taken Emma's advice and made a clean break and let her get on with her life.

She could be cute and quirky. One afternoon, she stripped naked on Morecambe beach and ran out with the tide, lucky not to be caught by the infamous Bore. She was inclined to determine the character of her daughters by their looks and wrote of her beloved son saying that he had the body of a tiny man. She was never on time. She loved the natural world as much as I did but she didn't like climbing. She mocked her little daughter's enthusiasm for gymnastics. She used her children to get her way with the Council. Almost always she discovered, after everyone else, that a neighbour was in trouble. Whereupon she often did something inappropriate too late. I said she had a kind heart and a bad eye. She could not read the city. She got on well with the middle-class neighbours who started moving in to the Gardens. She forgave men for actions she could never forgive women for. She could almost never say no but frequently begrudged others for taking advantage of her. She nursed long-lasting grudges against people she claimed to be friends and then blamed herself. When our daughter was attacked at knifepoint, Helena didn't tell me about it. The child kept phoning me asking to come and stay in Tower House. I told her we had guests and she could come later. Helena never said why the girl wanted to stay with me.

Helena spent hours on end barely working but talking and drinking with her dodgy friend Emma Tennant. Then she allowed herself to be interviewed by the *Sunday Times*, representing those successful authors who could no longer make ends meet on an income four times that of the average clerical worker. She paid her own bills with *New Worlds* cheques I had signed to pay authors. She took the money from writers who genuinely needed it. She told me she would split the proceeds of our Yorkshire house with me and then evicted me arbitrarily when I had nowhere else to live. No split. Then she bought herself a holiday flat in Brighton. She could spend prolifically, have nothing to show for it and send her children on holiday with me in worn, unwashed clothes. Another bit of passive aggression? I don't know. She called me a monster when I paid my teenage children's child support allowances directly into their own bank accounts so they could buy their own clothes.

At Cambridge her friends said she was known as a *femme fatale*. As she aged, her neighbours called her a saint. And, indeed, a martyr, sometimes. To me, she insisted, and I always tried to persuade her it was untrue, that she had the same mean, vengeful streak as her grandmother. The grandmother who bought a run of the *Windsor Magazine* at the Methodist bazaar and every year doled them out, one for her birthday and another for Christmas. When we met, she was as familiar as I was with *Sophie of Kravonia*, Ayesha and Quiller Couch. When we were breaking up, her mother sent Helena's brother to see me. His job was to persuade me to stay. He wound up reeling off a litany of reasons why he, too, would leave her in my position. By and large, she agreed with him. I tried hard to help her get rid of her self-loathing as much as I tried to help her understand how direct conversation beat passive aggression.

I tried to teach my children how to face and overcome their fears and to be the best they wanted to be. Helena wanted her son to become an admiral. She never really revealed what she wanted her girls to be.

And so Helena took control of the narrative. She came to hurt me through my children and taught them about anxiety.

I had honestly believed they would understand what had gone on, and if I didn't say anything, they would eventually see the whole picture.

Of course I still loved her. That was why I married her. I loved her more profoundly than I ever loved Jenny. Jenny was the girl my mother had wanted to be. My mother wanted me to be her father. I learned that early on. I was father and son to my mother; father and husband to Jenny; undead father to Helena. I really wanted to stop being a father to anyone but my children.

Idealism and actuality. I found it hard to make them work. Invention and reality. The comforts of romanticism. The terrors of sentience. Could they ever been be reconciled? I spent a life trying. Reconciliation was possible. But not for ever.

I came to learn this standing in that wonderful water garden as creature communicated with creature, when all our wounds were open wounds and sentience was at its purest. Communication. Not mere words or gestures, not simply mind, nor brain, nor spirit, but Sensibility. Sensibility speaking to sensibility. Mind to mind. And thus, at the Great Oasis and Sanctuary of Zaouia, I learned how even the great stars speak, how the minute atoms, which mirror those suns, speak: They speak as this mighty and everlasting consciousness which is the multiverse. Which contains itself and is contained by itself.

Seeking our sensibilities from somewhere behind us, as she drank and grew back to life in the oasis, *Spammer Gain*, the *spammaldjin*, the universal spirit, communicated with her glorious fry, her fishlings, whom she embraced as she was embraced.

For every mind is a mirror and every mirror shows us an identity.

"Now I see who you really are." Helena was in the Hall of Distorting Mirrors on Brighton Pier that day. When we visited

my mother, then my father, and the girls were three and four.
"If I had seen that first, I would never have married you."

That's how you get a long way from home.

25

The Great Wolf

THE BROTHERS HAD followed the giant wolf for years. They were from a tribe of trackers and hunters, the feared Bazuru, well known in the African hinterland, cousins to the Zulu and Matabele. Their N'nata'beli ancestors had been driven out of their original territories during a long, fierce war which ultimately established the ascendancy of the Zulu Empire.

The Bazuru branch of the N'nata'beli had settled in the lush highlands, an entire world of their own, on the great escarpment called the Blackstone by whites but Kono-Anu by the Naka aboriginals below. The Naka had farmed corn and cattle on the veldt before the Bazuru arrived with their more sophisticated and complex culture. The Naka contributed much of their customs, language and many of their legends to the united tribe, the Bazurunaka, which grew rich and strong and knew peace for many generations with the high escarpment becoming their safety from which the warrior tribe could fight. Until an earthquake destroyed the road upwards, the tribes were interdependent.

The Escarpment, from a distance, resembled two rounded breasts or the roofs of the great meeting houses where the tribe determined its laws and customs. Roughly, their Naka name

374

was said to mean Strife and Peace, the twin forces in their belief system. A very limited translation.

"Actually," Professor Consenseo told me next morning as we breakfasted, "I prefer the rather more sophisticated term 'Chaos and Law'. It's closer to the Naka meaning and, of course, exists in our Northern cultures, including the Persian, the Greek and the Norse. I'm no anthropologist but I have spent much of my life in Central Africa and have some understanding of the local languages and ideas. What would you say, M'natka?"

M'natka'mandunta, unlike his brother, had gone to school and university in England and spoke with an over-refined Tory accent, bearing only undertones of his warm, thrilling Bantu dialect. Next to him at the long breakfast table, his brother, Umsa'g'mandunta, known as On'beon, spoke in much stronger, African-accented tones. "I like what our people called the Escarpment when we approached it from the south – Two Shields – because its long rising heights resembled the convex surfaces of our cowhide shields."

The substance of that morning's conversations was exchanges of information between the various people now gathered at the Zaouia Sanctuary. These included Sheik Antara, Professor Consenseo, the Bazuru brothers, the Musketeers, Father Isidore, Imam Darnaud, Captain Barbarosa and the various monks, rabbis and sufis who regularly occupied the place. We ate in the great hall. The animals preferred to eat outside or in the stables. The great wolf had happily settled in with the others. He was by far the largest creature there, after *Spammer Gain*, as Professor Consenseo called her in English. The wolf had been terrified until Professor Consenseo had been able to communicate with him.

The eccentric Englishman could not talk to animals in the Doctor Dolittle sense. He could communicate, one sentient creature to another, in a predominantly wordless way. The brothers were unable to do this, except in the crudest terms. He was a kind of animal-whisperer. The giant wolf was gigantic only on this plane and, like many of the displaced animals and people, he was in constant pain. Professor Consenseo had recognised the dilemma at once.

"The planes of our universe are separated by scale and mass." I think he advanced his own theory. "The differences between one plane and another are minute. Apart from scale, one plane can be almost exactly identical to the next. But, should some unfortunate cross many planes at once, they may find they are gigantic or miniscule in comparison. That is why they feature so often in our folktales. Since I discovered this, and being from another relatively nearby plane myself (though fortunately feeling no discomfort), I have made it my life's work to help our animal friends cross back to their own. I have helped, conservatively, several thousand of sentients, including humans, find their native worlds."

I murmured congratulations. He shook his head vigorously. "Not my point, my good sir. Of late the gateways have altered, and even begun to disappear, as the so-called Conjunction grows nearer. Many gates will open, perhaps briefly, through the fulcra, then close quickly. That closure could mean that most gates will be shut. Perhaps all. So many will be stranded!" He spoke with considerable concern. Obviously matters were urgent.

Other animals in his strange menagerie shared their problems with the wolf. Everything was too large or small, out of proportion. These were the creatures who had not died. Gravity was wrong. The brothers had been tracking the huge beast ever since they had heard of him, trying to get him back to his original plane. The poor thing was in agony. Every bone in him radiated terrible pain. He had four times failed to destroy himself. He had a single hope of release. Like everyone, he had heard a rumour that *Spammer Gain* was on her way to the Escarpment. There might be a way home.

Consenseo had a bigger appetite than Porthos, who sat on my right in relative silence. The Musketeer was determined to make up for his recent starvation. He paused every so often to pour himself more wine, offer a brief, polite response between belches, and further apologies. He was somewhat in awe of this man of science. The Sufi were not of that sect of Islam which denied its followers alcohol, so Porthos gave them no offence.

The remaining musketeers had distributed themselves among the other breakfasters, as if to share their glory. D'Artagnan still insisted on shouting cheerfully to his comrades across several tables. Only Aramis did not respond. He was enjoying a quiet conversation with Sheik Antara.

The professor and the brothers were already acquainted. After we set off on our raid to save *Spammer*, they came together with the older monks, sufis and rabbis, as well as all the animals there. Somehow they formed a kind of group mind. From what I could tell, this was pretty much a literal *meeting of minds*. A *consciousness* is not necessarily the same as a *brain*. What I had seen had rather reminded me of a Quaker meeting. Everyone focused on calming and communicating with the gigantic timber wolf, trying to help him in his despair.

The wolf had not come from North America, as I had first thought. It came from the heart of Europe, from the Balkans. He was much larger than a grey wolf but equally beautiful and with similar markings. His huge bulk, always in pain, had carried him through Ukraine, Romania, Bulgaria, Turkey, Syria and Egypt, leaving shape-changing Dire Wolf and were-wolf legends and terror in his wake until, many hundreds of miles distant, he had reached equatorial Africa and almost found his goal. Then something had stopped him! The picture we had could be of frustration rather than fear.

This was how he came to the attention of the Bazuru brothers. As he fled towards the Nile they had tracked him into Chad for over a year. All around that part of Africa, they tried to force him back towards their homeland where they hoped they could return him to his own world through a gateway said to lie within the Blackstone Escarpment.

"He hates Africa," said M'natka in his Old Etonian drawl. "It is too hot for him. He is not difficult to follow. As he fled before us, he struck everyone as he must have struck you.

"The pain grew worse and worse," he went on. "What we sensed of it was unimaginable. Yet his will grew stronger. He was aggressive and horribly fierce. Quite honestly, my friend, I thought we'd met our match near Aswan when we first came face to face with him. We chased him for miles! Back and forth, back and forth, through the forest, the desert and eventually onto the low veldt and then the Sahara again. His pain made him intractable. Every time we cornered him, he snarled and howled and threatened us. We had tried to be gentle with him, but he simply would not respond. We could tell he was terrified but we had no way of calming him. He was just too big and strong for us to capture. His seventh sense told him he needed this Sanctuary but he had no clear idea where, or even what, it was. As you know, by the time he got here he was thoroughly out of his mind. Were it not for the *spammaldjin* he would have torn his own poor, tortured body to bits! I think he would have done some other damage, maybe even killed one of us, had it not been for Professor Consenseo and his superior wisdom!

"I am so thankful Professor Consenseo could get here when we did."

The professor beamed with a mixture of good will and a trace of patronage. "Happily, dear boy, I was on a mission of a not dissimilar nature. For over three years, on this particular

378

expedition, I travelled the world gathering together distressed creatures unable to reach their home plane. I had a happier experience because I knew there were many beasts desperate to return to their own environments as I was. When the big wolf got here I enlisted the help of all those creatures. The grey wolves, some foxes, coyotes and other wild dogs, who were immediately able to amplify their own sense of harmony and express it to him. Ultimately, by the time you returned, we were all in tune, so to speak. Sharing the same narrative. The violence out there in the desert was somewhat disturbing. Our mutual enemies, I fear, are determined people. But *Spammer Gain*, the *spammaldjin*, was able to let us know how you were faring. She is an impressive deity."

"Deity?" I had not really thought of the alien as a goddess. I could see how easily she might be considered one. How she might manifest, as it were.

Now that she had transferred herself from the outer tanks to the water garden, *Spammer*'s presence permeated the entire compound. She had not been seen since they erected another screen around her. I was unsure of the point of shutting her away from everyone's sight, unless it was for her safety. Every so often I still heard her voice. *My fishlings, sweet fishlings, what forms do they force upon us. It is hard, so hard to find the great gate again ... And we are tired, so tired ... We're tired of making love ...*

I think we all heard a snatch of that strange, melancholy voice.

"Oh, I know we're all gods in the eyes of others." M'natka answered, as if he had been caught in some naïveté. "But she ..."

"We were raised on her image as Mother of Gods. It is very hard not to show *some* superstition," added M'natka. "A certain awe, almost. For you it might be if one of your prophets appeared in the flesh." He laughed almost nervously. "As if Moses were to show up with the tablets of the Law under his arm perhaps." I believe he blushed at that moment.

I had a feeling he was condescending to me.

"She is that powerful, eh?" Next to M'natka, Father Isidore had leaned forward to listen. He was respectful. "Well, it is even more of an honour to have her here with us, if only for a little while."

They already planned to begin the next stage of *Spammer's* journey. Clearly most of us were gathered here to form an expedition to the Blackstone Escarpment. I had already come to understand that Lord and Lady Blackstone held a special rôle in this story. Even when I asked directly what that rôle was or who the Blackstones actually were. They were British gentry, apparently, whose ancestors had long since settled this part of the world. Nobody would tell me more. Largely, it seemed, because nobody really knew. They were as part of the ancient stones as the mysterious animal-gods who punished and protected. I understood that the Blackstones were greatly respected throughout Africa. They drew enormous loyalty from people on all sides of the continent's political divisions.

Growing up, I could not really remember ever reading about them or seeing them referred to on TV. This was surprising. I had gone to school when half the 'Dark Continent' was part of the British Empire (now the Commonwealth). Whatever happened, there was always news of the personalities engaged in running things. Blackstone sounded like a mixture of Allan Quatermain, Tarzan and Sanders of the River. They had the aura of Lord and Lady Mountbatten, who were believed to support colonial independence. I looked forward to meeting them.

Strange that people who were probably European were playing such a large part in African affairs. But then I realised that time was considerably distorted or, put another way, following a very different course to the one I had left behind in Paris with my wife and daughters! After all, here I was sitting at a long table with men who thought of home as seventeenth-century London and Paris, fifth-century Yemen, nineteenth-century England, thirteenth-century London, twenty-first-century Cape Town! And so on. I had come to accept it as normal.

Duval's absence concerned me. I hated the idea of his having been killed. A search was made for him, but Barbarosa's gunpowder had blown people to nothing. The scenes of our fights were marked merely by bits of bloody bone and flesh. We assumed that Madame Malady had fled with a few men back to Tangier. No doubt, those who had survived the gunpowder attack were also heading for some safer Maghrebi haven. Watch would still be kept for Duval by the Carmelites and White Sufis of the Sanctuary, but we must assume him killed in one of our desert battles. However, we would only mourn him when his death was confirmed.

We were agreed. We would leave in the next few days for the Blackstone Escarpment. Sheik Antara and the Bazuru brothers would lead us from the desert, across the veldt to where ultimately we should be able to see Kono-Anu rising out of the forest.

As soon as I had some sort of picture from the Bazuru trackers I became excited. This would be my first experience of the Africa I had read about in the Tarzan books and later in the stories of both H. Rider Haggard and Edgar Wallace, who had actually lived there. I would probably not be disappointed in the real thing. I had to admit that so far the Sahara had more than lived up to my expectations. I was not, however, especially looking forward to crocodile- and hippo-infested rivers.

The Bazuru brothers were most familiar with Lord and Lady

Blackstone. I was grateful when they decided to talk about them a little.

"Lord Blackstone is revered even amongst the most political of black Africans," said On'beon. "He was born and raised at the very heart of Africa by the legendary talking gorillas of the Deep Congo, the Hairy Men. His forest lore is greater than anyone's. He has lived on the Escarpment for many years. Some say he has lived there for ever, that he is as old as the world. Like you, professor, he can speak with the animals and can make the voices of the elephant, the lion and the gorilla!"

"Not *exactly* my skill," murmured the Englishman modestly. "Though I do have a certain expertise when communicating with the American bear." He was speaking about a special bond he appeared to have with the huge beast he called Bruno. Bruno certainly seemed amiable and to have a liking for the professor even more than most of the others in that bizarre menagerie.

"Gorillas! He sounds like Tarzan," I joked, but they looked at me in puzzlement. Clearly my childhood enthusiasms had not travelled. I have noticed increasingly how my early heroes have become no better than distorted memories. Certain stories are universal and become attached to changing heroes. The protagonists change frequently but the narratives do not. Others were not quite as widespread or did not outlast demographic realities. I suppose I should not have expected too much. After all, here I was, sitting at table with perhaps the greatest of all Arabia's legends, who had lived in the years before Islam.

Now talk turned to the expedition itself. *Spammer*'s 'carriage' would be repaired. The massive tank was already metal-lined, with several 'windows', like covered portholes, through which her water supply could be monitored. We would carry spare tanks. If she needed to, she could use her extraordinary eyes to see, physically, where we were taking her.

The oasis and sanctuary had existed for hundreds of years. Zaouia supported a good supply of experienced carpenters and blacksmiths now at work reinforcing the great cabinet. With luck, it would withstand the second stage of its journey to the Escarpment. No-one would say how were we supposed to haul the thing up the side of a very tall mountain? Perhaps there was an easy road to the top. All that mattered to me was that after we had helped the *spammaldjin* reach her destination I would return to Helena and the girls in Paris. How *that* was to be achieved I still had no idea. I was quietly determined.

The following week was spent in studying maps, planning our route, and creating the special extra vehicles for the animals which up to now Professor Consenseo had been forced to carry in increasingly cramped conditions. The crocodiles, the snakes, the smaller mammals were incapable of riding on the larger ones. I could tell that our caravan to the Blackstone Escarpment was going to be the strangest to make a road across Africa. But it would be considerably less difficult than it had been!

It did not occur to me to wonder how much time had passed in reaching the Sanctuary of the Zaouia Oasis. How long would the trek take? Were we following what Duval and others called the 'moonbeam roads'? Were there maps which did not show the obvious routes across the world? Had I failed to ask the right questions? Or notice what was obvious to others, perhaps because my attention was elsewhere?

Why had I made no serious effort to change the course of my experience? It seemed to me then that all my life I had taken the line of least resistance, just letting circumstances determine my next move. Maybe I was what Helena, half in anger, had once called an escape artist? Maybe I did care more for my work than for my family. Maybe I did try to control too much of my world, especially my domestic world, to ensure my work environment.

I suspected myself of writing fantasy to escape the whispering swarm of real-world responsibility. Then I criticised contemporary science fiction and fantasy for not achieving the seriousness they claimed. Was I that much of a hypocrite? That much of a coward?

26

Scarlet Sand

I WAS SHARING much of the journey with the great wolf and a cheetah almost as large. I called her Lizzie. They were companionable creatures, if a little introspective, preferring to eat and sleep when I did. We took to sitting and watching the horizon, usually at dawn or sunset. Like most cats, the cheetah had a tendency to sit down while thinking, while the wolf lay with his head upright, his forelegs stretched out in front of him. He bore his terrible pain with the stoicism of most wild creatures. The wisdom of all the apothecaries at the oasis, together with Professor Consenseo's powders, had combined to relieve his misery. His hunger was satisfied by the Englishman's mysterious elixir. Occasionally his tail would wag as he was struck by a pleasant thought. From the monster I had taken him for, he had turned into a rather grave, thoughtful beast.

The cheetah was a little more playful. From time to time she tried to get the wolf to join in her fun. When relaxed and, I think, glad of the distraction, the wolf would take a few passes at her and roll on his back, batting at the big cat and making little growling noises deep in his throat. Their personalities were not at all the same yet they were clearly friends. The cheetah enjoyed being scratched behind her ears, on her forehead and along her nose, and she would usually show

385

her pleasure by a deep thrumming purr followed by a kind of sigh. The wolf would lie down, resting his massive, warm body against mine and occasionally giving my hand or face an enormous, affectionate lick.

But the strangest thing about all the animals of this unlikely expedition was the sense of communion we had. Animals and humans shared minds in a way I would then have described as telepathic. We worked in concert, with great consideration, a kind of instantaneous democracy more common to insects than other creatures. Almost entirely unconscious. Even the beasts whose natural prey walked directly ahead of them showed no sign of wanting to attack. The gazelles, zebra or gnu had no fear of the predators, any more than the smaller monkeys, bats or rodents. Generally when we camped for the night, the animals moved close to our fires as the desert air grew cold, displaying nothing but a need for warmth, and lay down together near the flames. This was not surprising to Professor Consenseo, who knew his friends well. Bruno, the big brown bear, always chose to sleep outdoors with him. Every night the professor took off his tailcoat, his waistcoat, his flowing bow tie, folded his trousers neatly and place his cleaned boots beside them before slipping into the djellabah he used as a nightshirt. Then he and the bear would settle into a comfortable embrace. Bruno's grunts of affection would often be the last sounds I heard at night. Although Jumbo the elephant often kept them company, I could tell that Consenseo's friendship with the bear was in certain elements closer.

I was seriously tempted to try his 'elixir'. The clear brown liquid smelled strongly of beef, reminding me of Brand's Essence. My mother had given it to me when I was an invalid. Who would not want to try something which allowed you to keep going for weeks without eating? Just the stuff, I thought, for when I travelled on the tundra and mountains of remote

Scandinavia as Dave Harvey and I had done before I got married. I had enjoyed the trip, even if hitch-hiking back to Paris had been a bit depressing. George Whitman, predatory and kind at intervals, in Le Mistral bookshop had a habit of expecting young men to pay their rent with intimate services, so I had escaped into the Tuileries from rue de la Bûcherie. The French cops found me and took me to the British Embassy. The Brits in turn dropped me off at the Hôtel Madeleine and then put me aboard the boat train to London without anyone thinking to feed me so that by the time my mum met me at Victoria Station I was desperate for a plate of cod and chips and a pint of decent bitter which, of course, I couldn't hold down. Later that month I went to a party and met Helena. We started going out together. I got freelance work with Fleetway. I wrote fantasy stories for Ted Carnell. And then we were married and then we had the girls and then I was back in Paris and then I was out in the desert, part of a caravan of fighting Carmelite monks and white-robed sufis, several familiar figures of fiction, an eccentric English veterinary-zoologist of some kind, a bunch of unwild beasts of disparate sizes and a giant telepathic cephalopod who was worshipped as a goddess by two Bazuru trackers, one of whom at least was classically educated better than anyone else in the party.

What, I asked myself, was the best part of all that? And I thought of an August day in Holland Park in 1965 writing a scene for *The Wrecks of Time* for *New Worlds* as I sat on a bench, fence behind me, lawn behind that, peacocks on the lawn. And sitting in their big built-like-a-battleship double pushchair, one behind the other, pilot and observer of an old biplane, my two lovely girls, nodding off in the sunshine. Wearing identical Babygro suits, one was almost two and the other almost one. Fair hair, rosy cheeks, little, perfect hands grasping nothing, their blue eyes suddenly opening at the same time to look about them, wondering, surprised at the bright, busy world. As usual I had taken them into the park to give Helena a break. Pip, the Sheltie, ran around the pram, pink tongue lolling. I took descriptions for backgrounds and incidental characters from the park. I was writing a story about alternative Earths. Not many, I think. Maybe ten or twenty. My main character was a cross between Falstaff and Faust, who, as I recall, created and destroyed those alternatives. Not much of a story, really. My main interest had been in the character whom I'd revisit later, as Mr Kiss, in *Mother London*. I remembered more about the girls in the park. I yearned to be back there. I would yearn to be back there until my dying day.

Our weird caravan struggled on, wagons creaking, wheels squeaking, with the White Friars acting as guards. Those animals capable of it helped drag the great wood, metal and glass cabinet foot by foot across the Sahara towards the scrub of the low veldt and beyond that the green high veldt and beyond that the forest and the Blackstone Escarpment. I had to assume that we were in the region of Chad or Nigeria but all I could be fairly sure about was that we were in West Africa when we found a good, well-worn road. "An old Arab road," I was told. "A slaver's route. Discreet."

We were within a day of the desert's end, packing after breakfast and ready to get back on the road when I heard a half-familiar drone in the distance behind us. Unconsciously I looked up. The sound had reminded me of something I had not heard since my boyhood when the German bombers were coming over Britain. The day was a little hazy and the still air not especially clear. I tried to scan the sky but could see only misty cloud. I was amused by my own response. While I remained unclear about the dates involved, I was pretty sure this was the seventeenth century. Professor Consenseo, of course, was from Edwardian times, while the Bazuru brothers were also probably from the twentieth century. I mused on this, beginning to understand the ideas of time, mass and physical scale and also the notion of certain fulcra, whose 'spindles', as it were, passed through each separate scale, uniting them, perhaps helping to control their many orbits. Also they created a universal 'gateway' through which all could come and go, the only permanent and reliable passage between the planes. I talked to Brother Bertrand, one of the friars who accompanied the Sufis. They would all stay with us until we reached the Blackstone Escarpment. He had a big, square, tanned face, pale blue eyes and bushy brown eyebrows. I found his company calming. He was full of common sense. He could no more explain the mechanics of the multiverse than I could explain the workings of the human body. That was not his particular skill, he said. His job was of a more muscular kind.

Through him I learned a little more about the Carmelites. They were one of the few Catholic orders named not for a saint, but a mountain. The order existed thanks to the piety of late-Norman kings in England and France, and it was a tradition amongst many of them to offer sanctuary.

I asked Brother Bertrand what he thought of the aeroplane sound. Was it something he had heard from his time in London? He shook his wholesome, tonsured head. He knew nothing of planes. "The Sanctuary was never beset by the world's wars." A beaming innocence brightened his wide face. "Many remarked on it. We knew a zone of peace in the old Alsacia. All manner of events, many of them violent, took place beyond the walls of the Sanctuary," he told me, "but, within, normal life continued.

"Thieves and footpads, you know, even highwaymen! All manner of unrighteous folk, tried to make the Alsacia into a haven for their kind, but our Abbot was strong, as were many before him. While we cared for the injured and the sick and refused to give them up to the authorities, while wars or revolutions, skulduggery and so on, were banished from our Carmelite confines, we rejected the world more firmly than other orders. We had charge of Tompion's Great Orrery, after all. We ate and drank well, but we were pure. You'll find no public houses named after Carmelite brewers or victuallers, as you do, for instance, amongst the Black Friars or the Franciscans. We're a somewhat dour and meditative order, all in all, though our faction practise the use of arms. We have to defend ourselves, but we do not cultivate the sword or indeed the world. Often threatened, we are involved neither in politics nor wars."

While I did not believe him to be lying, my impression from all I had read about Alsacia (or Alsatia) in the eighteenth century suggested any thief could find sanctuary there, at least for a while. The Carmelite Abbots had been tolerant, some to the point of corruption. And before that, in the time of James II, who ruled after Elizabeth, the place was an infamous thieves' rookerie, as I knew from Scott's *Fortunes of Nigel*.

As I was about to ask Brother Bertrand another question, M'natka came running into camp. Partly from boredom, he had gone ahead to see how the land lay. From a hill he had seen something strange. At his description I thought he might have seen the plane, too, perhaps a helicopter. But he was adamant.

"It's definitely a whirlwind of some kind," he said. "I'm pretty sure I can tell the difference, Mr Moorcock."

"Those sand devils are common in the Sahara." Brother Bertrand shrugged. "The superstitious people of the desert believe them to be djinns or devils. I have seen dozens since I first came out here. I'm surprised we've not seen one sooner. This isn't their normal season."

"I've seen those," M'natka said. "But not like this one. It's the colour that's strange. It's different. High. The sky's otherwise clear. And the colour. A vivid scarlet. Have you ever seen anything like that?"

Brother Bertrand scowled. "Red? I don't believe so. Near Marrakech I once saw a pink tornado, what they call a red tornado in those parts, but the desert there is frequently of that colour, like the walls of the city itself."

"This one's scarlet. Bright scarlet. A big one, I'd say. And it's coming towards us. We've good reason for alarm, I think." He looked back to Sheik Antara for some sort of confirmation.

Sheik Antara got up and walked to where his horse waited for him, its bridle still on. "You never know with the Sahara. I'll take a look at it."

M'natka pointed to where the tornado had been seen.

Brother Bertrand said: "You rarely find such phenomena this far over. There's really no reason to panic."

A few minutes later Antara came galloping back hell for leather, dismounting as he brought his horse to a skidding stop. "It's a heavy one. It's coming our way. I've never seen a storm quite like it!"

"Should we take any special precautions?" Brother Bertrand asked mildly.

"If you value your life," shouted Antara above the rising wind. "And your soul, perhaps!" Turning his horse he went yelling into the main camp. The essence of his message was that we should all get down behind the wagons and heap ourselves and our animals with as many blankets and other coverings as we could find. "Keep it out of your eyes!" It was a bad sandstorm on the move. Not the kind Brother Bertrand was used to. At its core was a powerful tornado.

The noise I first heard had died away. D'Artagnan and the other musketeers were trying hard to catch a panicked horse. They moved farther and farther from camp. I decided to help but before I could Sheik Antara had ridden back and pulled me and my horse down behind one of Professor Consenseo's wagons, dragging with us the two zebra which had hauled it. Even the elephants were frightened. I think they knew what was coming as they tucked their trunks under themselves and fell on their knees before the approaching sand-djinn. The giraffes lay flat, long necks stretched out and long legs folded under them. Every animal understood what to do from the others. For a few moments there was a great braying and bellowing followed at once by a sudden silence.

Then we were hit by a screaming noise like a giant buzz-saw striking stone. A massive force hit my back and threw me flat on my face into the sand so that I narrowly missed one of the wagon wheels.

What I had mistaken for the roar of a large bomber was the sound of that approaching 'twister', a phenomenon I have become overly familiar with since I lived in 'Tornado Alley', Texas. It was easily mistaken for the approach of a powerful express train. There are few sounds more terrifying than that cackling, triumphant howl as the thing tears up everything in its path, hurling trucks and houses into the air and throwing them down. Witnesses often personify it as an angry supernatural being, a living creature of Chaos determined to leave nothing of mankind's manufacture in its wake.

All we could do was prostrate ourselves before it, hiding behind whatever shelter we could and hope that we were not caught at its epicentre. I saw Professor Consenseo pulling at Bruno. The bear seemed dazed and more concerned for the human than itself, wrapping the Englishman's ungainly body in those big furry arms, making reassuring grunts and growling noises in the back of his throat, pulling him down as he tried to help some small monkeys climb into a nearby truck.

It struck our camp with a blow like Vulcan's hammer! I could easily believe we had been hit by a nuclear bomb, furiously smashing and rending, picking up whatever could not find purchase, hurling wagons and creatures high in the air, breaking bones, boards and metal beams as if they were matches, wires, tiny mice or insects. I was reminded of the war when the houses around us had been hit by flying bombs.

Huge pieces of rubble rained down on us. Animals bellowed and roared. The tornado's terrible, angry voice spoke with a fury none could for a moment stand against. Mingled with its filthy violence, I could hear the screams and yells of the tornado's victims, innocent men and beasts who in no way deserved that end. Sickening as those mingled voices were, the rest was worse, an indescribable shout of sheer relish as the thing snapped bones, ripped and tore flesh and sucked the blood and life-force from its victims.

All this remained a shocking horror but I felt we were not experiencing an entirely natural phenomenon. This actually was what the poor souls who suffered from its actions understood: The whirlwind had been *summoned*. Set upon us by a thinking creature. Even as we died, we realised that an *intelligence which loathed all sentience*, perhaps even its own, which detested anyone who possessed hope, detested all virtue and despised anything kindly, considerate and good-hearted, loathed as weak and unrealistic all seeking to create tolerable and tolerant habitat for the multiverse's living inhabitants, whether they be atoms or planets, people or plants, amoeba or monsters. This *rage*, with its hatred of hope, desired to set everything against everything until existence itself ceased to be. Now I believed I truly understood the nature of Chaos in extreme and why certain intelligences, if that was what they were, could only hope to exist in such an environment of uncertainty, could not for a moment thrive in a world of Law.

How it screamed, voicing its crazed cackle! How it raged and roared and sought to slaughter all that was sane and certain and civilised! How it despised what we venerated! How it wished to destroy the essence of order and predictability! An order where every sentient being could expand its curiosity and knowledge for the benefit of every other being and be sure that creativity and consciousness could continue to grow for ever.

It clicked and clacked and growled and spat. It giggled and rattled and ripped at anything which stood before it. It chilled me to the core with terror! This sentient evil tried to claw down the very fabric of reality. It revelled in destruction, in the death and diminishment of all that was balanced and constructive in our near-infinite multiverse! For only in uncertainty and chaos could it ever thrive! Pierce that with an arrow and the effects of that arrow will be felt in the Higher and the Lower worlds of the multiverse and also in the Second Aether, the Grey Fees – and beyond!

This realisation struck me as, shivering with my fellows behind a fragile cart of wood and iron, I sensed a voice, a soft voice, as tender and sweet as its enemy was vicious. I could feel it physically resisting that force. It stood for sublime sanity and dynamic order, for creativity and empathy. It called for balance, for harmony and peace. It said:

"NO!"

And she gathered all her fragile energy. All she had been saving to re-create the multiverse. She gathered everything she needed to survive, everything she needed to flourish. She said:

'NO!"

And again she said:

"NO!"

Spammaldjin, our *Spammer Gain,* drew her tender power around us and protected every one of us who had survived that first terrible onslaught. She created a shield, the size of creation, a wall of energy which stood against the negativity of unchecked Chaos. Wrapping us all in her many arms she held us safe against the hate of the shrieking, bloody storm, made up of the remains of those it destroyed. Professor Consenseo was in tears, shaking his fist at the thing, which had taken his hat and threatened to tear the rest of his wildly flapping clothes. Antara and those friends I saw were safe enough, but it was clear *Spammer* would have a hard job defending us!

Time after time the horrible tempest flung itself against us, seeking weaknesses and flaws in the *spammaldjin*'s defences, trying for ruptures, for cracks and gaps, any little split which could be widened or forced open, to let the deadly blows in, to rain down on the ribs and skulls of those unable to defend themselves against her.

Yelping its frustration, the thing sobbed and began to spin faster, bringing all its foul, unwholesome energy against us, becoming first a dirty orange colour and then a brighter, deeper yellow, then a fluttering, burning yellowish green.

NO!

A scream of frustration and insane rage in retaliation against *Spammer* from the furious whirlwind! I could easily believe the thing was a living supernatural creature.

NO!

It seemed to me then that I could actually see *Spammer* as she wrapped her long, tender arms, as strong as our determination, around the wild, dancing, writhing, struggling thing which spat and yowled and threatened and screamed and made the surrounding sand blaze scarlet and undulate like some terrible, hellish nightmare ocean in the middle of a crazed and utterly unnatural storm! How she danced! How she attempted to frighten us.

And, again, she moved with all the authority of her mighty soul. *Spammer* was wounded and in agony, in a universe so unnatural to her she could barely stand to live. It pressed upon every part of her. The pain of the pressure constantly weighing upon her. The mass of the multiverse bearing upon a creature the size of a universe. And truly a goddess. Truly a mother. Truly a creator. And, being those things, and filled with our faith, she found the power to fight for us.

She told her story as she fought for her fry, her fishlings, her children, her responsibility. Born to maintain and serve us, to fulfil her aims and her destiny and make a stable environment, galaxy upon galaxy, universe upon universe, plane upon plane, on to faux-infinity, making up the vast and uncompromising multiverse. An irregular multiverse, existing in a state which could not abolish disorder, unless it abolishes itself. Therefore she was in a constant state of disorder. The trick was to limit chaotic effects never fully extinguished!

Again that voice, perhaps weaker but with just as much authority:

NO!

One of several enemies following *Spammer*, this bizarre living being sought to exploit a weakness in her. She grew increasingly tired. It screamed. It screamed in frustration. And again sought to drag *Spammer* down, down through scales smaller and smaller, heavier and heavier, down to that original Earth, unbelievably small, unbelievably heavy, from which all others came. Down and down the scales until the mass and size made her truly invisible to any world but herself. And the pressure must have been horrendous! I imagined a whirlwind down at that very first planet, attacking a caravan like ours? I knew it was unlikely. We were *billions* of scales apart. Even with the tiniest differences between so many worlds, the best one could imagine was a very distant variation, even if all parallels existed there. You could never close the doorways. But you had to follow the routes which led to them, however convoluted they were, for each moonbeam traveller had their own path to and from the gates.

Up and down the scales they struggled. Sometimes larger, sometimes smaller. Sometimes visible, sometimes not. I saw her great arms twisting and turning to hold and contain the spinning force. I saw her huge eyes glaring and that massive green-black beak tearing and ripping, breaking down and dissipating the sentient twister's ferocious energy. Again and again the red whirlwind, consisting of human and animal body parts, blood, pieces of wagons, weapons and clothing, struggled to escape those massive arms and failed, moaning and howling in its frustration. *No. No. No.* Time after time it attempted to break free from *Spammer's* grip, and time after time it failed, whining with fear and fury. *Spammer* squeezed once, strangling that creature of dust and débris. She squeezed again and again. I could feel her reserves failing. Another effort, wrapping her arms to contain the bloody twister. She squeezed, perhaps for the final time. Until I saw her become an enormous version of that cup they called the Fish Chalice, constantly changing colour, even, it seemed to me, metals, from silver, bronze to brass to iron and gold and within that cup I saw the magnified features of the many I had loved and the loved ones I had lost. And the sand struck my face, this way and that, like an angry cop, and I wept.

The thing broke up into thousands of smaller, whirling parts, flinging all its disgusting living charnel midden in all directions until the remains of our camp resembled an unholy shambles, streaked with gore.

Then *Spammer* returned to her tank, crawling wearily across the filthy sand. Her strange serpent skin rippling from gold to red to green, she climbed slowly up the boards to slide into the water. She lay, pulsing with a long regular beat, her complex eyes glazing as if in sleep. I think she sighed as she sank. The scarlet sandstorm died in an exhausted pattering of sand and stones.

And was gone.

And we were left, thankful and grieving.

I hated what must still be out there! I feared what remained to attack us. There were entities who needed to kill *Spammer*. In the Grey Fees, the spaces between the worlds, they waited. Sharks scenting blood. She recounted her history, explaining the nature of the multiverse and what our place was in it. How it was we could travel from one plane to another. How the gateways to the moonbeam roads opened and closed like lungs.

O, my fishlings. My greatest joy. My honest, sweetest, fragile fry. My aching children, my girls and boys! Let none determine how my children die!

The thing had gone. It had torn itself to pieces in its horrible ferocity. Trying to break from *Spammer*'s enormous restraining arms. I knew, if the djinn were not a living creature, it was in the control of one. I looked around me. There was much to do!

Sheik Antara cursed as he helped us dig the surviving animals out of the huge heaps of sand. We straightened those wagons unwrecked by the storm. And we judged the damage. Brother Bertrand and his monks saw to the wounded men and animals. Others buried what could be found of the dead. Many wept openly at the carnage. They stumbled about picking up fragments of the murdered people, gathering together pieces of our wagons. Luckily the main stock of food, buried in sturdy canisters, was unharmed.

The animals were mourning. Two elephants stood together with giraffes and the remaining rhino and hippopotamus. Birds and smaller mammals were clustered in the ruins of their carriage. The brothers came from their shelter with sand heaped on their shields. Their broad-bladed assegais were caked with the stuff, their ostrich headdresses crumpled. I looked for Consenseo and my friends, the Musketeers. The thing had happened so quickly that few of us had time to absorb the extent of the tragedy. Then I saw the dead bear.

Bruno had died protecting his friend. Consenseo was not unwounded, but he was alive. We helped him up. We sat him down on the ruins of a cart. He leaned forward, his head in his hands, staring at the bear. Then he reached out a hand as if to touch it. "Is it impossible for us to exist without strife?" he asked. "My beasts learned the value of existence without violence. Yet it is not true of the higher beings."

"Lower beings with great power are not *higher beings*," Brother Bertrand said. "They are simply cunning and greedy creatures who have learned how to imitate and steal and use the skills of those they envy."

"In all the decades of my life I have contended with such as these." Sheik Antara replied with a sigh. "It begins with envy, I think, or at least with a belief many stupid people have that the world is a simpler place and that there are easy answers to the world's problems or routes to power. They think any action has a simple reaction. That there is only one consequence to an action. A lack of imagination might also generate a stupid person's belief that they are as able as any other." He grunted as he pulled up a long board.

"Where could the Musketeers be?" I asked, scouring the sand in the direction where I had last seen my friends.

27

Tracker Van Geest

I DECIDED TO search for D'Artagnan and the others where I had seen them earlier. All four had disappeared with their horses and all their accoutrements. It was as if they had all been borne away together at the same moment. I became alarmed. I dug at the sand under wrecked wagons and dead animals. Nothing remained of my friends.

My search grew increasingly frantic. I felt physically ill. After a while, Sheik Antara, who had become their comrade, too, began helping me. All we found were a few caps, a pistol or two and one musket. It was as if they had been carried off all of a piece. I kept hoping to see D'Artagnan appear from behind some rocks or Porthos rise, laughing, from a ditch. But, beyond the few remnants we found, there was no sign of them. I went on searching until long after dark, while the others salvaged what could be saved. But they were gone.

I was weeping when Sheik Antara came to me in the moonlight, put his strong hands on my shoulders and spoke softly to me, telling me there was no longer any point in continuing my search. "Such things have happened before,' he said. "For all we know they were blown all the way back to the monastery."

"Maybe that thing came for them?" I suggested. "It was

sentient, evil. What if an enemy were looking for them, rather than us?"

"They were certainly caught up by the whirlwind, my friend," he said. "They should have stayed with us. They were trying to manage their horses and get them to safety. If they had remained with us they might well have been safe. Most of the time we were near the edge of the whirlwind. They were caught at its centre. Then I thought I saw them at the very edge over there. God alone knows what happened to them. Now God alone protects them."

"I can't help feeling the twister sought them out," I said. "There was no doubt in my mind that the *spammaldjin* stood against an intelligent creature."

"It was her," Antara muttered. "I know it."

"Her?" I asked him. "Are you suggesting that thing was a she? But, like me, you really do think it was alive?"

"The *maridjia*," he said. "A female djinn. You have already met her in human form. More than once, I believe."

"I assure you, Sheik Antara, although I have met some people of considerable intelligence and with strange powers, I do not believe they were actually *supernatural* creatures. True, some possess what seems to be telepathy and certainly an uncanny sense of empathy. Others have been a bit off the rails and a little crazy.

"Certain others have been distinctly unsavoury. But supernatural? I think not!" Yet I was remembering that bloody tornado and whatever might direct it. I did not doubt their nature. Decidedly evil. And what was *Spammer*? Not supernatural exactly but ...

And then I realised his meaning. "Mrs Malady is scarcely a vengeful ghost from the Arabian Nights!" I said. "Maybe inexplicable is a fair description." I was still pretty sure I associated her with somebody's mother, perhaps with a child in our general circle or maybe the mother of a former girlfriend. Malady? Her French name was strange, of course, and she was not exactly virtue personified, but for Antara to suggest she was an evil spirit was surely an exaggeration. Athos had known her. Maybe the others, too? I had accepted a great deal about this strange environment but most everything I saw had a physical explanation. Certainly the twister seemed a living thing, but there was a rational reading of that, too. I was actually of a very sceptical disposition. I had the talent of a fantasist but the scepticism of a scientist. I scoffed at people who saw fairies or thought they saw ghosts or who read crystal balls or predicted the future or anything like that. It would be some time before I could accept the supernatural. I could, however, believe that Madame Malady was an enemy who was able to track us and even kidnap our friends. That was credible, just as, to me at least, a 'multiverse' of interlocking quasi-infinities separated by mass and size was credible. But modern female demons were very hard for me to believe in.

I said all this to Sheik Antara who laughed openly at me. "Well, young Mr Moorcock, if you can believe in Eden, our destination, but not in unhuman spirits, you have a very odd intelligence indeed."

I accepted this, partly because I was still wondering if the Musketeers were alive or dead. I slept badly that night and awoke very early. The morning was overcast, as if yesterday's débris were blocking sunlight. There was still no sign of my missing friends. I breakfasted with the monks and then joined them as we continued to clear and, where possible, reconstruct the carriages and wagons. About half our original complement remained and we were forced to bury or even burn the dead more or less where they lay. We managed to rebuild wagons and found enough animals to pull them. Surprisingly, perhaps because it had been built so well to begin with, *Spammer's* huge tank had only sustained minor damage.

I still hoped I might find my friends trapped in a fissure or driven against a ridge. Or out in the desert trying to capture terrified horses. We found few further remains. I thought of them as indestructible. After all, I had written stories about them. They were immortal!

Professor Consenseo was not doing well. Bruno's death had shattered his nerves, and he had received several cracked ribs, many bruises and grazes and a bad cut across his head. He had recovered what was left of his hat and was constantly turning it by the brim. He was grieving.

We resumed our journey.

For some days I was very quiet, saying little, and, as often as not, riding on my own ahead of the main caravan. I needed time to absorb all I had learned when *Spammer* fought the tornado. I needed to work out exactly what Sheik Antara had meant when he spoke of superstition and rationality and my drawing distinctions which to him were strange. And did he imply that our expedition was to the Garden of Eden? My confusion was complete.

Over the weeks of our journey I did my best to forget my worries. The days went by and the desert turned again into barren plains country, bereft of trees and visible animals. Everything had died. It had tried to live and failed. I was very depressed by the time the landscape gradually changed into the lush high veldt with its great mixture of trees, grasses and shrubs, smelling of fecundity in all her forms. At dawn I breathed in the dew on the acacia trees and at midday tasted the rich air as the hot sun poured over the sage bushes, while in the evening I would become aware of a wonderful combination of scents, from animals as well as plants and men. The essence of Africa.

That was how I began to understand the profound appeal of the African bush. Its attraction had until then been primarily visual, as a background for adventure stories. Here, the narrative *was* the landscape, far more than any story of white hunters or noble savages or wild beasts who merely existed to threaten and be resisted.

Of course I had a broad idea of the evils of colonialism, but my romanticism made me think of emulating Allan Quatermain, on whom I'd based my own 'white hunter' character Lord Jim Caxton in *Tarzan Adventures* in the 1950s, completely oblivious, apart from a vague uneasiness, of the racialist and imperialist nature of the Haggard stories. For a while I had inherited from Haggard the common attitudes of British whites, the seductive paternalism which told you that your attitudes were good for the natives. You were doing them a favour by protecting and educating them while pinching their land and rights.

Even when challenged on these beliefs, you could argue that someone more ruthless had done it before you. Someone like the Zulu, who had built their empire just before you turned up. Or the Aztec. Or the Iroquois. Your empire might be as short-lived as the others before it, whether it be Chinese, British, Toltec or US. There was dynamic and there was decadence. You might as well not try. Better to trade for fair profit and never exploit another and, once you have put your own house together, concentrate your laws on ensuring that people were treated fairly in mutually beneficial terms. Fairness and justice began to transmute themselves in my young mind as something more complex than 'looking after' people. My mother and her mother easily saw past a person's colour, if they saw it at all, and were not intimidated by class. They identified with the underdog. I never knew two women with a greater sense of justice, even if their expression wasn't always very sophisticated.

I wondered if one day it might actually become possible to settle here, in this memory of childhood as it had never really been. Those close-cropped meadows of the high veldt set in rolling hills in a mild climate was some golden dream of the Shire for the English. Tolkien reconstructed his ideal world just as the British had tried to make an English paradise in South Africa. Those dreams are always built on inequality. They grew up on Rupert, Winnie the Pooh, Tiger Tim and Narnia and all those other dreams of middle-class security, the promises we were given in the 1950s which failed because we had believed in them without sustaining the belief. Because it was done at the expense of others. Because we left it to politicians to fix as they told us they would. We let them soothe us with their rhetoric, rather than work towards the common good. We had needed a shot of moral rigour and were demanding it when the '60s came and money was sudden showered upon us and we were granted some token concessions.

We had let them distract us! There was nothing wrong with the common dream as long as it was commonly achievable. Those safe hills and villages, those secure little towns where your anxieties were never allowed to thrive; where everybody had the best possible middle-class life? Scarcely a person in our overcrowded world didn't want that kind of life! Our maximum-security British dream was universal. No wonder so many wished to share it. A decent home. Decent healthcare. Decent food. Decent expectations. A decent future. Europe was too big for them.

As I rode and walked over those lovely hills and valleys so reminiscent of the endless drumlins which formed the backdrop of my peaceful fantastic childhood, I couldn't help feeling nostalgic for yet another magic, unthreatening England. You could not, in conscience, ever live in such an England. As often as I could I rode alone over rises, through copses of trees, beside rivers and watering holes. The languid air reminded me so clearly of my boyhood summers on holiday in Devon. A world of kindly aunts and decent old uncles. England had no men left. So many had died because of the war! Sometimes, in those days, our country could appear almost entirely deserted. That's when we invited West Indians in, to fill the jobs.

Years later Africa would be replaced in my nostalgic canon by California. I would get immediate comfort from the landscapes of Marin and the architecture of Los Angeles. I associated them with some of my happiest childhood years. London's greenbelt suburbs had been influenced by the architecture and trees of California which surrounded her tranquil golf links.

In Africa I came to see how England could be such a comforting miniature of the larger planet. We had defended the Shire. So much of the world was on our side. We had tried to extend the Shire throughout our environment. That was our moral descent, wishing to own what we loved. Green Line buses to Hobbiton. The All-Red Route was established so we could get a decent cup of tea anywhere in the world. Had so many died in terrible ways simply so the British Empire could extend its nostalgic Little England vision of the Shire? Securing trade was secondary. The largest empire in the world had been developed by people yearning to reproduce and maintain the security of the nursery. They would kill to defend it in Amritsar and Johannesburg. You're a better man than I am, Gunga Din.

As I mused on all this my mount suddenly snorted, screamed and reared. Not expecting anything, I was almost thrown, grabbing helplessly at the reins, before the horse took off, galloping as fast as he could. I managed to regain my seat and, looking back, saw that I was being pursued by a huge water buffalo, charging after us like an express train, its white eyes blazing, black nose dilating and red tongue lolling. I was terrified.

Ahead, a bearded white man rose up from the tall grass. He wore khaki, a wide-brimmed bush-hat, a shooting jacket, jodhpurs and riding boots. In his hands was a Martini-Henry rifle. I dragged on my reins but the horse refused to respond.

A loud crack!

I looked over my shoulder hoping to see the massive beast go down.

But it was no longer chasing us. It had raised its huge, snorting head and began to slow its pace. It was puzzled, staring at the man in front of me. Then it stopped altogether, head on one side.

The man was holding his arms wide, the smoking rifle in his right hand. "Hey, man! Slow down! You're fine. The poor old buff is feeling worse than you are!"

"I'm not convinced!" I yelled, still trying to control my horse.

"Don't worry, my friend." He had a faint Boer accent. "The buffalo's not after you now. I just had to get her attention. She kept running away from me. I needed to get her coming *towards* me so she saw me and I could look in her eyes. You flushed her for me! She's in a lot of pain, yes? You know she's not from these parts?"

I finally reined in my horse and dismounted. I was still breathing rather heavily. "Thanks for your help." I put out my hand. "Assuming that's what it was! I'm new to this country. My name's Michael Moorcock."

"One of the Durban Moorcocks?"

I had never heard of them. We shook hands. He grinned.

"My name's Van Geest. I think we're both a long way from home, eh? I've been tracking this beauty for quite a while, man. She's out of her regular environment and needs to get home." He strode towards the buffalo who was now breathing calmly, still snorting a little as she tore at the tough grass, her tail swishing. "I didn't want to have to dart her with this." He held up his rifle. "She's had too many shocks as it is." He rubbed her head gently and seemed to be whispering in her ear. Somehow I felt she was still feeling pain and said so to Van Geest.

"Oh, I think you're right, man. Poor old girl. She's aching in her bones. A lot worse than we'd feel, I think." Again he spoke to her. "Come on, old girl?" He turned to me. "She doesn't want to do anything but return to her own plane. She has no real idea what's going on. Because of her size, some bad people have hunted her. You can see two assegai wounds in her flanks there." He pointed.

He stopped rather suddenly, concerned that he had said too much.

"I believe you," I said, "but I could have done with a warning."

"Warning wouldn't have worked, man, I'm afraid."

He was a short, sturdy man with what we used to call a 'lived in' face. Tanned into folds of old leather, it gave him the air of a worried bloodhound. He told me that he actually was a bloodhound of sorts. He was known as 'Tracker' Van Geest all across South Africa, Kenya and the Blackstone territory, which was largely unmapped but secured by a deed between the Blackstone family and the British government. Parts of it were known as M'waniland, Pogoland and so on, the territories of various clans, mostly of Zulu or Masai descent. The inhabitants were very tall. They raised cattle and cereals. They hunted predators. They had also once hunted for meat, but only very rarely these days. Van Geest knew of the Bazuru brothers but had never met them. He told me all this as he retrieved his horse and encouraged the water buffalo to walk with us. I invited him to come back to our camp and meet Professor Consenseo and the brothers.

He said that he was looking forward to meeting them. "If the truth be known, old chap, I could do with a chinwag with a few fellow-spirits." He had stalked the water buffalo on his own for quite some time.

Van Geest's thick black beard was cut in the Imperial fashion. He had grey-green eyes and very small ears. His local nickname was *Macumazahn*, referring to his 'leopard ears'. I learned later that he was well-respected in the territory and often called *koos* or 'chief' by the locals. *Macumazahn* had led safaris out of Kampala and before that Pretoria and elsewhere. He specialised, these days, in trapping or drugging the unusually large or small wildlife sometimes found in the Blackstone foothills, which generally had wandered onto the wrong plane. "Though the lord only knows, man, how I'll get Bessy here back."

At the time I didn't really know what he was saying. I told him something of my own history which did not sound especially strange to him. "I have spent all my life, since I was a boy, out here in Africa," he said, "and have seen and heard a good many funny things, man, believe you me. There's no stories stranger than the ones you hear out here. Even the bloody grass talks to you!"

When he had finished retrieving his riding horse and pack mule from where they grazed under a tree and talked the enormous water buffalo down to a completely docile state, he asked me if I minded him writing a brief report. "Just a few notes for the District Commissioner." D.C. Sanders was stationed some eight hundred miles from where we were. It didn't take Van Geest long. "I promised I'd let him know what was going on. I'll send him the report as soon as I find a way of getting it back to him. It's best to write things up as I go. Otherwise I can easily get confused out here on my own." He was struck by a thought. "I say, old man, do you have any objection if we take old 'Bessy' back to your *kopje*?" That was what he called the camp. He had begun his career in the Transvaal before drifting north into what he called 'less civilised country'. "This professor friend of yours sounds my sort of fellow. And he knows a route up the Escarpment, you say?"

"So I'm assuming. Either he does or the Bazuru brothers do," I said, "because that's where they're headed, too."

"Then I'll hook up with your expedition, if I may," he said. "I'm a little worried about my old friends."

It was not my place to ask about them and he offered no more information as we returned. The camp was now made inside a *boma* of thorn bushes to keep wild animals at bay. His Martini-Henry was a welcome addition, and I think he understood that. He knew he was welcome.

Indeed, Brother Bertrand, various monks, Professor Consenseo, Sheik Antara and the Bazuru brothers were all more than pleased to see the South African. Van Geest had come with some supplies which everyone missed. We had lost many things in the storm and were particularly glad to enjoy the tracker's coffee. For his part he said our cooking made a change from his own, not very palatable, dinners. "Half raw mostly. You wouldn't believe the indigestion, man."

After listening to the rest of our story, he asked us where we had found our map.

"There is no map," said Sheik Antara. "I know the way across the desert and the Bazuru brothers know the way from here."

"You are familiar with the region?" he asked them.

"Yes," said M'natka'mandunta and Umsa'g'mandunta together. They had bonded almost immediately with Van Geest and knew much of the same country that he did.

"You know the road up the Escarpment?"

"I gather there's a relatively easy route up," said M'natka.

"Of course we'll have a hard time hauling *Spammer*'s crate all the way. Apparently, there's a second route, up the other side. A long trek around the whole escarpment."

"That's not a problem." Van Geest took a spoonful of soup. "There's a fairly easy pass *through* the mountains. A matter of a few days." He looked thoughtful. He glanced up at his fellow trackers. "But that might not be your trickiest problem."

"Problem?" I asked. His remark had an ominous ring.

"You've picked yourselves a bit of a bugger, my friends." Van Geest shook his shaggy head. "I'm so sorry to tell you this, but there's no longer an easy road *up* that mountain. The easy road *was* the one from the northern side. That's gone. The other more or less went up the middle. And that's gone, too."

"Gone?" Brother Bertrand looked about him, as if to find the answer there.

"There was a quake." Tracker Van Geest took a deep sigh, as if our bad news was also his. "A pretty big one, I'd say. Landslides. Bit unexpected. I was still a couple of hundred miles away in Bethlutho Town and we felt it there. I started hearing about what it had done almost the moment I set off the next day. Blackstone won't let them build a railroad – the telegraph was down. But I kept hoping. I have many friends around there, as I think I told you. And an old water buffalo needing to go through the Gates of Eden. I kept hoping, of course, that there was no serious damage. But I was surprised that I hadn't heard from them. I was in a pretty mess, I can tell you. I didn't know how much damage had been done. Or if any of them were hurt. There's no phone, see."

"How do they keep in touch with the rest of the world?" I asked.

"They don't need to. There's a sister. She's a doctor and she treats all local people. They have a plane and I think they use it quite a bit to come and go. They've a decent medical

411

surgery. The Blackstones have no great interest in the world. They have their own. They have limitless wealth. They enjoy their isolation. The climate's perfect. You can live a very long time indeed up there, I promise you. Occasionally Blackstone, his wife or his son or another relative, pays a visit to Paris or London. They are not unsophisticated people, but they have much to occupy them. The farm sustains them with a huge variety of food. They're vegetarians. Apparently Blackstone's parents were vegetarians. They are self-sustaining. They choose to live as they do. They enjoy visitors. The visitors bring them new books and so on ..."

"How do they get important news in and out?" I asked.

"We'd send runners when we needed to communicate. Or their runners would go to where the river boat puts in at Niranbe and drop a letter into the nearest Royal Mail box. The captain opens the box with his key, and the mail ultimately goes back via boat and plane to Mombasa. The service isn't as primitive as it sounds. We can get most main news in a week or so. As I said, they also have a small seaplane of their own. There's a lake they use almost in the dead centre of the plateau. It's moored there. It can land on the river or the lake if necessary. So they were in pretty good shape. We never think of them as utterly isolated. I am, however, worried about their well-being. I haven't heard from a soul up there. Naturally, we never expected something like this to happen. It's not really earthquake country, gentlemen, as I'm sure you know. Who could anticipate such an event? Anyway, I was hoping you had a map that might show other routes. Old roads I didn't know about or even a new road ..."

Glumly, Brother Bertrand told him what I had already said and he nodded. "Well—" the tight grin on his face must have seen him through a few scrapes "—I guess it's up to us to *look* for a route. Eh? Or make one." He put down his plate and treated us to a casual salute. "Goodnight, gentlemen. I'd best go and break the news to Bessy. At least she's not alone any more."

The bloody sun sank swiftly through an indigo sky. I watched Van Geest's slight figure, shuffling through the grass to where his friend, the giant buffalo, lay sleeping. She was enjoying the first relaxed hours she had known since she passed by some accident from her own plane of the multiverse into ours. Her big chest rose and fell slowly, and her black glossy nostrils quivered.

For some days, our journey across the veldt was made in a mood of considerable introspection.

28

The Blackstone Escarpment

T WO MONTHS LATER we watched our people bringing up water from a massive baobab tree. We had reached the forest edge. I was impressed. I had climbed several mountains but never one so massive. It could have been an entire range. Set against an intense blue sky, Kono-Anu, the twin shields, emerged from dense forest, her lowest slopes dressed in a slow, roiling haze rising from the unseen river, her flattened peaks softened by the sky. To me, she represented the front and back of a sleeping animal. The two peaks rose gradually from a green table of grass and forest. I marvelled at their size and beauty. Why had I never read about it? Or seen pictures of it? Was it really a forbidden zone of some sort?

We had feared another attack from that monster *maridjia*. It appeared *Spammer* had rid us of the thing. We travelled without further serious incident spending a good deal of our time discussing a strategy for scaling the mountain. The Blackstones had established their estate on the wide, flat central plain. They really had created a whole world up there. Sometimes, the clouds would be below them as they were from our Ingleton house. I was again reminded of the old Tarzan books. Tarzan had left his estate and travelled within that milieu at least once to visit Opar and renew his fortune. Burroughs's plots required Tarzan to travel frequently in Central Africa, I think not far from the sea. Never having read the books in order, I remained unclear of the particulars.

I had several times asked my companions why we were taking our animals all the way to the top of a mountain in order to return them to their original place in the multiverse. All Van Geest and Antara would say was that was where the Gates of Eden were located. I guessed I would find out the details when we arrived. We had been able to keep our *'Spammer'* alive and relatively comfortable. She and I had exchanged thoughts from time to time, as had Professor Consenseo, whose real name, I discovered, was Edward Prince, from Vauxhall, South London. He had no academic training but had become what we knew as a 'horse-whisperer' in mid-Victorian Kent.

I already knew his earlier story. How, from whispering to animals he had begun to communicate on other levels. To earn a living he posed as an animal trainer, showing off his complicit charges in several permanent fairgrounds and so-called winter circuses of the suburbs. Gradually he learned a little more from the lost beasts before he travelled around and had decided to make them his cause. He, the South African and the Bazurus spent hours together, discussing common strategies. They had heard of a group called Bêtes sans Frontières and wanted to know if I could explain it. I had a stab at what I thought it might be. I admitted I knew nothing about them but guessed they were connected to an across-borders animal rescue group.

Sheik Antara, the Carmelites, Sufi monks and I had spent long hours wondering how to get the *spammaldjin* up the mountain. It was our first priority. Few of us had engineering skills. We had a limited number of axes, hammers, spades, machetes and other implements. *Spammer* was the religious focus for the holy men. While I had no particular faith, I did feel I communicated with a spiritual entity.

415

Our immediate problem had been how to get *Spammer's* multistorey-tall cabinet through the forest. There were, of course, trails but they were not really suitable for such a wide wheelbase. We had some assistance from our larger animals, and while they had helped, I guessed we would have to clear jungle with what weapons and tools remained. The larger animals did what they could to help in pulling, pushing or even lifting. We had to deal with each problem as it arose.

Cutting and ploughing our way through that dense jungle took many days. We were plagued by snakes and ferocious biting insects. We cut down ancient trees and forced our way through prehistoric undergrowth day after day. At the end of the first week we had gone only one mile and were exhausted. All around us the living tropical forest thrilled with every kind of life. I saw gorgeous blossoms in a hundred vivid colours, tribes of monkeys chattering warnings, birds with unimaginably beautiful markings, and sensed rather than saw larger predators observing us. At night I heard a considerable variety of voices. We took precautions when we camped, posting regular guards, and we slept deeply.

Another two weeks and we were losing heart when the *spammaldjin* appeared to wake up from a long rest. We all caught fragments of her 'voice'. It was weak and failing.

O, fishlings, how grateful I am. We are close but it is hard for you. So hard. My heroic fishlings, my loyal fry. Is our existence completed?

Those animals extremely larger or smaller than normal felt the pressure worse and understood *Spammer's* misery. The large animals, particularly Big Wolf, as we called him, would even groan and growl in their sleep. They felt the oppressive mass of our universe pressing on their alien bones, creating agonising changes in their bodies. I saw hippos and rhinos shudder, whimpering. Great elephants trumpeted their constant discomfort. Few of the primates were ever truly still. And occasionally the voice of *Spammer Gain* would come to us. A gentle musical murmur. She talked to us all as individuals and, at the identical time, to each of us individually. What we heard was different, yet the same. As we had all discovered.

Spammer encouraged us. She comforted us. She soothed away the nightmares which came to so many of us in the jungle.

O, my clever little fishlings; my brave heroic sprats, my sweet and smallest fry, my unique, living darlings. Can any love be sweeter or so mutually consistent? Let not the selfish defeat you. Let them not escape the consequences of all their destruction. Let them vanish with their filth and superstition. Let them be gentled by their own religiosity. Let my children live. Let my children overcome and let my children flourish!

We understood then that one god addressed another.

And we understood how our people each carried our *spammaldjin* within. How the *Spammer Gain* was our universe, enclosing us, guarding us and relying on us as we relied on her. She was but one universe caring for another. And at the same time *Spammer* was contained in every individual.

She was one creature protecting her own as infinite numbers of other creatures protected *their* own. As every creature in the universe supported its spawn and in turn was supported. As we now found ourselves supported, as if within a gigantic seed-pod. A nut. We all felt such enormous self-confidence knowing that every thinking or feeling or sensate creature in existence had its place in the scheme of things. We were not what we wanted to be or what someone else wanted us to be; we were not what at some point in time we wished to be. We were what we most needed to be; we belonged to *Spammer* and she with us. One could not exist without the other, nor could any other universe in all that near-infinity of universes. In another universe, oblivious self-involved insects, reptiles and humans mated or died, as unaware of us as we were of them. Yet every action any of us took had consequences everywhere. That is how we were able with such glad hearts to carry our goddess through the tropical forest without serious accident.

By the time we broke through the last stand of trees and reached the river we had no more energy. For *Spammer*'s sake we had to rest. Although we had negotiated the jungle with few losses, we were barely elated. At least, however, we could replenish her water.

After we had made camp and eaten a sparse meal, I stood on the grassy bank of the river in a small clearing watching the racing water at the base of the Escarpment. We all were in relatively poor temper, especially as we now had no idea where or how we would be able to climb that steep escarpment. The road was gone. Van Geest and the trackers forded the river to take a look at the tumble of rock and earth where vegetation started to grow. Shaking their heads, Antara and Van Geest both studied the now unfamiliar terrain.

Unsure that we had the resources left to get *Spammer* to the top. I craned my neck to look up. The rock was what in my climbing days they used to call 'dirty'. Treacherous and liable to crumble. Was it even possible for the larger mammals to climb? We were willing enough to go on but were all as tired as *Spammer*. The determination and good humour of our party had given us magnificent morale for a while, but for the moment we were wiped out. Only Antara seemed unruffled.

The Arab knight had led the way much of the time. He was now deep in thought. He was going over a plan of some kind but was unwilling to discuss it until he was certain he had a safe route. He rode along the banks until he found a crossing in a shallow spot where the waters quietened. He dismounted to get close to a waterfall apparently coming from a fissure in the rock wall and emptying into the river. He kneeled on the ground, inspecting pieces of flint and igneous rock. He had some idea he was still not sure he wanted to share, perhaps because he had no wish to raise our hopes. Every so often he became excited, jumping off his horse again to look at the ground or clear away undergrowth and inspect what lay beneath. Sometimes he muttered to himself or even burst into a short song becoming unusually cheerful. When he was nearby I did occasionally remark on his good mood. He would reply cryptically.

I hoped that the *spammaldjin* would have a solution, but the battle with the tornado had exhausted her powers.

Next morning we broke camp and moved the huge, creaking cart up to the good fording place. We had already replenished *Spammer*'s tanks and made her a little more comfortable. Everywhere were signs of the recent earthquake. We could also make rollers to help us over the worst parts.

"When we're sure she's not harmed by the crossing I'll go over and have a look at all that rock again." Antara walked across the black, rounded stone, washed by the clear river, his shining boots reflecting the long shale slopes, thin layers of dark grey slate which tumbled down to the fast moving water. He put his hands on his hips. "I hope they arrived in time." He was now speaking to his private thoughts as he stared down the river. All along the wide stretch of the crossing the hippos, rhinos, water buffalo and other larger animals were enjoying their baths. The elephants stood up to their knees, spraying water over one another, and the bears were playing in the deeper pools created by the powerful stream which came bursting out of the rock about ten feet overhead. Only Mr Jumbo did not join in. He was still mourning his loss.

When he reached the other bank again, Antara stumbled over the slate until he stood beside the waterfall, looking up.

Elsewhere the Bazuru brothers were climbing a small rock face, testing it to see how hard it was to scale. It was fairly difficult and only went higher and higher. From here there was no way of seeing the top past impossible overhangs.

Van Geest stepped up beside me. He was smoking a smelly Turkish tobacco in his old, stained Meerschaum pipe with his Martini-Henry under his arm, his battered bush-hat on the back of his head. He pointed to a fissure running down the grey slab joining a place where two small green bushes pushed themselves out of a crack in what looked like recent growth. The rock then fell into a tangle of moss-grown pebbles and earth. "That's where the old road was, man. It went in a series of steepish terraces all the way to the top. It wasn't an easy bugger. I hadn't looked forward to going up it with a bloody oversize buffalo in tow. Now, well, you can see for yourself. The whole thing came down almost from the very top. I've been just about the whole way round and if there's a new pass formed, I swear to God I have not seen it. What we're doing here now strikes me as pretty hopeless. It's a long bloody climb, man!"

Antara came splashing back. "There's a chance we'll not have to go up that way at all."

"Don't tell me you've found a hot-air balloon just big enough to carry your *Spammer* here all the way to Nairobi," laughed Van Geest.

"I wish that I could tell you that, Mr Van Geest," replied Antara, arranging his robes. "But it's worth trying."

Van Geest laughed at the knight's remark but said nothing. Antara walked on downriver, peering at something in the overhead rock. A complete mystery to us.

The Bazuru brothers had continued climbing looking for a route up. They had found what seemed a good road that turned into a tumble of broken slate sliding down into a gorge. There were no other routes. In despair, Brother Bertrand slumped down on the riverbank and tried to think.

"At least *Spammer* has water." My banal attempt to look on the bright side.

Water's the way to the moonbeams. I can help you as you help me. Before we made you there were others. Rock thinks, as do trees. A brain is quite different to a brain. It carries all our memories does the sentient magma. Nothing is nothing. Let the old rocks think and speak.

Spammer tried to reassure me. I could not understand what she meant. Brother Bertrand's big, square face turned to me, frowning, asking a question. I nodded. We both knew. And we both did not know.

That's how the water comes down at Lodore.

What did she tell us? Could she be failing mentally? The life-span of cephalopods in earthly waters was very short. Could she be dying?

The cataract strong then plunges along, striking and raging ...

I recognised it ... what today I'll often declare as the first rap lyric. Southey's poem, which I had muttered to myself on that disappointing day when I had scrambled to Lodore near Keswick and found that a passing drought had left the Falls dry as a bone. And now *Spammer* was recalling it. Was our goddess being ironic?

"How does the water Come down at Lodore?" My little boy asked me Thus, once on a time; And moreover he tasked me To tell him in rhyme. Anon, at the word, There first came one daughter, And then came another, To second and third The request of their brother, And to hear how the water Comes down at Lodore, With its rush and its roar, As many a time They had seen it before.

So I told them in rhyme, For of rhymes I had store; And 'twas in my vocation For their recreation That so I should sing; Because I was Laureate To them and the King.

I found myself quoting the poem with some relish. I was fond of nineteenth-century light-verse and frequently quoted Southey's *Lodore*, Meredith's *Woods of Westermain* and *The Ruined Maid* by Hardy to my children. Somehow *Spammer* knew this and was sending us a message. I found myself wondering at a being who could know everything about me and everything, it was fair to presume, about every other individual in the universe.

But why was *Spammer* spouting Victorian poets at me? Presumably, by the way our companions were frowning, something similar was happening. But there seemed to be another factor involved, perhaps another voice. Only Antara seemed to have some clue what she meant.

I looked around me to see if something new had presented itself. All I could see, a few feet up on a wide sheet of slate, was Sheik Antara, and he was grinning all over his face.

"Have you thought of a way up?" I called.

"Not quite," he said. "But I think I know someone who can help. Do we have any of that gunpowder left? Did we bring more with us?"

I did not know so I called downriver to where Brother Bertrand sat talking to a few of his coreligionists and the White Sufis.

They had some gunpowder. Not a great deal. One of the monks had packed a few guns and some shot with about half a barrel of the stuff. The guns had been lost during the whirlwind but we still had the powder.

He jumped down, motioning behind him with his thumb.

"I heard something. Something from up there, behind that big rock. Did you hear it, too? You wouldn't know the Arabic. A snatch of my own poetry. Not especially good. Everyone has such a poem. About the rocks and the water gardens and the deep green of the grass, the foliage, the moss, the peacock's

422

eyes of beauty. Thus in the desert our spirit takes us to the holy presence where we know only the oneness of the river which must take us all ultimately to Eden's Gates!"

He spoke in French. I found it hard to understand him but I took his meaning.

Eventually we had all listened to the sound behind the rock and were agreed that we could hear water rushing. This was too much water just to be feeding the stream behind us. This had to be a serious torrent coming down within the mountain, very likely from the top. Perhaps there was a way to the top from inside?

Antara was overhead now, still muttering to himself and intermittently pressing his head to the rock, almost as if he were in conversation with the mountain.

We had all become very excited arguing about the best way of finding the truth. Eventually Sheik Antara and Tracker Van Geest took charge of their particular specialities and began setting charges and gunpowder tubes and making calculations. Eventually, Antara climbed up to the shelf and again listened, again murmured to the rock face itself and appeared to be listening to the musical sound of the unseen waterfall.

When the powder and fuses had been carefully packed, we all drew back into the protection of the forest. The fuses were lit and, without much idea of what would happen, we waited.

The noise was louder than we had expected: A dull, resonating *BOOM* which echoed into the distance. It seemed to go upwards, rather than outwards, but rubble scattered over us nonetheless. The two experts were not especially puzzled as the rock could be seen to *fold* down the cliff face. We were peppered with stray stones and heavy rock dust, but most of the slabs and boulders slid down into the stream, diverting it so it was suddenly running around us, resuming its course some distance downstream.

Sheik Antara and Tracker Van Geest were grinning like schoolboys at their success. Huge stones were piled pretty high into a huge fissure in the rock which rose in a black, V-shape down which a waterfall could be seen running as if from a widening mouth. For a moment I saw a huge face in the cliff, irregular and yet benign, as if that mouth were smiling as well as sending down cascades of water. I wondered if every rock which had seemed to have some kind of animal shape were actually alive.

What we saw at once was a possible way up. A number of ledges rose one after another, like a series of gigantic steps. We all came cautiously out of cover as dust and pebbles continued to fall. I brushed some of the stuff out of my hair and climbed over the fallen rock to see the result.

We had exposed a waterfall which rushed down from a great black opening high above. We could see a long way up, where it climbed higher and higher into the rock, the water pouring steadily down. But could we be sure it was a way to the top?

I saw shadows moving in the gloom behind the water. I thought I recognised them. I began to understand. Antara knew exactly what I was looking at. He climbed down to the other side and walked into the darkness towards them.

I heard an odd crooning. The water became bright with the full spectrum of a rainbow. None of this felt artificial. The light glared in my eyes. I had to shade them to see what I thought might be there.

Antara spoke in that strange Old French of his. He embraced the first of the people he found there. And I knew who they were. They were the people I had met almost a year earlier in the cavern world below Tangier. Antara had known them then. Their names were as strange as their origins. Had not Duval considered them to be the first humanoid life on Earth? He had called them the Off-Moo. They lived within the rock, eating many forms of lichen, living on clear water. They had survived extinction events. From the living rock, they built asymmetrical houses like 'skyscrapers'. They lived beside lakes of mercury and were able to conjure beings like giant rays into the air to spread themselves or rippling sheets of near-transparent silk to settle on two battling factions and carry them about until they stopped fighting. They wore robes of cloth-of-gold and -silver and woven stone and sang their language, when they spoke at all.

They were the people who had lived here before mankind, before Nature found a dominant species even more adaptable. In fact they could mingle easily with many other life forms and had done in the past. I envied the quiet, contemplative life of the Off-Moo, the last people of Atlantis. I knew Antara had made good friends with them, presumably over the centuries, for he had lived before the time of Jesus and Mahomet and might have seen the world of Oor in all her new-raised glory. The soldier was both poetry and poet. He was the epitome of the Syrian knight and knew the world at her best and her worst. He raised his voice in that same rising and falling song which was part of the Mu-Oorian way of speaking.

Antara gestured towards me and one of the scholars signed for me to enter. Now that we were inside I saw that the cave formed a natural cathedral with jagged green-yellow light falling to pool on the jumbled surface of the system we had opened. I walked into the light, coloured, as far as I could tell, by the various forms of luminous lichen growing in the upper reaches of the cave. I saw something move, step out and then hide. A shadow. Nothing I recognised.

My attention was drawn back to the scene before me. Antara was gesturing, asking questions, pointing up at a waterfall course surely driven long since by the action of the ice on the rock. Thus creating not one huge fissure but several smaller ones, as well, so that the shale formed peculiar folds between layers of harder rock. Somehow the magma had flowed inside the rocks, pushing a course down the thrusting mountain and its exterior. My ill-informed theory explained things as I stood staring at the writhing twists of frozen volcanic lava and the sheer, unstable sheets of shale over both of which the golden water poured, gorgeous drop upon gorgeous drop, like so much sugar syrup. I could smell its sweetness; the stuff looked wonderfully drinkable! But, of course, it was really no more than various kinds of hard and soft rock, miraculously brought together to form a very dangerous staircase which, the Off-Moo assured Antara, would take us all the way to the mountain's table.

This environment was not in regular use by the Off-Moo. It had not been visited by many for centuries. They had taken the route here which we would have taken had not everyone's plans gone awry. In spite of conditions not being suitable for us, our stone friends had made our original journey knowing that when we arrived we should need help.

Antara turned to me. "There's a new problem. *She* can climb it pretty easily. However, it's no fun for anyone else. Our animals must be left or somehow hauled to the top with us!"

Van Geest had heard him. "I don't know about you other fellows, but it's pretty simple for me. Either they all go up or I stay. I thought you had told us we were in this for the long haul, man?"

He looked over to the trees where Professor Consenseo and the White Brothers stood together closely, murmuring among themselves and wondering what was happening. "I'm not going without Bessy and I very much doubt most of our religious friends or our good professor will want to leave their charges behind. We can't afford to leave our horses here, can we? They'd be in danger. So about the only beasts who might want to stay are a few camels, who very likely would eventually go back to the veldt and mix with a wild herd. Some of the monkeys can easily climb the outside with the other apes. Lastly there is whoever else is indigenous to these parts, some of whom have already slipped away."

In another short conference we brought together everyone from the *spammaldjin* to the smallest reptile, we talked about the way in which we were going to get our charges up the mountain road! We would take days, to get to the top. We all hesitated. We still could not be sure we had reliable information. Someone suggested the goats, sheep and other natural rock climbers could also make their own way up, but Professor Consenseo pointed out that several, including our great wolf, were in too much pain to be able to execute the path. Many would die, he feared. Others would not try the ascent at all. The arguments continued back and forth until we were all more or less ready to begin our climb.

We decided *Spammer* would go ahead with some of us, marking the widest ledges and then returning to help haul platforms up the slippery cliff, so that bit by bit we would all ascend the Staircase of the Cascade, as Professor Consenseo called it. The ascent was going to be difficult, but it would have been impossible had we not, with the help of our Mu-Oorian friends, been able to create that staircase.

A certain amount of light from the glowing lichen lit the gloomy route and water made it slippery. The whole exposed part of the stair still consisted of narrow and wide ledges and glowed with a deeper green where the water touched it. Exposed to the outside light for perhaps three or four hundred feet, it then retreated into the mountain where, the Off-Moo assured us, it continued all the way to the top. In other words, we would be climbing up a kind of monstrous funnel, whose darkness would be relieved only by phosphorescent fungi.

This required some consideration and a great deal of planning. They assured Antara they would help get all our animals to the top.

Again some suggested that we should ascend before the animals. Perhaps just take the creatures which could be carried. I recalled the responsibilities we had taken on before we knew what we faced. It wasn't much of a word to give if you pulled out as soon as things got difficult. It reminded me of what I had been experiencing in the UK before I left. I hated England at that point. I hated the juggling tricks people did with their consciences. What fine hypocrites we become, the better educated we are.

Next day, as that disparate group sat around the fire for breakfast – one which could possibly be our last – I wondered if my marriage was based on hypocrisy, or at least convenient lies. Did it actually matter to whom we were married? Did the institution itself impose a set of rules or conditions? I know that I had not expected to feel such a weight of anxiety at the age of twenty-two when Helena grew pregnant. I suppose I should be glad I'd taken out all that life insurance believing that I might die young or go mad and leave my family all but destitute. I could still leave them my royalties and trademarks and know they'd have a bit to live on if it came to a pinch. At that time and age I was a lot better off dead. Assuming anyone knew where I actually was when time came to write a claim. If I died here, for instance, Helena would be welcomed back at the British Council and continue her job, even if she had to wait a few years, until I could be declared dead, before she inherited my royalties.

Now we wheeled *Spammer*'s massive cabinet, at least four times the size of a London bus, as close as we could get to the rock face. It was, as ever, a monumental task. I could only think of the Pyramids or Stonehenge and how they were

428

bigger problems than moving something that size over such rocky terrain. Later I would see a clip from *Fitzcaraldo* and feel a certain sympathy. *Spammer* encouraged and praised us the whole time we were in communication with her. Shouldering the wheels, we pushed as hard as we could. Slowly she began to move.

O, my sweet fry, my darling children, my fishlings, my off-spring! Soon our fortunes shall be reversed and restored, dear fishlings. Soon we shall know Balance. Be of good heart, tender ones, for the Gates of Eden shall open for us and we shall be restored to our rightful places in the multiverse.

Then we gave a final heave, the cabinet creaking and protesting like a flight of captured geese. We came full against the rocks with no other way of moving forward.

Flitting here and there within the caves exposed by the fallen walls, the Off-Moo found Sheik Antara and spoke to him.

Antara gave instructions for the monks to release the sealed locks which had kept the cabinet watertight and *Spammer* safe. There came a strange noise from the Off-Moo, like a single slow aspiration, and water began pouring from the gigantic casket. At last, the front fell forward with a massive, reverberating crash – and the monster emerged.

First came a huge, dark, multicoloured arm, its underside covered in suckers the size of dinner-plates. This reached forward, feeling for the bright rocks of the waterfall. Then, colours forever shifting, it felt upwards. Another arm followed, and another, until six of those great, predominantly soft green and golden arms were outside the cabinet, feeling all over the rocks, shifting colour as her surroundings changed, processing information that was meaningless to us.

But not until one of *Spammer*'s huge green-gold eyes emerged out of the cabinet did gasps came from the watchers. Her vast, indeed, breathtaking substance: a huge, elongated

'W' in green, black and yellow was constantly moving, eyes looking in every direction at the same time. Her arms now carried her forward, functioning as legs might, and quickly found the cool, wet rock. The monster, reducing us to the size of small frogs in comparison, drew her last arm from the tank, which fell on its side, sending more echoes through the rock and tumbling for a few feet backwards as she climbed slowly, gracefully upwards, not pausing until, flickering with rainbow colours, that entire body was moving. Seeing her like this for the first time I was astonished at how gigantic she was! Bigger than the largest whale, bigger than any living creature on Earth! Or perhaps any fictional monster as well. A benign kraken, she flowed out of her cabinet with the water she had lived in. She flowed up the rock, arms and tentacles undulating as she went. She turned her great benign head to look at us. We were prepared.

We threw her the long ropes we had ready. She caught them easily, dragging them to her. We stepped away from the cabinet as she took the rope and then, with astonishing agility, swarmed up the cataract. Water poured over her coruscating ever-changing body as, using arms and tentacles, she climbed the gleaming rock and then disappeared into the gloom above, into a tunnel or chimney which the water had carved over millennia and which the earthquake had revealed.

Somewhere high above we heard her working until at last the tetherings were secured in place, while we tied the first animals into modified wagons or platforms. Then some of the fittest of us began to scale the ropes.

Of course we found it much harder to climb that waterfall than *Spammer*. But she had made our task possible. Perhaps the most miraculous thing I saw that day was a series of wagons full of miniature elephants, gigantic hippos and goats rising very slowly into the darkness where a supernatural octopus, normally the size of a universe, and a group of contemplative sufis and fighting monks, had rigged a crude winch.

Our wolf was one of our worst climbers. Vertically he had a dreadful sense of balance and was feeling very sick. The other canines, particularly the pet dogs, had a terrible time as well. In the end, so many brave dogs volunteered to try the climb that it was a mercy to send them up on the rafts. However, one little black-and-tan terrier called Kalila had a gravity-defying sense. She could climb anything. She reminded me of the little terrier mutt who had turned up at the Battersea Dogs Home the day my mother and I went looking for a pup. Brandy followed me everywhere, even chasing buses I caught, finding his way home on a bus route after I forgot him. He never lost me, but I'd taken him for granted. The guilt recurred throughout my life. Kalila, though a little larger, was the spitting image of Brandy. She had the same joyous willingness to try anything. The same unquestioning trust. Watching her climb I wondered where and how such coincidences occurred. Could we chart them? Was there a easy way of mapping the multiverse? Mandelbrot would come close. But we should never abolish sorrow. Or guilt.

Eventually as we had trodden our road to arrive at the Escarpment, I came to know why erratic roads remained undiscovered before they were travelled.

And now I chart them again, story by story, similar but dissimilar. I do wonder about Brandy whom I had lost as a boy. If I lost a dog on my own plane but found a new one, exactly the same, on another plane, who knew me as I knew him, from the next plane, was it the same dog? Could I make amends? If I understood that I made another self, knowing the same bitter emotional pain of loss I felt, could I take that dog from its own plane? Perhaps that was what *had* happened. How Brandy had vanished.

431

Something occurs when you become familiar with the multiverse, because potentially you are confronted by a million mirrors, which doesn't exactly make you self-conscious but it does make you think about your actions and their consequences. Whether it makes you a better person is another matter. *'If I had seen you as you really look in that mirror, I would never have married you.'* Sometimes you follow your conscience. Sometimes, perhaps, you don't. Sometimes you lick your wounds.

With men positioned at every point, we piled the smaller animals into the wagons and pulled them to the first stage. The big elephants and mammoths went up last on the platforms we constructed for them. In this, as well as other efforts, *Spammer* did much of the physical work, using her arms, tentacles and beak in ingenious ways to bring the swaying platforms to the first level wide enough to take all of us except *Spammer* herself.

Until I die I will remember that climb through the semi-darkness over bright, reflective rock gleaming with water making the erratic music of the falls as they flowed and skipped to join the river below where the Off-Moo still stood silently observing us. *Spammer*'s monstrous bulk, pulsating with every subtle shift of colour in the glowing mosses, crawled slowly upwards, her gentle sensitive suckers feeling for every rock firm enough to bear her weight. I felt an unimaginable bond with her even though I was in proportion no larger than a vole compared to a man. It had often surprised me how small animals could live side by side with creatures of my size and feel no anxiety. That particular bonding was no longer a mystery to me. The bond between us had begun many months before when I lay in the desert, winded and bemused beside an endangered *Spammer*'s first crate while a battle raged everywhere around us and her subtle intelligent suckers had touched me with such loving delicacy I could not feel afraid.

At intervals *Spammer* paused to wait for me, making sure that I could catch up with her, that I was safe. The tip of one of her arms would encircle my waist, enfolding me with concerned and careful strength. It was easy for me to see something in her huge, unhuman eyes that reminded me of the love I felt for my own children, the protectiveness, the wish to see them standing brave and independent, going before me. I had thought myself free of such impulses, but Nature still has rules no amount of thinking can regulate. I felt very proud to be in her presence as we climbed up through that endlessly echoing chimney. Far below and above I heard men's voices, the whines, barks and growls of the animals responding to them, all amplified by the natural chimney through the rock. I was under the protection of a benign universe. She longed to return to her natural state. She was vastly larger than any of us and yet much smaller, too. On the planes of the multiverse we are mites or giants! This apparent paradox was a central truth to existence, and for some reason I had never had any problem with the idea. As Mandelbrot would tell us, and as I had known from a very young age, what was contained in the other also contained the other. I have no doubt that this has informed all my work, even my non-fantastic fiction in which the multiverse is used more in the Jamesian sense. William not Henry.

Those endless arms, the undersides covered in rows of suckers, sometimes pink-yellow, sometimes green or scarlet, moved very gradually, very deliberately past. They filled my entire field of vision. I remained amazed by *Spammer* climbing with such delicate precision up the centre of the falls while the water washed over her, constantly changing colour, and her gorgeous, benign eyes regarding me as she passed. I have already said how like a cathedral the interior of that escarpment was. I have to say that the 'monster' Jake Nixer had sworn to destroy could have filled both the Houses of Parliament and Buckingham Palace.

When she paused to rest, as she must sometimes do from her earlier exertions and from being cooped up for so long, she might occasionally answer my questions or tell a story of her own. Generally this was by association and on whim. She would turn that massive head and look through those strange, colour shifting 'W's of gold and black eyes and make a small, protective space for me, modulating her vast brains so that I should not be blasted. Even an earthly cuttlefish's brain can be considerably larger than a human one. I would receive thoughts, not always in English at first (for she was not only communicating with me).

For too long I was safe. Carefree, you might say. Simply drifting up and down scales I had no business visiting. Exploring. Idle curiosity, without substance. There is a region called The Second Aether where some of us could go to roam and be free. I had good friends like Pearl Peru and the Universe of Roses. Buggerly Otherly and even Oakenhurst the Mountie! We had not reckoned with enemies. Never suspected there were forces which planned to destroy us. I speak, of course, of those who wanted to build what they called the Only Way, the Empire of Law. The Original Insect, their chief representative, knew how to pierce through our defensive music and her straight arrow battlecraft were close to defeating us. Of course this could not be, for the Balance is all that sustains us. A legend.

Baron Greenfellow was prey to envy by then. He respected a thousand beliefs and their variants. How it had happened I could never discover, but there was a moment when the House was beaten in the Game of Time. On the banks of the Gulf of Mexico, we were all threatened, not with extinction, which is the loss of

434

consciousness. But with witnessing the stopping of Time, where-upon the conquered live the same single moment for eternity. O, fishlings, this is a story which cannot begin or end for thus the Balance is destroyed and Law determines the end of all songs, all form, save imitation. Whereas Chaos, by offering narrative without form, determines the end of form, save whatever is random. Time herself loses substance and meaning.

So in balance we are assured stories, told over and over again, and so giving shape to Time and weight to Space. These are the myths and the legends by which we are enabled to live in linear time. The order is maintained by repetition like music. As Repetition reassures our inner child, so Disorder is maintained by distraction, a cacophony of constant novelty. Neither is sustained without the other. That is why there are no ordinary or predict-able routes on the moonbeams and why the roads change all the time. There can be no maps, only visions and co-ordinates. Only intentions. If Law has her way, then all roads will run straight and be predictable. Leading to Oblivion, or worse. An agony of Now.

And that was one of the things *Spammer* told me suddenly, as we scaled the Blackstone Escarpment after travelling so slowly for so many months.

Climbing, as we did, as quickly as the weakest of us, it took us four days to follow the rushing waterfall until we reached a gentler diversion from the main river to emerge in the shallow waters of a meadow pool, with a pale sky above and little clouds bringing the possibility of rain. Sandy banks and soft grass made it all look as if we had arrived in an English field. For a second it occurred to me that we had emerged from Alice's rabbit hole! I was home again in Surrey or Oxfordshire. Then I saw the horizon, the trees, and knew I was still in the African highlands.

"Looks like we made it, man," said Van Geest, climbing

up behind me. He could not help himself. He threw back his leathery head and began to laugh.

29

Lord of the Mountain

EVENTUALLY WE ALL assembled in that tranquil mountain meadow, a great herd of different animals of different sizes and native environments, from our huge grey wolf to a miniature English cow. Around us the ground sloped gently upwards, the grass like an English lawn, showing that animals grazed here. Beyond the hilltops were signs of a deciduous wood. The massive *spammaldjin* had moved to the edge of the wide pond which fed the stream. She sat there splashing herself with water, trying to submerge, while elephants and hippos, tiny in proportion, watched with mild astonishment. We no longer needed to travel in wagons. Our bizarre herd filled most of the wide meadow, with Professor Consenseo doing his best to organise it. The majority of our intrepid climbers avoided further exposure to water and lay sunning themselves all over that broad expanse. The Bazuru brothers and some monks remained behind to haul and stow the ropes and platforms. While I was still wet, I went back to see if they needed help. I climbed a short distance down the side of the waterfall, now running less steadily, thanks to the activity above. The exhausted monks on the last wide ledge of rock near the top were laughing and coiling long sections of rope into 'bells' large enough to be carried on their backs with reasonable safety, while stacks of planks stood waiting to be pulled upward.

I abseiled past that ledge and down to the next one. From there I could see a few torches lit. I wanted to thank the Off-Moo before they disappeared back into their caverns. According to Sheik Antara they had sent him a message when they understood we would be in danger if we climbed the Escarpment without help. They had anticipated our problem. This suggested that they been monitoring us all along? We knew that we were disqualified from the swift, secret routes available to these odd, pre-human people.

From my ledge I called down to where, far, far below, Brother Bertrand was supervising the monks. He was a nimble climber and had gone up and down several times. I was not worried about his safety.

I barely heard the monk reply to me, he was so far down. He was agitated for some reason. I called to him that I would come down to the next level so I could hear him. His voice seemed to weaken. Alarmed for his safety, I began quickly climbing down.

I heard Brother Bertrand's voice again. Then some shouts whose words I could not understand. Just as I reached a narrower ledge not far above, where one of the Off-Moo stood looking down, there came a tremendous *bang*. Again I was briefly deafened. The rock shook. Shale fell. I turned to the Off-Moo for enlightenment, speaking French. But he did not understand me. I swung outwards, meaning to descend. A long, rocklike arm, surprisingly strong and firm, shot out in front of me and stopped me going further down on the rope. It tried to sign to me that I should be careful and stay with him, or so I thought. Again I tried to descend further. This time came a confusion of shouting voices and again the tall, grey-blue Mu-Oorian held me back. He was pointing. Evidently he wished me to return to the top.

I tried to see what was happening when blinding smoke came pouring upwards. The strong smell of gunpowder rushed into my nostrils making my eyes water. I could now hear a voice. I was pretty sure it belonged to Brother Bertrand. I called to him:

"Are you injured, Brother?"

There came a muffled reply, too distant to understand. I called again. Into silence. Still no response save the sense of something preparing to attack.

I struggled with the tall Mu-Oorian just as one of the Bazuru brothers reached the ledge. It was M'natka, a slender spear between his teeth. "It's that pilgrim!" he said. "Nixon, is it?" He swung off the rope onto the ledge. He was panting a little. "He shot Brother Bertrand. Disgusting. Not bloody cricket, I know that. It was horrible. Blew a hole clean through him, poor chap!"

"He's dead?"

"Nothing could survive that awful cannon the man carries. What is it? A naval weapon? Antara said the Persians used to mount them on camels. On *camels*!" He was masking his own response. I could tell he grieved as I did.

I could not reply. I mourned for the murdered Carmelite. I struggled in the Off-Moo's grip. His stony, long thin fingers were too strong. The other brother came up the rope. "I was on my way here when the shooting started. That creature almost killed me with his pistol. I threw a couple of spears at him and he hid behind a rock, probably reloading. Well, everyone was safe except me."

I heard another shout, a sudden sharp crack, a throaty yell, another reverberating shot, but nothing came up that chimney. Then On'beon tugged hard on the rope he had climbed.

There came a deep rumble which quickly grew deafening and ended in the sound of rocks rattling downwards in a landslide. Thick dust filled our noses and mouths before we could cover them. Then there was silence again. No longer ominous. On'beon smiled quietly to himself. "I suspect that he'll shoot no more decent old Carmelites in this life. It's a trick I learned from a Matabele hunter who used it to kill a rhino! Well, I learned it from the hunter *and* a film I saw a few years ago in Natal."

"I ought to go down there," I said. "Brother Bertrand could be alive ..."

"Together with Nixer, he's under a few tons of granite now, I'm afraid," said M'natka flatly. "Pretty thoroughly buried, I'd say. They both are. That priest is keeping company with his coreligionist for eternity."

"I suspect they'll have very little to talk about," I said. "Two Christians, with nothing in common except the name of their prophet!" I stupidly presumed that if Nixer survived the desert he would return to the coast obsessively determined to continue his pursuit of us. Though grieving for Brother Bertrand, I was glad to see the back of that hypocritical Puritan and his disgusting weapon. Those people were bad enough when they were sincere. I remembered the Thanksgiving joke I used to tell about the board game I planned to market. '*Save America from her most terrible danger!!*' The game was called *SINK THE MAYFLOWER!*

I drew a deep breath and said goodbye to the Off-Moo who had joined their fellows on the ledge. Again I thanked them for their help. They responded with their familiar quiet good grace. Although we did not share a language I had little doubt we understood each other well. Almost apologetically they took several steps backward into the darkness and then had vanished.

As we climbed slowly back up the side of the waterfall, I asked the Bazuru brothers what they intended to do once they delivered Big Wolf to the Gates of Eden.

"Oh," said M'natka, "I suspect we'll spend some time up here. There's always plenty to do for Lord and Lady B. and if they are in need of help after that earthquake we'd be happy to volunteer."

"So you know them very well?"

I saw him smiling in the light from the luminous fungi.

"You've worked for them for many years?"

"Oh, yes. Many. And before that my grandfather. And before that my great-grandfather."

"A long relationship," I said.

"Over a hundred years. Ever since they came here. Long time!"

"Lord Blackstone was born here?"

"Oh, yes. As were his mother and father."

They seemed amused, as if they shared a private joke.

Finally we reached the pond again. The scene was overshadowed by the bulk of *Spammer Gain,* as if someone had built a shopping mall while I had been away. I could have sworn I heard her humming as she continued to pour water over herself.

After some discussion we all decided to make camp in the meadow and continue on to the Blackstone bungalow first thing in the morning.

Later that evening, Van Geest, Consenseo and the rest of us sat around a good fire and discussed events of the day. The Carmelites and the White Sufis were mourning their dead brother. Beloved for his physical courage and stamina as well as for his robust spirituality and intellectual rigour, Bertrand was admired and liked by everyone. I had enjoyed his company very much and now grieved deeply for him. He had been an important part of our expedition and I had enjoyed many good conversations with him. I could hardly believe he was gone. In an atmosphere of muted sadness, we talked about him and his accomplishments.

Faraq Haad, one of the younger scholars at the medrasa, had been very close to him. They were almost inseparable. He described how he had learned so much, in many disciplines, from the older monk. Eventually he decided to leave our group as his grief overcame him. He went off to mourn alone.

"Tough bugger, that Quaker," mused Van Geest, puffing on his powerful pipe. The only pictures of American pilgrims he had ever seen were on packets of Quaker oats. "He must have been, to get over the desert and trail us through the jungle. I kick myself for not posting some kind of sentry at the opening of the chimney as we went up. Who could have guessed, eh?"

I nodded. "I thought of that man as my nemesis, nobody else's," I said. "I'm not sure why. I hardly knew him. But he hated me for some reason, and he seemed to incorporate everything I hate about the modern world. His greed, his hypocrisy, his religiosity, his murderous nature ..."

"Everything, in fact," said Van Geest with a slow smile, "that's sinful, eh, man!" He knocked his pipe out on a rock. "I never knew him, of course, but guess I know the type! He's like the DRC preachers I grew up with in Bloemfontein. Nose in the air and boots in the slurry, as we used to say. They know all there is about sin because sin is all they really know. If you take my meaning. They think we're all like them!"

With a friendly pat on my shoulder, he, too, headed for bed, leaving me with my thoughts. It took me some while to go to sleep.

I woke early to find several ranks of ebony warriors squatting around us. Every man was dressed like a chief. They were splendid in their white ostrich-feather headdresses, gold-and-lion-claw necklaces and white cowhide shields. All had kilts of leopard skin and short lionskin cloaks. Crack warriors, they carried both broad-bladed, short-shafted stabbing spears and long-shafted throwing spears. At their hips were short swords in heavily decorated leather scabbards. Their long throwing spears and knobkerries, among others, seeming to identify them as a branch of Zulu or Masai, I wondered if they belonged to the Wad'ira tribe of legend. All had close-cropped hair and most had extraordinary good looks. The majority of the warriors were men but there were some women amongst them, dressed identically. As I opened my eyes to observe them, they remained expressionless, though I thought for a moment I saw humour in their faces as well.

I certainly hoped they were friendly. Was it possible that the Blackstone Estate had been raided during a period when it could not get news out to the world? Were these the conquerors?

I heard Van Geest and the Bazuru brothers nearby. I could only think of one word of greeting: *Sanibowani*. When they all replied with the single *Yebo*, I felt I had made some progress but could not be completely sure. I remembered the word, I think, from a *Sanders of the River* West African story, or maybe the Paul Robeson version of the film, or perhaps some other childhood adventure story read when I was young, maybe Edgar Rice Burroughs, who was certainly no expert on Africa or her languages.

Van Geest saw that I was awake. I think he was amused by my expression.

"These chaps are here to escort us to the estate, apparently. You would not believe me if I told you what was going on, man."

I grew a bit gloomy at this news but, seeing my expression, he laughed loudly. "It's nothing for you to worry about, but it's bloody big news in this part of the world. The Wad'ira have always had a special relationship with the Blackstones. You probably know that. Goes back a hundred years or more, I gather, to a time when the Blackstones were rumoured to be going in and out of some sort of Atlantean Lost City! Populated not by the blokes who helped us, the rockies, but humans of some sort. I know! Crazy, isn't it? But it explained their fortune, I guess. I myself explained a certain amount by the distraction of King Solomon and an immortal falling in love with me. Everyone loves a good tale, Mr M.! Eh?" He contemplated his stained meerschaum. "The English Blackstones aren't hugely wealthy. Anyway, the Off-Moo were expecting us, as you know. The Wad'ira were also making their way to help us but were still on the other side of the plateau. They arrived just before dawn. Anyway, they're pleased to see us. They were afraid we were going to be late. We're all supposed to get together at the homestead, as soon as we can. They are here to guard our safety. I know. A bit late for that." He shrugged.

"They'll carry anything or herd anything or do whatever we need. They want us to hurry. Something about an important 'coming together', a kind of congress. They speak a version of Bantu but too different from anything I understand very easily. We'd better have some breakfast and get on the road! Apparently Lord Blackstone will explain everything. He's in a bit of a hurry, too. We're almost too late! I think we'd better save any questions until we get to his place."

"Is it far?" I began to get out of my sleeping bag.

"No, man. Barely a hundred miles from here."

I was surprised. I looked around me. All I could see was a wide plain, some mountains in the far distance, a forest to the west and the east and a wide sky. "How big is this plateau?"

"I'm not sure. I once heard it called the Endless World in Bantu. Pretty big, I'd say. We're on the farthest edge I know.

It's a whole bloody *planet* up here. You know. Different micro-climates and terrain. Something of every kind of weather. Mostly I'm reminded of home. Strikes a chord here—" thumping his chest "—here, you know. Blackstone once talked of getting a team up to survey it properly. But when I raised the idea a couple of years ago he'd become much less enthusiastic. I'm not sure anyone's ever really mapped it. Unless it was Blackstone or one of his people." He kicked at a loose stone. "It goes on for ever, man. At least some of the Wad'ira don't believe it has any boundaries at all! They say it's an entire plane of the multiverse. They call it the Cloud World. It's huge. There are whole civilisations out there, undiscovered by anyone from ours. See that distant peak to the West? I heard there's another mountain grows out of it with a whole prehistoric world on top of it! Like that one Conan Doyle set in South America. With monsters, pterodactyls and all that. Maybe King Kong on the top!" He laughed loudly and slapped me on the back. "Believe you me, man! Every story you ever heard about Africa has its beginnings there."

"Is there any way of getting out of here?" I asked him. I was again beginning to think about my family. "That's what's really worrying me!"

He chuckled. "We got here, didn't we? I've been up and down a few times, as have the Bazuru brothers and several others. And so has Blackstone and his family, of course. So you really shouldn't worry, man. Don't forget they've got a radio *and* a plane *and* god knows what else. Keep your hat on, old boy. If you're worried about seeing your people again, you're going to be fine! Fine, fine, fine." His broad Boer face broke in a grin.

Something about his tone, however, was not entirely reassuring.

We set off on the remaining stage of our journey. I could

not help thinking again, as they expertly guided our great herd over the plain, singing as they went, how we could have done with the help of those fine-looking warriors earlier in our journey. I was distracted from any regret by what really was an extraordinary scene. We moved over the wide, high escarpment table towards the snow-topped Western mountain. The *spammaldjin* was back in her refreshed and remade cabinet. Most of the other animals moved by themselves and carried smaller beasts. Some dragged ramshackle carts and sleds, while many rode on the horses or elephants. The plain was now thick with life, most of it brought from below. Our many feet began to kick up dust as we moved. I could look in any direction: Animals and people moving at a steady walk. I thought of an exodus. The peoples of Israel or Germany or Mexico or Burundi, all pressing on into the dusty darkness attempting to find assurance of safety or food. But these creatures were going home!

Most of the time we were led by Big Wolf. He was reinvigorated by his successful ascent, loping ahead of us, the most anxious to get to our destination. At our centre was *Spammer*. On our flanks were the Wad'ira. The dust rose and fell like an ocean. I was still unsure exactly where we were going or what the so-called 'Gates of Eden' were. If expectations were based in past adventures we could actually be heading for the Gates of Hades!

The animals were moving a little more eagerly now, acting as if time were running out, as if the coming 'Conjunction' were only hours away. Even I picked up on their sense of urgency, sometimes riding a distance ahead with Mabira, the chief of that particular detachment of Wad'ira. He knew excellent English and was full of praise for Lord Blackstone and spoke warmly of Blackstone's love for Africa and the African people. Without bothering to check the crude maps Mabira carried, we followed Big Wolf, who seemed certain of his destination, keeping a steady, loping pace before us.

Perhaps it was the most extraordinary sight Africa had ever known. The massed Wad'ira moving at a jog, their ostrich plumes nodding, their glittering brass, gold and lions'-teeth ornaments jingling on their wonderful bodies. Sometimes I was blinded by those blazing steel spears, magnificent in the rising sun. Meanwhile the Bazuru brothers and Sheik Antara, mounted again on his camel, continued amongst them. Occasionally I made out Professor Consenseo riding with Tracker Van Geest amongst that huge medley of oddly sized animals from every part of the world. Sometimes I rode with the White Sufi and their brothers the Carmelites, all now on horseback at the rear.

In spite of my misgivings I was intensely proud to be part of that party, especially when, a couple of days later, I saw at last the beautiful Blackstone farm ahead.

The main building was a long Palladian-style bungalow, with Jeffersonian eccentricities, built at the crest of a gentle hillside and shaded by spreading acacias. A clear stream curved beside it, watering the dark banks and bright blossoms of rhododendrons. The water reflected the bright, blue sky. The sheltering branches of massive old trees shaded English flower beds, surrounded by gentle, green-gold meadows in which horses and cattle grazed. I might have been back in England on an Oxfordshire farm, save for the dimensions of those trees.

A small group of people waited for us outside that elegant 'Monticello' of a house. We signalled our horses into a canter and moved to the front of the procession, hearing distant English voices calling a greeting from the house's long verandah. Surprisingly most of the whites wore vaguely Edwardian clothes. Straight from the set of a BBC poshstalgia series.

Outside the house the Wad'ira came to a sudden, disciplined

stop. Stamping their spear shafts upon the hard ground, they let out a deep staccato roar. Evidently this was a sign of their respect. The animals, especially the larger reptiles, paused cautiously. The rest of us reached a more ragged halt as the Wad'ira ranks parted to let Tracker Van Geest and our visiting party approach the verandah's steps where stood a handsome, square-jawed man more than six foot tall. His black hair was long. He was muscular, tanned, wearing a white shirt, cravat and white linen suit with a pigskin waistcoat. Beside him was a lovely woman, presumably his wife. She was also tall, her fair head coming to above his shoulder. They reminded me of illustrations in *The Strand* for 1899. By now I had become used to such anomalies. She, for instance, wore a pale blue Edwardian day dress cut to just above a pair of white kid boots and on her fair, pretty, head a 'boater' with a floral band. On her delicate hands she wore white lace gloves. A perfectly informal daytime costume.

They made an extraordinarily handsome couple. I felt a strong frisson of recognition as if I visited relatives not seen for many years. We dismounted and ascended the verandah steps. As I did so I caught a powerful scent of flowers. There, on one side of the house, with a distant view of a wild forest and the snow-topped mountain peak behind it, was a lovely rose walk bearing displays of roses in a variety of shades. I took a deep breath of that reassuring air. The whole house bore a sense of tranquil civilisation. I could easily comprehend what Van Geest had told me about the place.

We shook hands and the tracker performed the introductions. *Spammer* was taken off to their big swimming pool. Lord John Blackstone spoke an easy English with what I thought was a faint French accent. Lady Jane Blackstone had the cultivated American accent I associated with the Edwardians. Behind them stood a beautiful dark-haired younger woman in a pink and white costume, introduced as Miriam Claybourne, the couple's daughter-in-law. They apologised for their son not being present.

"Jack's over at the lake fixing the planes," Lord Blackstone told us. "We had a bit of a rumble here a while ago. A tornado went through just as we felt the aftershocks. We're surprised anyone was able to get up the Escarpment, even with expert help. Rather glad to have your company, I must say. If only for this very short time. We feared we'd not be ready for the Conjunction, you know. The radio went out and all our valves were broken so we can't send or receive signals until the planes can get running again. We'll go over there in a bit."

While the Wad'ira dispersed to their own village, just visible beyond the rose bower, we were invited to freshen up in the Blackstones' surprisingly modern bathrooms. At length, after taking turns and being shown our overnight quarters, I eventually re-joined our hosts on the verandah.

I felt in better shape than I had in ages. I found the old-world atmosphere of this Edwardian tea party both seductive and a touch repellent. Dignified and happy, all of the servants seemed Egyptian, with round heads and light brown skins. I had never been very comfortable with that particular *status quo*. I found somewhere to sit. It was for me a terrific chance to rest in relatively comfortable conditions after so much stress. It was civilised. Lord John explained, *sotto voce*, that it was important to the women. He did not seem very comfortable in his well-cut suit which failed to hide his masculinity. We were all served our choice of tea or lemonade and fresh-baked scones. This was the most familiar moment I had experienced since I had left Paris.

Enjoying everything about this incongruous tea party, I was reminded rather sadly of all the comrades I had lost on the way to the Blackstone house, so far from the world of war and insane capitalism, of sentimentalised virtue and demonised humanity. I thought of Claude Duval, my Musketeers, Bruno the bear and Brother Bertrand. At the back of my mind I had rather hoped that some of my friends, at least, might have found a means of going ahead of us and reaching the Blackstone plantation before we did. That they were not really dead. As it was, the verandah was a bit crowded with the Blackstones and their current guests.

Of course it had not taken me long to believe that I was in reality meeting the man who had not only been my second-most admired fictional hero while growing up (after the same author's John Carter of Barsoom) but who had also given me a living as the editor of *Tarzan Adventures* with my first job in national publishing. I must admit I again felt a little dizzy and life took on a dreamlike quality. I made conversation easily enough!

"I gather you were born in these parts, sir." I sipped tea as good as the best Darjeeling. Lady Blackstone told me it was grown on their own plantations, as was their coffee.

He replied pleasantly, "I was a young man before I saw England. My parents were going to farm out here but were marooned over on the West Coast and my mother died, sadly, before I spoke my first words. My father was killed soon afterwards but I had the good fortune to be fostered by, of all things, a mountain great ape belonging to a tribe whose territory is not far from here. I was something of a wild beast, I have to admit, before the Wad'ira found me. After my foster-mother was also killed they raised me. My story was a bit of a sensation for a short while before the Great War."

"I believe I know it a bit," I told him, trying to suppress my astonishment. "Weren't you known as Tarzan?"

He shook his head, smiling. "I can guess where you found that rather sensational account," he said. "No, I had a rather unpronounceable name in my earliest years, until the Wad'ira saved me. Not really a name in our sense. There was an American chap fictionalised a tale for an American magazine a few years back. I met him briefly in Chicago. He wanted me to see Mr Kipling in Sussex and tell him my story. He was a little agitated about it. Apparently Kipling swears the chap stole that Tarzan story which is a pity, since quite a lot of it is true. He didn't mind my adoptive mother being an ape but drew the line at a black foster-family! In fact, it's fair to say he rather toned things down."

"Mind saying what sort of things?" asked Professor Consenseo, I thought a little rudely. Blackstone, however, was very charming.

"I can demonstrate, if you like. If everyone's ready for a bit of a surprise." He looked around at all the people enjoying something of an animated tea party. Raising his voice he addressed the guests. "Is everyone ready to meet some of the other Blackstone residents?" And as soon he had received a murmur of consent (with Lady Jane offering a mild protest), he put his head back a little and cupped his hands, making a strange, almost inhuman noise, half-growl, half-whistle. He turned to me with a grin and glanced towards the entrance of the rose bower.

I saw a movement. Two of the berobed sufis, closer to the bower, gave a cry and quickly backed away. They looked down as something scuttled past their feet and I saw a flash of pink, then green and yellow, then blue – all different colours. We found it impossible not to smile, not to cry out in astonishment at the collection of living creatures suddenly appearing on the verandah.

I wasn't sure what to call most of them. They were reptiles but they had the manner of enthusiastic dogs, red mouths gaping, red tongues lolling, white teeth shining, their tales clattering and their scales, if anything, brighter, more variously feathered than those of the local birds. They were clearly at least as clever as crows, hopping and perching all over the Blackstones and behaving only slightly more cautiously towards their guests. They were dinosaurs. In miniature. Without doubt. Tyrannosaurs and triceratops and stegosaurus and brachiosaurus and parosaurolophus and velociraptors and spinosaurus like so many varieties of pets! Ferrets came to mind.

The scampering reptiles clearly loved Blackstone (I had a terrible urge to call him 'Tarzan') and the guests loved them, welcoming them with cries of delight as if suddenly introduced to a collection of cockatoos, immediately taking pleasure in the friendly creatures, then gasping again when an entire flock of glittering, multicoloured pterodactyls perched on the verandah's balustrades. Lady Blackstone, however, was not prepared to let the pterodactyls stay and waved them gently away when they tried to settle on the extended arms, hands or proffered shoulders of the guests. Catching my eye, she held her nose then grinned and winked at me.

At that moment I knew what Tarzan saw in Jane. I might feel something like it when Jenny came along. I wasn't really in love with her, but she represented something I had lost, the companionship of my female self, my cousin, who had died of polio and had been my best friend. I had been conditioned to respond to her in certain ways. I discovered a kind of comradeship in her that I had never really known before. My own immediate fascination with Jenny had much of the frisson of recognition I felt when I first saw Jane. Jenny had the instincts but lacked Jane Blackstone's moral strength to back it up. I once suggested she and her family should join hands and form a vacuum. Never to her face, but I suspect she saw that cruelty in me and was afraid of me. And attracted to me.

She was forever trying to attribute to me a cruel streak I didn't have. What I had might have been worse.

Jenny was exactly the sort of kid I used to send back to their parents from gigs or parties. Girls who should have stayed at home and got their A-levels. She won a great scholarship to one of the best schools in the country and would have gone straight to Cambridge to do her studies, get a good degree and become self-confident. But she lived too close to the line between fantasy and reality. She would have been happy if she had not lived in Notting Hill and turned fourteen in 1966. I was twenty-six. She had an abortion in 1968. "You should have seen the other girls in the clinic! Almost all their boyfriends were famous!" Different days. Everyone was doing it. I fiercely denied she was a groupie. Weren't we in Paris? Helena and I?

Watching the bright miniature dinosaurs I suspected that Blackstone was showing off a little. "I found the little chaps in a most unusual adventure," he told me. "This entire part of the world is heavy with what I can only term a kind of magic. More to do with its precise position in space and time and given to anomalies. So many unlikely things happen because we're cut off from normal reality here. As if nothing tests their nature or even *raison d'être*. We find many more odd phenomena than there used to be. That's part of why we stay here. One's rarely bored."

I smiled. "Where do they come from?"

"Well, you see, there's another underworld. More than one as far as I can tell. Not the same as the Mu-Oorian one."

"You're familiar with Mu-Ooria, sir?"

"Of course. Those are the chaps who came to help you get up the waterfall? We were afraid the Wad'ira would not reach you in time. I have a way of contacting them, as has Antara."

"Your little fellows didn't come from Mu-Ooria, surely? You said—"

"I said it was another, very different underground world. The dinosaurs come from a world which lies in a kind of air-pocket below our own, heated by the earth's core. It's pretty vast. A world of jungles and mountain ranges and oceans. But as a result of the physics applying there, the creatures and plants never grow very big! I think it's to do with the gravity. Actually, they might not be directly underneath us. Not necessarily. What if they are in another universe in which such things are far more likely to occur?"

"Connected dimensions?"

"The narratives act like physical roads. Pretty much anything that Chicago chap can think up, we've experienced here! Ancient civilisations. Temples of gold. Beast men. Ononoes. Queens of strange races. Whatever you could find in, say, Jules Verne or Rider Haggard. I don't know why the Escarpment is so special. Odd! As I say. It can be pretty ordinary if you don't go down to the lake at certain times. Or follow certain rivers. Or enter certain parts of the forest. Or become involved in certain stories! The Wad'ira aren't native to the area around the Gates of Eden. We call the Gates by that name, but this land has had plenty of other names.

"The Wad'ira's lowland ancestors used to call this the Haunted Plateau and were scared of the place. The game is plentiful but they refused to come up here. Many other tribes still fear it. So we cultivate its mystery. It can be very dangerous sometimes. We've grown used to it. We have learned how to protect ourselves. These days we have made some helpful friends we can call on. We can't always offer the same safeguards to newcomers. We can, however, teach them how to survive." He sighed and smiled, looking off towards the distance where a flock of tiny pterosaurs circled in the air like gnats.

For a moment I felt a chill.

I thought I had heard the Whispering Swarm.
And it was not antagonistic.

30

The Gates of Eden

I WAS DISTURBED for a moment by Blackstone's declaration that he preferred his fantastic retreat to the outside world. I was wary of escapers in those days. I felt we had entered a period when vigilance was required of us as citizens, not escape. I loved the modern world in all her intricacy and wonders. My first response was to continue with my determination to leave. Suddenly I feared the Haunted Plateau. Not for its dangers but for its delusions. Those were too much at odds with my familiar reality, my sense of what was most valuable and desirable. What were my responsibilities as a father and partner? Life here was too vividly attractive. Too easily distracting from problems I had already engaged in. By betraying those commitments, I betrayed myself. I had already learned that lesson, when I had behaved in a cowardly or betrayed a trust, like leaving my dog tied to a bush and returning to school. Of course I was partly tempted to stay with these magical people. To live a life of high adventure and distraction and somehow fall in love with a woman like Jane, a sweet, companionable, down-to-earth girl who would be a perfect mother. But then, of course, I would get bored with bucolic escape and spend the rest of my life trying to free myself from a narrative without any substance but the quest for thoughtlessness and a kind of oblivion.

I asked Blackstone if he ever missed London and he replied: "Not nearly as much as I miss the jungle."

I told him that I still missed London more than anywhere else. While I loved travelling I would not willingly leave the city of my birth.

"Well," he said thoughtfully, running his finger down a scaly back belonging to a tiny saurian. She reached out a forked tongue to smell him and then put her delicate hands over her own disproportionately large eyes. Suddenly I could see what the creature must look like to a small mammal occupying a space between the earth's surface and the earth's core. "I wonder which London you like now and whether you'll continue to like it. Dreams change quite as much as reality, as you know." He flashed a glance of good-humoured intelligence.

I wondered how, when entering that world of the earth's core, the Jungle Lord had managed to shrink to the appropriate size. I simply couldn't believe it, in spite of experiencing so much fantastic adventure. I was a rationalist at root. To me Blackstone seemed faintly demonic. Should I blame Hogarth, who had depicted him as a forest spirit, avenging and invisible? I became suspicious. Unable to distinguish between dream and reality, suddenly I saw Blackstone as Mephistopheles trying to seduce me. To keep me as a Peter Pan in Neverland. I had resisted so many attempts to make me compromise my goals. Had I already been tricked, step by step, for something so trivial? Was I bait in some supernatural ritual? Tricked so that a giant cuttlefish could play a goddess? I could believe I existed on a world which was merely one tiny part of a section of a near-infinite series of fulcra travelling sideways through a multiverse that is both circling and swinging in eccentric orbits, kept roughly in balance by the narratives of mankind, who might be the only creatures common to the entire

457

multiverse, a kind of storytelling *bug*. Not merely exploring space. But making shapes in mirrors. Making shapes that are the elements of other human lives. And living in seeming chaos like small animals often do. Like metro-mice, utterly careless of the electrified trains constantly coming and going above.

That's what I thought. The ravings of a madman, eh? Acid freakburn?

"Every exploration expands essential elements in a blunt narrative that refuses to make itself, as it claims, as sharp a surgeon's stylus," said Sam on my shoulder. *"In other words, the game is always to some degree rigged. If you want to adjust that, then try it."* He gave an enigmatic croak. *"Just remember, idealists are rarely pleasant people. Or, rather, they are often not liked by their nearest and dearest. The kulaks control their poorer brethren and are in turn controlled. I have seen it. They call it working democracy. I call it feudalism. Just a thought. Some modern Russians made restoring serfdom a cause."*

"I—" I began.

"That's what they all say," he told me, and flew away. I was remembering the jackdaw I had met in the same short alley where I had left Brandy. Only at that moment did I realise where both events occurred. The alley ran from the other side of the road, where our school was, to the road which more or less paralleled it. Why did I so rarely use that alley? I've since tried to find it. It's not on Google and neither is Belmont prep school. They have probably been built over.

I was beginning to believe that *only* creatures like us – mammals, fish, reptiles, cephalopods, birds – were replicated across the multiverse. The plane of the multiverse I now shared was the tiniest of fractions. If we moved we would barely be shifting a microbe's width, if that, in multiversal space. Then why was it worth doing? The answer came quickly: Because our actions were replicated. Our function was to replicate, even

458

multiply, our narratives. Repetition was order, and if one action was replicated, if one action was repeated, then perhaps all knowledge could be replicated, perhaps exactly, perhaps not, throughout the multiverse. *Which is why it isn't always a good idea to mow the grass too short*, said an odd voice in my head.

Had Sam returned? No. It was *Spammer*. Making a joke? The valuable and wise *spammaldjin*, the goddess who was a universe. Like every good mother she took dreams as seriously as she took reality. She honoured all existence and had created the scales to measure and control a multiverse constantly shifting her geometry, symmetry and point of balance. Maintaining enough order for Chaos to flourish. Surviving as everything survives, between darknesses. On the pinpoint of matter between dreams and non-dreams.

So I asked Blackstone, the Lord of the Haunted Plateau, if he had ever feared death at the hands of the dead. And he told me that while the dead could not steal the life of a free spirit, they could sometimes steal a soul. The chief Wad'ira medicine man, one of the other guests, agreed enthusiastically.

I became still more uneasy.

I missed my family intensely, remorsefully. I hoped those who loved me would forgive me for anything I had done to wound them. I struggled between intellect and emotion. I knew Helena would dismiss what I was thinking as sentimental bullshit, but it was upon such bullshit I had to base my actions. Upon my sentimental actions the extravagant pain of whole worlds might be based. Countless souls might suffer for near-eternity. So logically, I leaned towards a less demanding interpretation, an assumption of empathy. Perhaps this moral and spiritual struggle was good for me? I tried to put my idealistic beliefs to practical use. Since I was a teenager I struggled with moral ideas. The consequences of actions. I believed the arts, and especially writing, to be action. I believed every action carried a moral meaning. Did context always define the action?

I was burdened.

Here, on the Haunted Plateau, I found moral choices superficially easy. There again, the chance of enjoying magical adventures and extraordinary sights was very attractive. As was the endless opportunity to satisfy my curiosity. What if my wife and children *wanted* to join me? I imagined how exciting the children would find all the exotic animals and people. I couldn't abandon them. I knew Helena's common sense would overrule any romantic dream. The girls might get bitten by something or eaten by something or catch something. Mocking references to slavery, colonialism, and corruption.

She would speak with increasing rapidity as she became nervous and ashamed of her own anxiety. She didn't want to travel so far from home when it came down to it. Faced with a chance to take a camel-train into the Sahara, she would rather stay a night at the Ritz. Fair enough. She was driven by nostalgia. Her lost land was the one she had shared with her father, the dead Vickers-Armstrong manager. I still wonder if that informed her later decision to have another child. A child which eventually I seemed to welcome and take responsibility for more than she did. I have since wondered about our decisions and if they were ever made for our children at all. I don't know, and I rarely enjoyed enough clarity to think deeply about it in coming days.

I began to wish Blackstone had lent us a Land-Rover rather than horses. How old was he? I suspected him of a kind of tree-hugging ostentation and nostalgia for Edwardian times as we trekked wearily following the magnificent cephalopod across the plateau towards the lake. Dwarfing us all, *Spammer* travelled on a kind of shallow, water-filled cart which she moved with her arms, showing every sign of joy as, with occasional stops to bathe, she led us towards the Gates of Eden.

When we walked our horses, Lord Blackstone was with me much of the time. He assured me that I was welcome to stay with them as long as I liked. "Do send for the family. We've a great library and children love it. No-one's ever bored. We even have a cinema at the back of the house. Radio. Records. We take only what we enjoy from the outside world. And, of course, our uplands are cool and our rolling downs go on for ever! Jane's even planted a bluebell wood in spring. Many English flowers grow perfectly here." He paused briefly to breathe in that sweet earth. "Do consider it. Perfect for a writer." *Not*, I thought, *a writer who thrives on their curiosity about the modern world.*

I knew, of course, what he meant. The low hills and woods were strongly reminiscent of Surrey and Kent settled by my many aunts, who, like my mum, all had green fingers and were wizards with roses and hollyhocks, lupines and tulips. I saw quite a bit of them during the war. I think mum was told to leave London because of the bombing. Before the Blitz many did the same. Mum left me at my Aunt Rose's in Haywards Heath, playing with my cousin Pauline. What a lovely little girl she was. My first love! Those calm mock Tudor houses and parks with their poplars and cedars and spreading chestnuts were amongst my strongest early memories. I sometimes yearned for my childhood days. I wasn't more than three, barely out of my pushchair. Sweet-smelling hedges and a mass of colour. And this was wartime. Silence. Only the rare air-raid warning. And Aunt Rose, so unlike my mother, calm and easy but not much good at playing monkeys.

Blackstone was being very generous. I was curious to know how he could afford all these amenities. I had never read of a Blackstone fortune. I asked him. He did not mind my question.

461

He smiled. "One of my luckiest adventures involved an ancient decadent city whose stores of gold are vast," he said. "Probably the real King Solomon's mines! Anyway, it provided me with all the wealth I've needed. This land was never claimed by anyone else. Only the Wad'ira came to hunt. They shunned it for the most part. We have cultivated it. Civilised it. Nurtured it. We have good generators powered by the upstream waters above our house. The cinema and an electric phonograph are my chief extravagances. That and our plane, I suppose. You'll see it at the lake."

"Your son flies, you said?"

"Oh, we all do."

I relaxed again beneath a big sky. All the animals and people were spread across the wide landscape. They moved together like a dignified tide. This really was one of the most beautiful places on earth! I breathed in more of her vibrant air.

We had left the Blackstone women at the house, together with a couple of learned sufis and Carmelites who, remarkably, had studied various manuals and believed they could fix one of the radios. I had no idea how they were going to make a vacuum tube! No doubt they would try to salvage one from the ruins. I did not find their explanations especially credible, but Blackstone seemed happy enough! Sheik Antara was ready to go back to his beloved desert but decided, from curiosity, to come with us to the lake.

Soon the distant peak was to our left and just behind us. Blackstone said we were nearing the centre of the double escarpment. "The lake's bang in the middle," he said. "Must have been a bit of a big thump when the asteroid hit, don't you think? Set the whole volcano off again! Created the entire bloody anomaly, I'd say."

"So this isn't – normal ..." I said.

He seemed amused. "What do you think?"

I suppose I'd been lucky to find it. Maybe this 'anomaly' was my only chance of getting home.

Making an excuse, I climbed into my saddle and soon I rode beside *Spammer*. Her huge mournful, unhuman eye looked down at me. Her arms, the diameter of a Tube train, as sensitive as a lover's touch, rose and fell laboriously. Her great clacking beak opened and closed as if she breathed with difficulty.

I wondered why I felt so comfortable in her presence.

"*You have taken a long diversion in service of the Balance.*" I was astonished. She rarely addressed me directly.

"We could not have got here more directly, *Spammer*, dear."

"*Oh, indeed no. Not once you left Paris. You went straight as an arrow, all things considered. As the Corporal Pork flies! Only Fearless Frank Force himself could strike a quarry so quick to the core. Very few can navigate the reality you witness. All the fine fleets of straight arrows could not fly faster! Pearl Peru was not braver. It is why you were chosen, for you walk the coiling moonbeam trails so well, with such certainty of step, you and your stories, you and your tarot, you and your music diddly diddly. O, we love my sprat, my sweet fry of fries.*"

And she stopped to clean her eyes with her arms, like a fly, with deep satisfaction, back, front, up, down and sideways. Soft in a self-caress. "*Thanks.*"

"*I wonder what you are thanking me for, Spammer dear.*"

"*Oh, for the realities and wonders and the stories which have been and which are still to come, which lie frozen still beneath the ice of Limbo or scatter elements upon the twilight winds; the winds we shall never never see, the winds shall never never be and the fleece that Jason steals shines dear ones and reels from axle to axle and wheel to wheel like the onion Poor Peer peels and all the waves from the snows of yesterday rise up and the waves fall so are you prepared to die for that, to weave your carpet and*" expire, consumed by unquenchable fire and run for ever under perfect skies. What do we hold but a ball of golden wool? There are few maps to the Labyrinth."

"I hold nothing, dear Spammer, save a dreaming mind, a silver wand, a sword engraved with my name."

"And flesh, my darling fishling. The power to reproduce. The power of rage and pain. The power to smile and betray. The power to struggle and survive."

"You flatter me, Spam. Or fatten me for glory. For sacrificial glory. For the melancholy life."

"Not you, my crackling."

I think she was amused. I could not sense the same suspicions of her that I had of Blackstone. I was suspicious of all who turned their backs on the city to find sweet escape in shires and ditches and even forests and mountains. I neither hated, feared nor despised them, for we choose our routes if not our roots, but I could not help mistrusting their *understanding*. In my eyes, part of my responsibility as an adult in a democracy was to inform myself about the world's issues and to take some action to affect a solution. While I sympathised with the flight impulse, I still needed to hear the murmuring presence of the outside world. Now we crawled and swaggered and trudged and flew and wriggled towards the lake. Following the *spammaldjin*, whether for revelation, revolution or resolution, through the Gates of Eden.

So 'her crackling' drops back and on we march and strut and ride and slither and slide. All writhing or walking on our way back to Eden reaching with open arms and tight closed eyes to squat and stare beyond the light and colour swirling and gyrating about our happy heads, for *Spammer*'s to be saved and the mighty multiverse set to spin again in every direction at once and another story's started and another story ends. "*Spinning*," says Spammer, "*is what we do*."

Sheik Antara, who was speaking to Professor Consenseo, comes riding up to grin through his dusty face and point ahead to where columns of ivory steam rise in the distance.

"The gates," he grins. "We are almost there! And now your adventure, my friend, begins and ends. A flourish! You will do what you must all do on the moonbeam roads, but I am committed to my duty elsewhere. To throw another die in the Game of Time. This is what we all must all do! So the multiverse renews!"

I felt sudden disappointment. Even though I had always known he intended to remain on his home plane, I had still hoped he would come with us through the gates.

The Bazuru brothers and the holy men also intended to stay, since this was their natural plane, and Antara had his own commitments, of course, as we all did. Why would an Arab hero not want to remain in his beloved Sahara and his native deserts? He had been clear since I met him. His love of the desert was palpable. Yet I sensed something else, some mysterious and urgent desire to return. I almost wanted to go with him. But I had enjoyed my share of danger! I wondered what he knew, this man of two ages. What did he see beginning that he did not want to be involved in? I forced myself not to wonder. I had been promised a chance to get home and I was determined to go. Now I trusted *only Spammer*!

Sheik Antara handed me a decorated tube, beautifully made of tree-bark. Then he turned his horse, blew me a cheerfully sardonic kiss, and rode rapidly away, back towards the distant house. He was the last of my desert comrades to leave. I like to think that he had gone to join Duval, D'Artagnan and the others on a wild adventure in Syria. Another narrative, another buttress added to the great cathedral of wisdom and knowledge built from our shared experience. But what has he given me? I tucked the tube inside my shirt.

465

Blackstone was next. Would I care to go for a gallop with him? We rode for the pleasure of it, cantering until quite suddenly we mounted a short promontory overlooking the green-blue waters of a wide, tranquil lake reflecting the blue and white pallor of the sky. And there, dragged to the beach beneath a wooden awning protecting it from the sun, was one of the largest flying machines I ever saw! A tall airliner, fit to rank beside the great ones. That was the first time I saw the predecessor of Hughes's marvellous Spruce Goose and Britain's Princess. Those two dreams of flying were superseded by jet-liners before they had a chance to solve their technical troubles. This plane also clearly had problems with her power-weight ratio. She was the DoX, Doktor Dornier's huge flying boat, commissioned before the Nazis came to power, but part of their prestige. Like the Goose and the Princess, she had flown into mists of legend, leaving us the duty of making their myths. With few curves she looked as if she had been built from a giant Meccano set. I could hardly believe the forest of engines and propellers on her top wing! She was pale blue with Dr Dornier's name prominent on her bow where someone had made a recent, almost invisible, repair.

Drawn up near the big boat-house was a smaller plane, a scarlet Hawker Osprey two-seater. She had clearly been damaged. She had an irregular hole in one of her wide floats and another in her side. Standing near her, a wrench in one grease-covered hand, wiping sweat from an equally grease-covered face, was a woman I recognised. Before I could speak to her, a big window in the larger plane's control cabin was drawn back and a good-looking young man stuck his tousled blond head out of the plane to address the 'Forest Lord' as he started to dismount. "What ho, Dad! You're just in time. We've got 'em all going in sync at last! Wait till you hear 'em!" He ducked back into the big control cabin to make an adjustment and, one after another, start the twelve propellers. The independent engines, mounted in fore-and-aft pairs on the plane's high wing, began to cough and vibrate. I had never experienced so much power in a conventional engine.

Blackstone's expression suggested that he did not take the same pleasure in noise, but still he grinned back at the man who was evidently his son. Down from his horse he motioned for me to do the same.

With a whoop, Jack Blackstone disappeared from the window. A moment later he appeared above the low wing and waded towards the narrow shingle beach. "Hullo, pater! Ain't they sweet?"

The 'Forest Lord' and I made our way along the sandy path to the beach. A woman walking towards us was exactly who I thought she would be. I had left her in a very different place and time. I was delighted to see her. She was smiling, too. She wore an oil-stained white shirt, jodhpurs and boots and was trying to wipe her face with an already oily towel. It was the Rose of Las Cascadas! With her hair bobbed in a fashionable 1920s cut.

"Lady Rose." I put out my hand. "What a pleasure! We met at Las Cascadas. You were in command of an abbey and a ship, then! A schooner, as I recall."

"I do not forget you, Mr Moorcock. Guide Sensers have excellent memories." She spoke in a low, pleasant, English-accented voice. "Has everyone come to see my plane take off?"

Lord John chuckled. "You did rather isolate everyone when you crashed into our little sea-hawk," he said. He turned to me to explain. "Rose came here looking for you. She intended to get you back home. That whirlwind caught her in the desert and buggered her engines! Sadly, the water in the lake had gone down a great deal since she was last here and she had some trouble landing that monster of hers. She knocked the

Hawker sideways, threw out her props and put a hole in her fuselage, making both ships unskyworthy!"

"Because you hadn't followed regulations," she insisted. "And parked your little plane on the water into the sun. I hardly saw her until I was coming in to land and did my best to straighten up. Too late! Nice to see you again, Mr Moorcock. You're bringing our *Spammer* home, I see. I had always dreamed of doing that myself. But as long as someone does ..."

In the lake shore's sandy grass animals of all sizes were standing. Expectant and alert, they looked to where, in the shallows, the *spammaldjin* cast her Leviathan shadow over the water. Lord Blackstone pointed with a half-smoked cheroot to the middle of the lake.

Something was shimmering there. At first I thought it was a fountain sending up a shower of golden droplets, but then I realised I saw a gigantic globe, a bubble growing more clearly defined with every moment. Our animals became nervous, letting out a chorus of cries, barks, howls, hisses, grunts and roars in their agitation. Some shuddered from head to foot, anticipating their pain and discomfort ending at last. They were hardly able to restrain themselves from plunging into the water and swimming out to the great pulsing sphere.

Nearby, Professor Consenseo made no effort to hide his schoolboy pleasure. He guided his elephant, Mr Jumbo, into the calm waters of the lake, throwing his head back and calling out to me.

"It's the Conjunction, old boy. It's the great reckoning, when all lost travellers find their way home! The same story plays out! Some champion must end the world! This is happening everywhere. Now we reset the universe. The multiverse vibrates. Isn't it wonderful? We follow our star!" I felt a great wave of joy. I loved the sight of Professor Consenseo on the back of that pint-size pachyderm. He and the elephant were in proportion. Perhaps he was not of the same plane as mine, but he came from a world closely similar. I felt an intense bond and affection for him.

I watched the tall eccentric, still in his ruined top hat and frock-coat, guiding Mr Jumbo towards the golden glow. I had begun to see events as a series of cameos. I lost track of sequence. In the light of my experience I abandoned all notions of linear time.

I gasped as the globe, radiating first a pale blue light, continued to glow, as it were, *under* other gorgeous and varied colours. They rose like drifting spoors from the water. The air around the globe pulsed with new, bright colours, unique colours I had never known before and would yearn to recall for the rest of my life! I was seeing in the avian spectrum! Birds see many more shades and varieties of colour than we do. The display of colours, wave after wave, one gorgeous explosion after another, poured out of that enormous globe as it gradually divided into two. Intangible columns of ivory turning to dark gold. I could easily see why they called it a gate. As the halves split wide, the magnificent waves of colour brought music. I was reminded of Messiaen and perhaps Mahler in its grandeur. The Gates of Eden.

We were just in time.

The sight was magnificent. For me it resonated like a myth, as if the ancient stories of the Bible were being enacted in life. All our animals in their vast variety were entering the water, moving towards the shining gates to return to their own planes, like animals boarding the Ark.

Some lumbered through the churning waters, for they were too large to swim. Others could only be identified as part of a tiny swarm. I saw the monsters moving with unexpected agility over land and I saw them wallowing in rivers and ponds,

469

but this was the first time I saw them truly swim. The crocodiles were wonderfully graceful, as were the snakes and other reptiles. Why did this feel like redemption?

Barely speaking, we watched that astonishing exodus towards the now blue and golden gateway, radiant and shimmering in the pale sunshine. Animals which could not readily swim sat upon or floated beside those who were more at ease in the water. Those who could fly – birds and bats – began to darken the sky. Penguins continued their endearing waddle until they entered the water, joining the seals and walruses, some of them barely larger than one of my toy soldiers! The small seals formed a pod as they slid into the lake.

"You were just in time," said the Rose. "An hour later and the gate would have closed for good. Some of those beasts have been waiting for years and risked much. I came here for this. I had to abandon my schooner. The *spammaldjin* would have been stranded and heaven knows what chaos would have ensued. As it is ..." She came to stand beside me, watching.

The gates opened wider and wider. The colours were now deeper, like a rich yolk, and the pillars had begun to pulse, though none of the creatures had yet reached the gate. I thought I heard new music coming from the other side. A deep, thrumming single note reminding me of all the glorious music I had ever heard. Complex, shades of Berg, Ives, Schoenberg, Mahler again.

Spammer quivered. She put two arms in the water and turned to regard the lake, I saw something emerge from a stand of trees behind me and to my right. I thought it was one of our people. Perhaps a monk. I recognised the figure. He was short, dressed in ragged and stained broadcloth, his breeches hanging loose over his filthy white stockings. He had bruises and red welts all over him. I shouted and, without thinking, started towards him. He had lost his tall black Puritan hat but still carried miscellaneous guns and a couple of spears. He limped as he took aim at us. I began to run towards him. I thought only of *Spammer*. It was stupid and probably suicidal, but I meant to kill him if I could. For what he had done to Brother Bertrand. For all the cold evil he represented, if for nothing else!

31

Resurrection and Death

I RAGED AT Nixer, that undying brood of Satan! How had he survived the explosion and landslide? And climbed the waterfall? I wanted to tear his eyes out and rip his head from his body. I found myself screaming at the creature. People were shouting. Nixer laughed, levelling his huge tromblon as he did so. For me, he was the very embodiment of all that was evil in our world. By now most of the animals had entered the water. *Spammer* continued to slide off the beach, her colours reflecting her changing locale as, with stately dignity, she crawled towards the pulsing, multihued gateway at the lake's centre.

Nixer was not aiming at me. "The sight and stink of your joint corruption clouds my eyes and clogs my nostrils! God has spared me, so I alone shall drive that disgusting, unchristian horror from all corners of Creation!"

I strained to reach him. He was all that she was not. In contradicting his beliefs, she contradicted his existence. He lusted to kill *Spammer* as I lusted to kill him. I did not know if he could do it, but I had no wish to test him.

The great gun went off! I felt the burning powder singe my face. I was deafened. I fell, turned, saw *Spammer* shudder and a huge red wound blossom in her side. Knowing Nixer, I was convinced the monster had loaded his gun with shot designed

472

specifically to kill *Spammer*. Colour raced over her body broadcasting her pain. I got up and continued to run towards him, but fell again. I looked back and saw the Rose not far behind me. Like me, she was unarmed. I did not want either of them to die. Another shot. I heard men yelling, then a figure darted past me at tremendous speed.

As I rose to my feet for a second time I saw that someone between me and Nixer had gone down. Blackstone. His arm was drenched in blood. He was struggling to rise. The Rose and Jack were close behind me. I saw Nixer grin as he levelled a second blunderbuss. At this rate he would kill us where we stood! Again I ran towards Nixer.

A long red-grey arm, covered in those same sensitive suckers that had stroked my face and comforted me in the desert, lashed past me and found Nixer as he calmly stood with his back to a tree reloading one of his weapons. He saw that arm reach towards him. He abandoned the gun and leaned to pick up a spear. Jack Blackstone and the Rose were almost upon him. He drew back his hand to throw the spear.

Spammer's arm now ran with flashing colours signalling a score of emotions. It encircled Nixer, curling round his body until only his crazed face remained! Lord John, stumbling to his feet, made a grab for a spear. Blood gushed from *Spammer*'s wound, staining the water blue and black. *Spammer* shuddered but did not lose her grip. It tightened. She lifted Nixer high, partially released him, staring with puzzled compassion at his antics as he kicked and spat and swore and called on his God to destroy this Lucifer incarnate, screaming and screaming in rage, his face flaring and twisting as he struggled to get free of her.

There was an explosion. The gun went off, hitting no-one.

Reacting, *Spammer* flung the Puritan high up in the air and back to the ground and then threw him away from her in disgust. Out over the lake. Far over the lake.

Towards the welcoming Gates of Eden.

Most of the animals had passed through. Some remained and had to be encouraged to accompany Professor Consenseo. I like to think they actually did find the Garden of Eden beyond the gates or at least somewhere pain-free. Could sentient creatures in the near-infinite dimensions of the multiverse actually live in peace together? At least there? In Eden nothing could easily change a predatory carnivore into a vegetarian, but Professor Consenseo had fed all his animals on his mysterious potions. Could we live without obeying the aggression we still carry deep in our memories? I once believed it possible for all creatures to communicate and live harmoniously. I saw nothing unrealistic in believing that sometimes it came down to the simple rule about not eating your own. And then defining our own! I always believed, I hope robustly, that humanity could work for mutual good, given the will. Now the exception had just sailed through the air, his arms and legs waving wildly, his horrid guns going in all directions, his stained coat-tails in another, and passed through those gates to vanish with a red splash.

We stood there, staring in silence at the gates as the animals continued to flow slowly through.

"In all my adventures across and within Africa, I had never thought to witness a sight so strange," said Blackstone. "Or, indeed, so moving." His shirt-sleeve was soaked in blood, but his wound did not seem too serious. He watched as our *spammaldjin* turned towards the lake. Her flesh was livid around the gaping wound in her side.

"*You are not all the same kind of creature,*" I heard her say. "*Some, poor spirits, are exceptions. They have no stories of their own. They cling to shallow narratives borrowed from sensational fiction. Because they cannot understand complexity, they try to destroy it, simplifying the world until it collapses into a few sterile elements and destroys us all. They have no interest in the stories of others. You must always make sure they do not gain power over you, for if they do, they will try to bring all you find glorious to an end."*

Maybe I had never given enough credence to the Jake Nixers of the worlds: The insensitive, the incurious, the judgemental, the jealous, those with petty ambitions, with unimaginative minds, the narcissists and those incapable of empathy. I had once mistakenly thought that everyone could potentially at least learn empathy, could be shown how to feel for others.

And yet my faith in the world was undiminished. If anything it was reinforced. For there really was no difference in fantasy or reality, only in the defining context.

Context defines, said *Spammer,* slipping into the water again. *Context determines.*

Perhaps that was all I ever needed to learn.

The Rose stepped up beside me. "We have no more time here," she said.

I was startled, as if the Grim Reaper had put a hand on my shoulder!

We walked down to where the DoX lay rocking in the shallows underneath her shed. We waded through the water, and the Rose stepped up onto the stubby lower wing, opened the door and helped me in. The control cabin was glorious in ebony and silver art deco with silver trim and dark enamelling. It smelled of new leather and faintly of metal polish. And, of course, whispers of Guerlaine Florals. A Universe of Roses. White tile panelling and black trim. It might have been a ship's bridge from the Golden Age of Ocean Liners. Fred and Ginger could have danced across those wings. I had always dreamed of flying in a DoX.

"Lady Abbess," I began, but she interrupted me.

"I'm Mrs Rose von Bek now," she said, leaning to pick two

sets of helmets and headphones from beside her. She handed me one and put hers on, made an adjustment, flicked toggles, turned a key, "or will be soon. I am the jugador, Rose von Bek! Welcome to my world!"

"Yours?" I had no trouble with the helmet, fixing the chin-strap.

"The world of the Female Ace, Mr Moorcock. Yet another fantasy neither of us can afford to indulge for too long! Did you know poor Amelia could barely fly?" She looked back, flashing me a smile.

The great engines roared and shook the whole plane.

"Keep your fingers crossed," she yelled. We vibrated so much I felt we would fall apart before we could become airborne.

The huge seaplane taxied slowly forward. Rose eased the throttle. The vibrations were less violent. We sped over the lake heading for those shimmering golden semi-spheres. My last sight was of Professor Consenseo on Mr Jumbo leading some mammoths and followed by the slow-swimming *Spammer Gain*. Both passed through the Gates of Eden.

I saw them vanish. Then our ship lifted. Joyously Rose von Bek laughed with joy as we followed them into the blue and gold pulsing Gates of Eden. We banked once over the vast African veldt. Then the Sahara. Then the Mediterranean sea. And then we were in France, driving into a silvery darkness, following a pale path for the capital.

We were in Paris within two hours. We landed silently, late at night on the quiet widest part of the glimmering Seine in deep shadow, somewhere upriver of Île St-Louis. Few saw us and only one or two people appeared to notice our aircraft. Perhaps they could not see it.

Mrs von Bek kissed me lightly on the cheek. "I won't stay," she said when I asked. "I shouldn't be here. I must quickly get the plane back. It's rented. You know, I'm not normally bothered by anomalies really." A further quick kiss on both my cheeks. An embarrassed glance away. Without another word, I climbed from the big passenger door and onto the pontoon. I stood there balancing for a moment, then made a quick jump for the shore and landed smack in the water. With a couple of hasty steps I was out and crunching along the riverside until I found steps to the top. I continued to walk through near-deserted streets, wondering if by a trick I had been abandoned in some other Paris.

For a while a while I made my way through almost deserted streets and was lucky to find a taxi.

I arrived back at Le Grand Hôtel de l'Univers just as they were unlocking for the dawn deliveries. I was received by the staff as if I had been seeing a mistress rather than M. Caveliero's final performance. I was allowed in with a knowing grin and a whisper. I almost felt guilty.

Helena and I shared an amiable bed. She rather wished she'd come with me. Their own evening had been a bit dull, she said. The memory of the Winter Circus was so vivid, I had an enthusiastic time recalling it!

The girls had breakfast with us in the hotel's tiny restaurant. Helena poured delicious coffee from an old pewter jug, I handed orange juice to the girls. Everything had suddenly become normal and domestic. If I talked about my adventures now, my family would believe me to be telling them one of the vivid dreams they were always laughing about. A few hours earlier I had been flying in an ancient, legendary plane over the Sahara Desert and I was so glad to be there! I didn't mind if it was ordinary or came with a lot of obligations. I was relieved. I could still hear the Swarm. Constant. Unrelenting. Like the voice of conscience. Nothing had changed.

"How was the show?" Helena asked.

Epilogue

O N THE TRAIN *up to the Dales, Blackstone practised his part.* *He had set such great store on it, and he hated to embarrass his cousin. He needed to rest. He closed his eyes, listening to the steady rhythm of the Newcastle Flyer, falling slowly into sleep.*

THEY CALLED FOR ME.

That is all I really know.

They called for me across the teeming multiverse and I went to them. I could not do otherwise.

Why was I chosen?

I still do not know. All names but one are unfamiliar.

Now it is done and I am here. I shall always be here. Time is only cyclic when we choose it to be. And I suppose I choose it to be. Guilt is a great guide for those like me. We pick paths through apparent chaos. We pay a price that for us is forever due! For others, Time is an agony of Now and I fear that most. Should I come to that part of the cycle I know as the twenty-first century, no doubt I will be called Michael Moorcock and my story will be much the same as this one. And that, I suppose, makes me immortal.

Next

The Wounds of Albion

I THINK THEY might have called my name, or at least a familiar one, because I had the impression I answered them, reassuring them. Everyone has at some time been under the illusion, between wakefulness and sleeping, of hearing voices, scraps of conversation, phrases spoken in peculiar tones. Déjà vu? Echoes? Sometimes we attempt to attune our minds to hear more, but usually aren't successful. These are called hypnagogic hallucinations, the beginning of the dreams we shall later experience as we sleep.

There was a woman. Three children. A city. A name which occasionally changed: Michael Moorcock. They called in voices I did not recognise, in a language I did not understand. It might have been Sioux.

Erekosë ... Erekosë ... Erekosë

I heard distant steady, insistent drumming ...

Had I hung for ever in Limbo? I was not being torn away, but I could not see who was calling me. I felt that all humanity had a voice. I begged for it to pause. I saw a wooden fort made variously of palisades and heaped rocks. Mounted Norse and Napoleon's hussars. A group of brightly dressed samurai. The fort was manned by soldiers of many kinds – British cavalry from Waterloo, infantry of around the same time, French

Mamelukes, English Forest Rangers, eighteenth-century armed civilians, a massive Carthaginian war elephant, its howdah packed with contemporary British nurses, American natives from the eighteenth century, American frontier scouts and trappers, while outside the fort massed Sudanese warriors from the time of the Mahdi and Ottoman Turks. Other armed men were mounted on dinosaurs lumbering through the relatively low shrubland around the fort. This was like a scenario I laid out for my collection of toy soldiers as a boy and I was fascinated by the moving details of those living little warriors. I was being drawn down to meet them and I struggled to escape. I felt I was being drawn into yet another great battle which would rob me of all I valued.

"EREKOSË EREKOSË VON BEK! VON BEK! We need you, Champion!"

I was being drawn into this dreamland, and I was reluctant to go. There were still things I had to do. Other narratives to write. Commitments to readers and my family. I had promised a third memoir in the sequence. I had to stay to write it.

The call was stronger now. I turned to tell Helena what was happening. My wife was gone. I was helpless. Their call was stronger. *Champion ...!!*

Erekosë ... Erekosë ... Erekosë ...

The voices were insistent and irresistible. I could do nothing else. I gave myself up to them. I let them draw me down ... Down for yet another terrible conflict. Perhaps, this final time, I would redeem myself.

— *The Wounds of Albion* (forthcoming)